Gasolina

CREATED BY SEAN MACKIEWICZ & NIKO WALTER

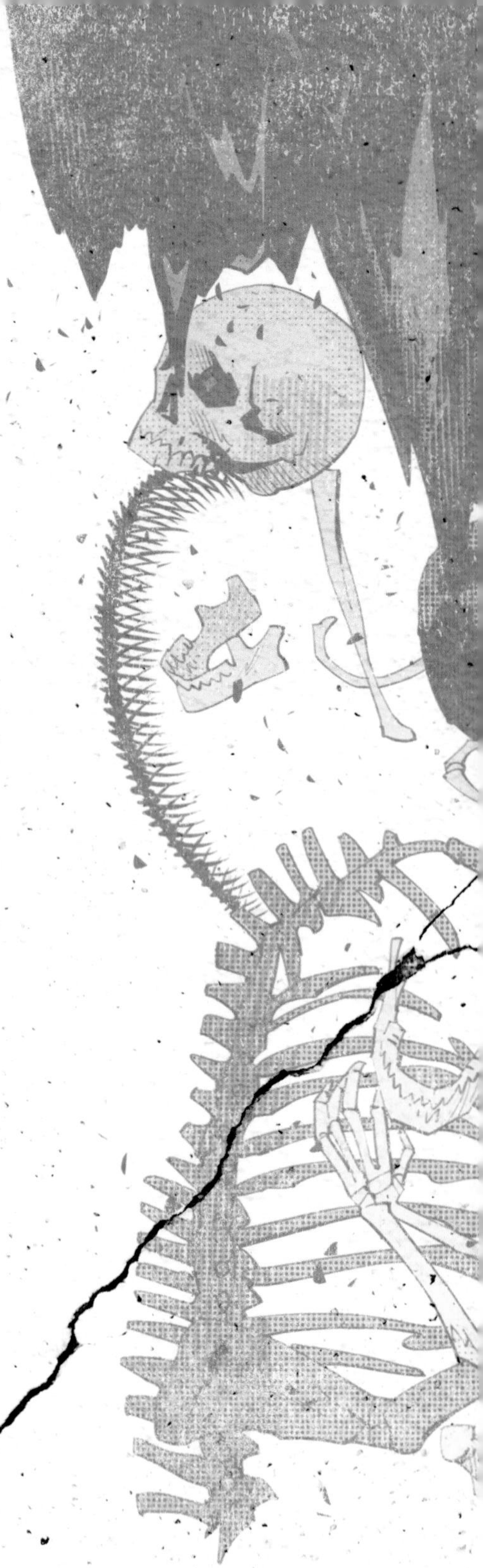

SEAN MACKIEWICZ
CREATOR, WRITER

NIKO WALTER
CREATOR, ARTIST

MAT LOPES
COLORIST

RUS WOOTON
LETTERER

ARIELLE BASICH
EDITOR

FOR SKYBOUND ENTERTAINMENT

Robert Kirkman *Chairman*
David Alpert *CEO*
Sean Mackiewicz *SVP, Editor-in-Chief*
Shawn Kirkham *SVP, Business Development*
Brian Huntington *Online Editorial Director*
June Alian *Publicity Director*
Andres Juarez *Art Director*
Jon Moisan *Editor*
Arielle Basich *Associate Editor*
Carina Taylor *Production Artist*
Paul Shin *Business Development Coordinator*
Johnny O'Dell *Social Media Manager*
Sally Jacka *Skybound Retailer Relations*
Dan Petersen *Director of Operations & Events*
Nick Palmer *Operations Coordinator*

International Inquiries: ag@sequentialrights.com
Licensing Inquiries: contact@skybound.com

WWW.SKYBOUND.COM

IMAGE COMICS, INC.
Robert Kirkman *Chief Operating Officer*
Erik Larsen *Chief Financial Officer*
Todd McFarlane *President*
Marc Silvestri *Chief Executive Officer*
Jim Valentino *Vice-President*

Eric Stephenson *Publisher*
Corey Hart *Director of Sales*
Jeff Boison *Director of Publishing Planning & Book Trade Sales*
Chris Ross *Director of Digital Sales*
Jeff Stang *Director of Specialty Sales*
Kat Salazar *Director of PR & Marketing*
Drew Gill *Art Director*
Heather Doornink *Production Director*
Branwyn Bigglestone *Controller*

WWW.IMAGECOMICS.COM

GASOLINA VOLUME 1. FIRST PRINTING. March 2018. Published by Image Comics, Inc. Office of publication: 2701 NW Vaughn St., Ste. 780, Portland, OR 97210. Originally published in single magazine form as GASOLINA #1-6. GASOLINA™ (including all prominent characters featured herein), its logo and all character likenesses are trademarks of Skybound, LLC, unless otherwise noted. Image Comics® and its logos are registered trademarks and copyrights of Image Comics, Inc.

Printed in the U.S.A. For information regarding the CPSIA on this printed material call: 203-595-3636 and provide reference # RICH – 782024. ISBN: 978-1-5343-0506-9

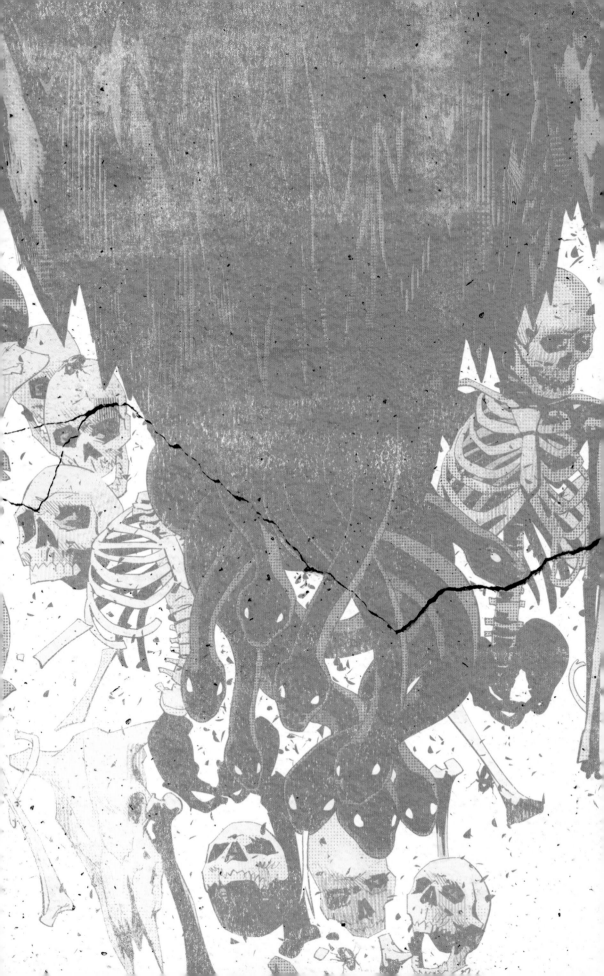

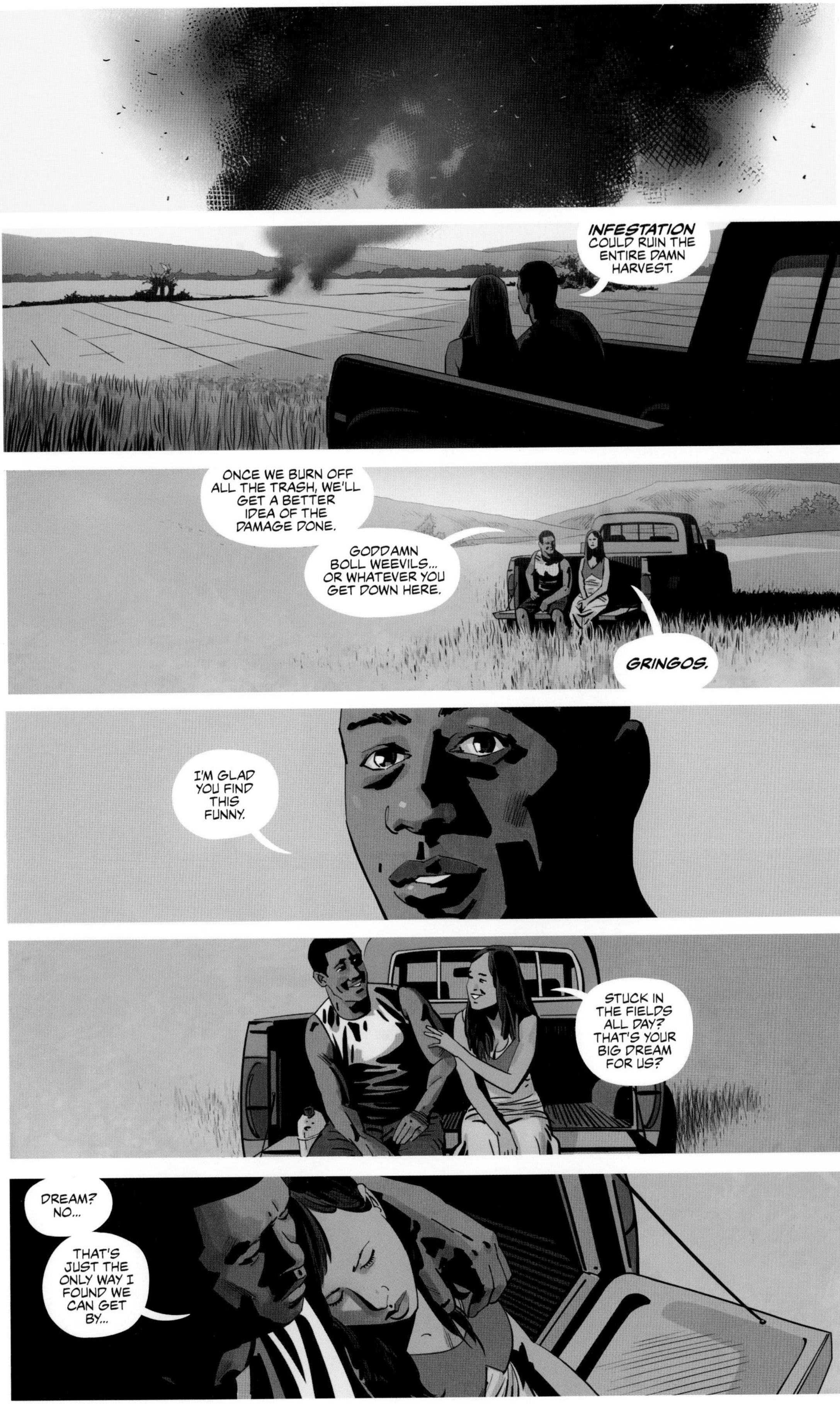
INFESTATION COULD RUIN THE ENTIRE DAMN HARVEST.
ONCE WE BURN OFF ALL THE TRASH, WE'LL GET A BETTER IDEA OF THE DAMAGE DONE.
GODDAMN BOLL WEEVILS... OR WHATEVER YOU GET DOWN HERE.
GRINGOS.
I'M GLAD YOU FIND THIS FUNNY.
STUCK IN THE FIELDS ALL DAY? THAT'S YOUR BIG DREAM FOR US?
DREAM? NO...
THAT'S JUST THE ONLY WAY I FOUND WE CAN GET BY...

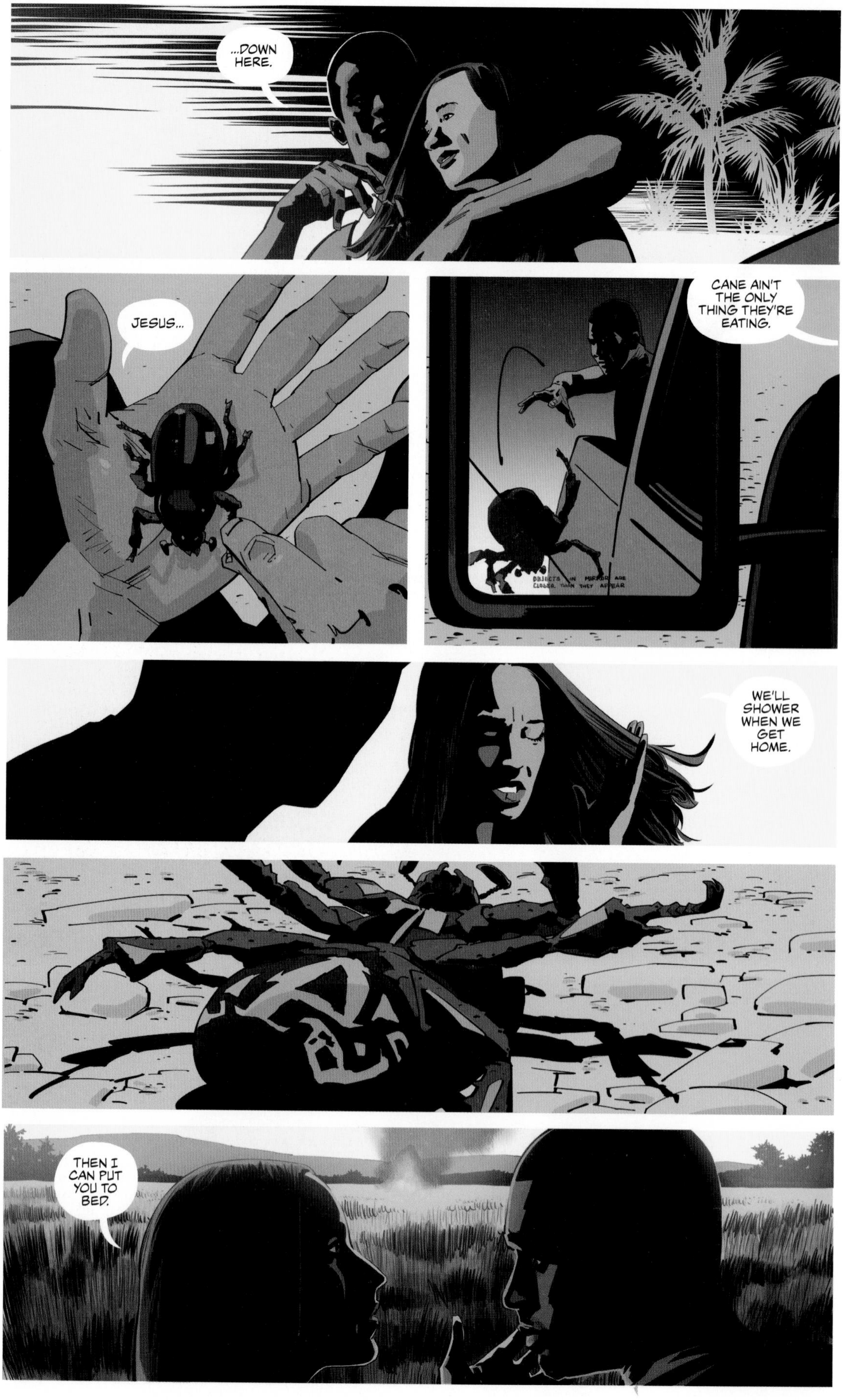
...DOWN HERE.
JESUS...
CANE AIN'T THE ONLY THING THEY'RE EATING.
OBJECTS IN MIRROR ARE CLOSER THAN THEY APPEAR
WE'LL SHOWER WHEN WE GET HOME.
THEN I CAN PUT YOU TO BED.

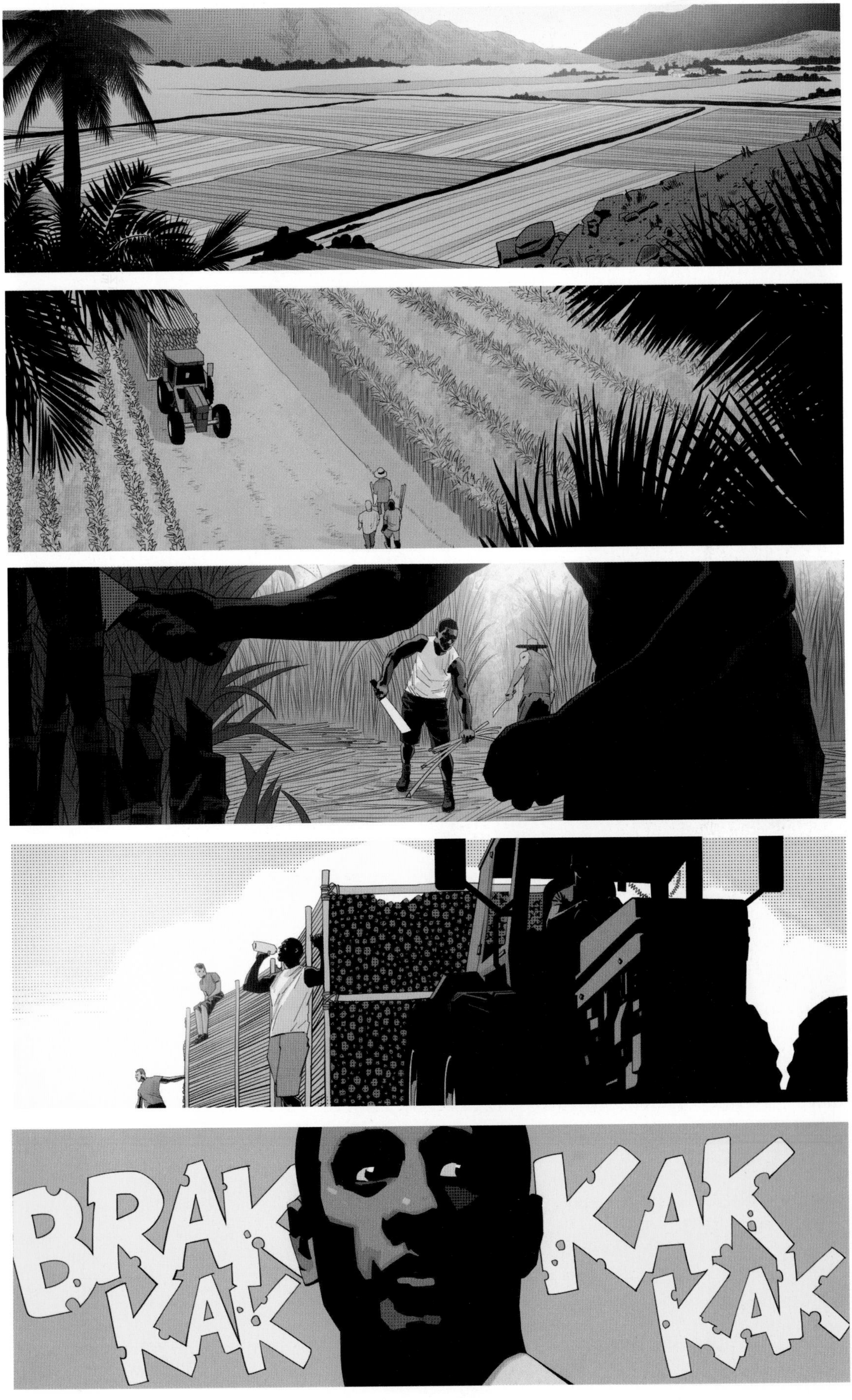

BRAK KAK
KAK KAK

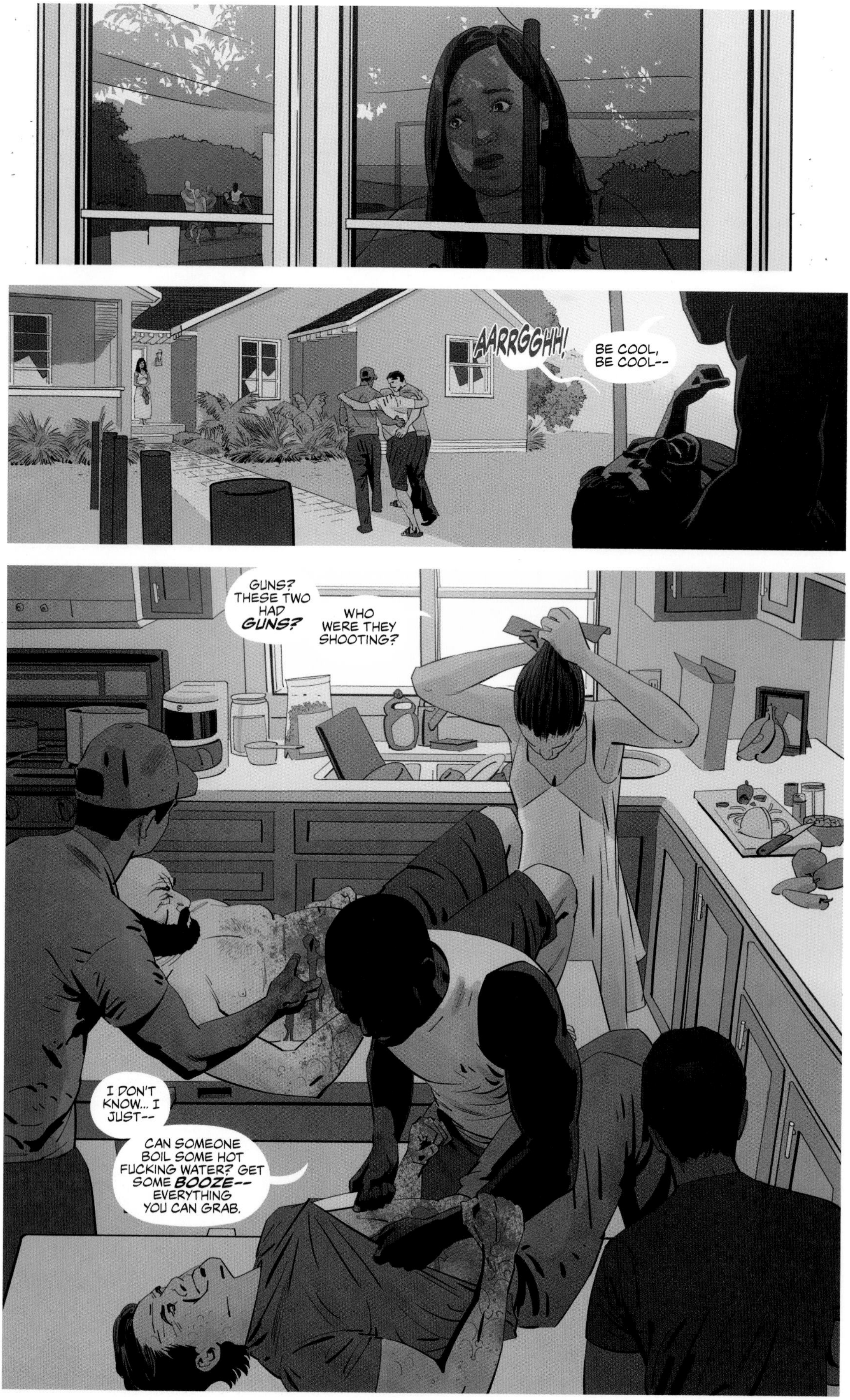
AARRGGHH!
BE COOL, BE COOL--
GUNS? THESE TWO HAD GUNS?
WHO WERE THEY SHOOTING?
I DON'T KNOW... I JUST--
CAN SOMEONE BOIL SOME HOT FUCKING WATER? GET SOME BOOZE-- EVERYTHING YOU CAN GRAB.

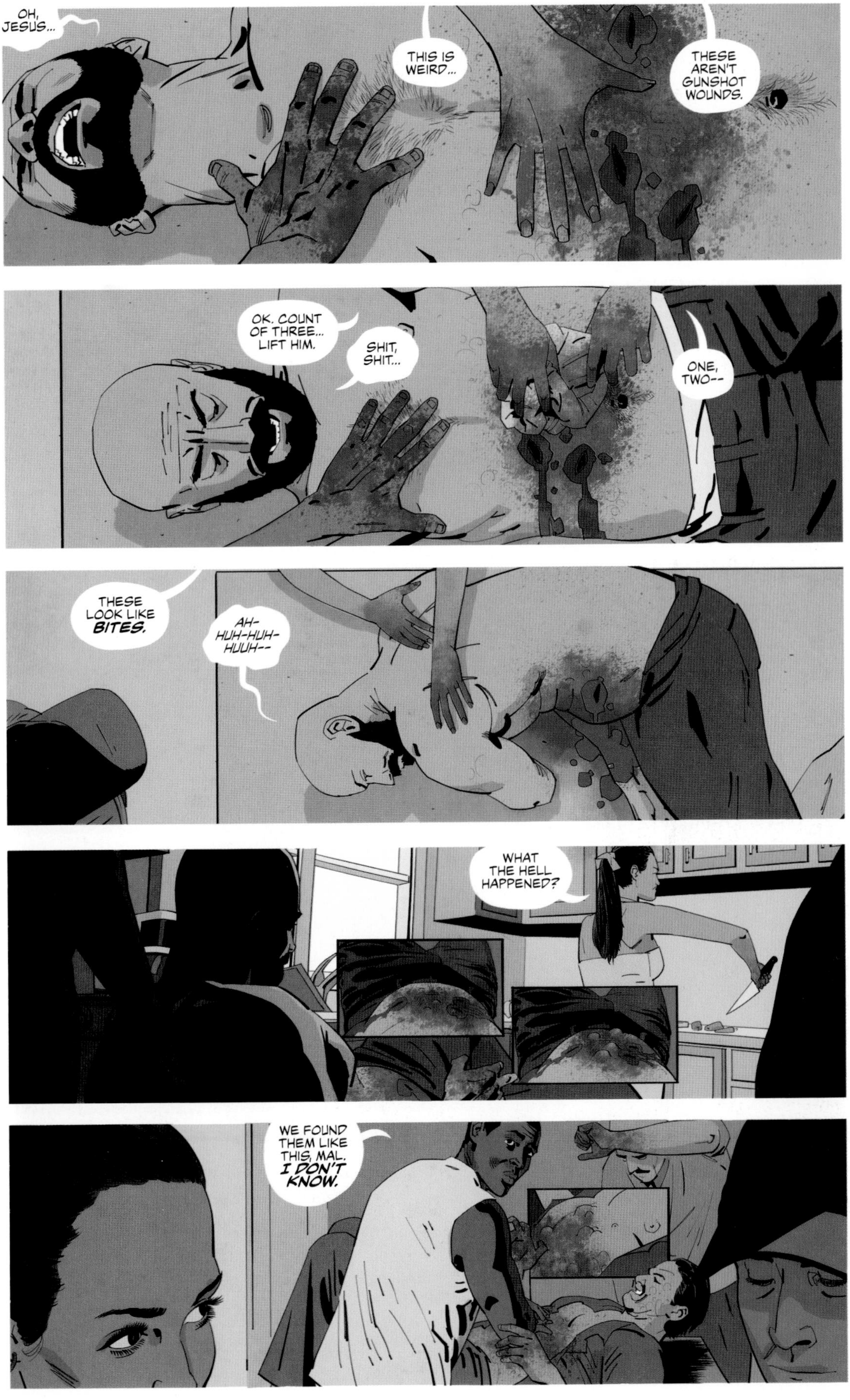
OH, JESUS...
THIS IS WEIRD...
THESE AREN'T GUNSHOT WOUNDS.
OK. COUNT OF THREE... LIFT HIM.
SHIT, SHIT...
ONE, TWO--
THESE LOOK LIKE BITES.
AH-HUH-HUH-HUUH--
WHAT THE HELL HAPPENED?
WE FOUND THEM LIKE THIS, MAL. I DON'T KNOW.

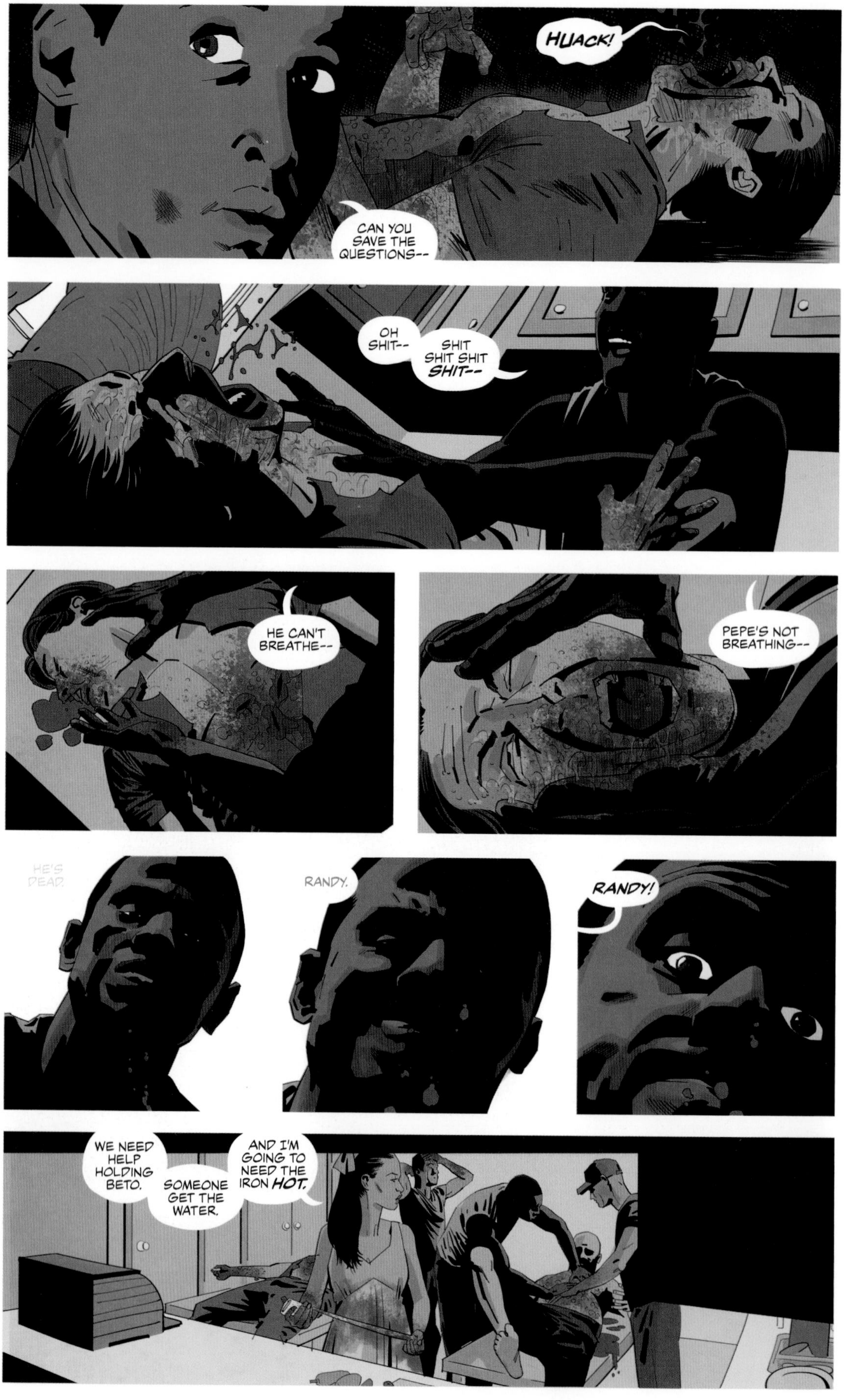
HUACK!
CAN YOU SAVE THE QUESTIONS--
OH SHIT--
SHIT SHIT SHIT SHIT--
HE CAN'T BREATHE--
PEPE'S NOT BREATHING--
HE'S DEAD.
RANDY.
RANDY!
WE NEED HELP HOLDING BETO.
SOMEONE GET THE WATER.
AND I'M GOING TO NEED THE IRON HOT.

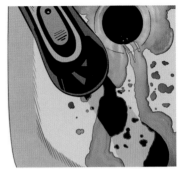

YOU OK?

YEAH, I JUST, *UH...* GOT IN MY HEAD A LITTLE.

HE WAS DYING, NO MATTER WHAT WE DID.

I KNOW.

AND BETO'S GOING TO BE FINE.

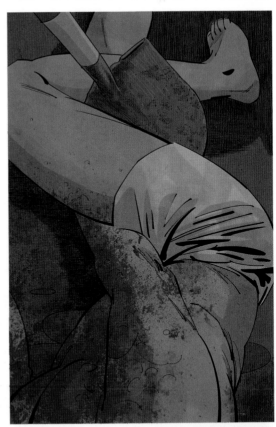

HECTOR WOULD LIKE TO SPEAK WITH YOU.

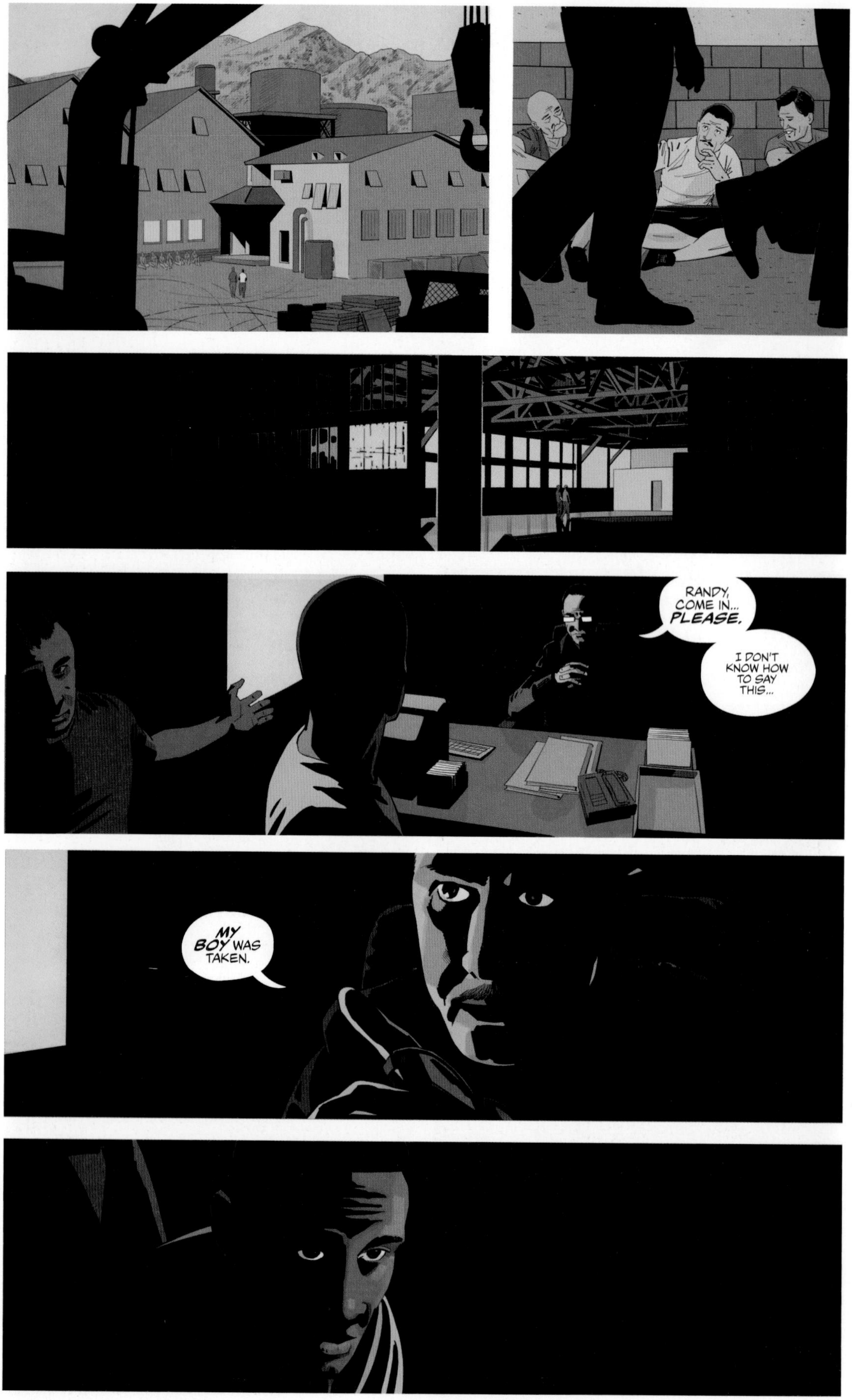

RANDY, COME IN... PLEASE.
I DON'T KNOW HOW TO SAY THIS...
MY BOY WAS TAKEN.

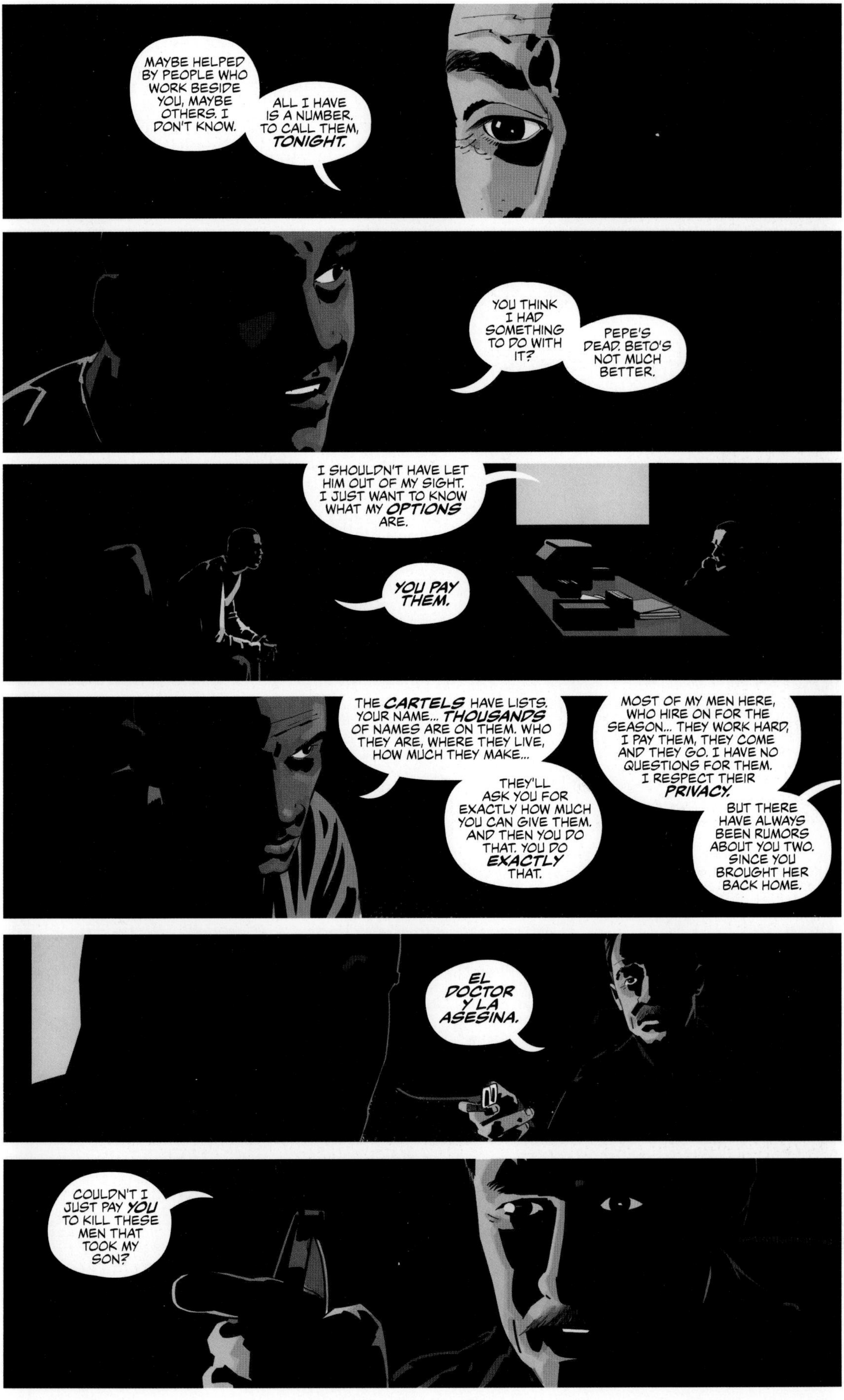
MAYBE HELPED BY PEOPLE WHO WORK BESIDE YOU, MAYBE OTHERS. I DON'T KNOW.
ALL I HAVE IS A NUMBER. TO CALL THEM, TONIGHT.
YOU THINK I HAD SOMETHING TO DO WITH IT?
PEPE'S DEAD. BETO'S NOT MUCH BETTER.
I SHOULDN'T HAVE LET HIM OUT OF MY SIGHT. I JUST WANT TO KNOW WHAT MY OPTIONS ARE.
YOU PAY THEM.
THE CARTELS HAVE LISTS. YOUR NAME... THOUSANDS OF NAMES ARE ON THEM. WHO THEY ARE, WHERE THEY LIVE, HOW MUCH THEY MAKE...
THEY'LL ASK YOU FOR EXACTLY HOW MUCH YOU CAN GIVE THEM. AND THEN YOU DO THAT. YOU DO EXACTLY THAT.
MOST OF MY MEN HERE, WHO HIRE ON FOR THE SEASON... THEY WORK HARD, I PAY THEM, THEY COME AND THEY GO. I HAVE NO QUESTIONS FOR THEM. I RESPECT THEIR PRIVACY.
BUT THERE HAVE ALWAYS BEEN RUMORS ABOUT YOU TWO. SINCE YOU BROUGHT HER BACK HOME.
EL DOCTOR Y LA ASESINA.
COULDN'T I JUST PAY YOU TO KILL THESE MEN THAT TOOK MY SON?

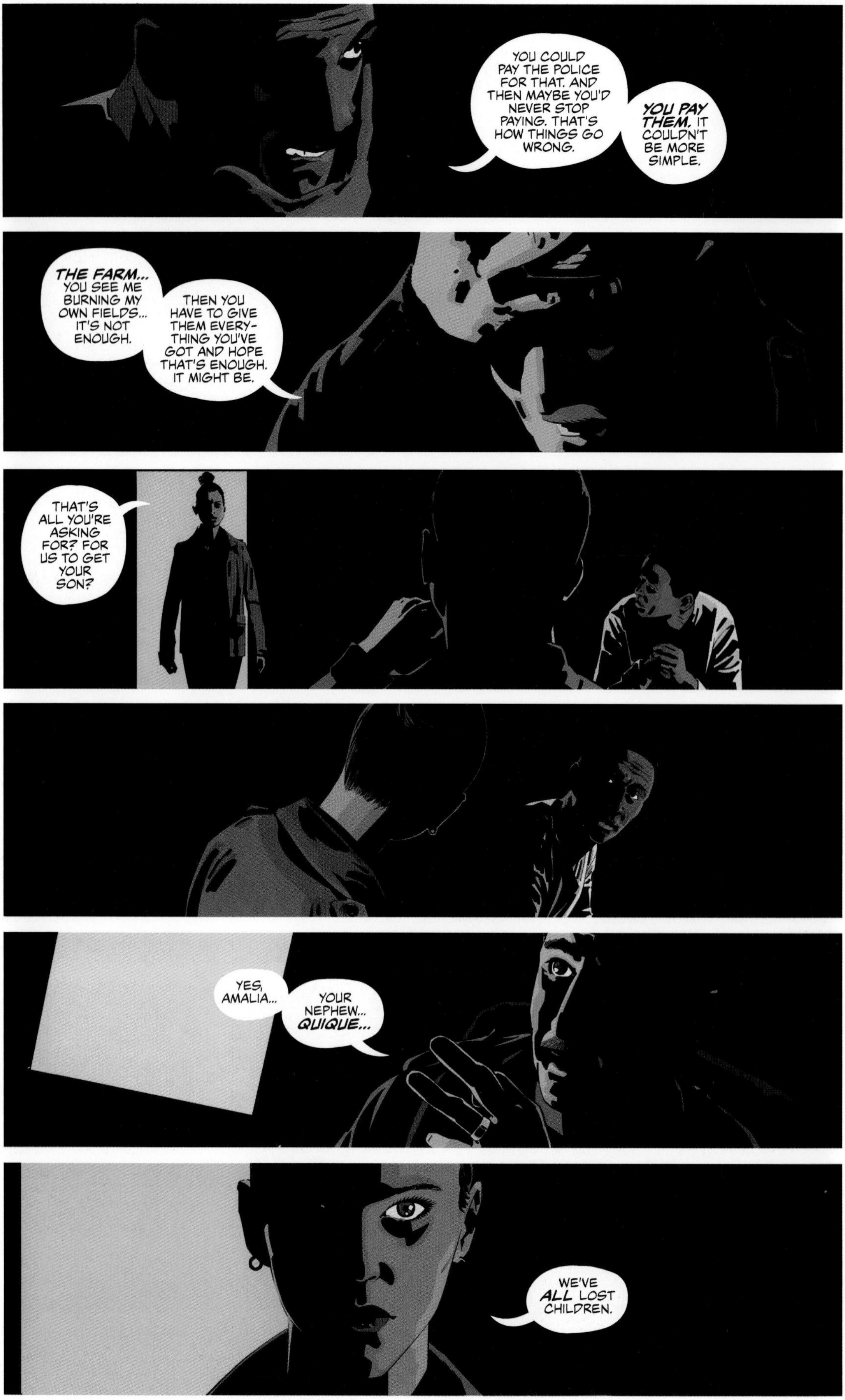
YOU COULD PAY THE POLICE FOR THAT. AND THEN MAYBE YOU'D NEVER STOP PAYING. THAT'S HOW THINGS GO WRONG.
YOU PAY THEM. IT COULDN'T BE MORE SIMPLE.
THE FARM... YOU SEE ME BURNING MY OWN FIELDS... IT'S NOT ENOUGH.
THEN YOU HAVE TO GIVE THEM EVERY-THING YOU'VE GOT AND HOPE THAT'S ENOUGH. IT MIGHT BE.
THAT'S ALL YOU'RE ASKING FOR? FOR US TO GET YOUR SON?
YES, AMALIA...
YOUR NEPHEW... QUIQUE...
WE'VE ALL LOST CHILDREN.

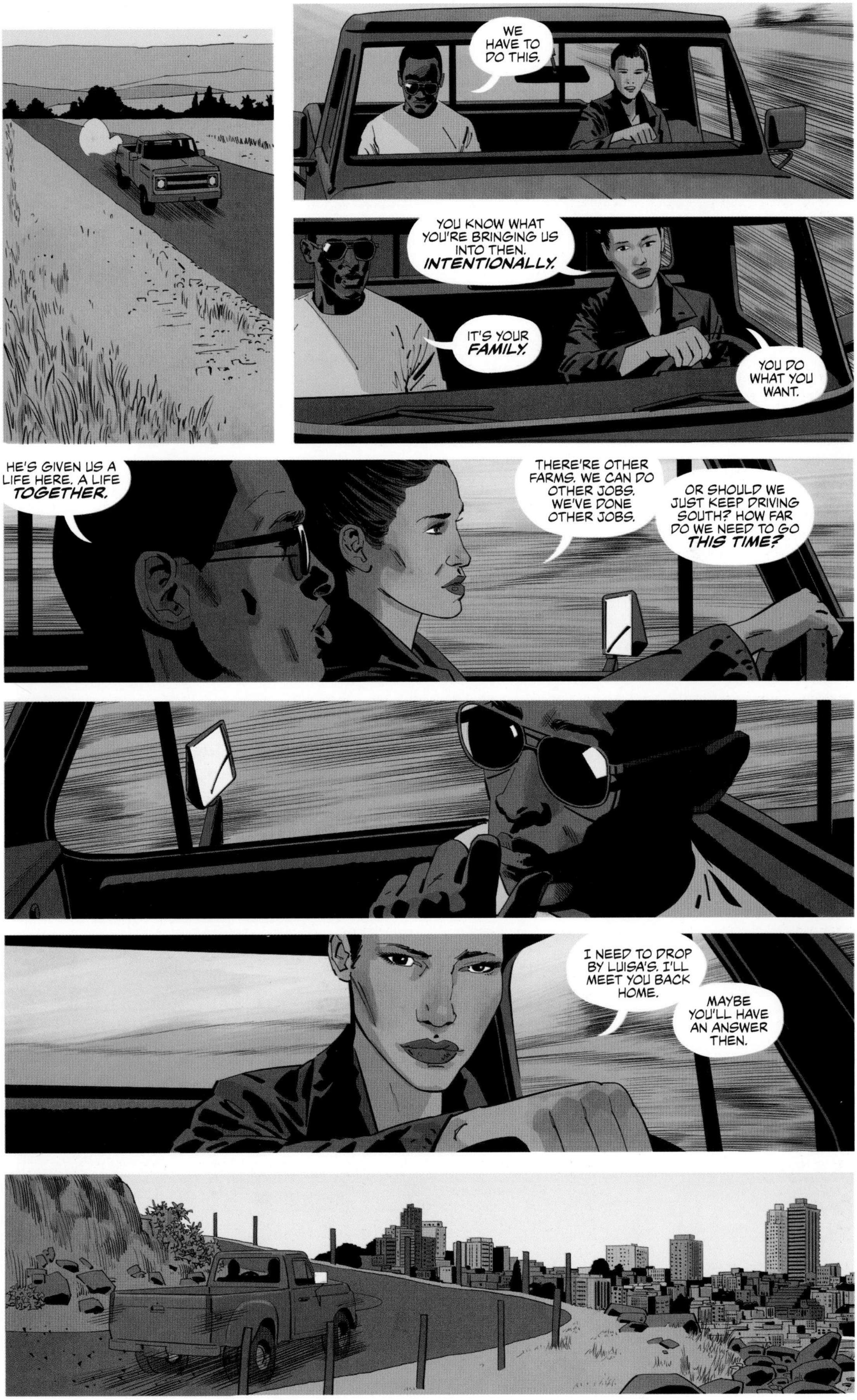

WE HAVE TO DO THIS.
YOU KNOW WHAT YOU'RE BRINGING US INTO THEN. INTENTIONALLY.
IT'S YOUR FAMILY.
YOU DO WHAT YOU WANT.
HE'S GIVEN US A LIFE HERE. A LIFE TOGETHER.
THERE'RE OTHER FARMS. WE CAN DO OTHER JOBS. WE'VE DONE OTHER JOBS.
OR SHOULD WE JUST KEEP DRIVING SOUTH? HOW FAR DO WE NEED TO GO THIS TIME?
I NEED TO DROP BY LUISA'S. I'LL MEET YOU BACK HOME.
MAYBE YOU'LL HAVE AN ANSWER THEN.

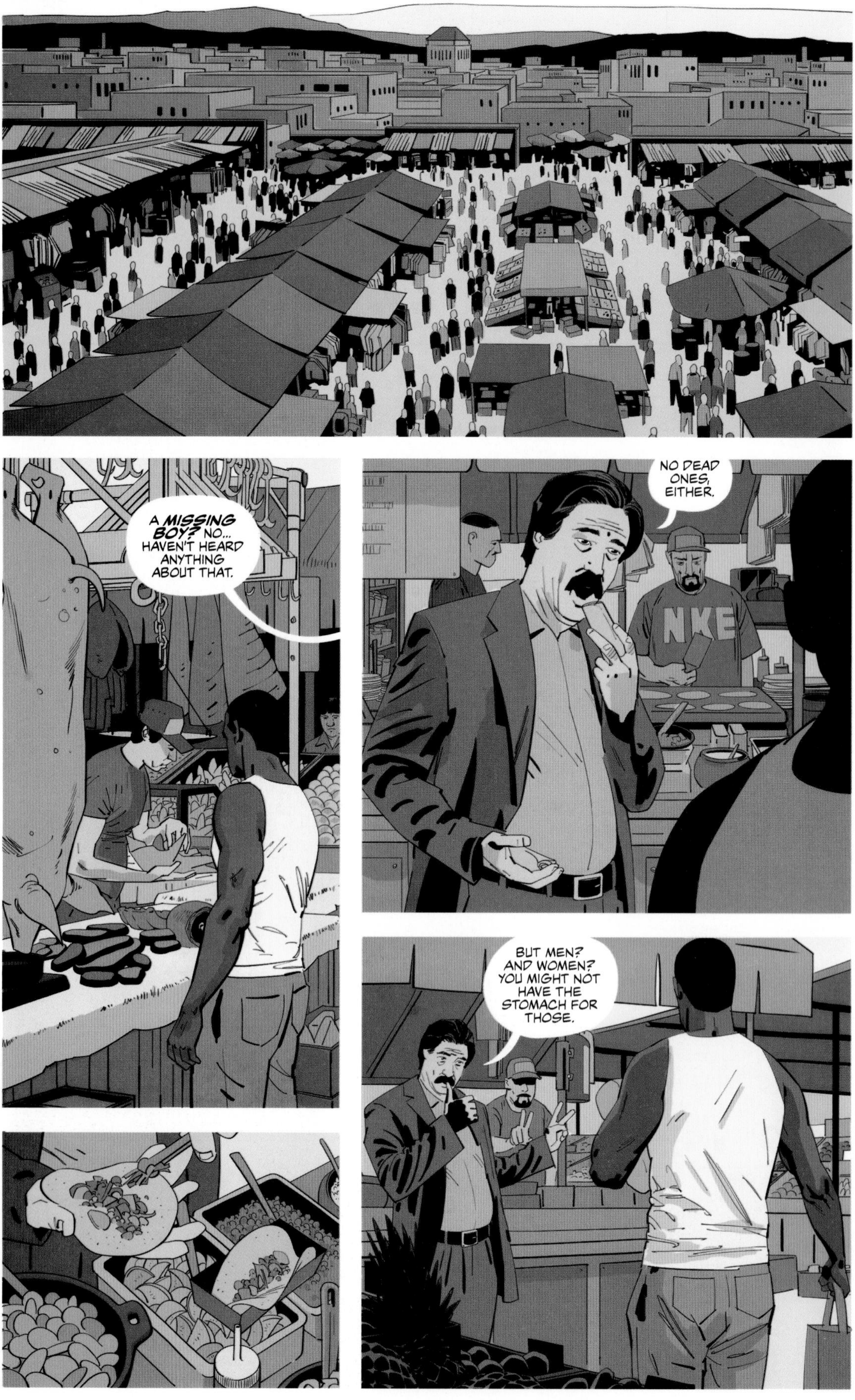
A MISSING BOY? NO... HAVEN'T HEARD ANYTHING ABOUT THAT.
NO DEAD ONES, EITHER.
NKE
BUT MEN? AND WOMEN? YOU MIGHT NOT HAVE THE STOMACH FOR THOSE.

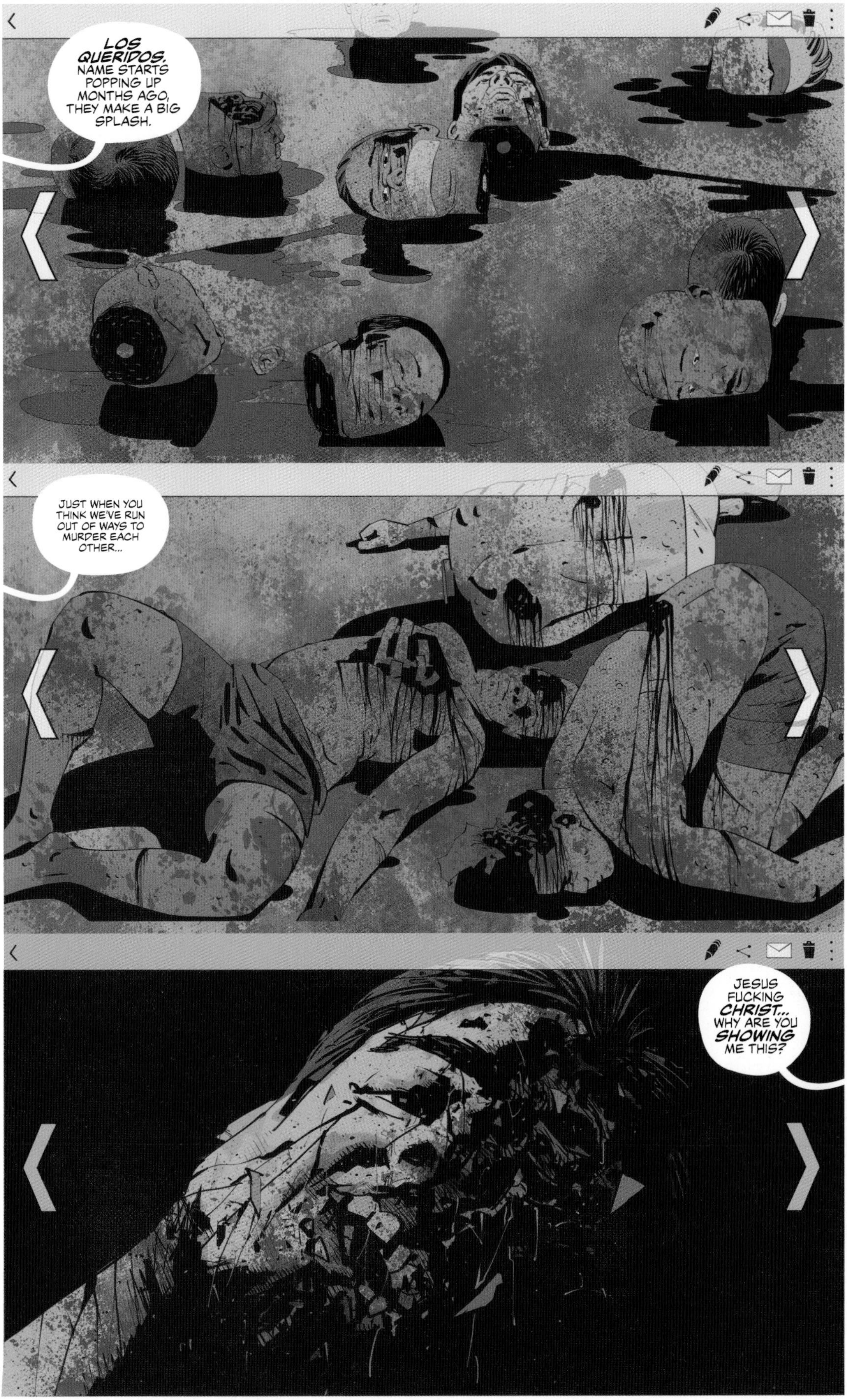
LOS QUERIDOS. NAME STARTS POPPING UP MONTHS AGO, THEY MAKE A BIG SPLASH.
JUST WHEN YOU THINK WE'VE RUN OUT OF WAYS TO MURDER EACH OTHER...
JESUS FUCKING CHRIST... WHY ARE YOU SHOWING ME THIS?

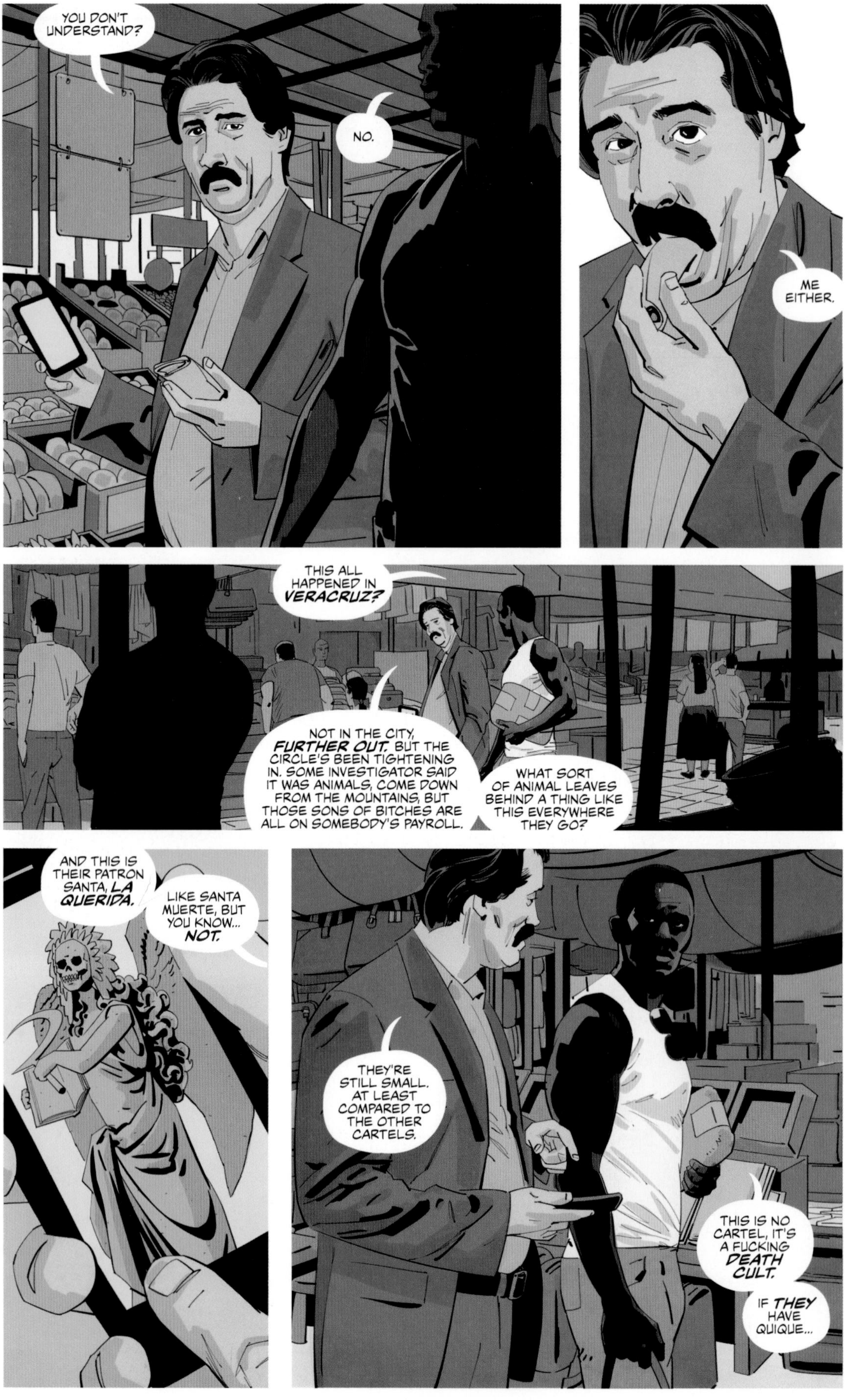
YOU DON'T UNDERSTAND?
NO.
ME EITHER.
THIS ALL HAPPENED IN VERACRUZ?
NOT IN THE CITY, FURTHER OUT. BUT THE CIRCLE'S BEEN TIGHTENING IN. SOME INVESTIGATOR SAID IT WAS ANIMALS, COME DOWN FROM THE MOUNTAINS, BUT THOSE SONS OF BITCHES ARE ALL ON SOMEBODY'S PAYROLL.
WHAT SORT OF ANIMAL LEAVES BEHIND A THING LIKE THIS EVERYWHERE THEY GO?
AND THIS IS THEIR PATRON SANTA, LA QUERIDA.
LIKE SANTA MUERTE, BUT YOU KNOW... NOT.
THEY'RE STILL SMALL. AT LEAST COMPARED TO THE OTHER CARTELS.
THIS IS NO CARTEL, IT'S A FUCKING DEATH CULT.
IF THEY HAVE QUIQUE...

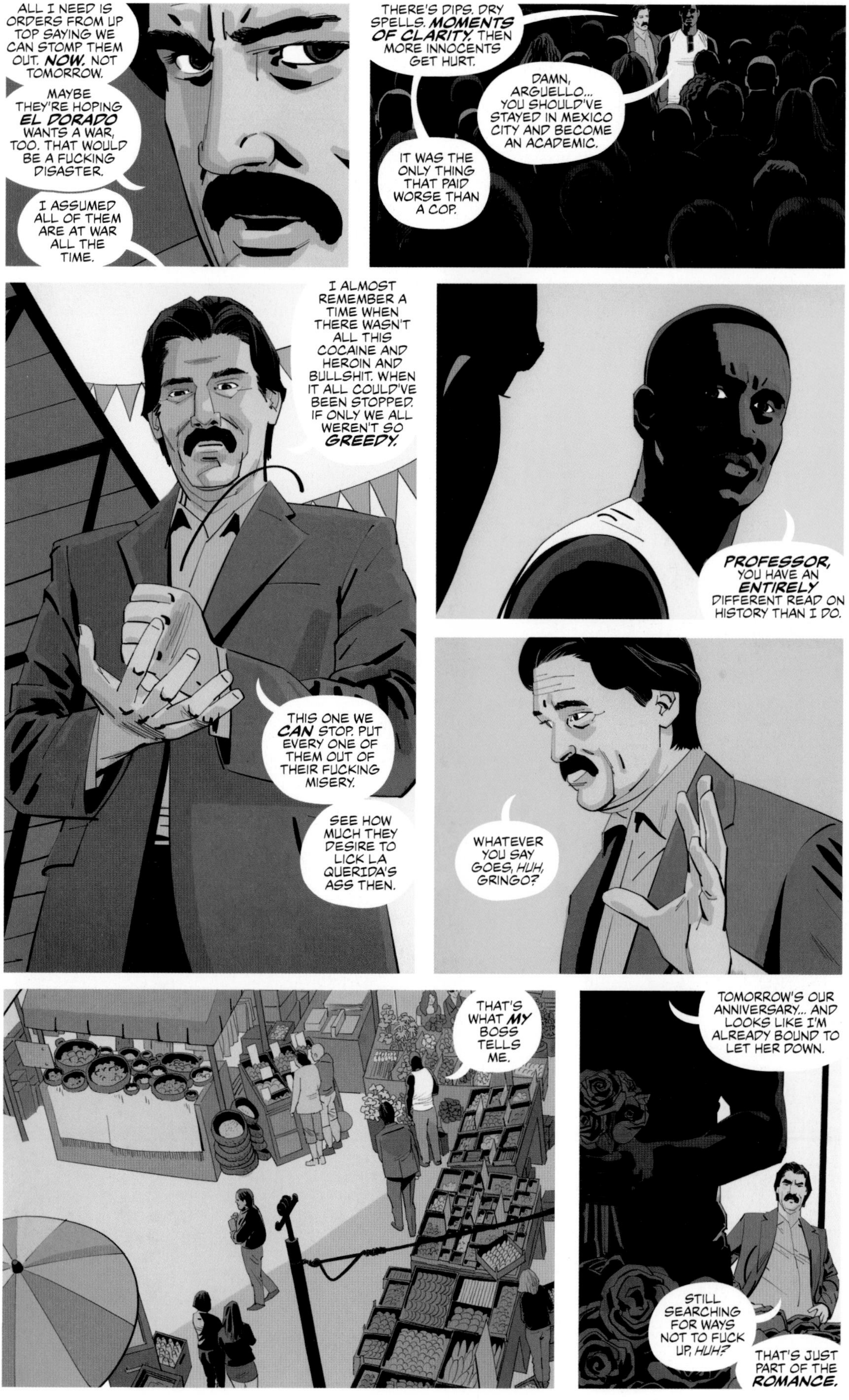
ALL I NEED IS ORDERS FROM UP TOP SAYING WE CAN STOMP THEM OUT. NOW. NOT TOMORROW.
MAYBE THEY'RE HOPING EL DORADO WANTS A WAR, TOO. THAT WOULD BE A FUCKING DISASTER.
I ASSUMED ALL OF THEM ARE AT WAR ALL THE TIME.
THERE'S DIPS. DRY SPELLS. MOMENTS OF CLARITY. THEN MORE INNOCENTS GET HURT.
DAMN, ARGUELLO... YOU SHOULD'VE STAYED IN MEXICO CITY AND BECOME AN ACADEMIC.
IT WAS THE ONLY THING THAT PAID WORSE THAN A COP.
I ALMOST REMEMBER A TIME WHEN THERE WASN'T ALL THIS COCAINE AND HEROIN AND BULLSHIT. WHEN IT ALL COULD'VE BEEN STOPPED. IF ONLY WE ALL WEREN'T SO GREEDY.
PROFESSOR, YOU HAVE AN ENTIRELY DIFFERENT READ ON HISTORY THAN I DO.
THIS ONE WE CAN STOP. PUT EVERY ONE OF THEM OUT OF THEIR FUCKING MISERY.
SEE HOW MUCH THEY DESIRE TO LICK LA QUERIDA'S ASS THEN.
WHATEVER YOU SAY GOES, HUH, GRINGO?
THAT'S WHAT MY BOSS TELLS ME.
TOMORROW'S OUR ANNIVERSARY... AND LOOKS LIKE I'M ALREADY BOUND TO LET HER DOWN.
STILL SEARCHING FOR WAYS NOT TO FUCK UP, HUH?
THAT'S JUST PART OF THE ROMANCE.

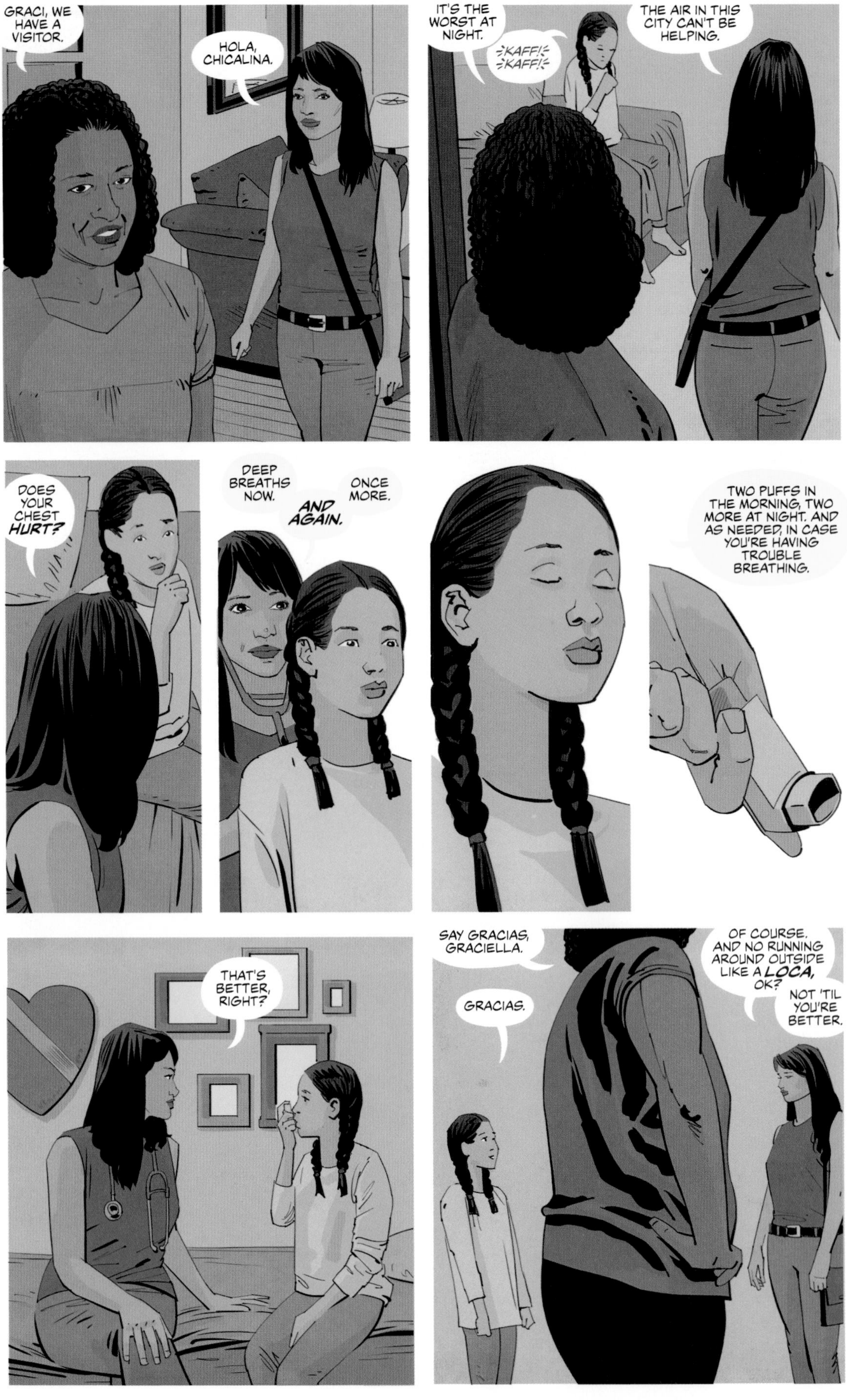
GRACI, WE HAVE A VISITOR.
HOLA, CHICALINA.
IT'S THE WORST AT NIGHT.
KAFF! KAFF!
THE AIR IN THIS CITY CAN'T BE HELPING.
DOES YOUR CHEST HURT?
DEEP BREATHS NOW.
ONCE MORE.
AND AGAIN.
TWO PUFFS IN THE MORNING, TWO MORE AT NIGHT. AND AS NEEDED, IN CASE YOU'RE HAVING TROUBLE BREATHING.
THAT'S BETTER, RIGHT?
SAY GRACIAS, GRACIELLA.
GRACIAS.
OF COURSE. AND NO RUNNING AROUND OUTSIDE LIKE A LOCA, OK?
NOT 'TIL YOU'RE BETTER.

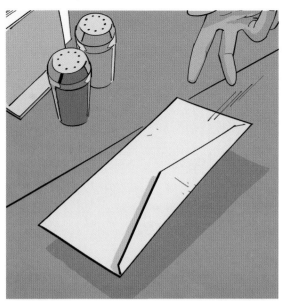

NO NO NO...

IT'S NOT MUCH, BUT IT'S ENOUGH. PUT IT SOMEWHERE SAFE.

SAFE?

I HAVEN'T BEEN TOUCHED IN YEARS.

AND YOU?

HE CAN'T KEEP HIS HANDS OFF ME.

NO, I MEAN--

I'M THE SAME... AS ALWAYS.

GRACIAS.

YOU ALWAYS HAVE A PLACE HERE. IF YOU'RE NOT ON TOP OF HIM.

LUISA'S COOKING?

I WAS GOING TO SAVE IT FOR TOMORROW. SO I DIDN'T HAVE TO COOK.

WE COULD DO THAT.

...HERE.

I RAN INTO ARGUELLO AT THE MARKET.

DID YOU NOW...

HE SAID SOME THINGS.

IS THAT ALL THE MONEY WE HAVE LEFT SAVED UP?

MY MIND WAS ALREADY MADE UP. YOU KNEW THAT.

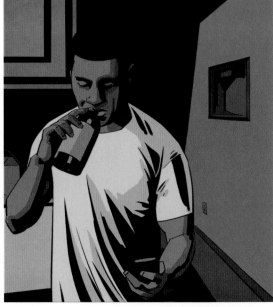

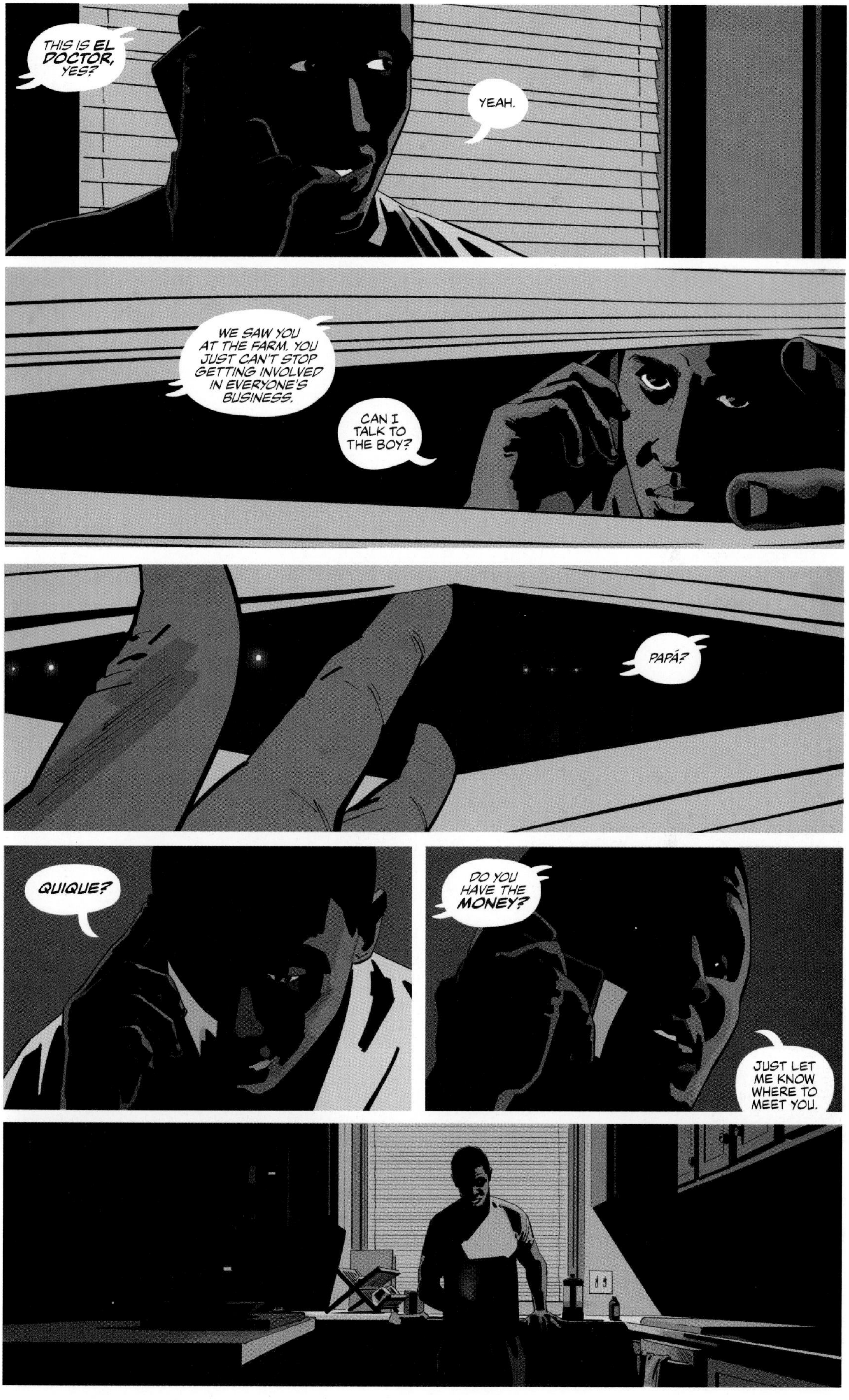
THIS IS EL DOCTOR, YES?
YEAH.
WE SAW YOU AT THE FARM. YOU JUST CAN'T STOP GETTING INVOLVED IN EVERYONE'S BUSINESS.
CAN I TALK TO THE BOY?
PAPÁ?
QUIQUE?
DO YOU HAVE THE MONEY?
JUST LET ME KNOW WHERE TO MEET YOU.

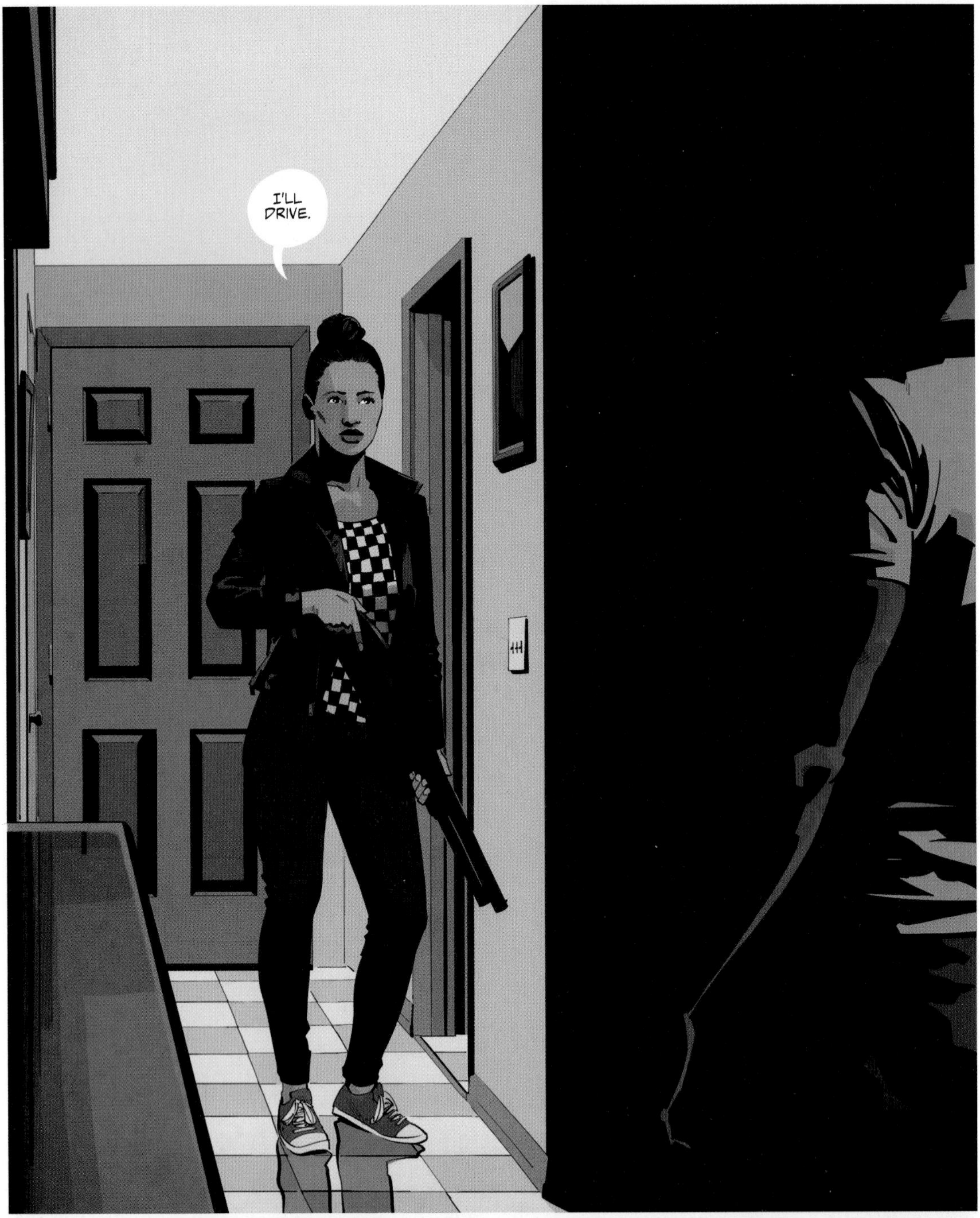
I'LL DRIVE.

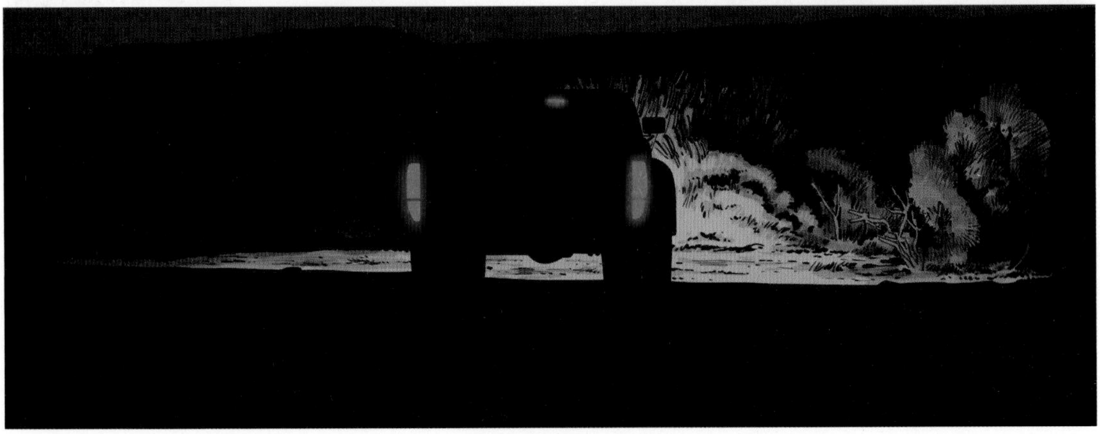

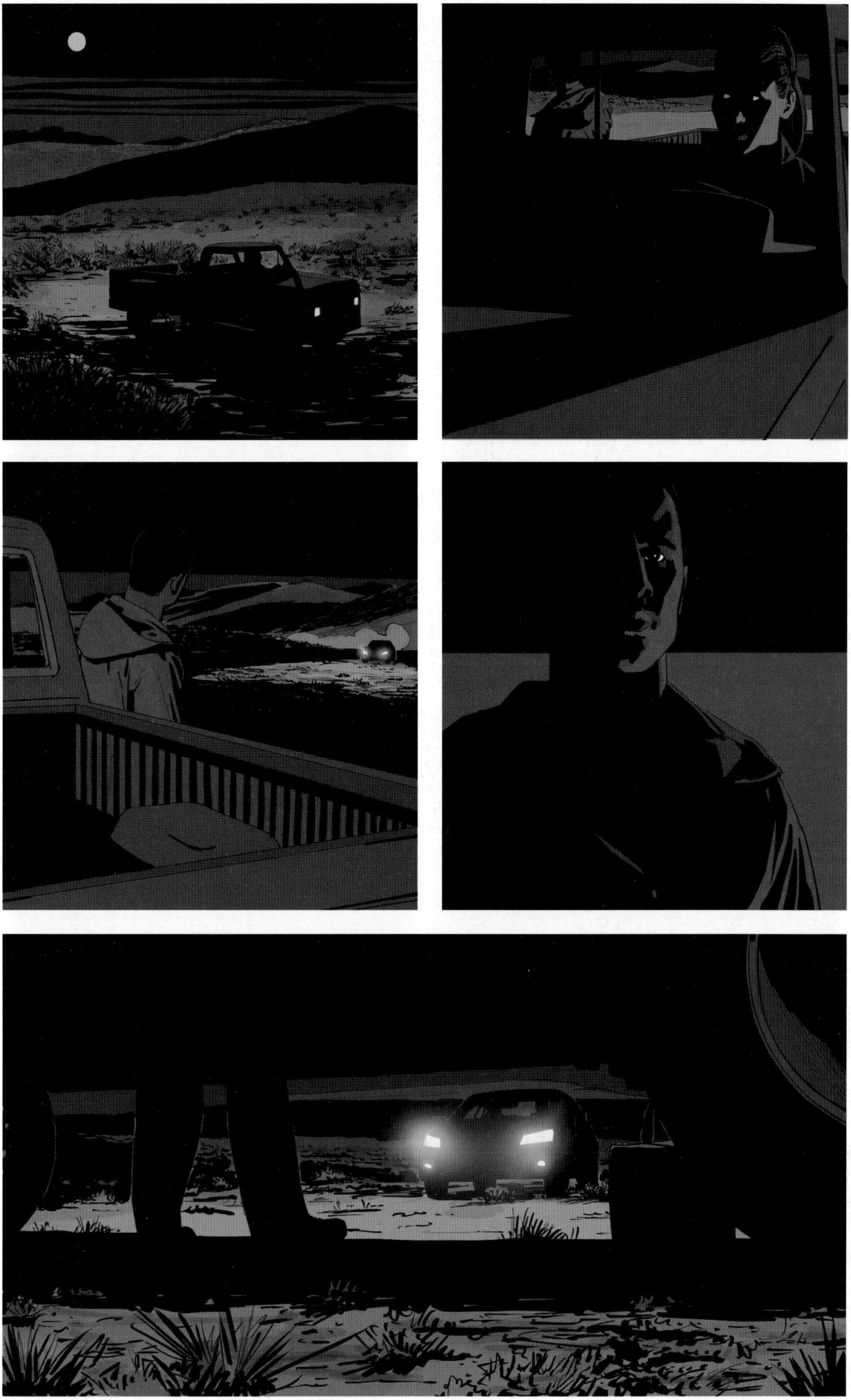

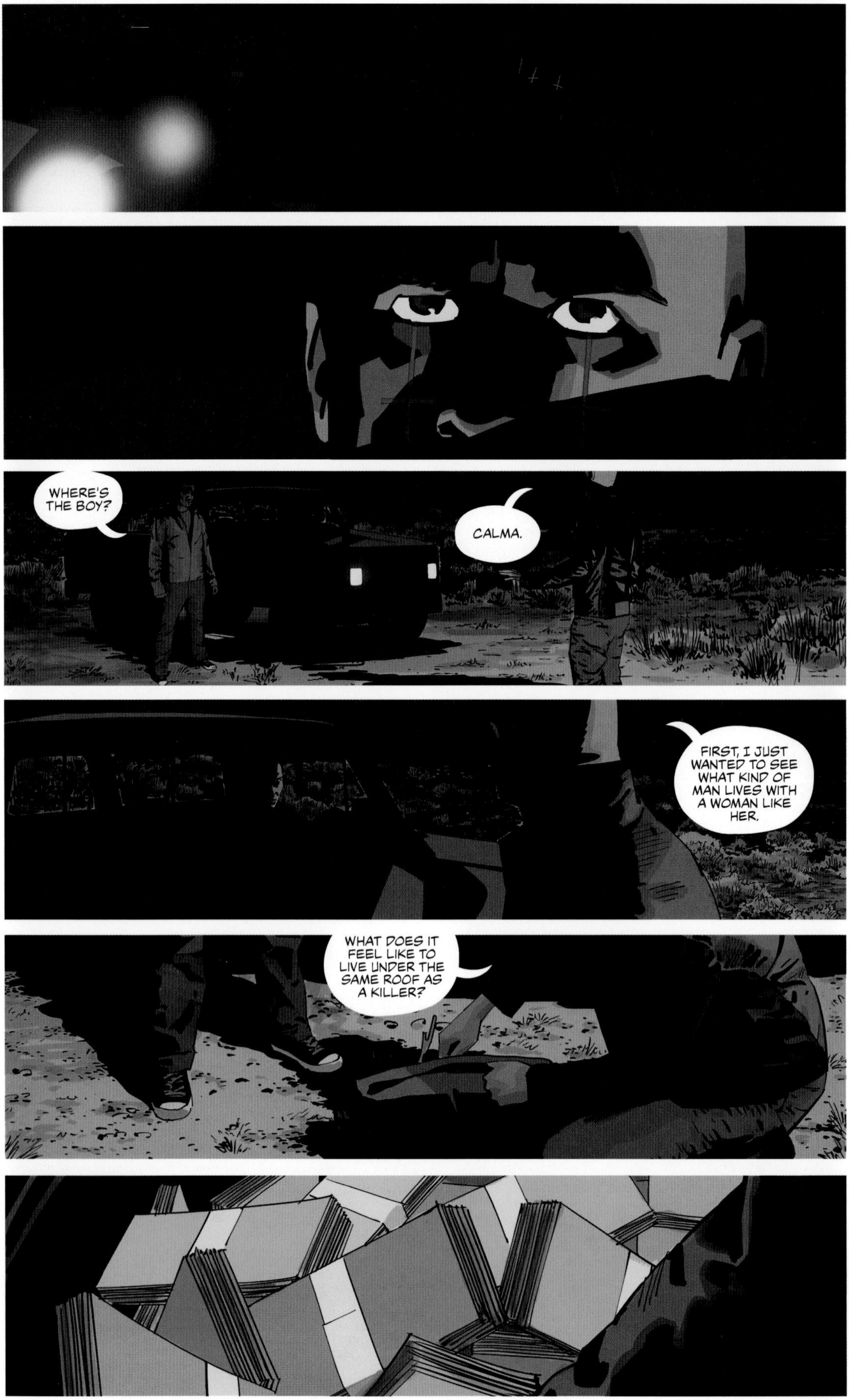
WHERE'S THE BOY?
CALMA.
FIRST, I JUST WANTED TO SEE WHAT KIND OF MAN LIVES WITH A WOMAN LIKE HER.
WHAT DOES IT FEEL LIKE TO LIVE UNDER THE SAME ROOF AS A KILLER?

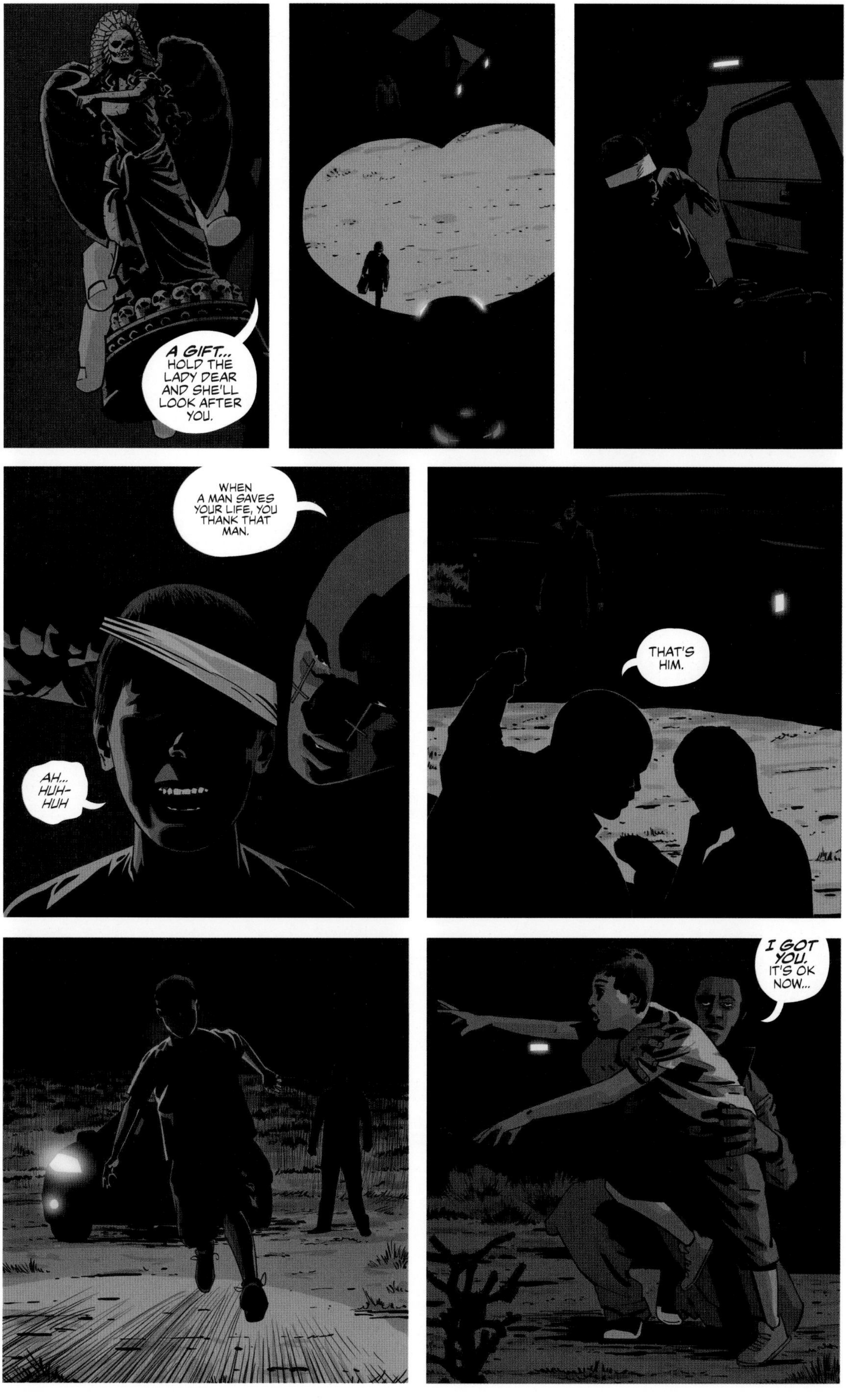
A GIFT... HOLD THE LADY DEAR AND SHE'LL LOOK AFTER YOU.
WHEN A MAN SAVES YOUR LIFE, YOU THANK THAT MAN.
AH... HUH-HUH
THAT'S HIM.
I GOT YOU. IT'S OK NOW...

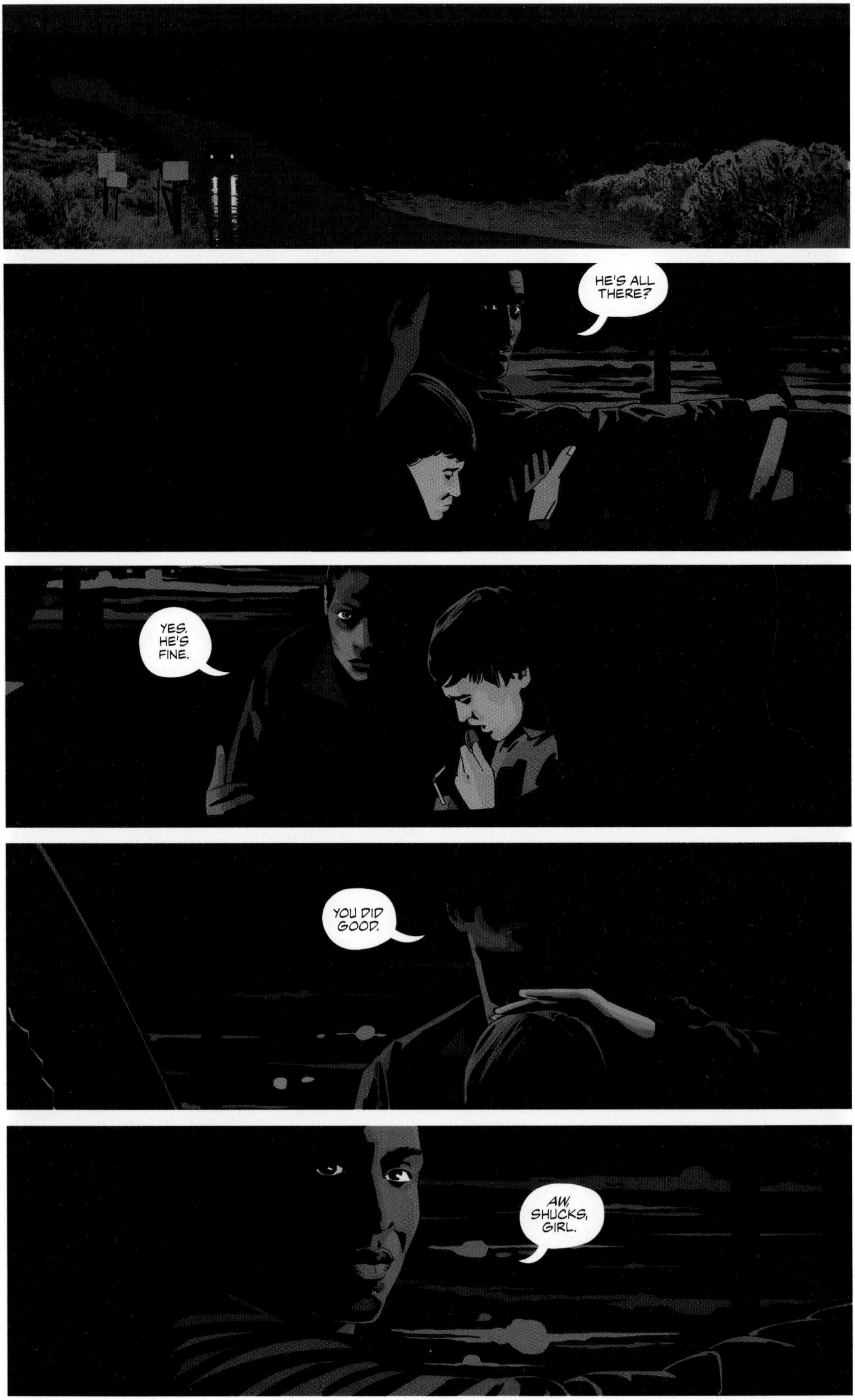
HE'S ALL THERE?
YES. HE'S FINE.
YOU DID GOOD.
AW, SHUCKS, GIRL.

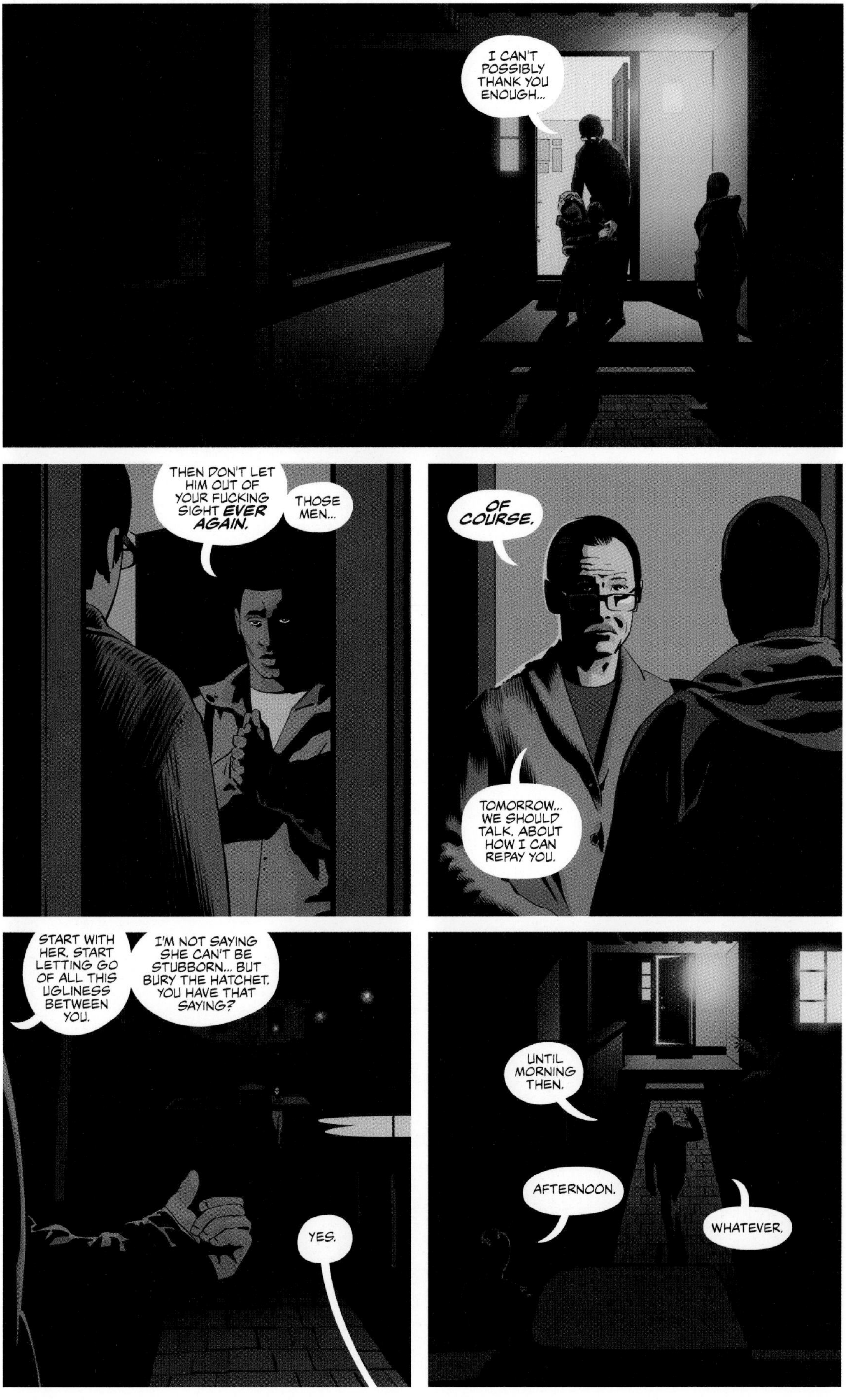

I CAN'T POSSIBLY THANK YOU ENOUGH...
THEN DON'T LET HIM OUT OF YOUR FUCKING SIGHT EVER AGAIN.
THOSE MEN...
OF COURSE.
TOMORROW... WE SHOULD TALK. ABOUT HOW I CAN REPAY YOU.
START WITH HER. START LETTING GO OF ALL THIS UGLINESS BETWEEN YOU.
I'M NOT SAYING SHE CAN'T BE STUBBORN... BUT BURY THE HATCHET. YOU HAVE THAT SAYING?
YES.
UNTIL MORNING THEN.
AFTERNOON.
WHATEVER.

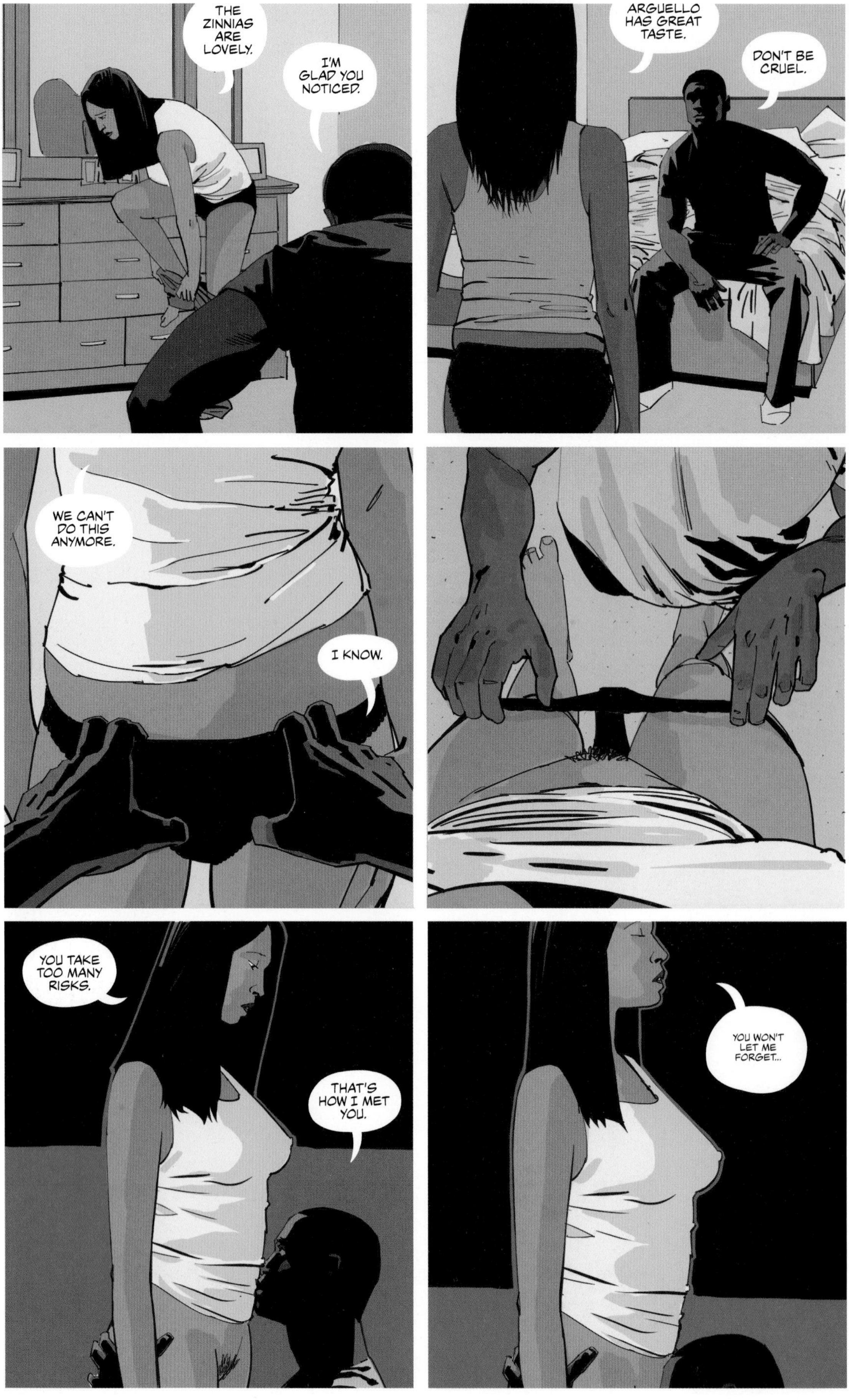
THE ZINNIAS ARE LOVELY.
I'M GLAD YOU NOTICED.
ARGUELLO HAS GREAT TASTE.
DON'T BE CRUEL.
WE CAN'T DO THIS ANYMORE.
I KNOW.
YOU TAKE TOO MANY RISKS.
THAT'S HOW I MET YOU.
YOU WON'T LET ME FORGET...

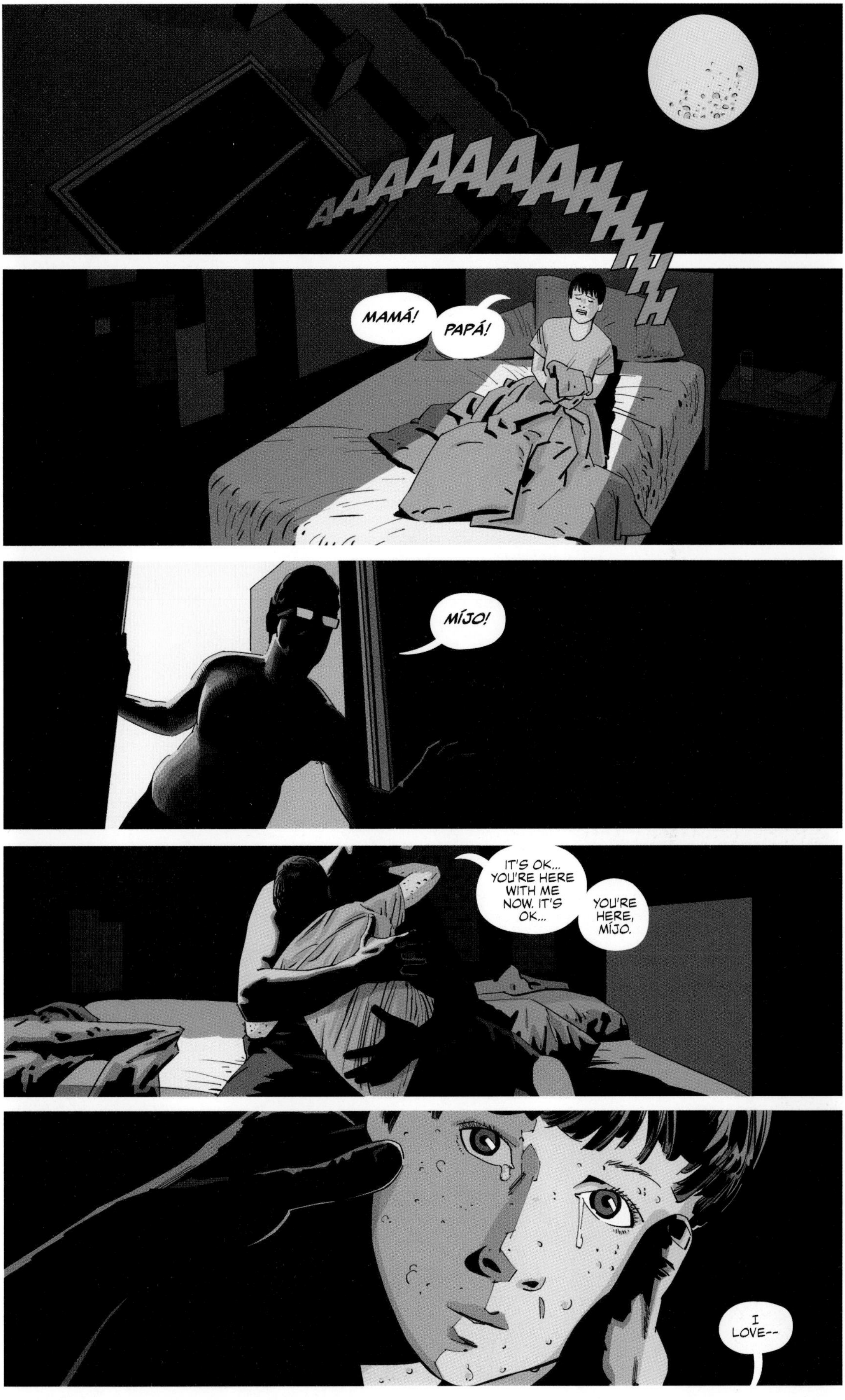
AAAAAAAAHHHHHH
MAMÁ!
PAPÁ!
MÍJO!
IT'S OK... YOU'RE HERE WITH ME NOW. IT'S OK...
YOU'RE HERE, MÍJO.
I LOVE--

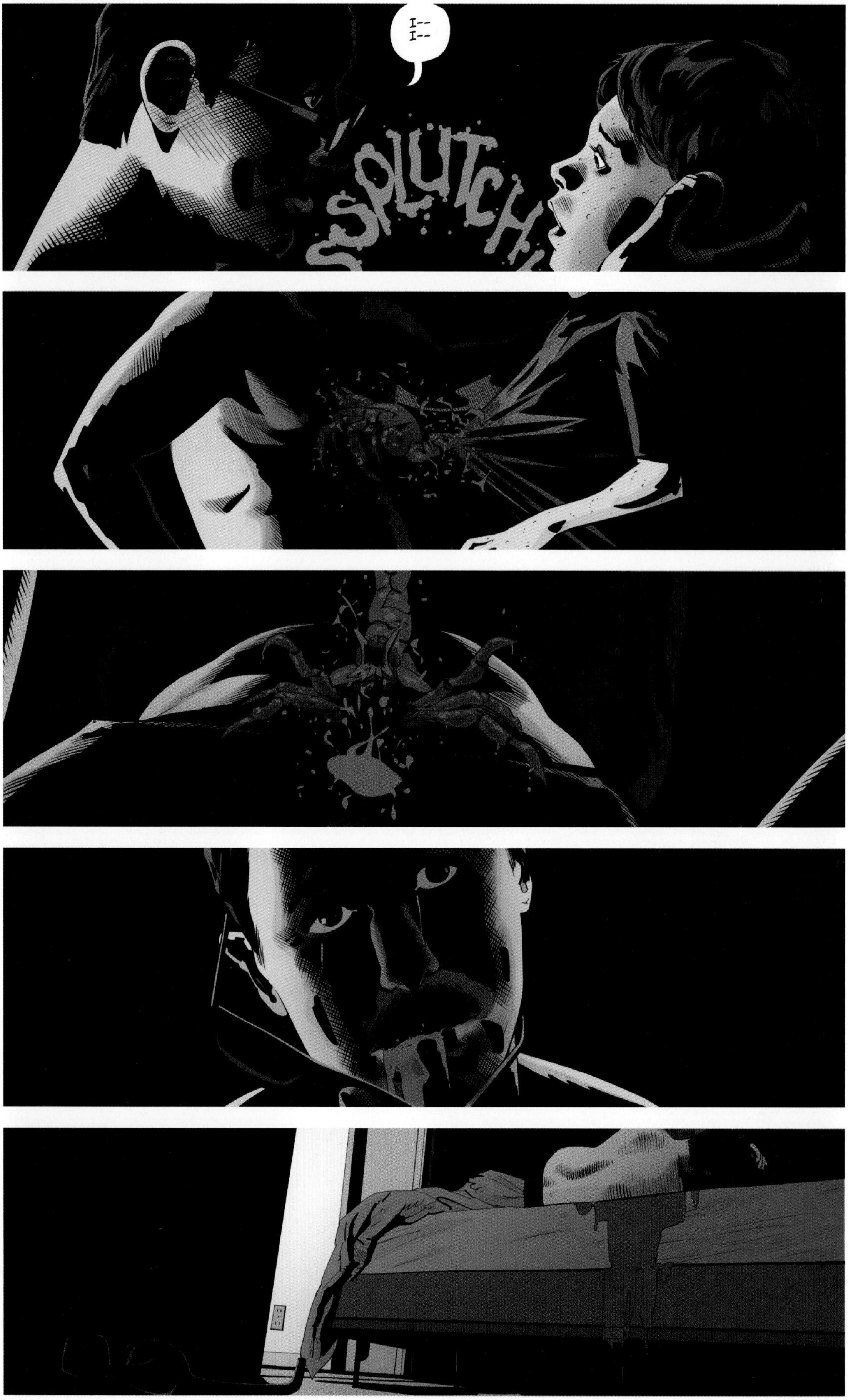
I--
I--
SPLUTCH!

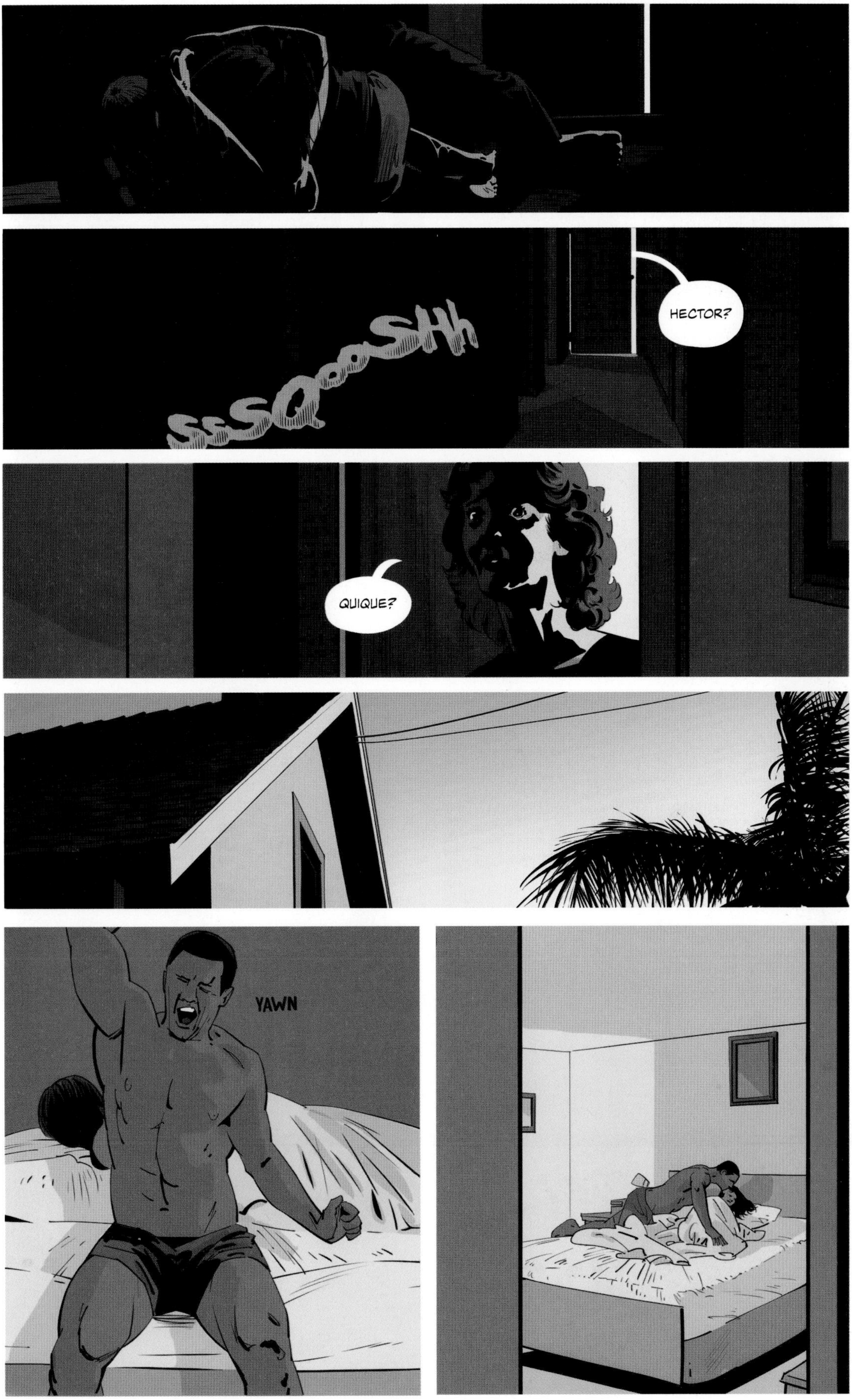
HECTOR?
SSSQooSHh
QUIQUE?
YAWN

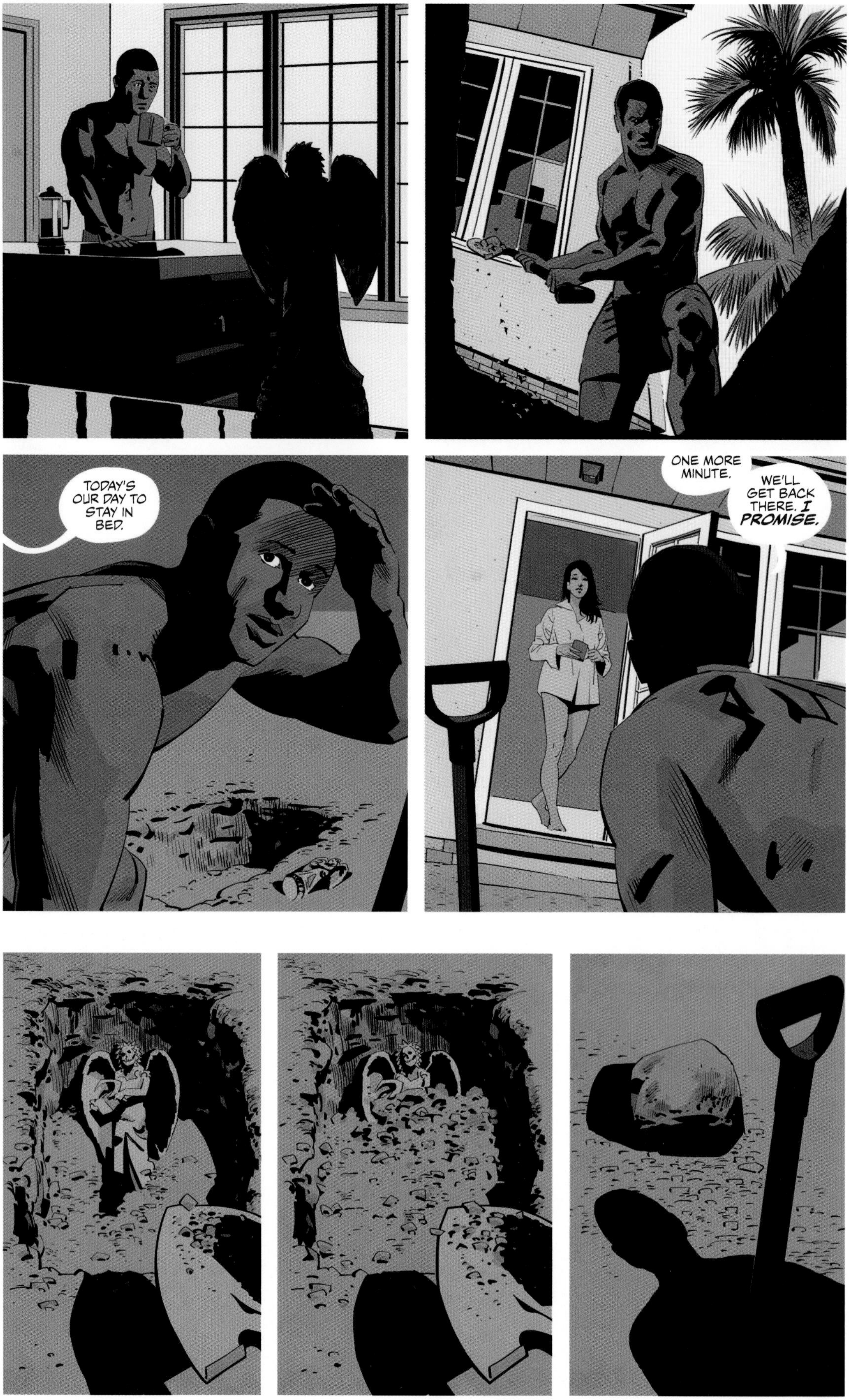
TODAY'S OUR DAY TO STAY IN BED.
ONE MORE MINUTE.
WE'LL GET BACK THERE. I PROMISE.

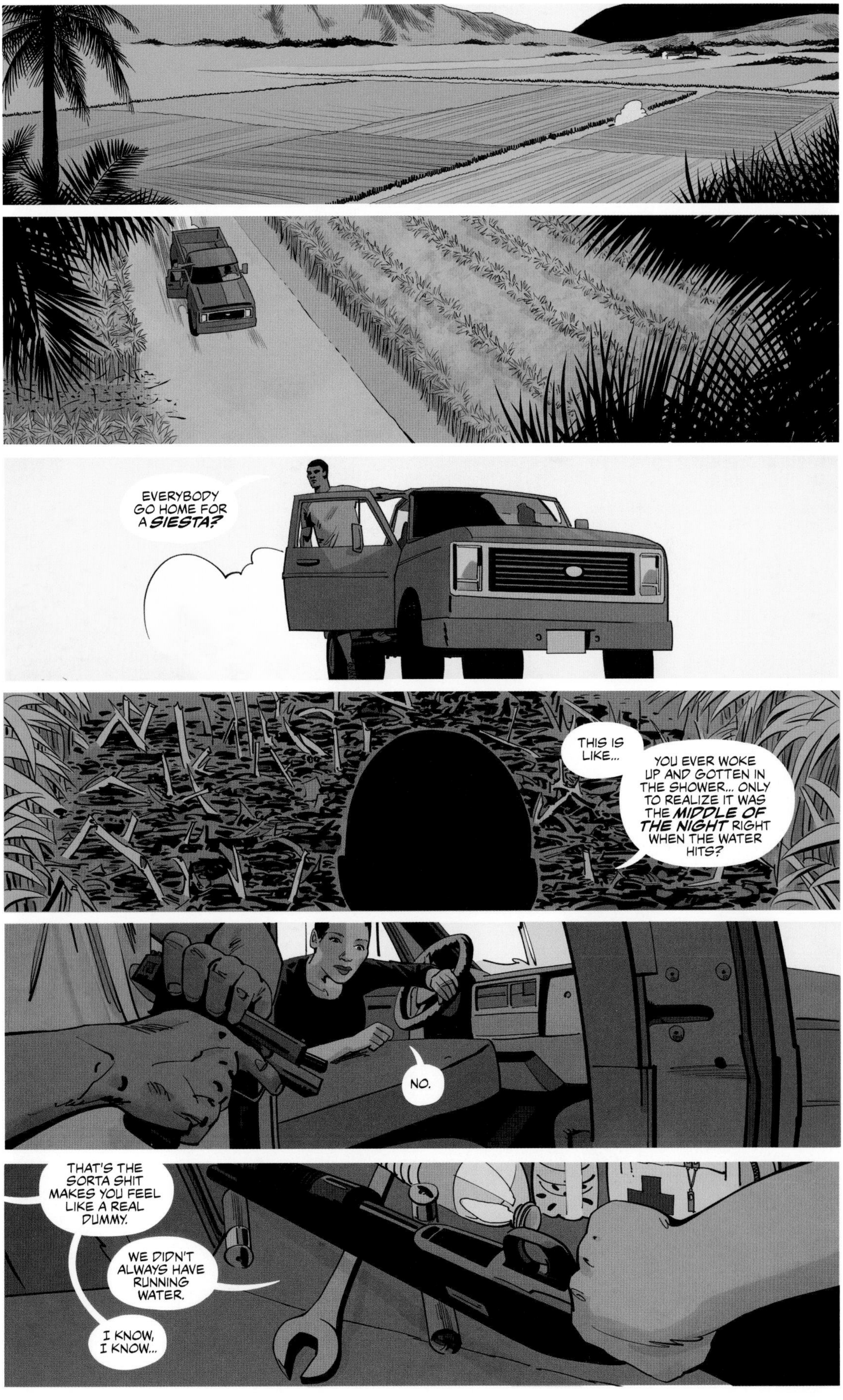
EVERYBODY GO HOME FOR A *SIESTA?*
THIS IS LIKE...
YOU EVER WOKE UP AND GOTTEN IN THE SHOWER... ONLY TO REALIZE IT WAS THE *MIDDLE OF THE NIGHT* RIGHT WHEN THE WATER HITS?
NO.
THAT'S THE SORTA SHIT MAKES YOU FEEL LIKE A REAL DUMMY.
WE DIDN'T ALWAYS HAVE RUNNING WATER.
I KNOW, I KNOW...

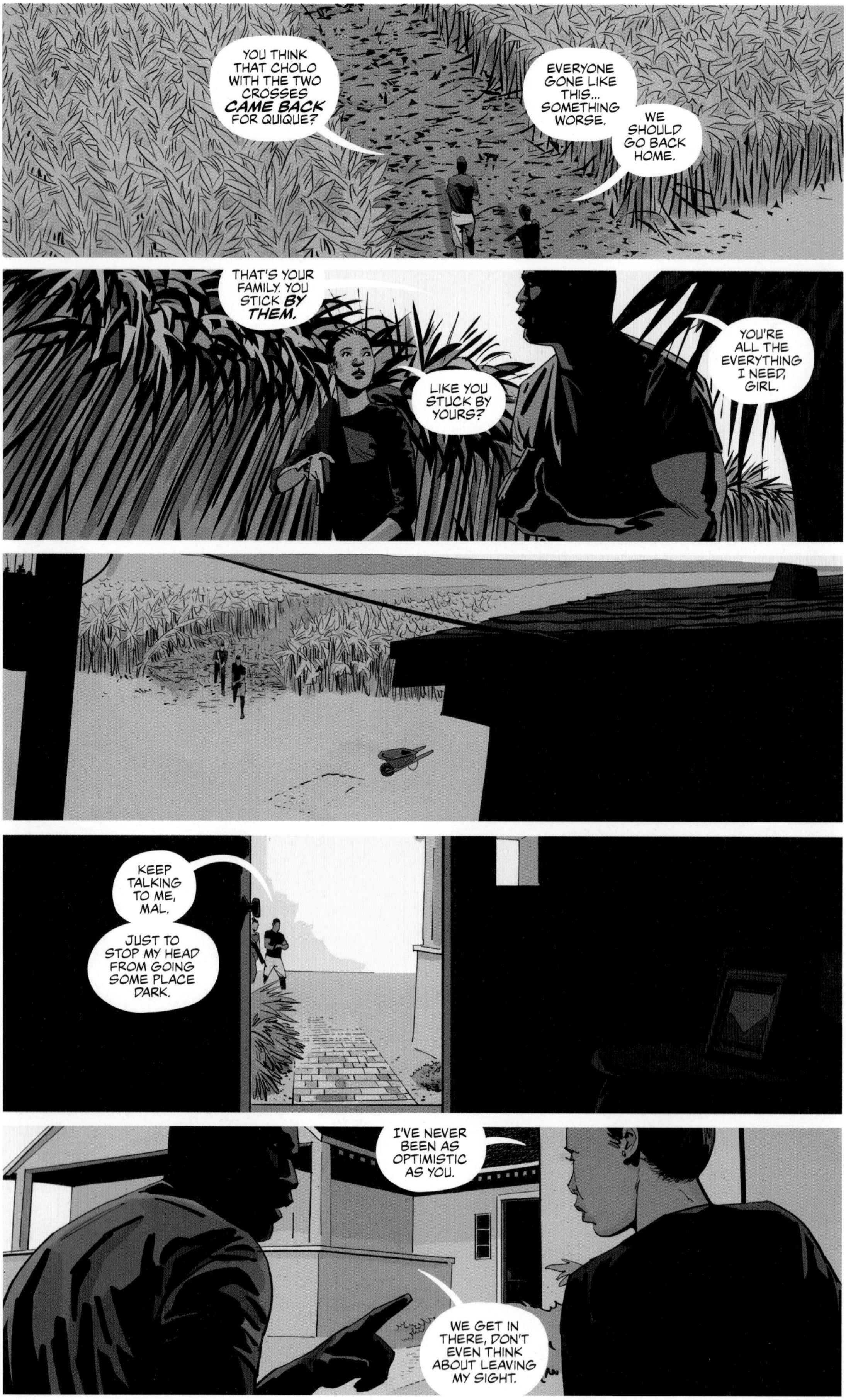
YOU THINK THAT CHOLO WITH THE TWO CROSSES **CAME BACK** FOR QUIQUE?
EVERYONE GONE LIKE THIS... SOMETHING WORSE.
WE SHOULD GO BACK HOME.
THAT'S YOUR FAMILY. YOU STICK **BY THEM.**
LIKE YOU STUCK BY YOURS?
YOU'RE ALL THE EVERYTHING I NEED, GIRL.
KEEP TALKING TO ME, MAL.
JUST TO STOP MY HEAD FROM GOING SOME PLACE DARK.
I'VE NEVER BEEN AS OPTIMISTIC AS YOU.
WE GET IN THERE, DON'T EVEN THINK ABOUT LEAVING MY SIGHT.

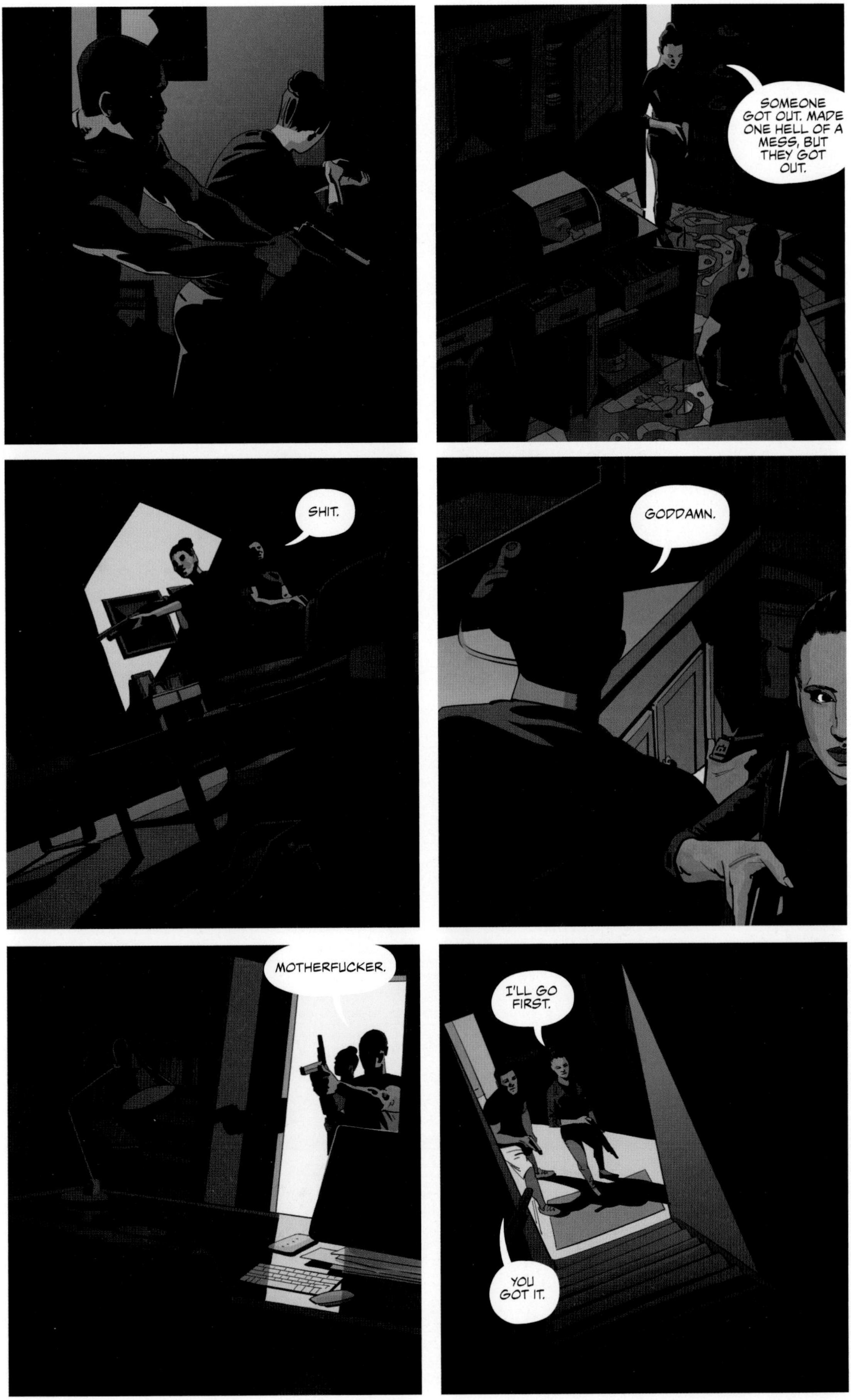
SOMEONE GOT OUT. MADE ONE HELL OF A MESS, BUT THEY GOT OUT.
SHIT.
GODDAMN.
MOTHERFUCKER.
I'LL GO FIRST.
YOU GOT IT.

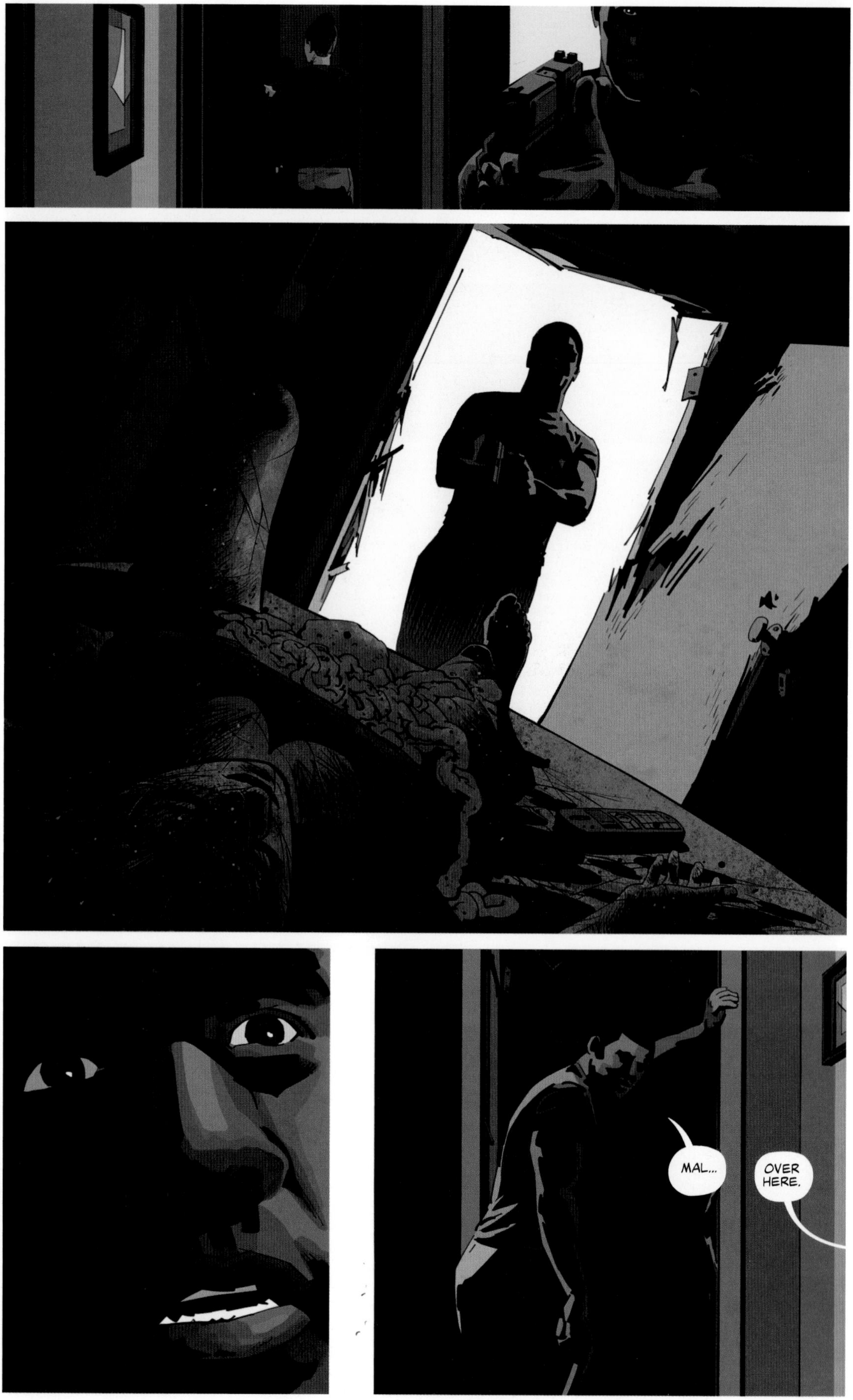
MAL...
OVER HERE.

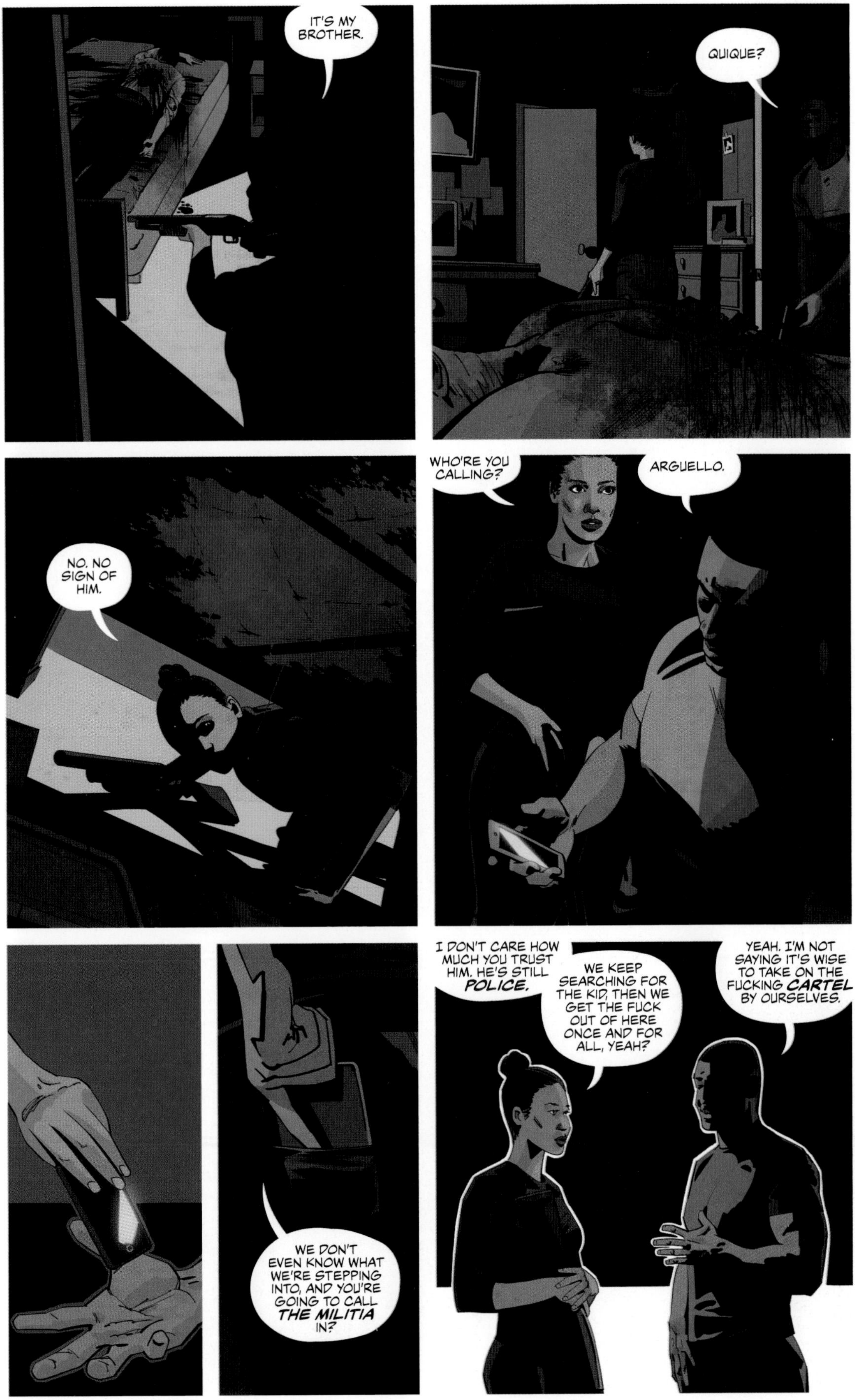
IT'S MY BROTHER.
QUIQUE?
NO. NO SIGN OF HIM.
WHO'RE YOU CALLING?
ARGUELLO.
WE DON'T EVEN KNOW WHAT WE'RE STEPPING INTO, AND YOU'RE GOING TO CALL THE MILITIA IN?
I DON'T CARE HOW MUCH YOU TRUST HIM. HE'S STILL POLICE.
WE KEEP SEARCHING FOR THE KID, THEN WE GET THE FUCK OUT OF HERE ONCE AND FOR ALL, YEAH?
YEAH. I'M NOT SAYING IT'S WISE TO TAKE ON THE FUCKING CARTEL BY OURSELVES.

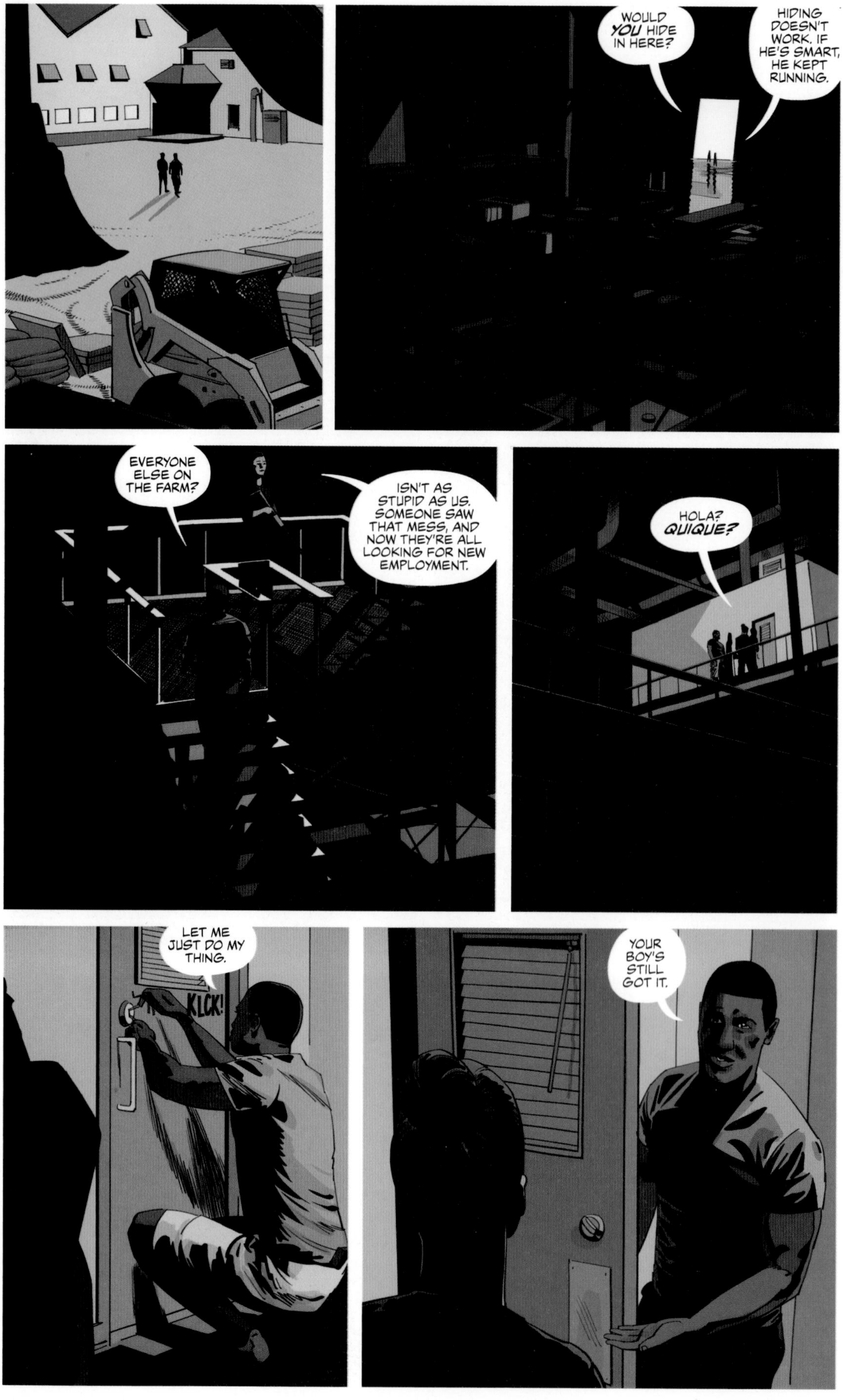
WOULD YOU HIDE IN HERE?
HIDING DOESN'T WORK. IF HE'S SMART, HE KEPT RUNNING.
EVERYONE ELSE ON THE FARM?
ISN'T AS STUPID AS US. SOMEONE SAW THAT MESS, AND NOW THEY'RE ALL LOOKING FOR NEW EMPLOYMENT.
HOLA? QUIQUE?
LET ME JUST DO MY THING.
KLCK!
YOUR BOY'S STILL GOT IT.

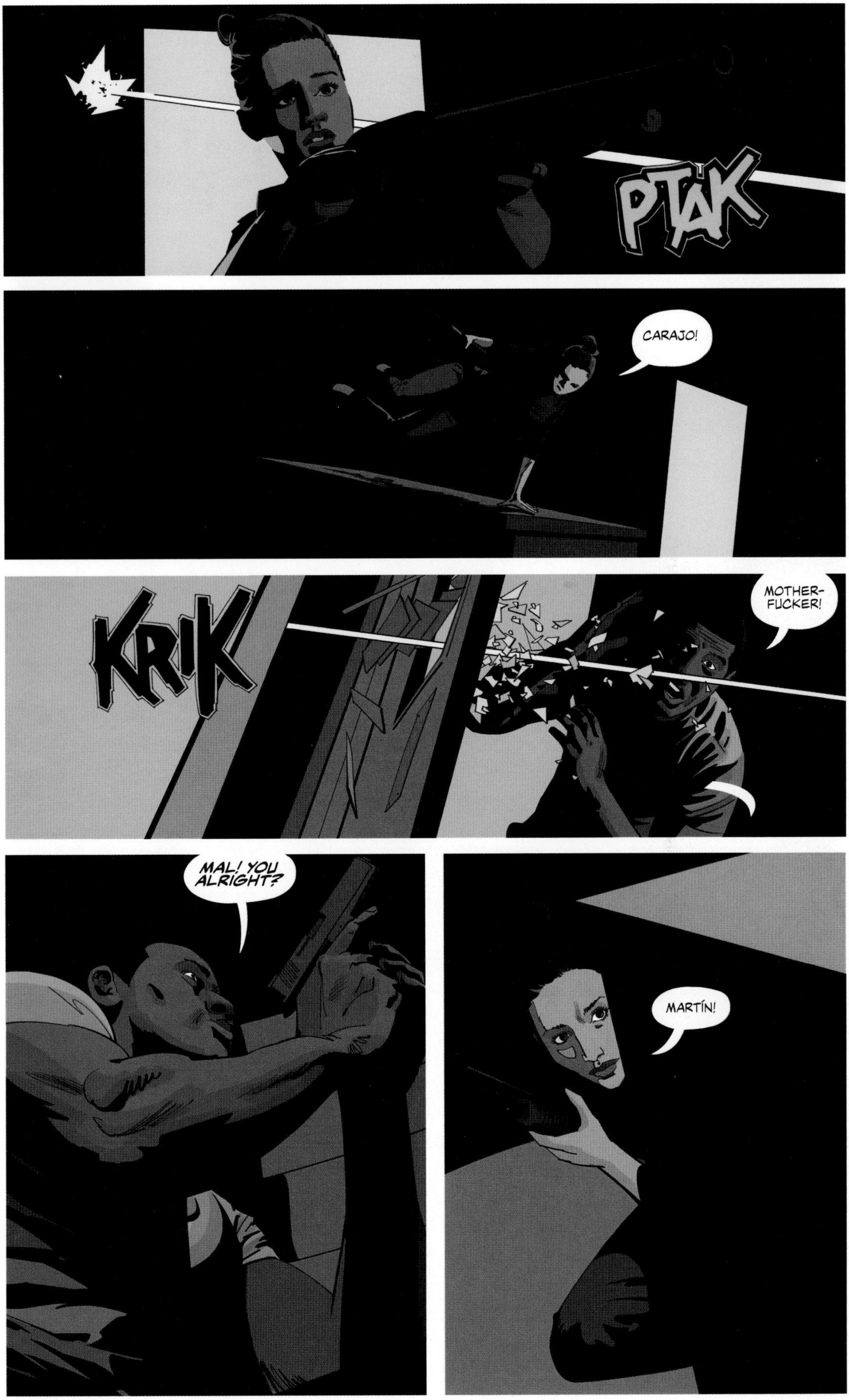
PTAK
CARAJO!
KRIK
MOTHER-FUCKER!
MAL! YOU ALRIGHT?
MARTÍN!

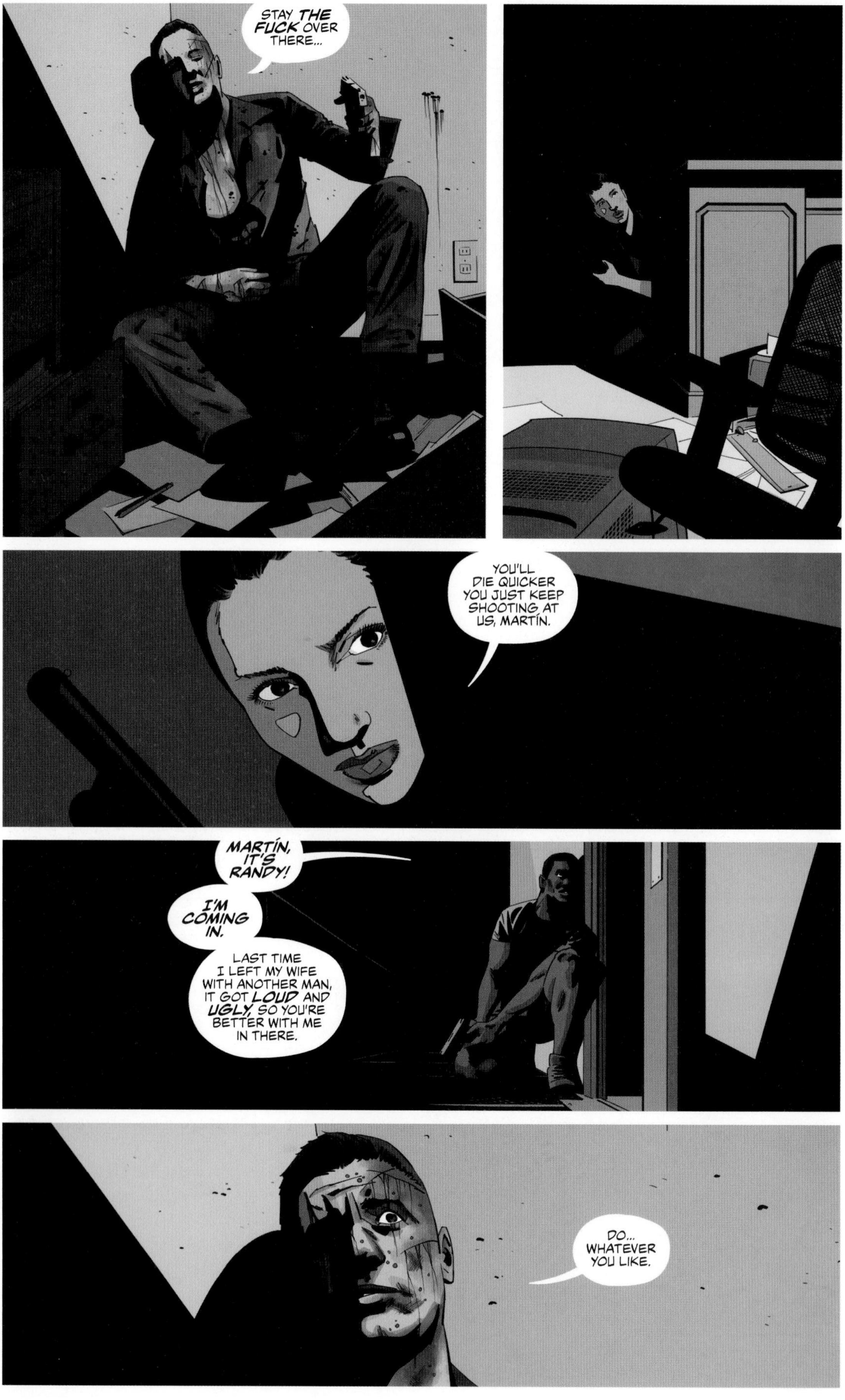
STAY THE FUCK OVER THERE...
YOU'LL DIE QUICKER YOU JUST KEEP SHOOTING AT US, MARTÍN.
MARTÍN, IT'S RANDY!
I'M COMING IN.
LAST TIME I LEFT MY WIFE WITH ANOTHER MAN, IT GOT LOUD AND UGLY, SO YOU'RE BETTER WITH ME IN THERE.
DO... WHATEVER YOU LIKE.

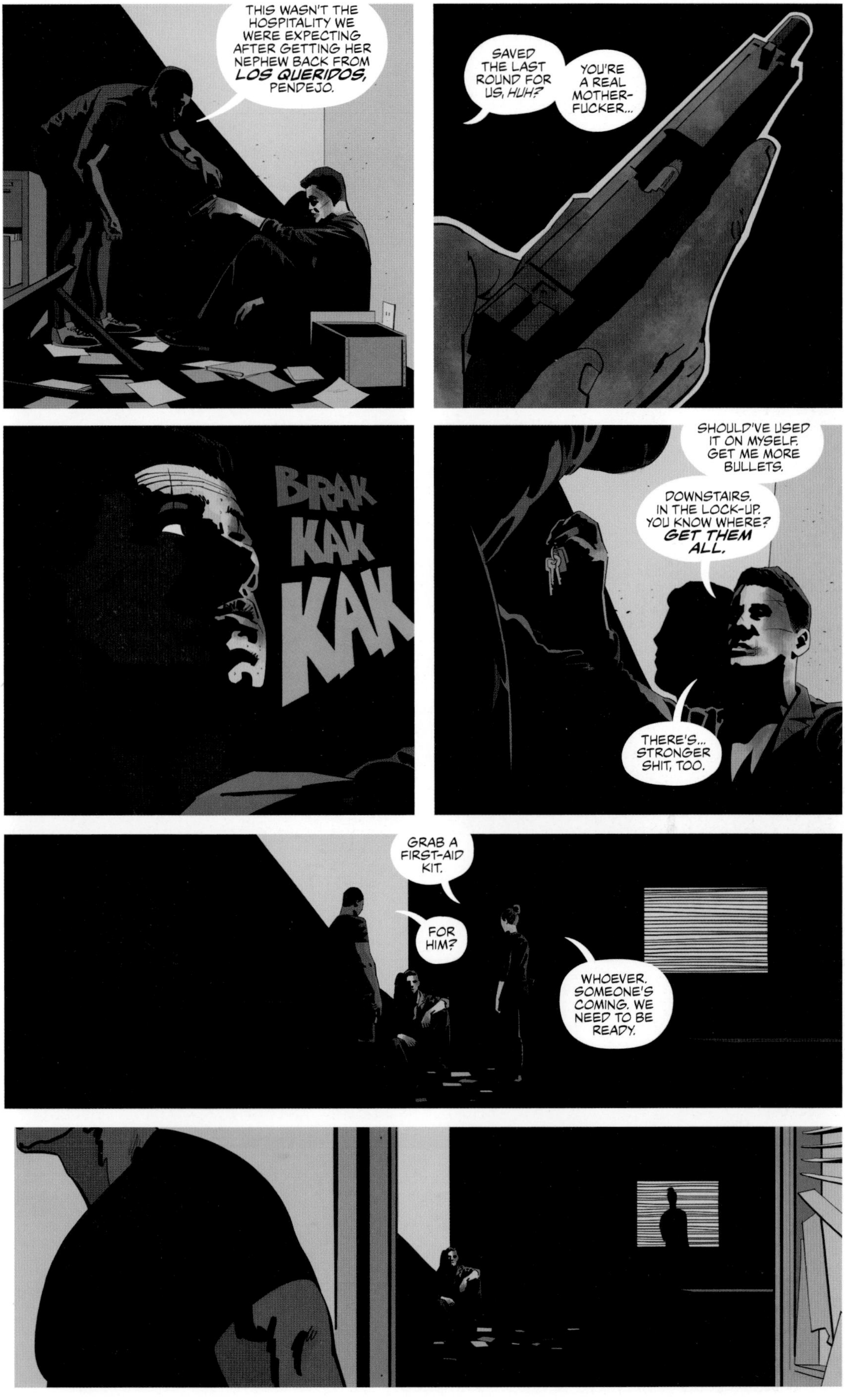
THIS WASN'T THE HOSPITALITY WE WERE EXPECTING AFTER GETTING HER NEPHEW BACK FROM *LOS QUERIDOS,* PENDEJO.
SAVED THE LAST ROUND FOR US, *HUH?*
YOU'RE A REAL MOTHER-FUCKER...
BRAK
KAK
KAK
SHOULD'VE USED IT ON MYSELF. GET ME MORE BULLETS.
DOWNSTAIRS. IN THE LOCK-UP. YOU KNOW WHERE? ***GET THEM ALL.***
THERE'S... STRONGER SHIT, TOO.
GRAB A FIRST-AID KIT.
FOR HIM?
WHOEVER. SOMEONE'S COMING. WE NEED TO BE READY.

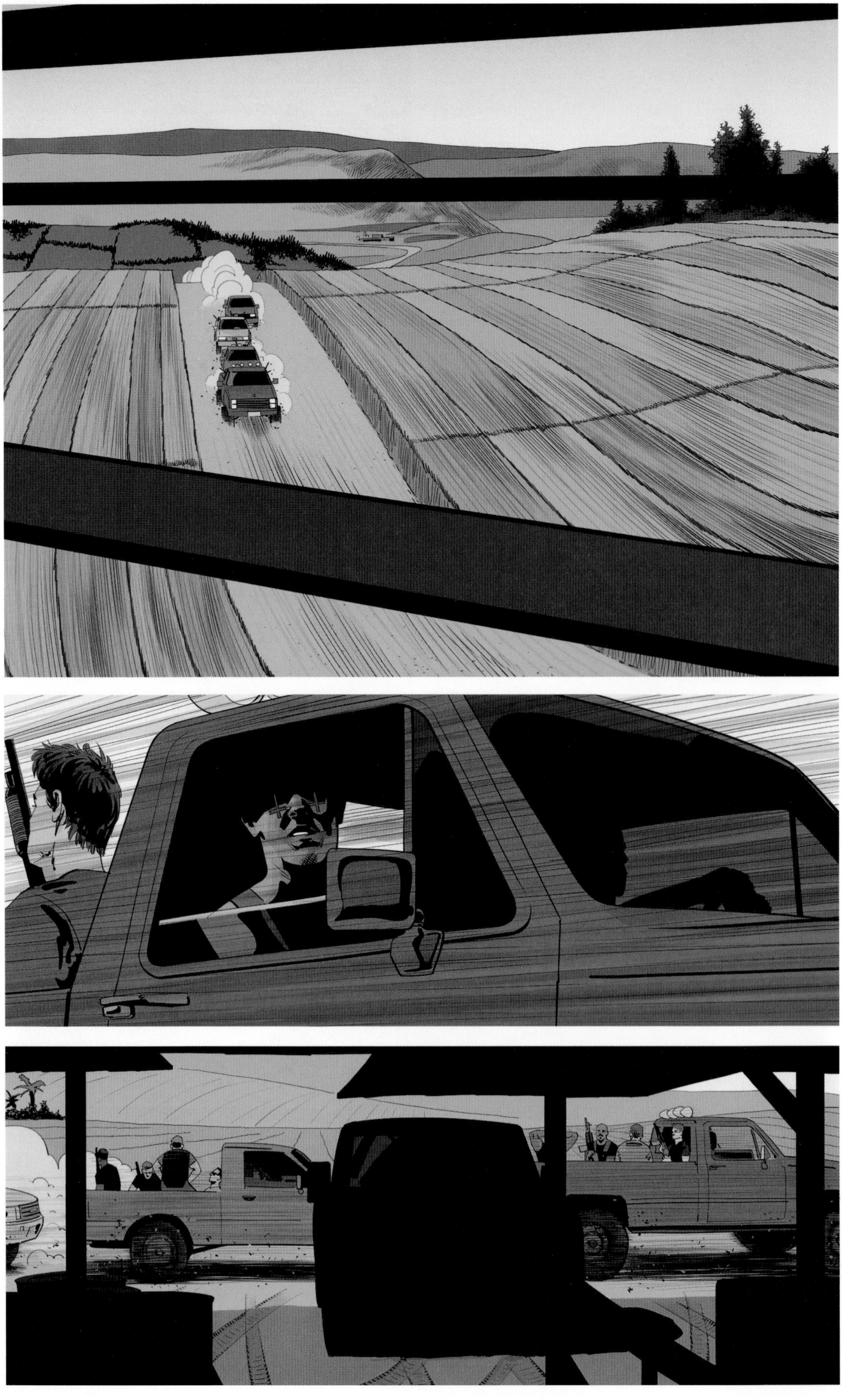

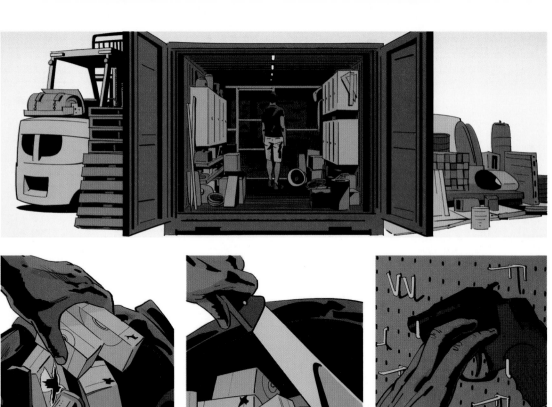

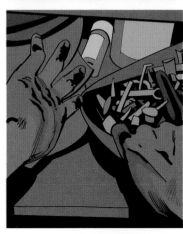

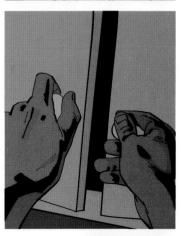

DAMN, DAMN... GOOD *GODDAMN...*

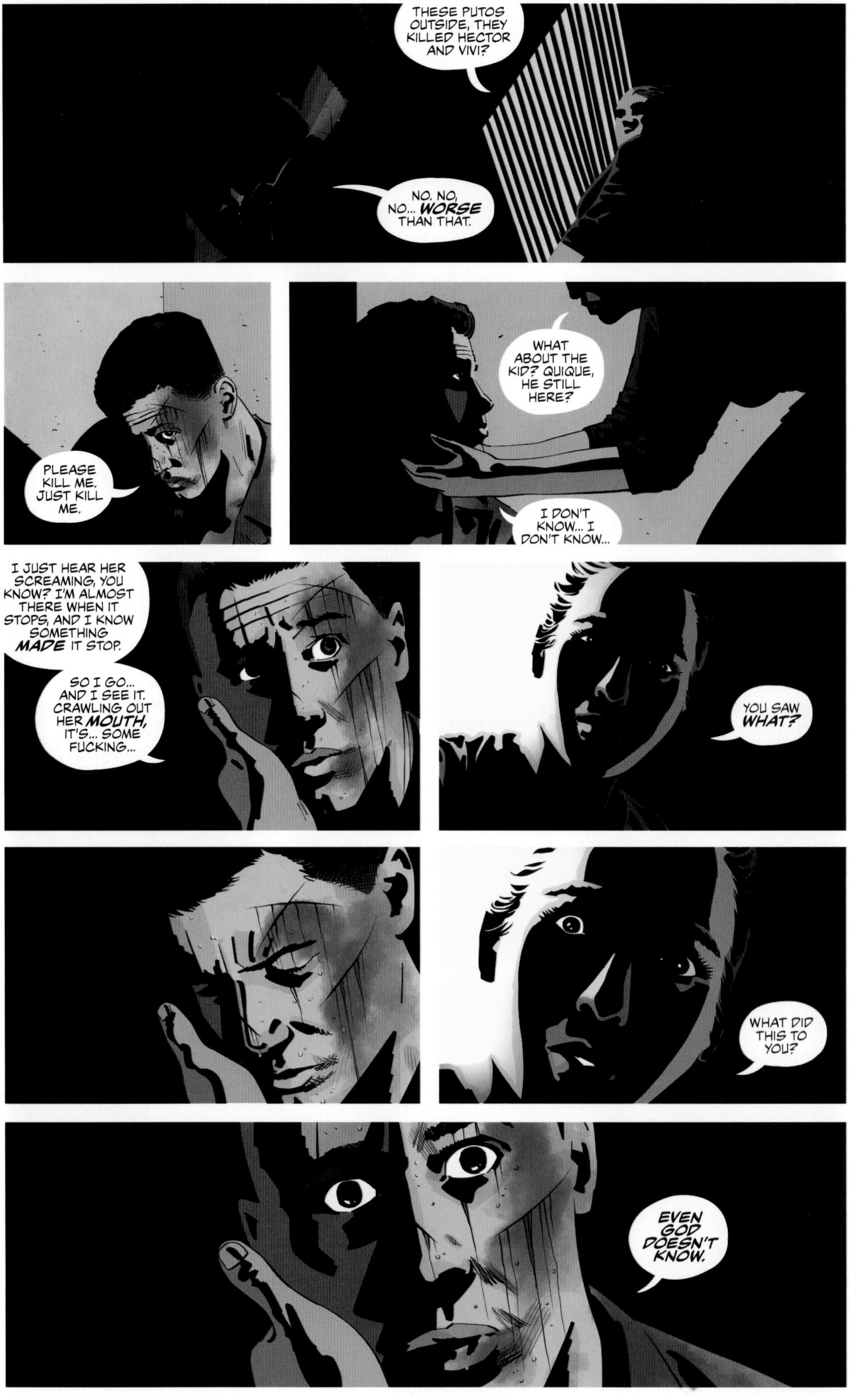
THESE PUTOS OUTSIDE, THEY KILLED HECTOR AND VIVI?
NO. NO, NO... WORSE THAN THAT.
PLEASE KILL ME. JUST KILL ME.
WHAT ABOUT THE KID? QUIQUE, HE STILL HERE?
I DON'T KNOW... I DON'T KNOW...
I JUST HEAR HER SCREAMING, YOU KNOW? I'M ALMOST THERE WHEN IT STOPS, AND I KNOW SOMETHING MADE IT STOP.
SO I GO... AND I SEE IT. CRAWLING OUT HER MOUTH, IT'S... SOME FUCKING...
YOU SAW WHAT?
WHAT DID THIS TO YOU?
EVEN GOD DOESN'T KNOW.

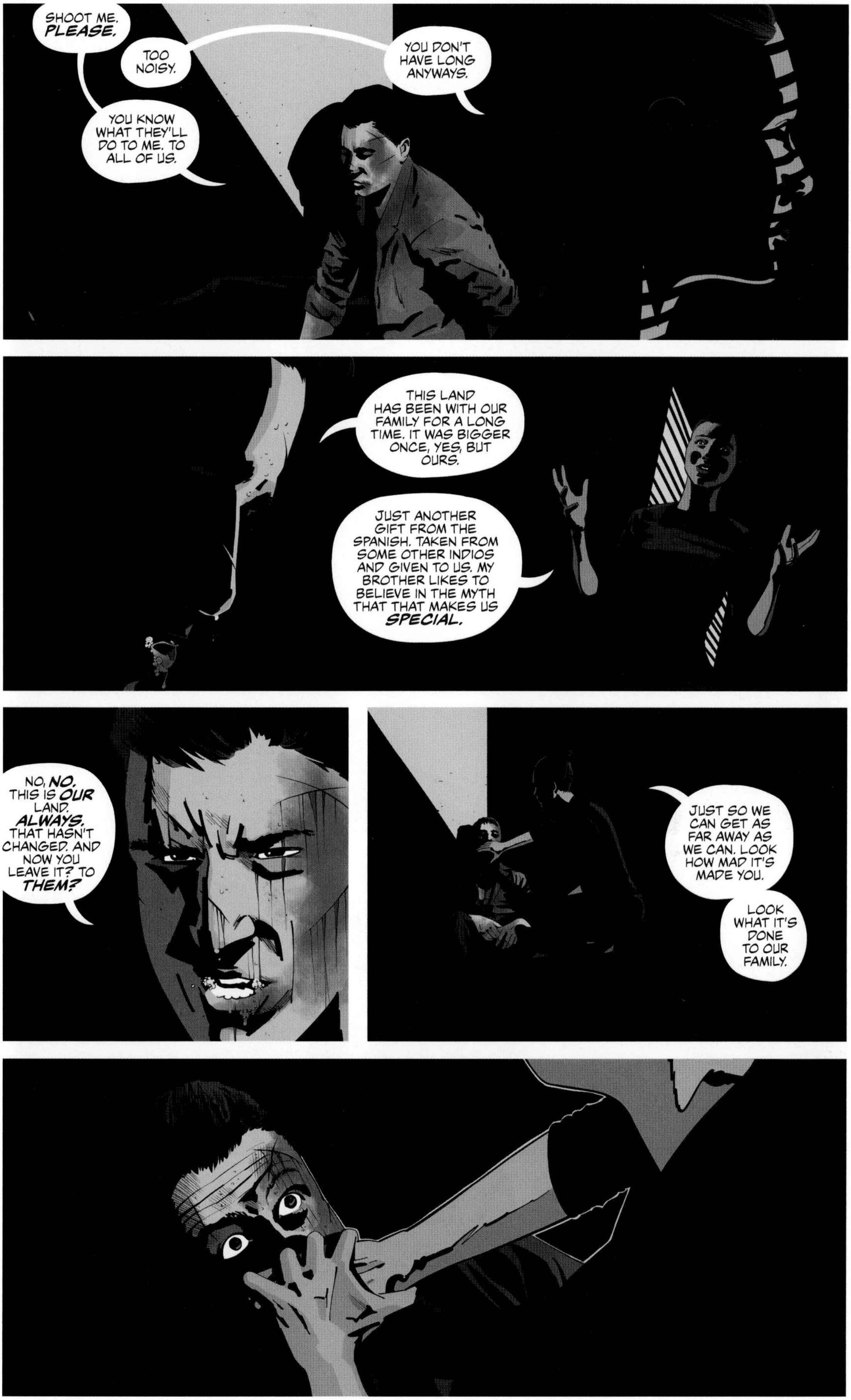
SHOOT ME. *PLEASE.*
TOO NOISY.
YOU DON'T HAVE LONG ANYWAYS.
YOU KNOW WHAT THEY'LL DO TO ME. TO ALL OF US.
THIS LAND HAS BEEN WITH OUR FAMILY FOR A LONG TIME. IT WAS BIGGER ONCE, YES, BUT OURS.
JUST ANOTHER GIFT FROM THE SPANISH. TAKEN FROM SOME OTHER INDIOS AND GIVEN TO US. MY BROTHER LIKES TO BELIEVE IN THE MYTH THAT THAT MAKES US *SPECIAL.*
NO, *NO.* THIS IS *OUR* LAND. *ALWAYS.* THAT HASN'T CHANGED. AND NOW YOU LEAVE IT? TO *THEM?*
JUST SO WE CAN GET AS FAR AWAY AS WE CAN. LOOK HOW MAD IT'S MADE YOU.
LOOK WHAT IT'S DONE TO OUR FAMILY.

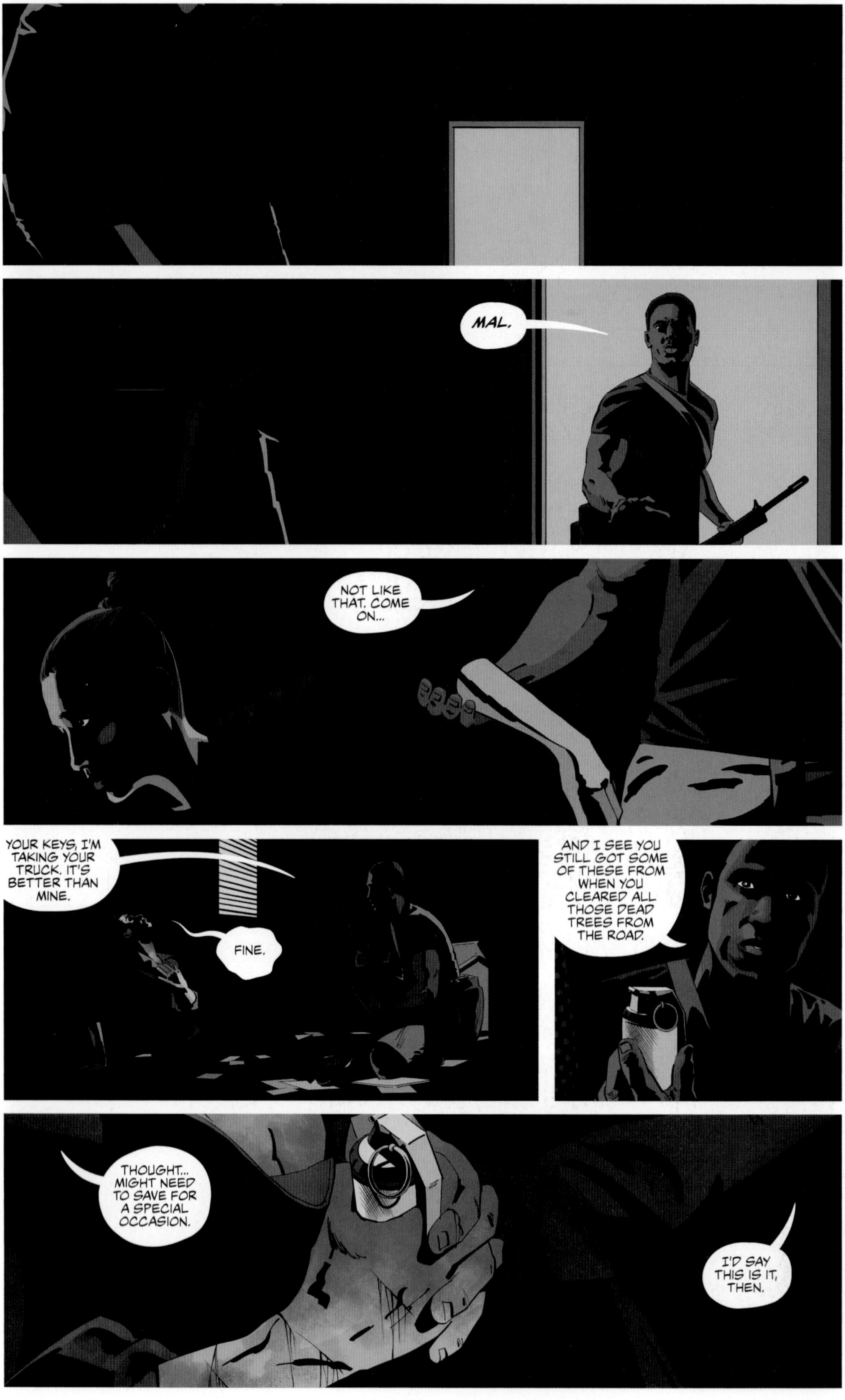
MAL.
NOT LIKE THAT. COME ON...
YOUR KEYS, I'M TAKING YOUR TRUCK. IT'S BETTER THAN MINE.
FINE.
AND I SEE YOU STILL GOT SOME OF THESE FROM WHEN YOU CLEARED ALL THOSE DEAD TREES FROM THE ROAD.
THOUGHT... MIGHT NEED TO SAVE FOR A SPECIAL OCCASION.
I'D SAY THIS IS IT, THEN.

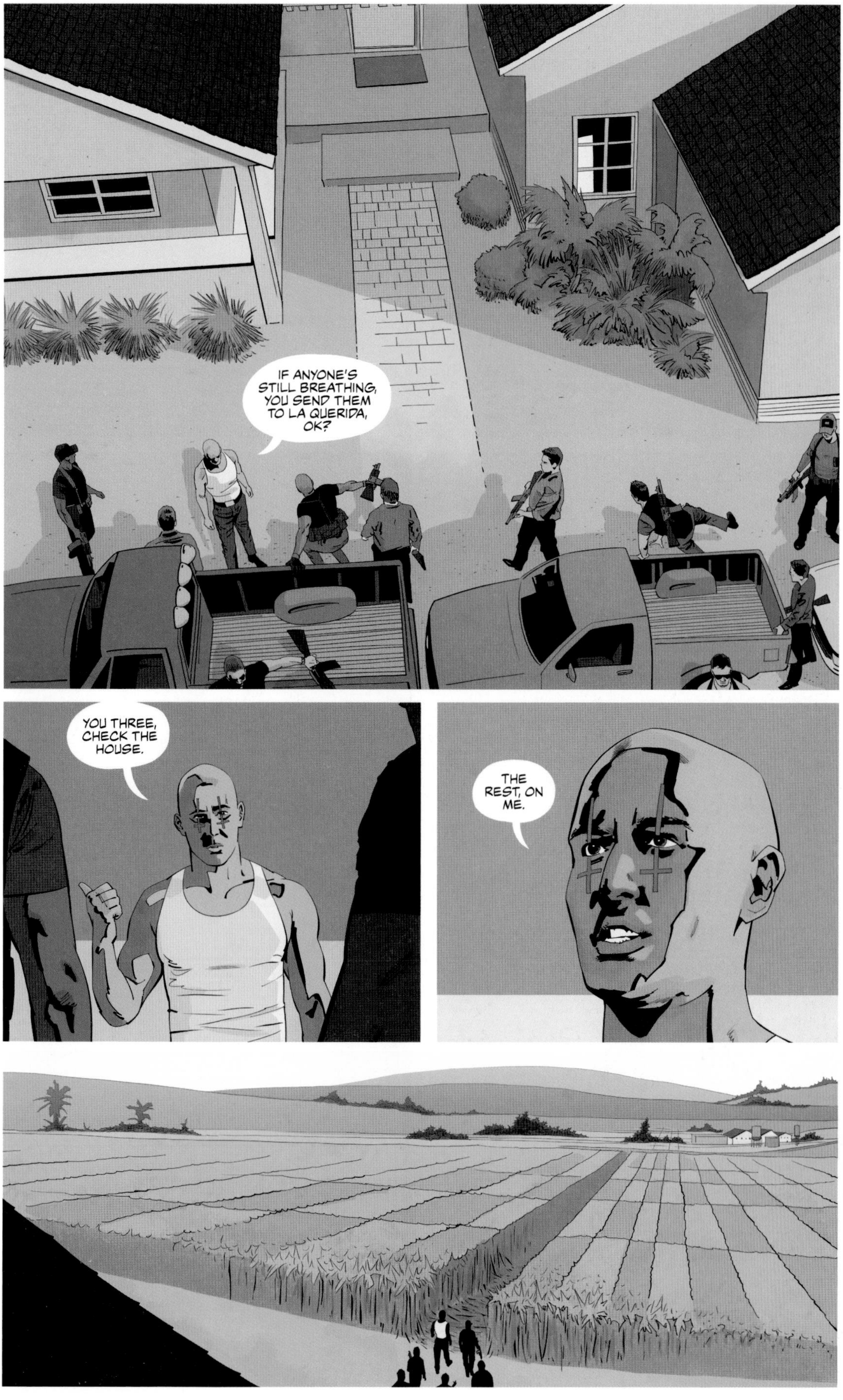
IF ANYONE'S STILL BREATHING, YOU SEND THEM TO LA QUERIDA, OK?
YOU THREE, CHECK THE HOUSE.
THE REST, ON ME.

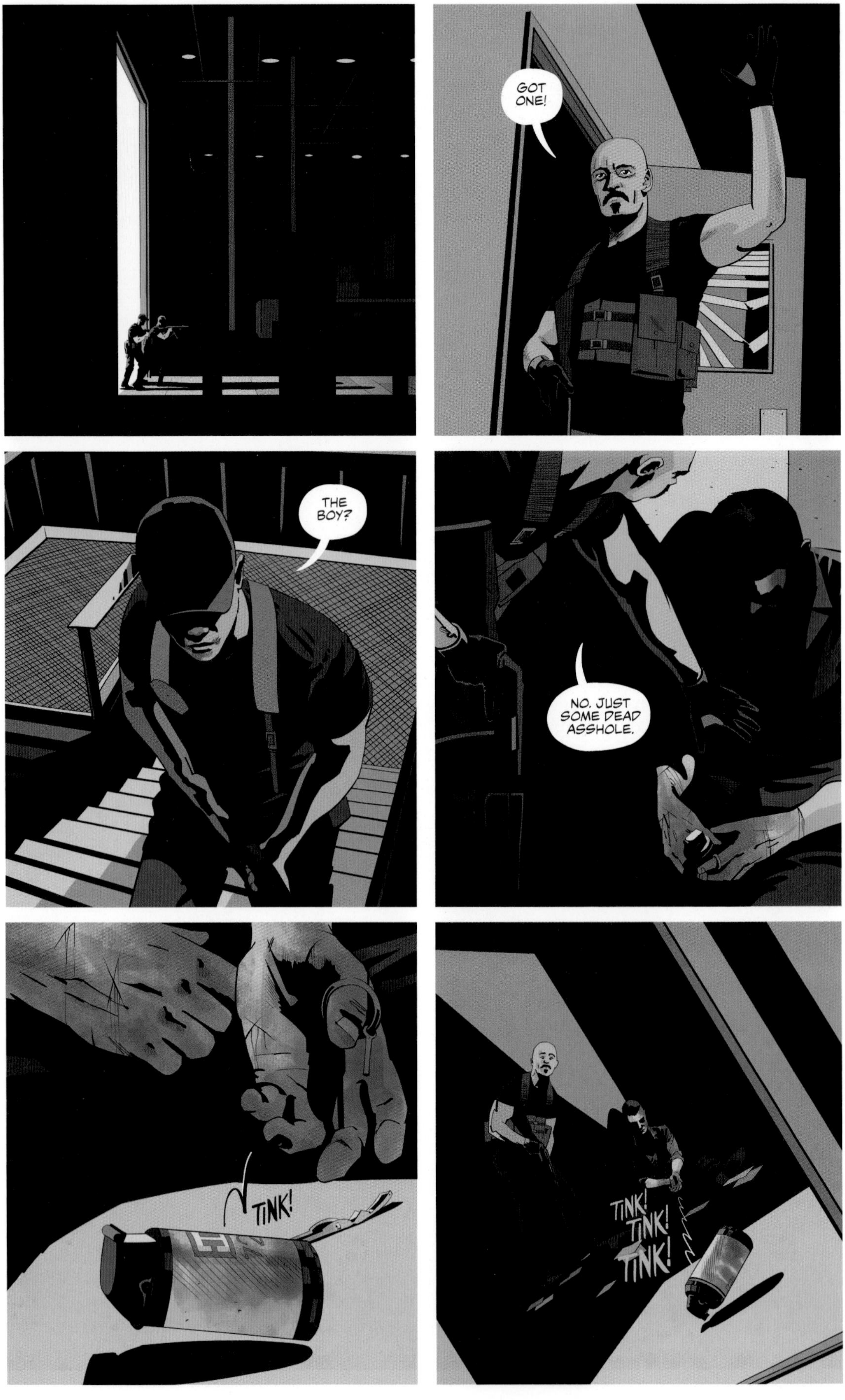
GOT ONE!
THE BOY?
NO. JUST SOME DEAD ASSHOLE.
TINK!
TINK!
TINK!
TINK!

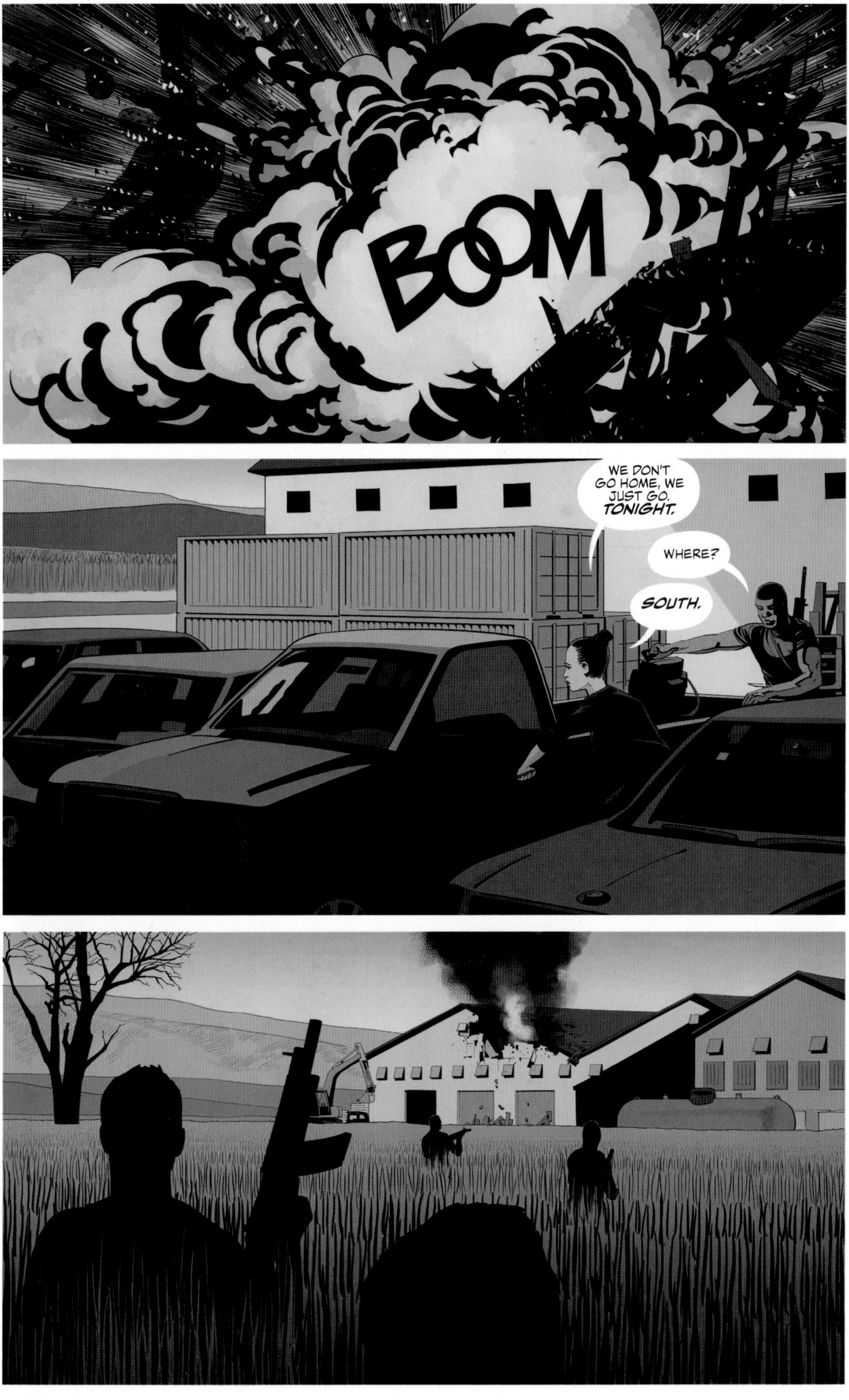
BOOM
WE DON'T GO HOME, WE JUST GO. TONIGHT.
WHERE?
SOUTH.

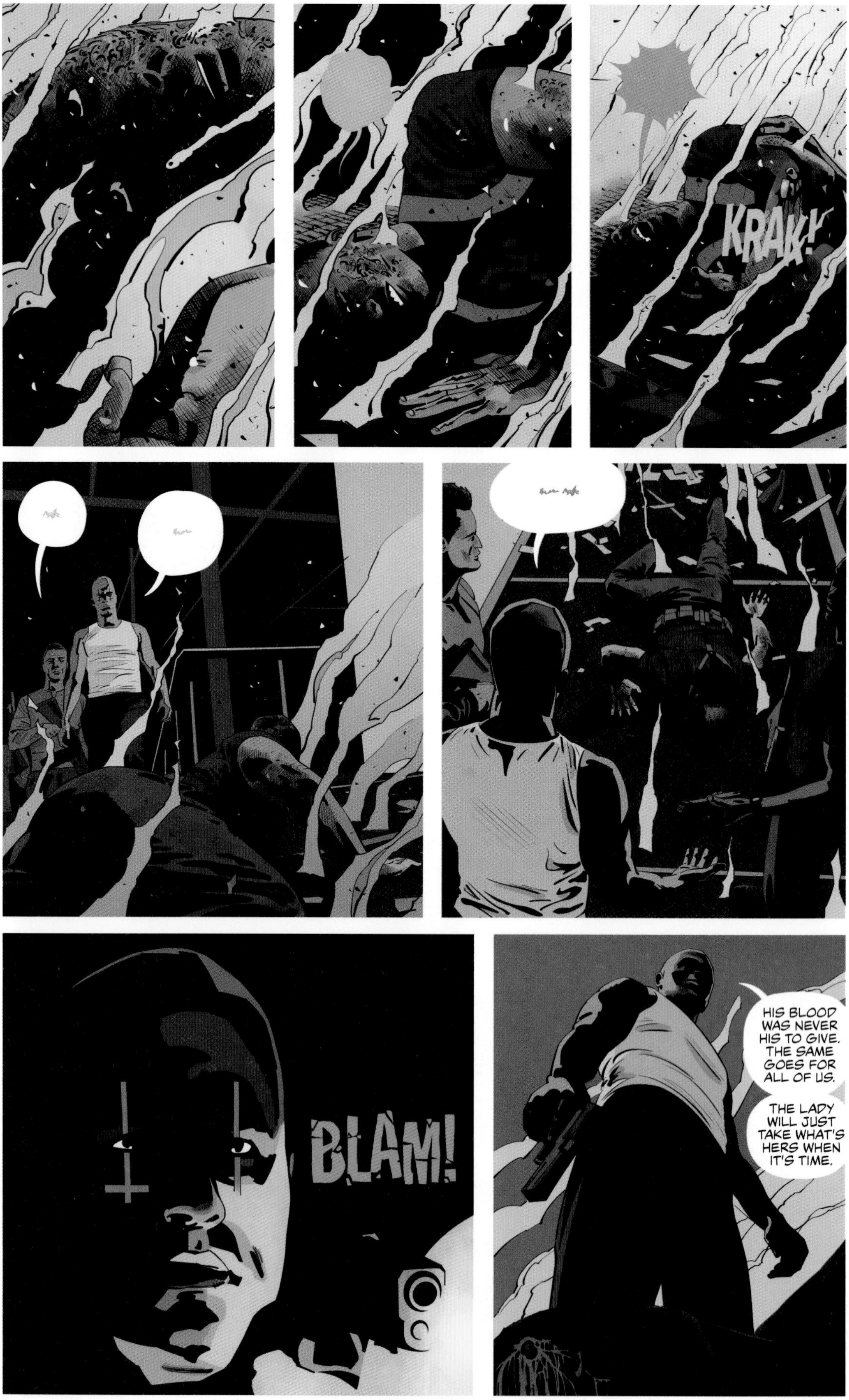
KRAK!
BLAM!
HIS BLOOD WAS NEVER HIS TO GIVE. THE SAME GOES FOR ALL OF US.
THE LADY WILL JUST TAKE WHAT'S HERS WHEN IT'S TIME.

"BRING THE BODIES HERE AND LET THEM BURN.

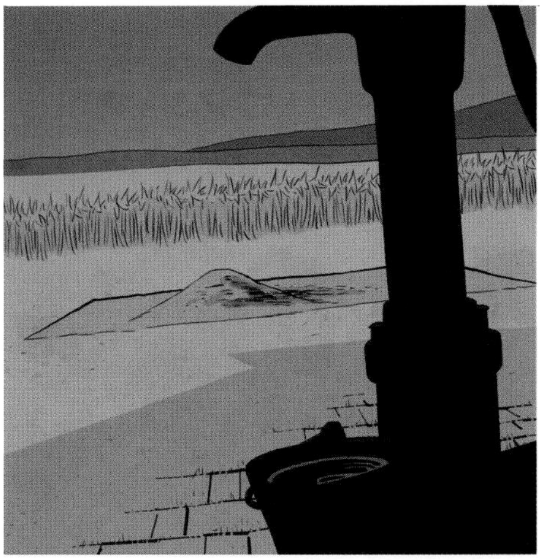

"IF THE FIRE GOES OUT AND THERE ARE NONE LEFT TO BURN...

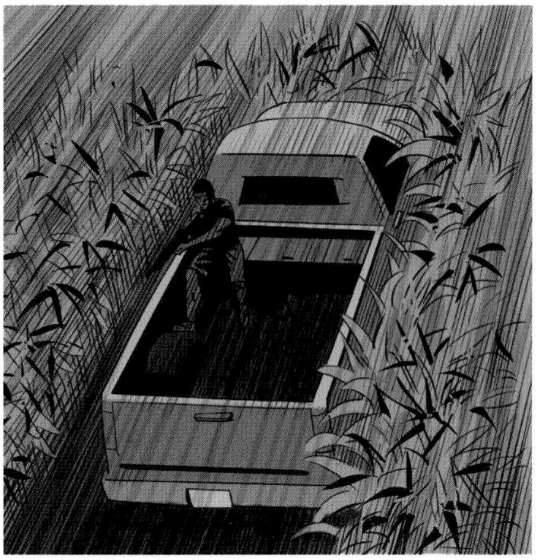

"GIVE YOUR WEAPON TO THE BROTHER BESIDE YOU AND WALK INTO TO THE FLAMES.

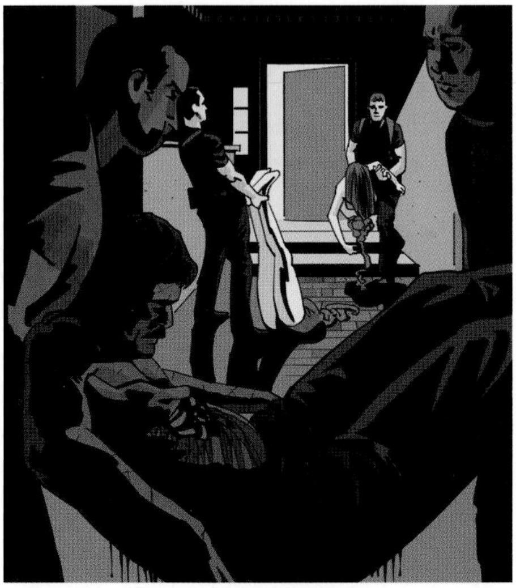

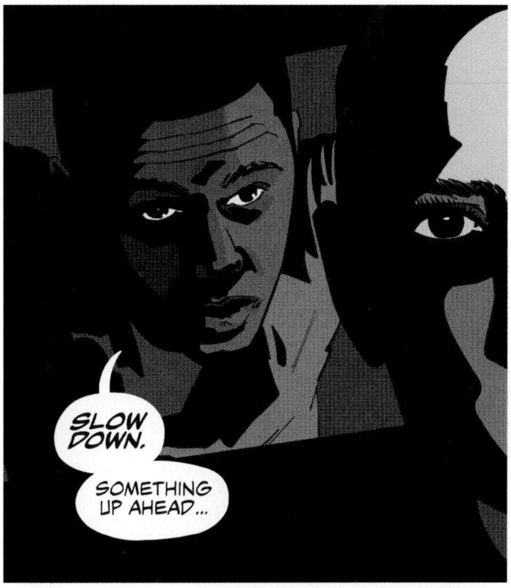
SLOW DOWN.
SOMETHING UP AHEAD...

"IT MUST NEVER DIE DOWN. WE WILL WARM THE EARTH TONIGHT AND PREPARE OURSELVES.

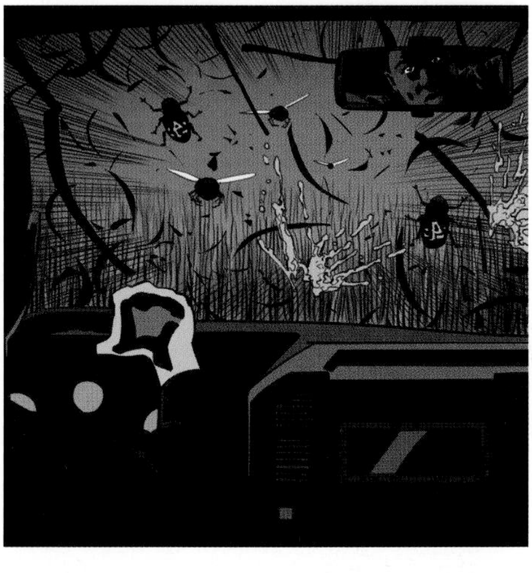

"MORE WILL JOIN US. MANY MORE.

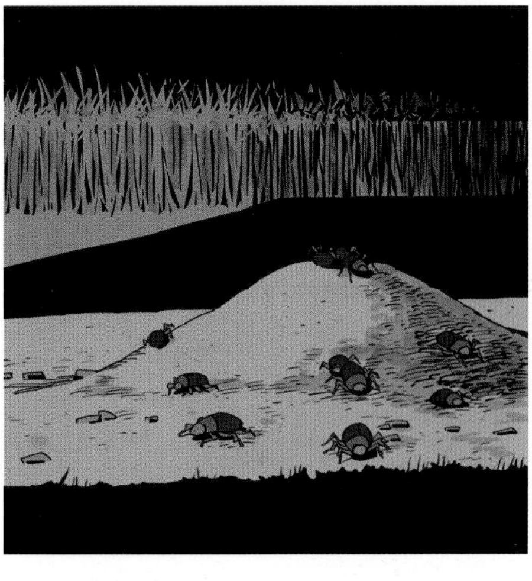

"TO ***BLESS THIS LAND*** WITH FLESH AND BONE AND FIRE.

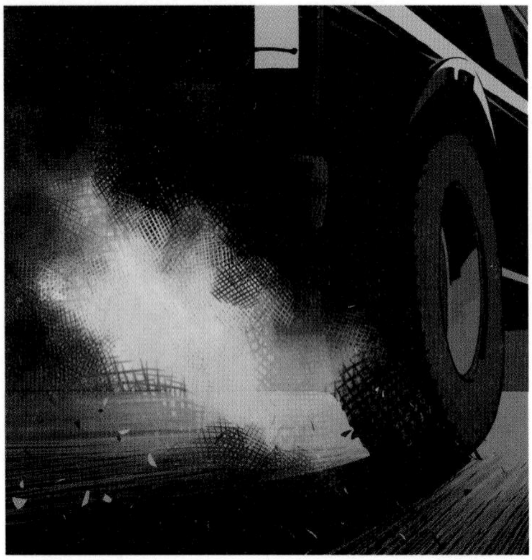

"FOR WE SEEK NOT DEATH NOR FEAR IT...

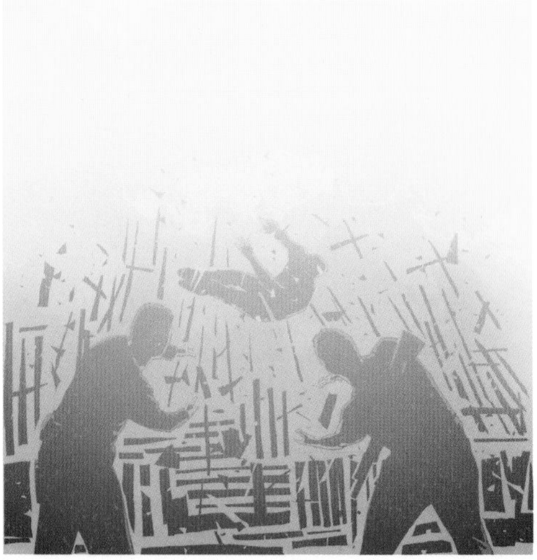

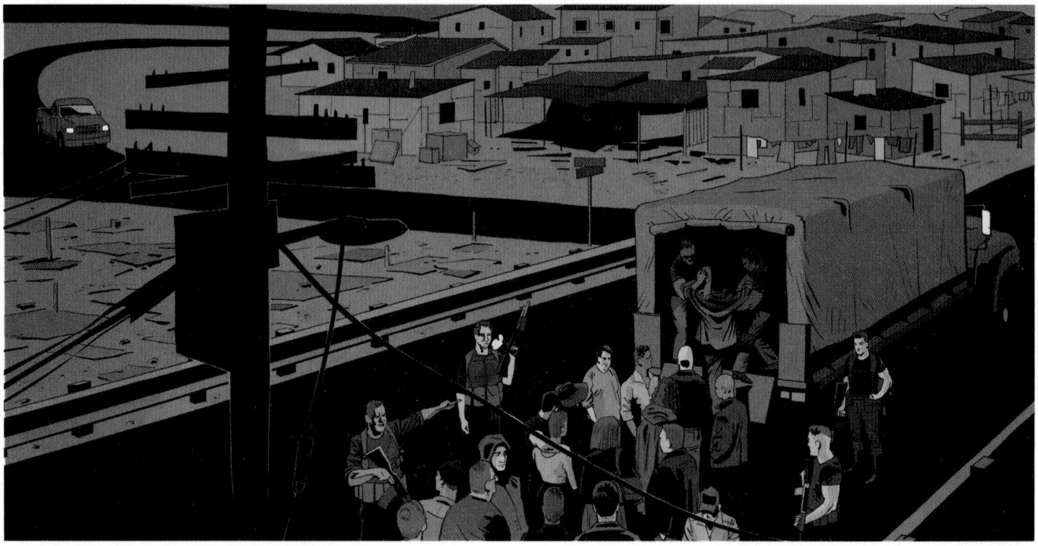

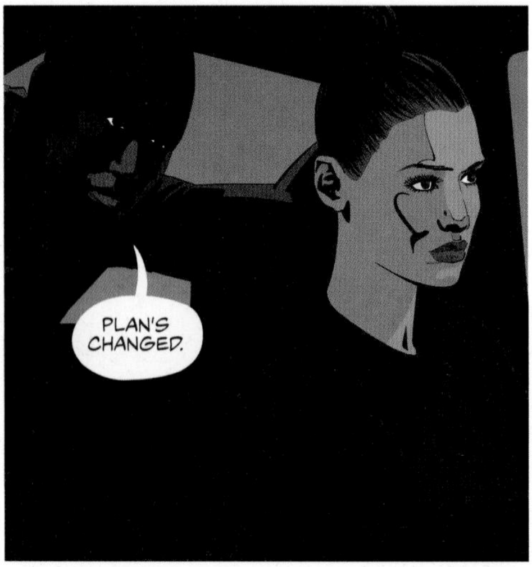
PLAN'S CHANGED.

"FOR DEATH IS BUT THE GATEWAY TO OBLIVION."

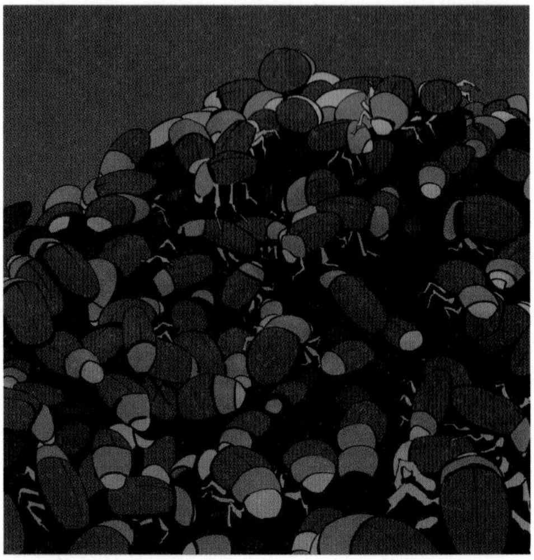

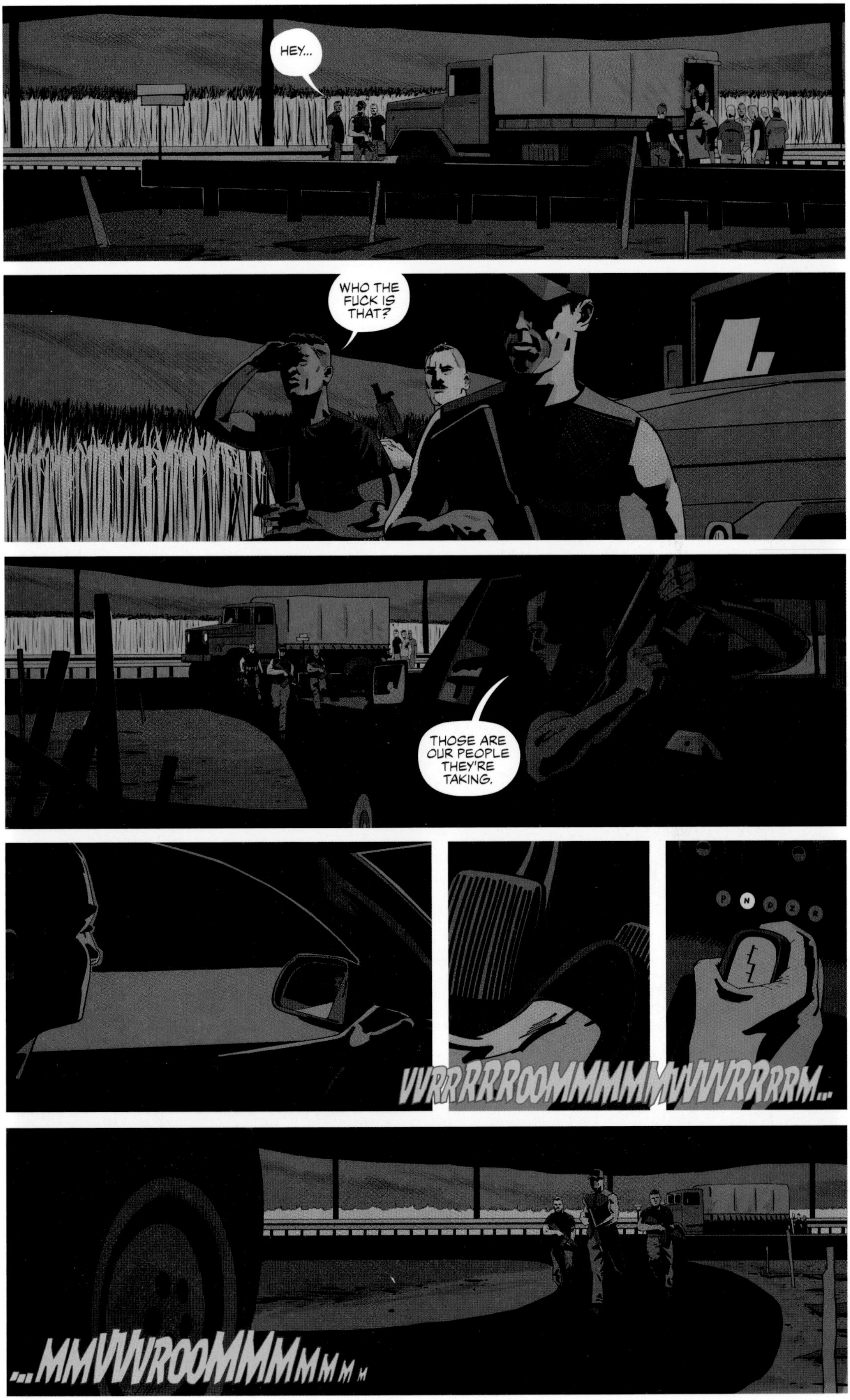
HEY...
WHO THE FUCK IS THAT?
THOSE ARE OUR PEOPLE THEY'RE TAKING.
VVRRRRROOMMMMMVVVVRRRRM...
...MMVVVROOMMMMMMMM

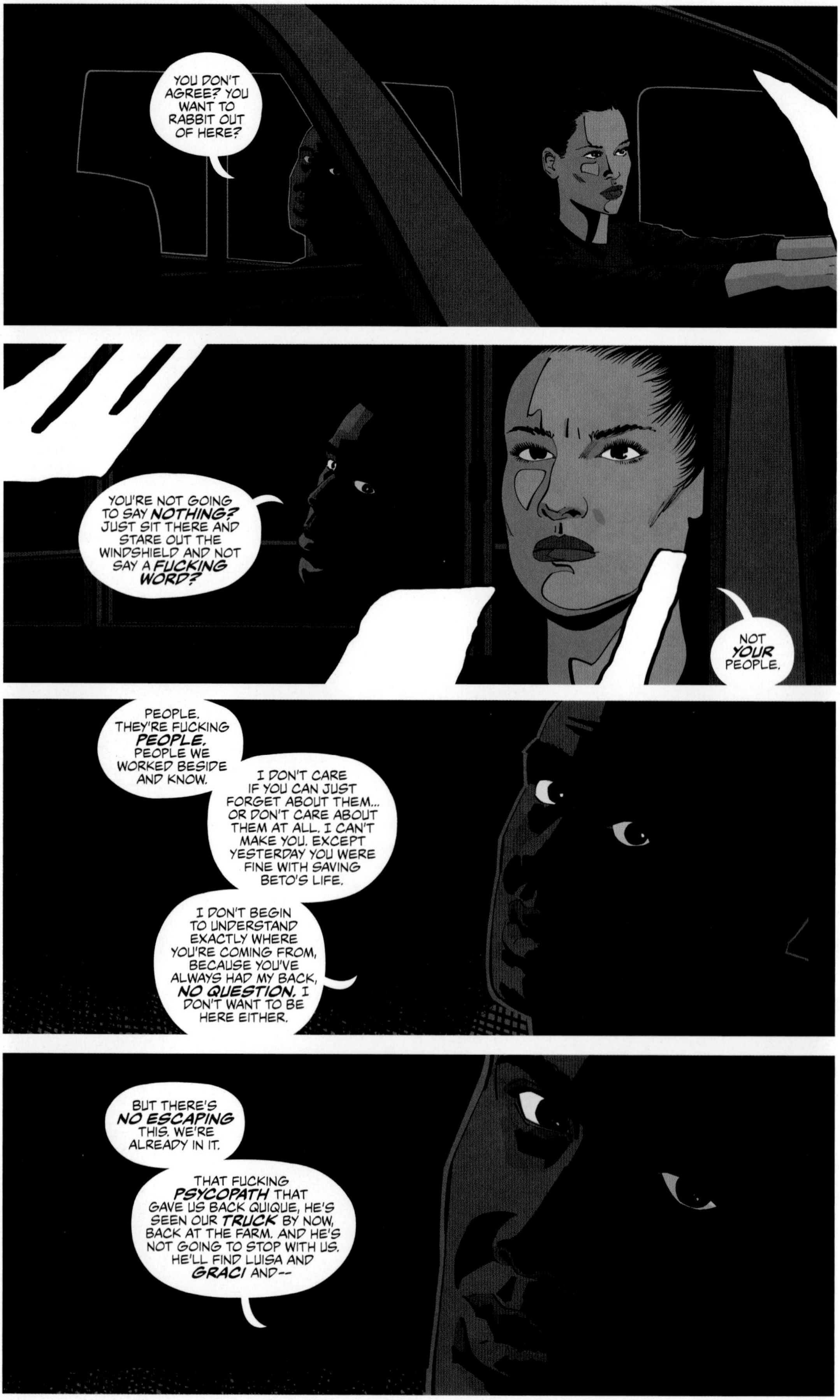
YOU DON'T AGREE? YOU WANT TO RABBIT OUT OF HERE?
YOU'RE NOT GOING TO SAY NOTHING? JUST SIT THERE AND STARE OUT THE WINDSHIELD AND NOT SAY A FUCKING WORD?
NOT YOUR PEOPLE.
PEOPLE. THEY'RE FUCKING PEOPLE. PEOPLE WE WORKED BESIDE AND KNOW.
I DON'T CARE IF YOU CAN JUST FORGET ABOUT THEM... OR DON'T CARE ABOUT THEM AT ALL. I CAN'T MAKE YOU. EXCEPT YESTERDAY YOU WERE FINE WITH SAVING BETO'S LIFE.
I DON'T BEGIN TO UNDERSTAND EXACTLY WHERE YOU'RE COMING FROM, BECAUSE YOU'VE ALWAYS HAD MY BACK, NO QUESTION. I DON'T WANT TO BE HERE EITHER.
BUT THERE'S NO ESCAPING THIS. WE'RE ALREADY IN IT.
THAT FUCKING PSYCOPATH THAT GAVE US BACK QUIQUE, HE'S SEEN OUR TRUCK BY NOW, BACK AT THE FARM. AND HE'S NOT GOING TO STOP WITH US. HE'LL FIND LUISA AND GRACI AND--

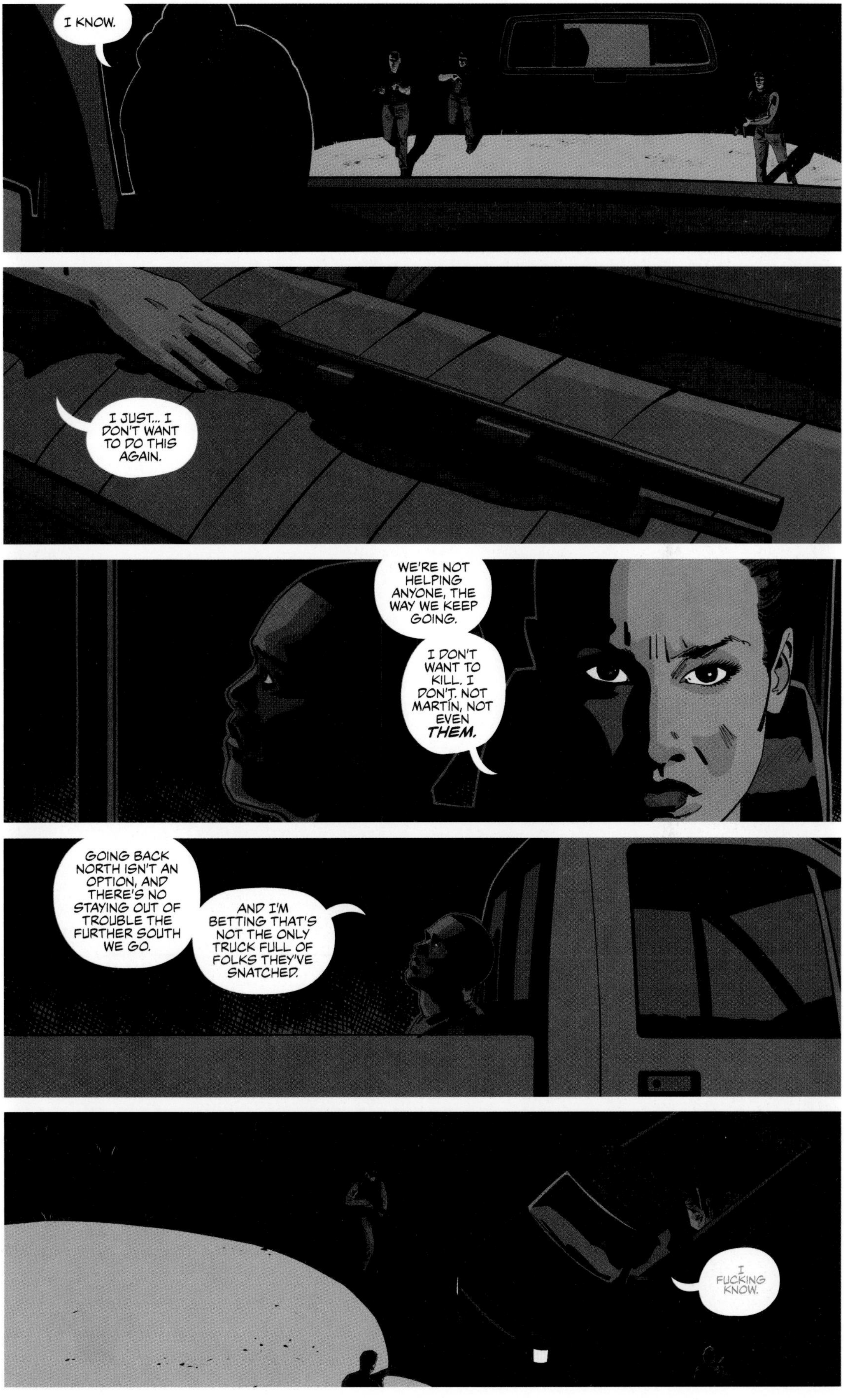
I KNOW.
I JUST... I DON'T WANT TO DO THIS AGAIN.
WE'RE NOT HELPING ANYONE, THE WAY WE KEEP GOING.
I DON'T WANT TO KILL. I DON'T. NOT MARTÍN, NOT EVEN *THEM.*
GOING BACK NORTH ISN'T AN OPTION, AND THERE'S NO STAYING OUT OF TROUBLE THE FURTHER SOUTH WE GO.
AND I'M BETTING THAT'S NOT THE ONLY TRUCK FULL OF FOLKS THEY'VE SNATCHED.
I FUCKING KNOW.

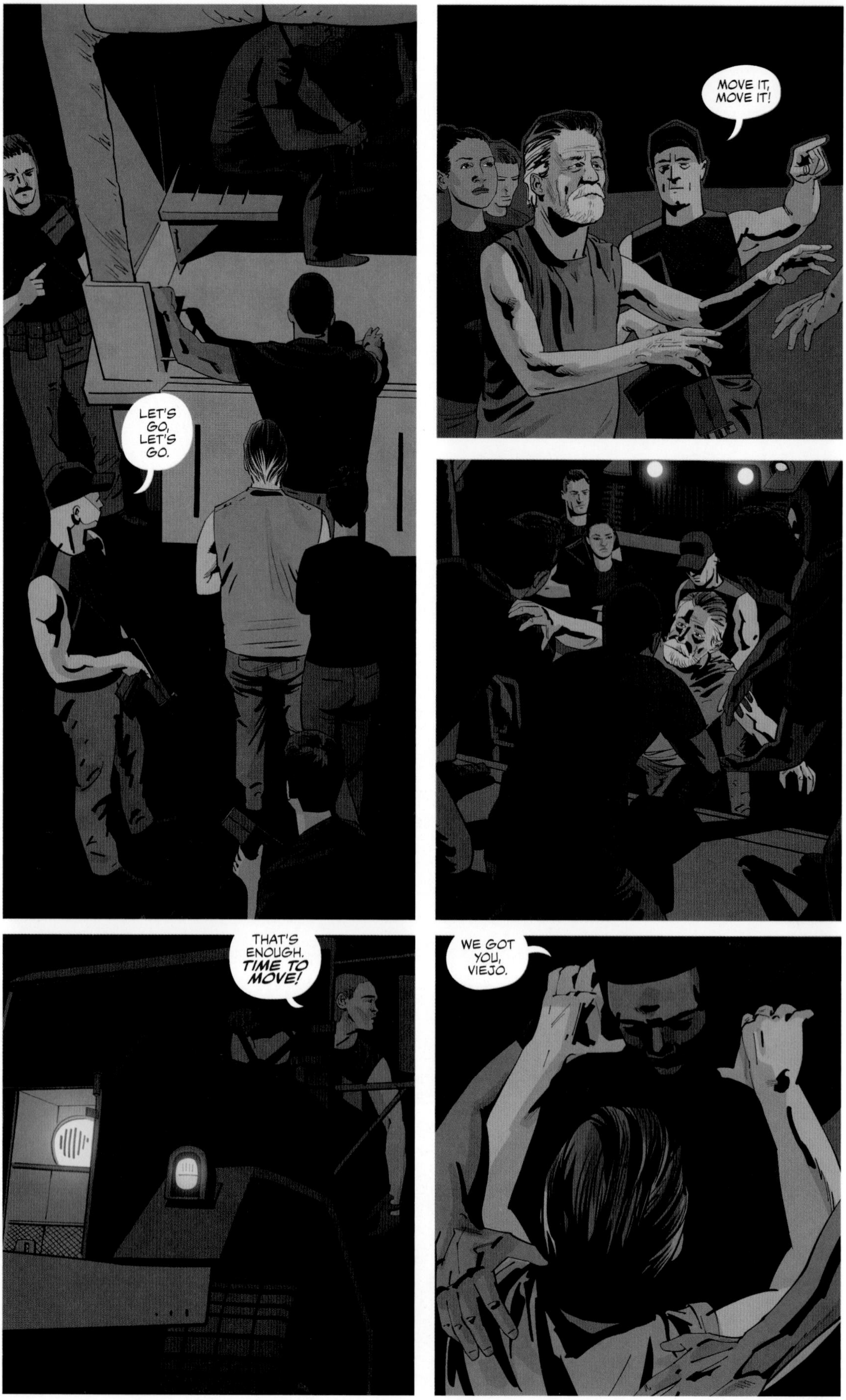
LET'S GO, LET'S GO.
MOVE IT, MOVE IT!
THAT'S ENOUGH. *TIME TO MOVE!*
WE GOT YOU, VIEJO.

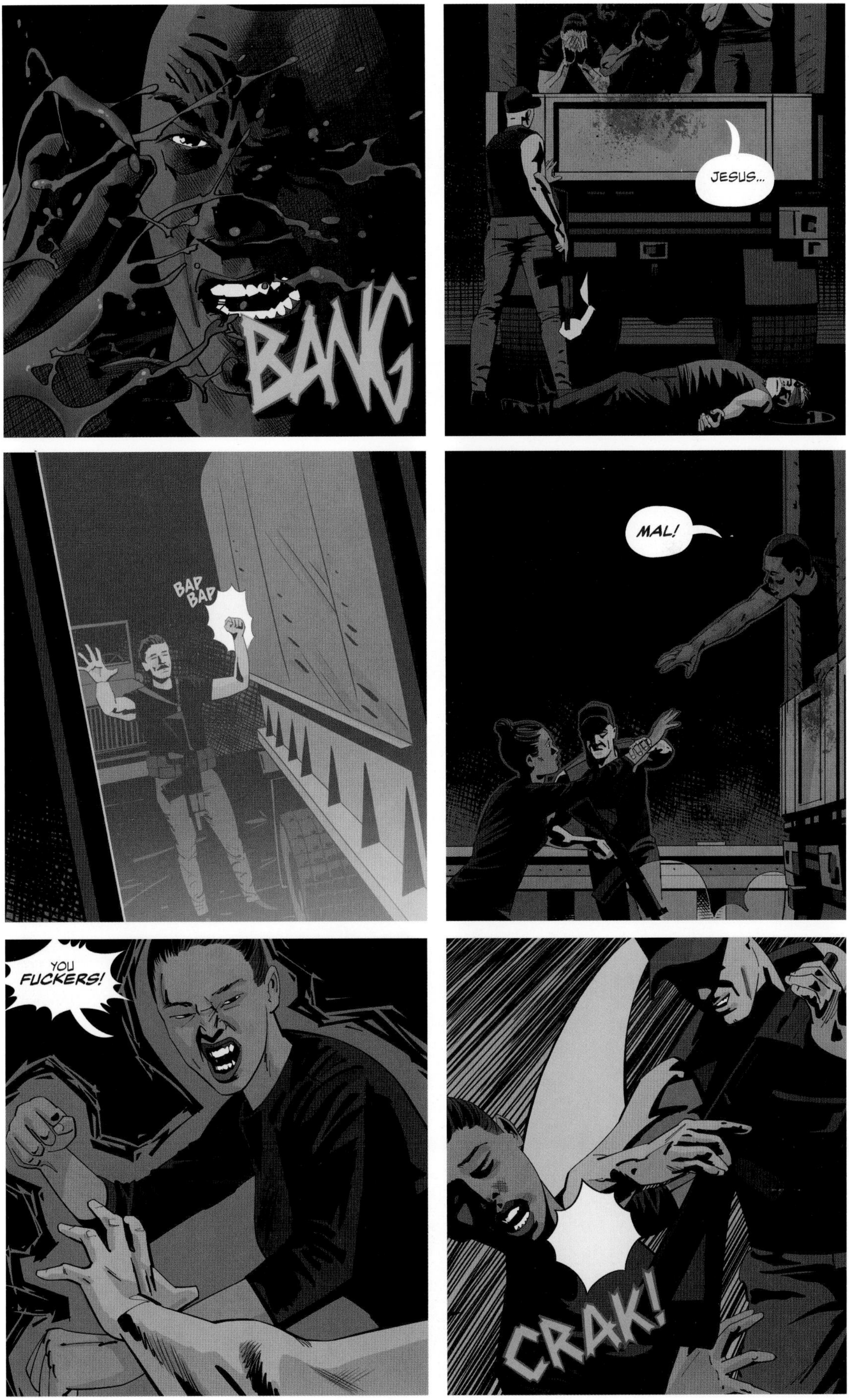
BANG
JESUS...
BAP
BAP
MAL!
YOU FUCKERS!
CRAK!

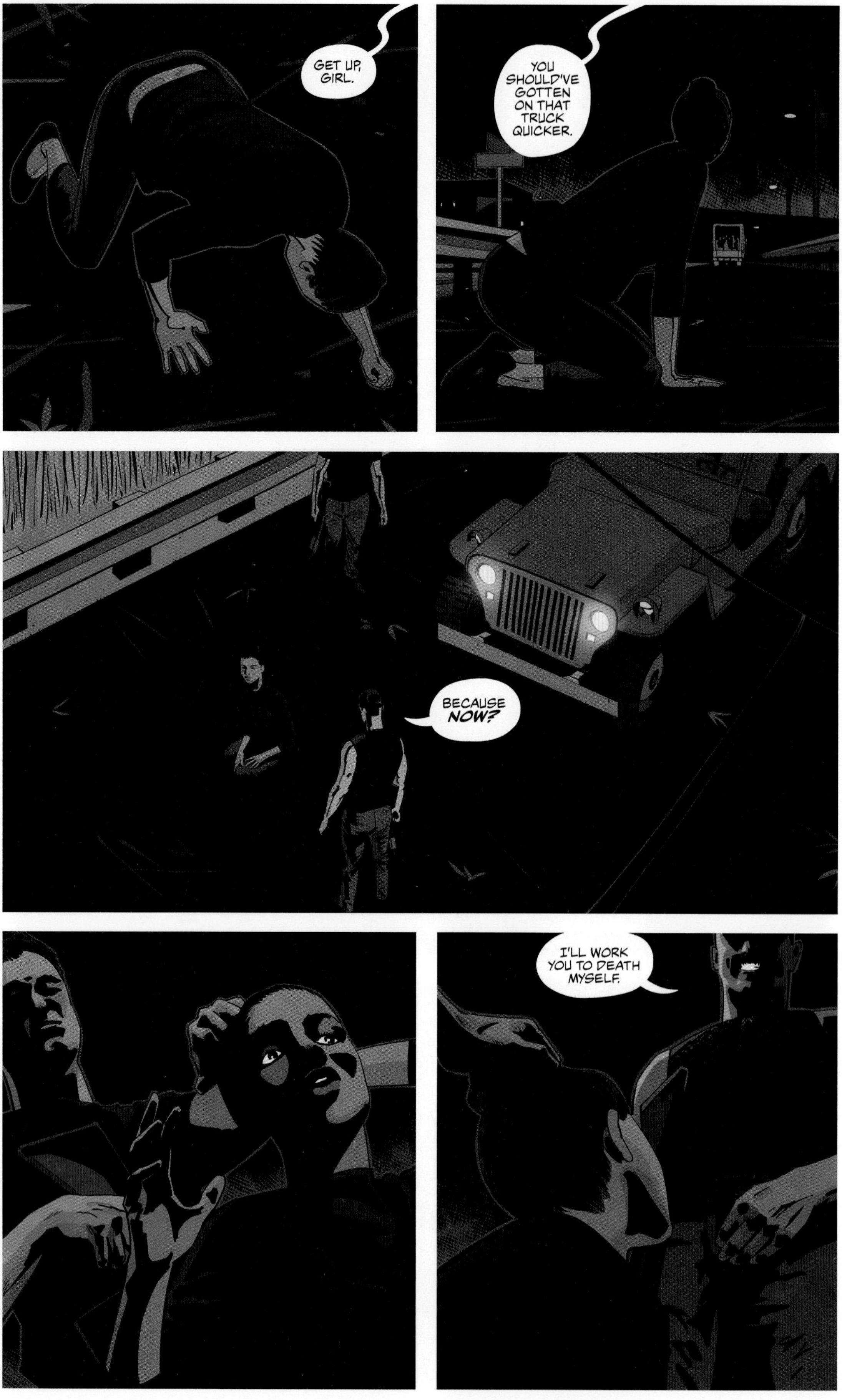
GET UP, GIRL.
YOU SHOULD'VE GOTTEN ON THAT TRUCK QUICKER.
BECAUSE *NOW?*
I'LL WORK YOU TO DEATH MYSELF.

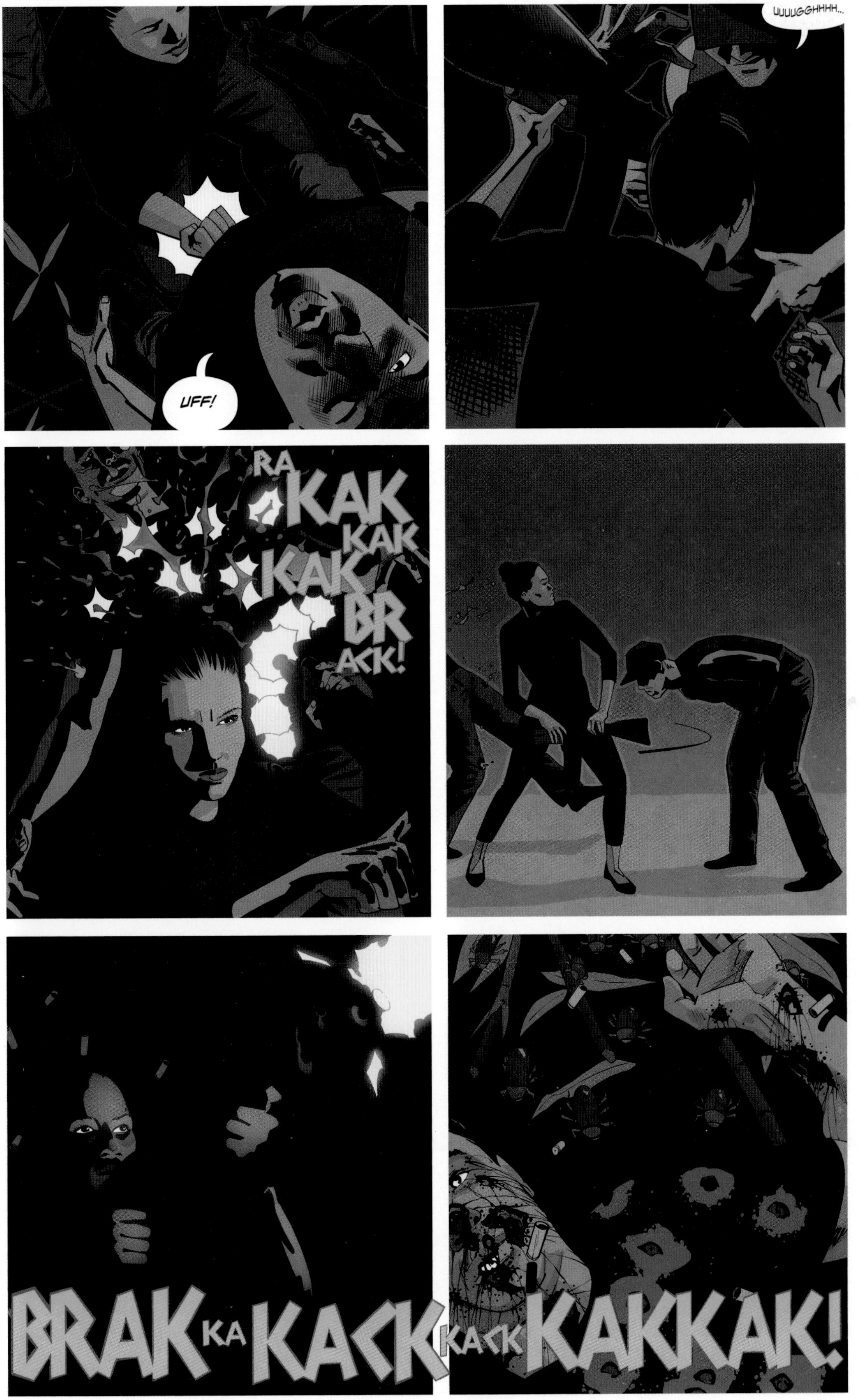
UFF!
UUUUGGHHHH...
RA
KAK
KAK
KAK
BR
ACK!
BRAK KA KACK KACK KAKKAK!

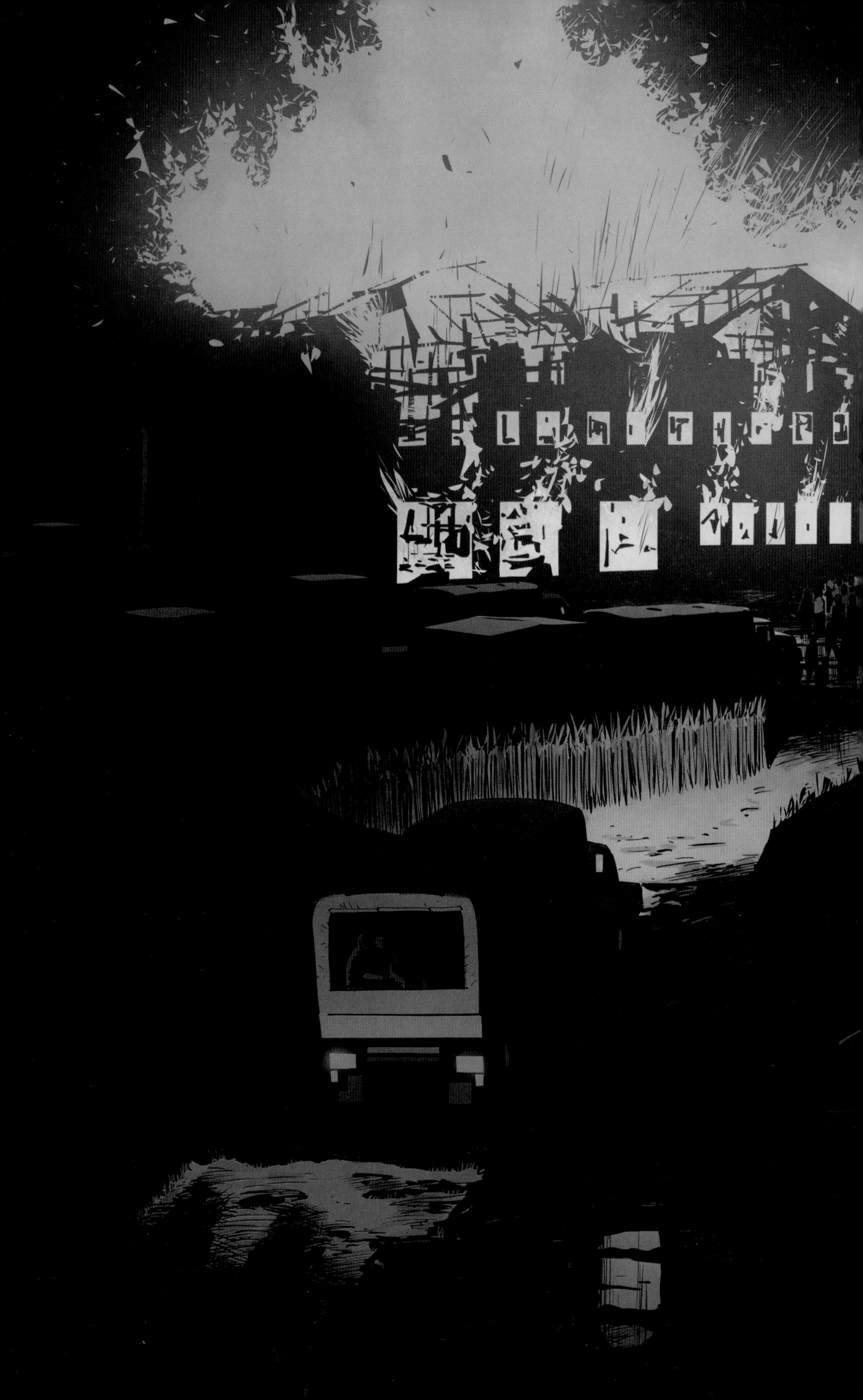

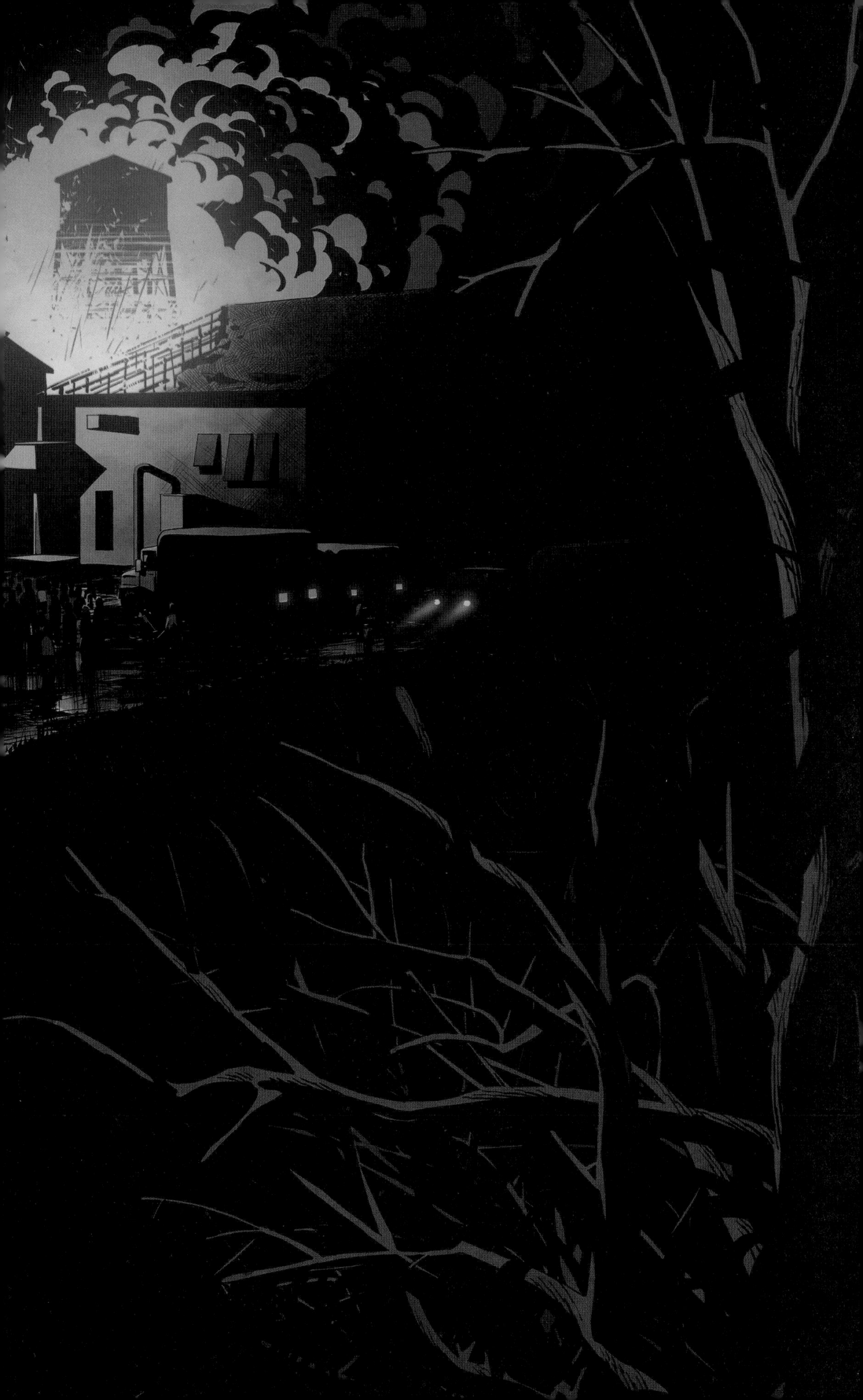

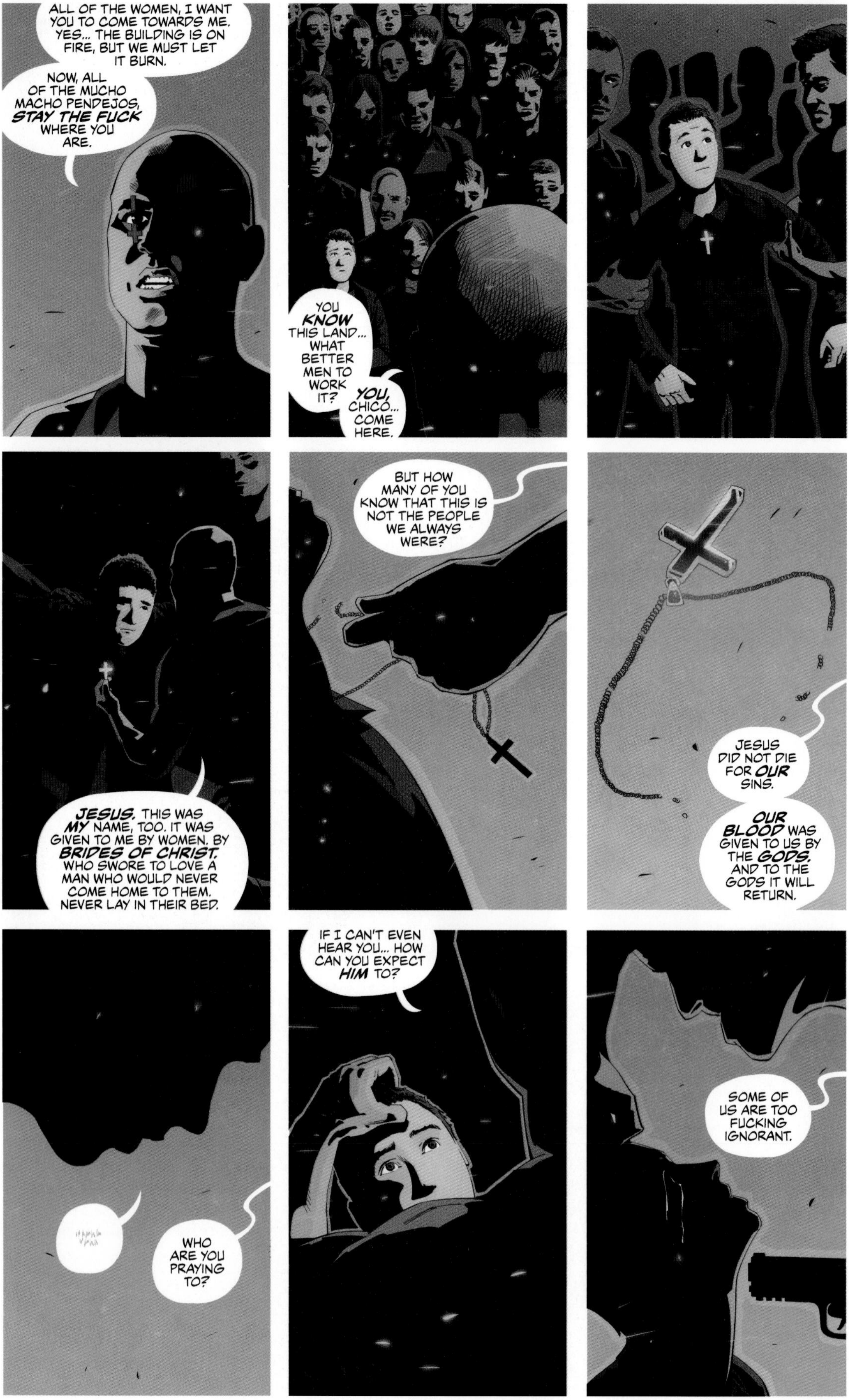

ALL OF THE WOMEN, I WANT YOU TO COME TOWARDS ME. YES... THE BUILDING IS ON FIRE, BUT WE MUST LET IT BURN.
NOW, ALL OF THE MUCHO MACHO PENDEJOS, STAY THE FUCK WHERE YOU ARE.
YOU KNOW THIS LAND... WHAT BETTER MEN TO WORK IT?
YOU, CHICO... COME HERE.
JESUS. THIS WAS MY NAME, TOO. IT WAS GIVEN TO ME BY WOMEN. BY BRIDES OF CHRIST. WHO SWORE TO LOVE A MAN WHO WOULD NEVER COME HOME TO THEM. NEVER LAY IN THEIR BED.
BUT HOW MANY OF YOU KNOW THAT THIS IS NOT THE PEOPLE WE ALWAYS WERE?
JESUS DID NOT DIE FOR OUR SINS.
OUR BLOOD WAS GIVEN TO US BY THE GODS. AND TO THE GODS IT WILL RETURN.
WHO ARE YOU PRAYING TO?
IF I CAN'T EVEN HEAR YOU... HOW CAN YOU EXPECT HIM TO?
SOME OF US ARE TOO FUCKING IGNORANT.

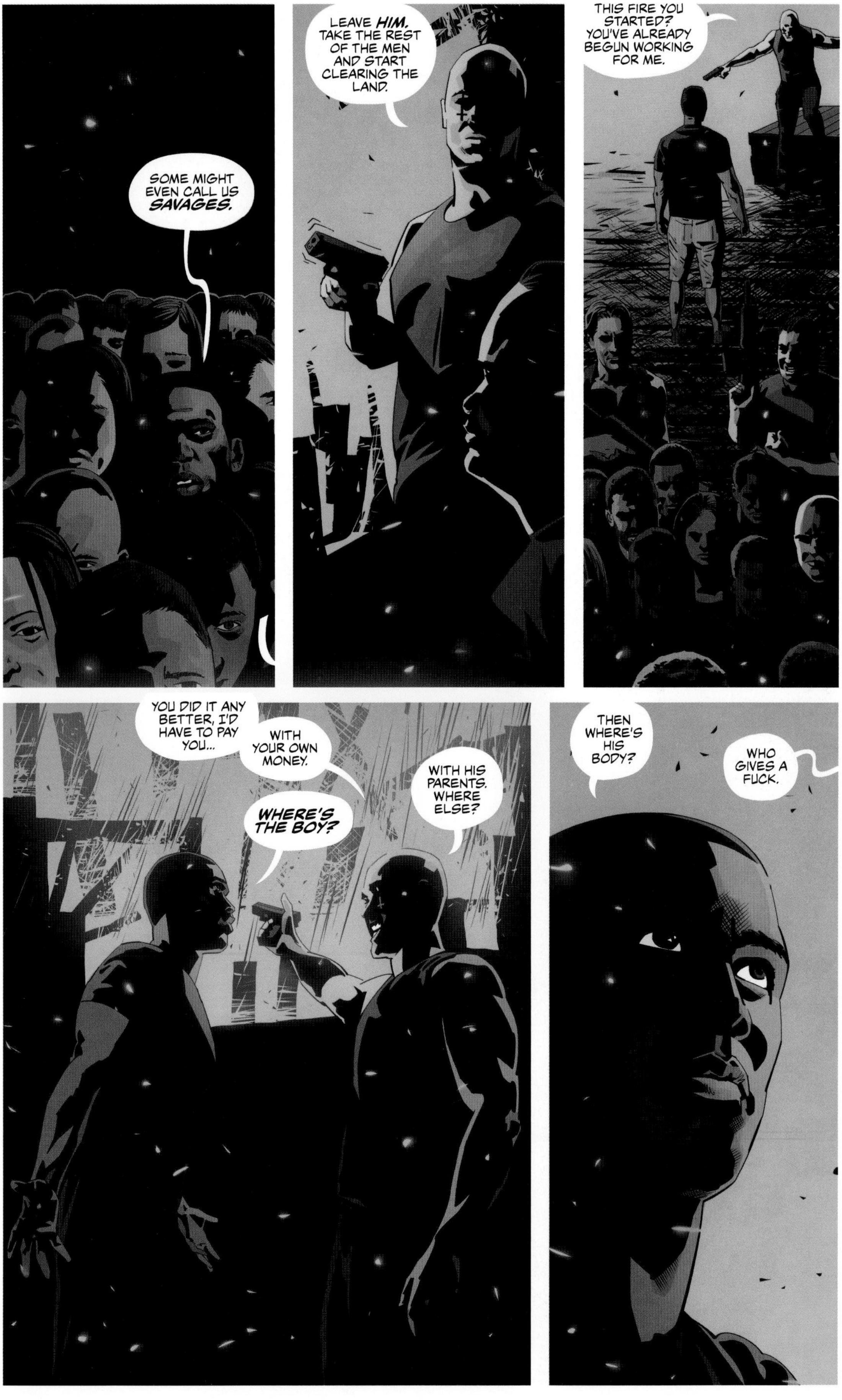
SOME MIGHT EVEN CALL US SAVAGES.
LEAVE HIM. TAKE THE REST OF THE MEN AND START CLEARING THE LAND.
THIS FIRE YOU STARTED? YOU'VE ALREADY BEGUN WORKING FOR ME.
YOU DID IT ANY BETTER, I'D HAVE TO PAY YOU...
WITH YOUR OWN MONEY.
WHERE'S THE BOY?
WITH HIS PARENTS. WHERE ELSE?
THEN WHERE'S HIS BODY?
WHO GIVES A FUCK.

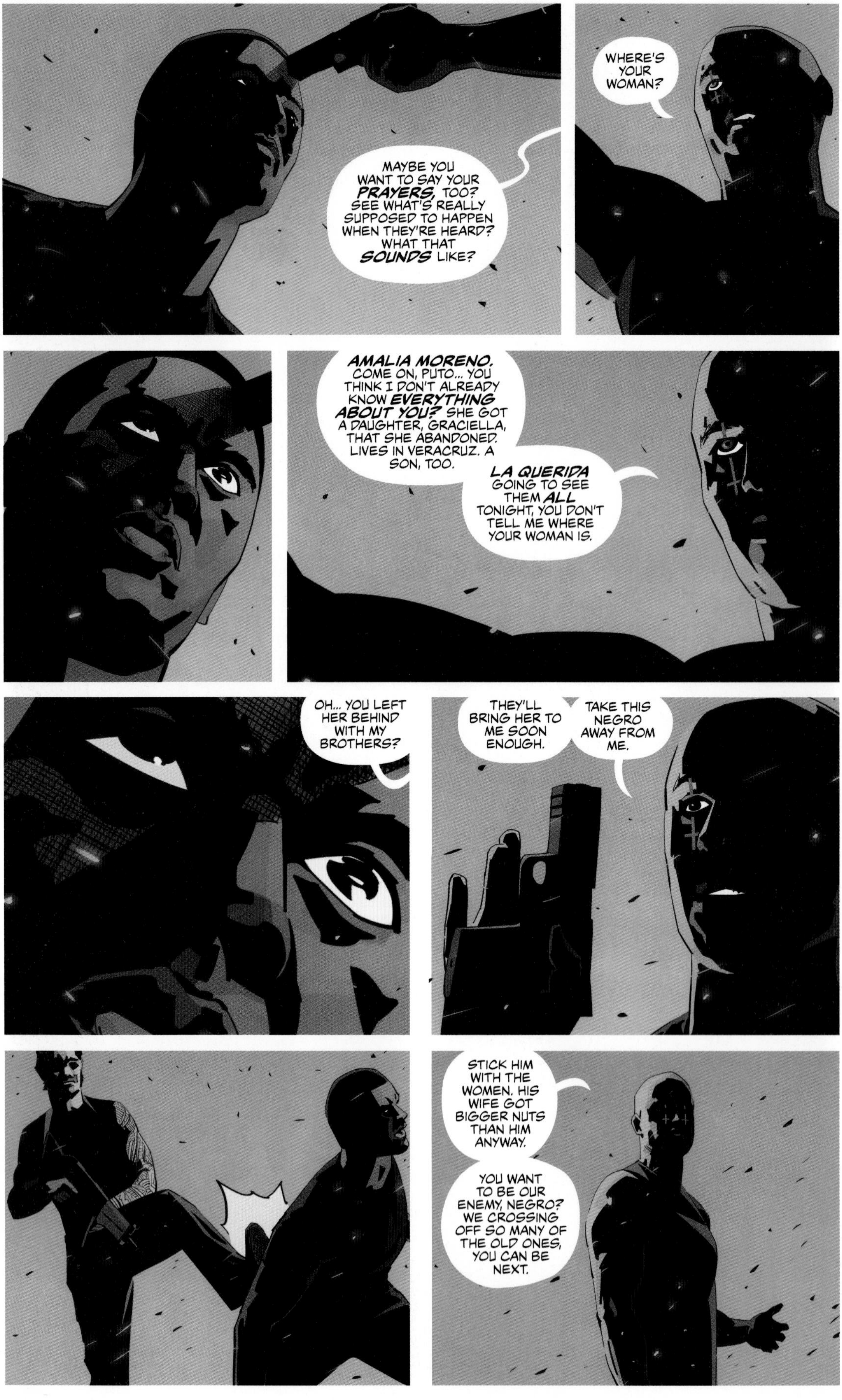
MAYBE YOU WANT TO SAY YOUR **PRAYERS,** TOO? SEE WHAT'S REALLY SUPPOSED TO HAPPEN WHEN THEY'RE HEARD? WHAT THAT **SOUNDS** LIKE?
WHERE'S YOUR WOMAN?
AMALIA MORENO. COME ON, PUTO... YOU THINK I DON'T ALREADY KNOW **EVERYTHING ABOUT YOU?** SHE GOT A DAUGHTER, GRACIELLA, THAT SHE ABANDONED. LIVES IN VERACRUZ. A SON, TOO.
LA QUERIDA GOING TO SEE THEM **ALL** TONIGHT, YOU DON'T TELL ME WHERE YOUR WOMAN IS.
OH... YOU LEFT HER BEHIND WITH MY BROTHERS?
THEY'LL BRING HER TO ME SOON ENOUGH.
TAKE THIS NEGRO AWAY FROM ME.
STICK HIM WITH THE WOMEN. HIS WIFE GOT BIGGER NUTS THAN HIM ANYWAY.
YOU WANT TO BE OUR ENEMY, NEGRO? WE CROSSING OFF SO MANY OF THE OLD ONES, YOU CAN BE NEXT.

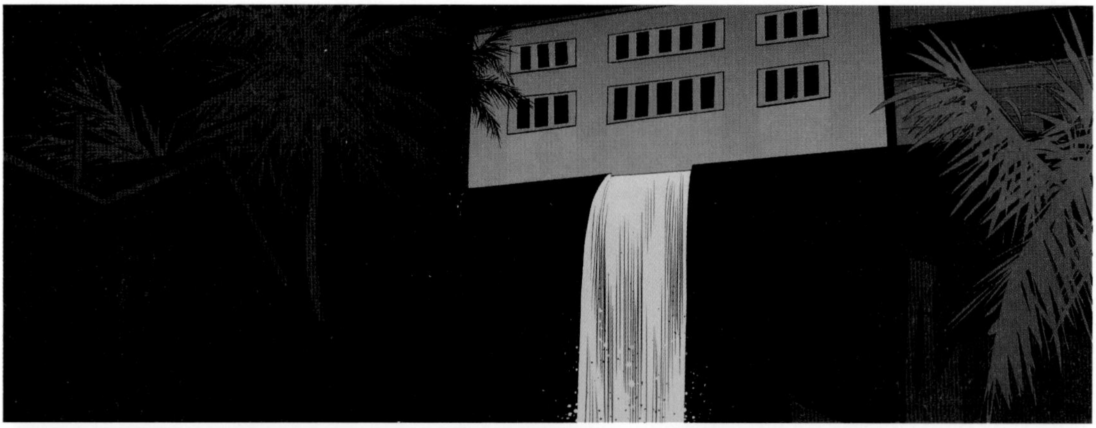

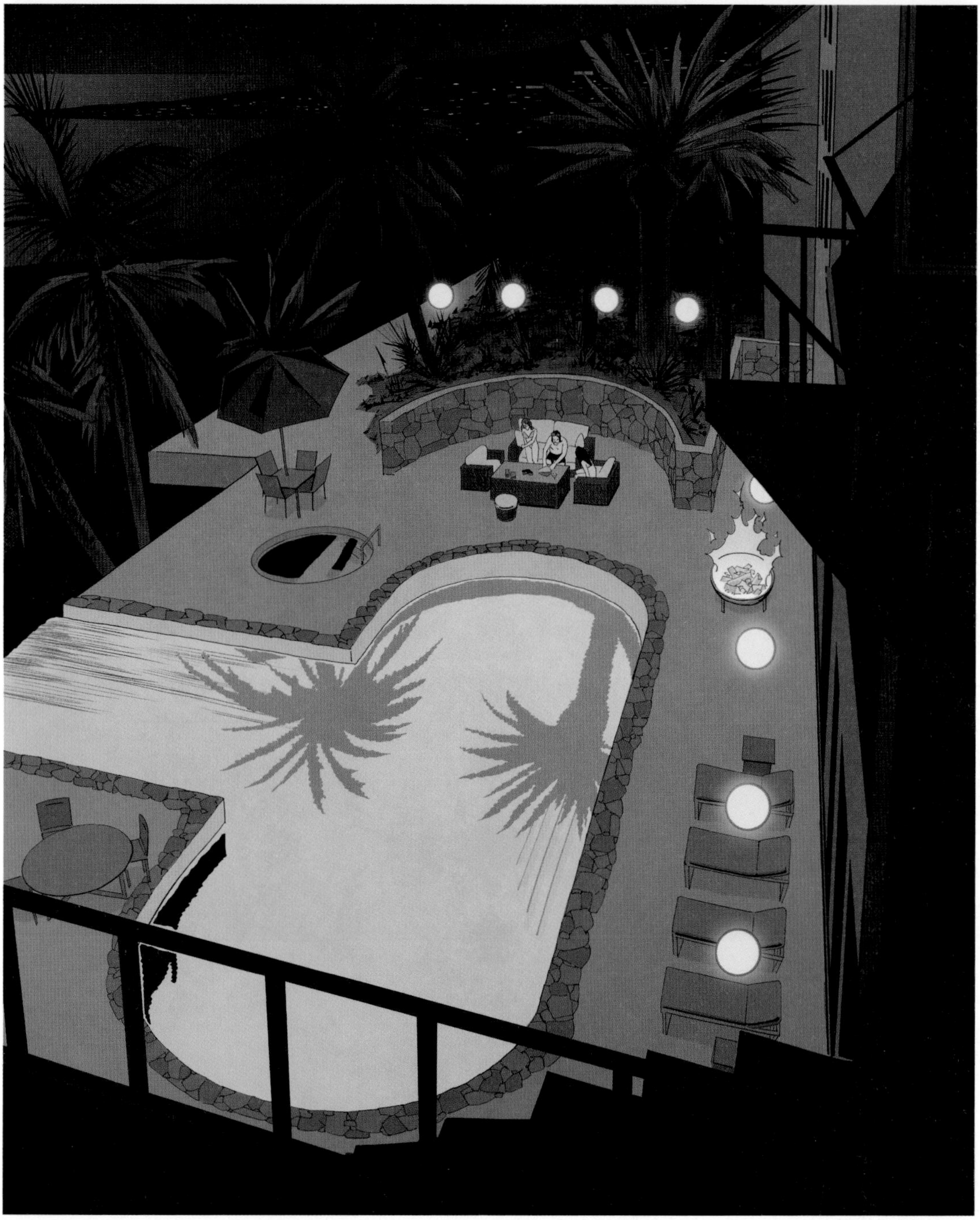

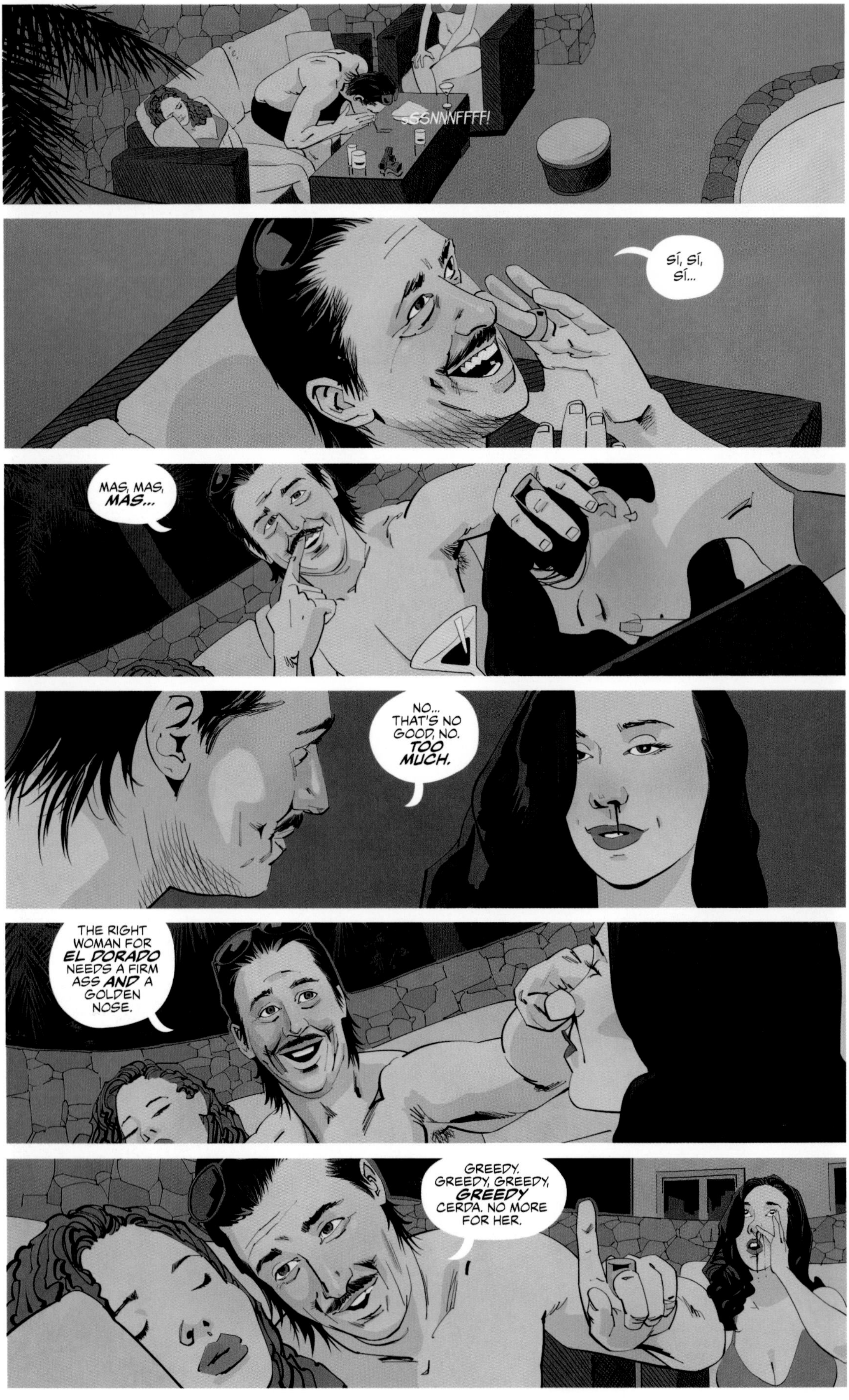
SSSNNNFFFF!
SÍ, SÍ, SÍ...
MAS, MAS, MAS...
NO... THAT'S NO GOOD, NO. TOO MUCH.
THE RIGHT WOMAN FOR EL DORADO NEEDS A FIRM ASS AND A GOLDEN NOSE.
GREEDY. GREEDY, GREEDY, GREEDY CERDA. NO MORE FOR HER.

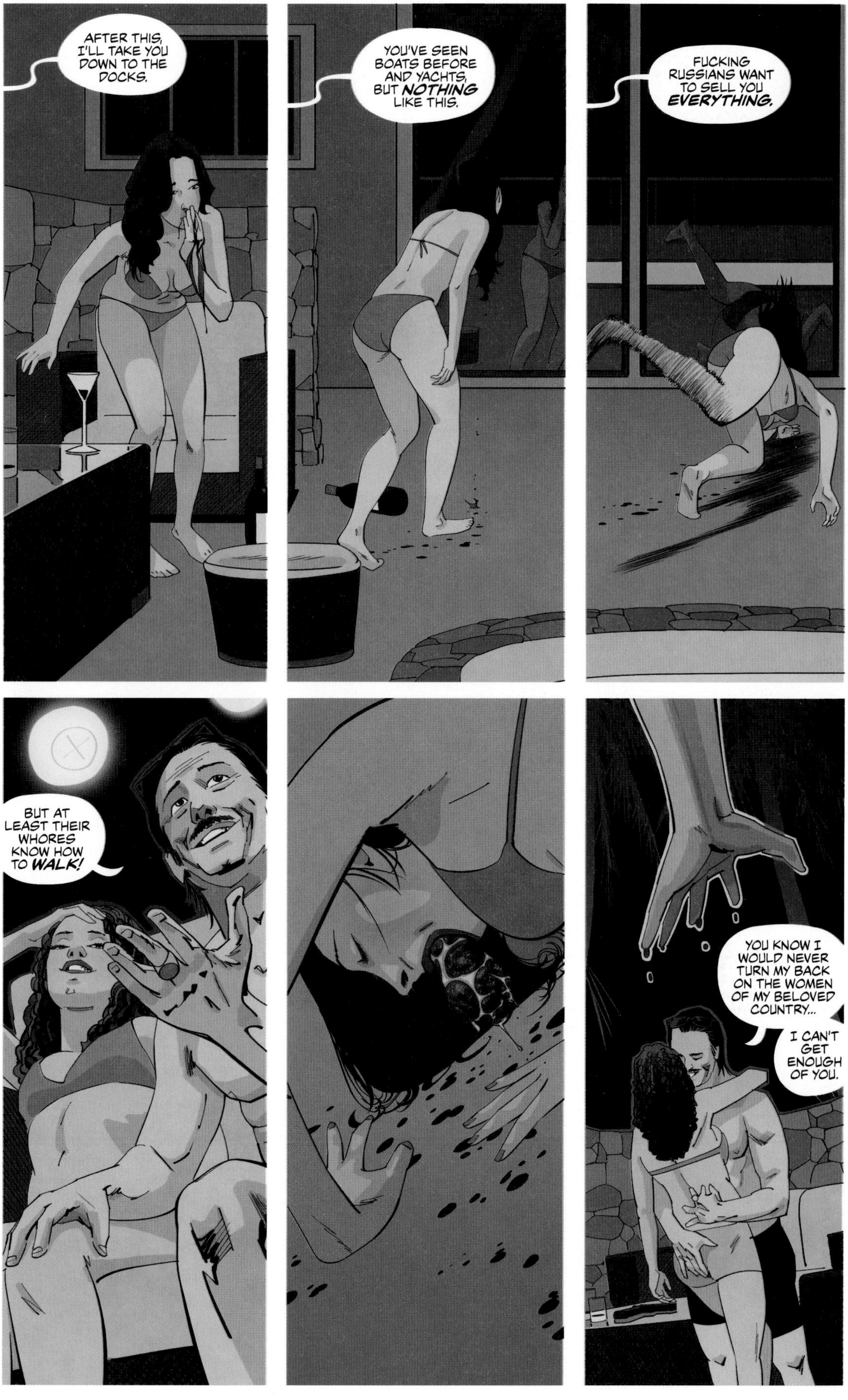

AFTER THIS, I'LL TAKE YOU DOWN TO THE DOCKS.
YOU'VE SEEN BOATS BEFORE AND YACHTS, BUT NOTHING LIKE THIS.
FUCKING RUSSIANS WANT TO SELL YOU EVERYTHING.
BUT AT LEAST THEIR WHORES KNOW HOW TO WALK!
YOU KNOW I WOULD NEVER TURN MY BACK ON THE WOMEN OF MY BELOVED COUNTRY...
I CAN'T GET ENOUGH OF YOU.

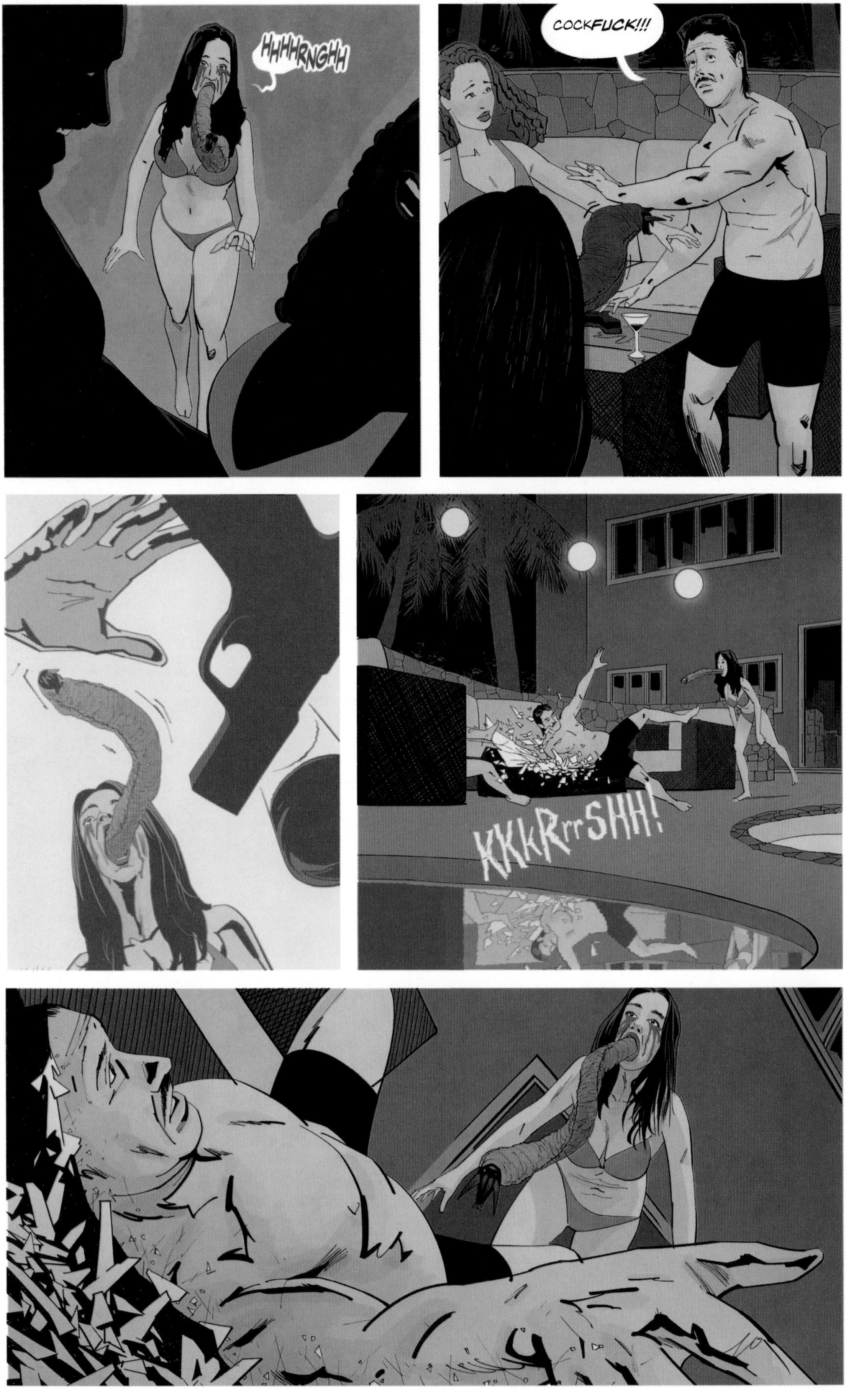
HHHHRNGHH
COCKFUCK!!!
KKKRrrSHH!

HUP!

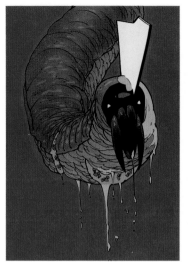

I *SHIT* ON EVERYTHING THAT MOVES, DEVILFUCK--

KLACK KLACK KLACK KLACK KLACK KLACK KLACK KLACK

AHHHHHH!!!

DID YOUR MOTHER DRINK THE DEVIL'S MILK, TOO? YOU *SUCIA* LIKE HER?

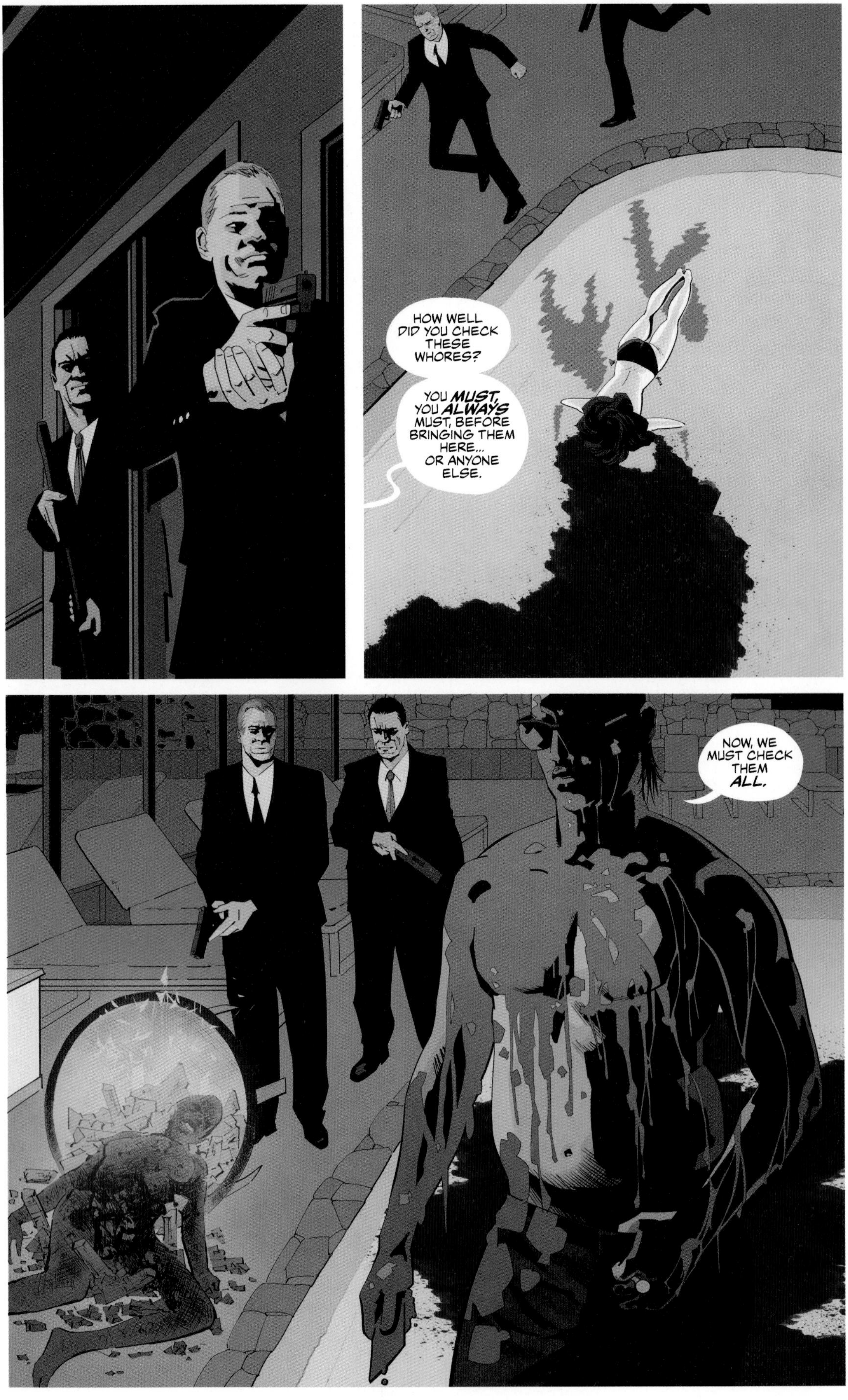
HOW WELL DID YOU CHECK THESE WHORES?
YOU MUST, YOU ALWAYS MUST, BEFORE BRINGING THEM HERE... OR ANYONE ELSE.
NOW, WE MUST CHECK THEM ALL.

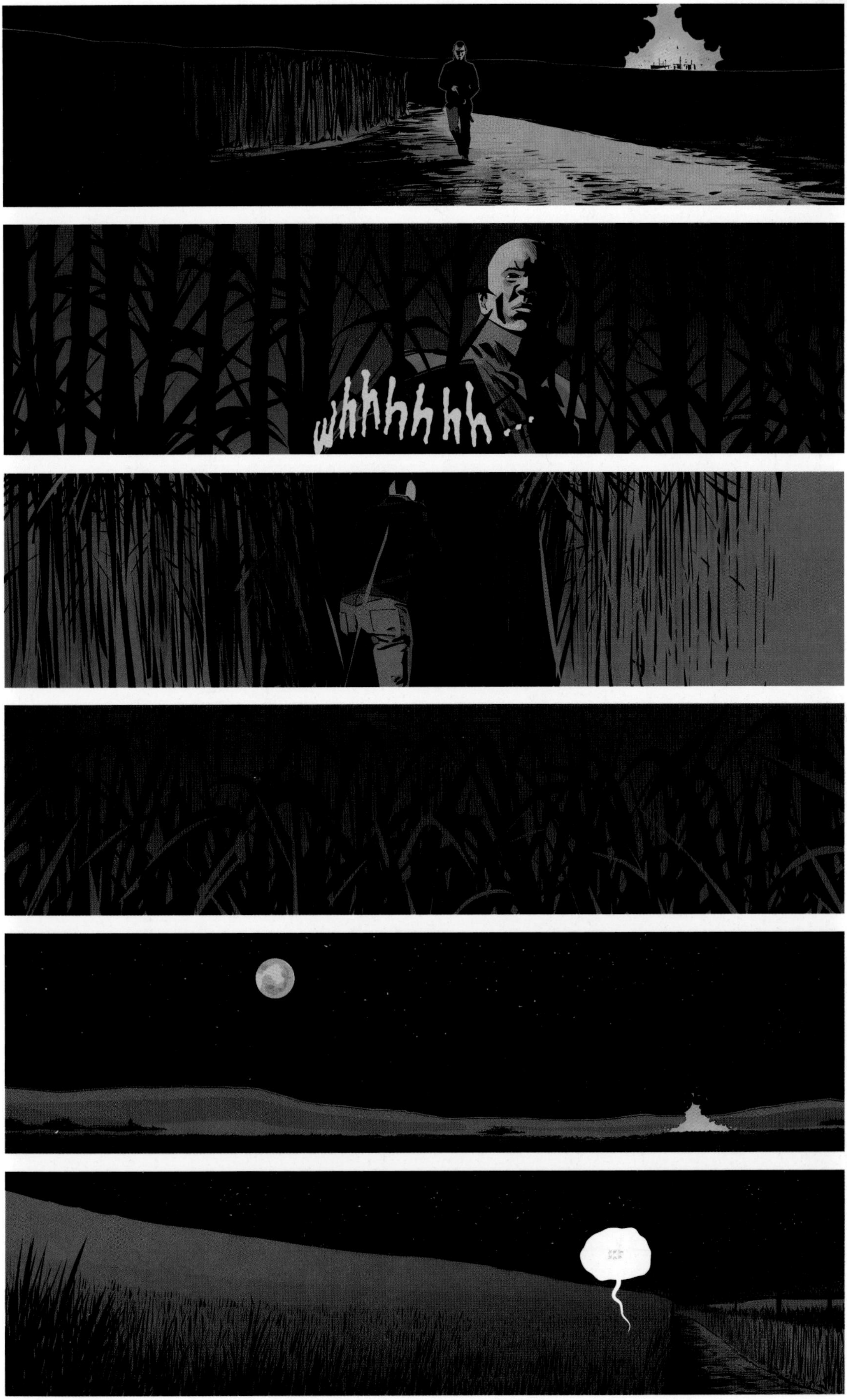
whhhhhh...

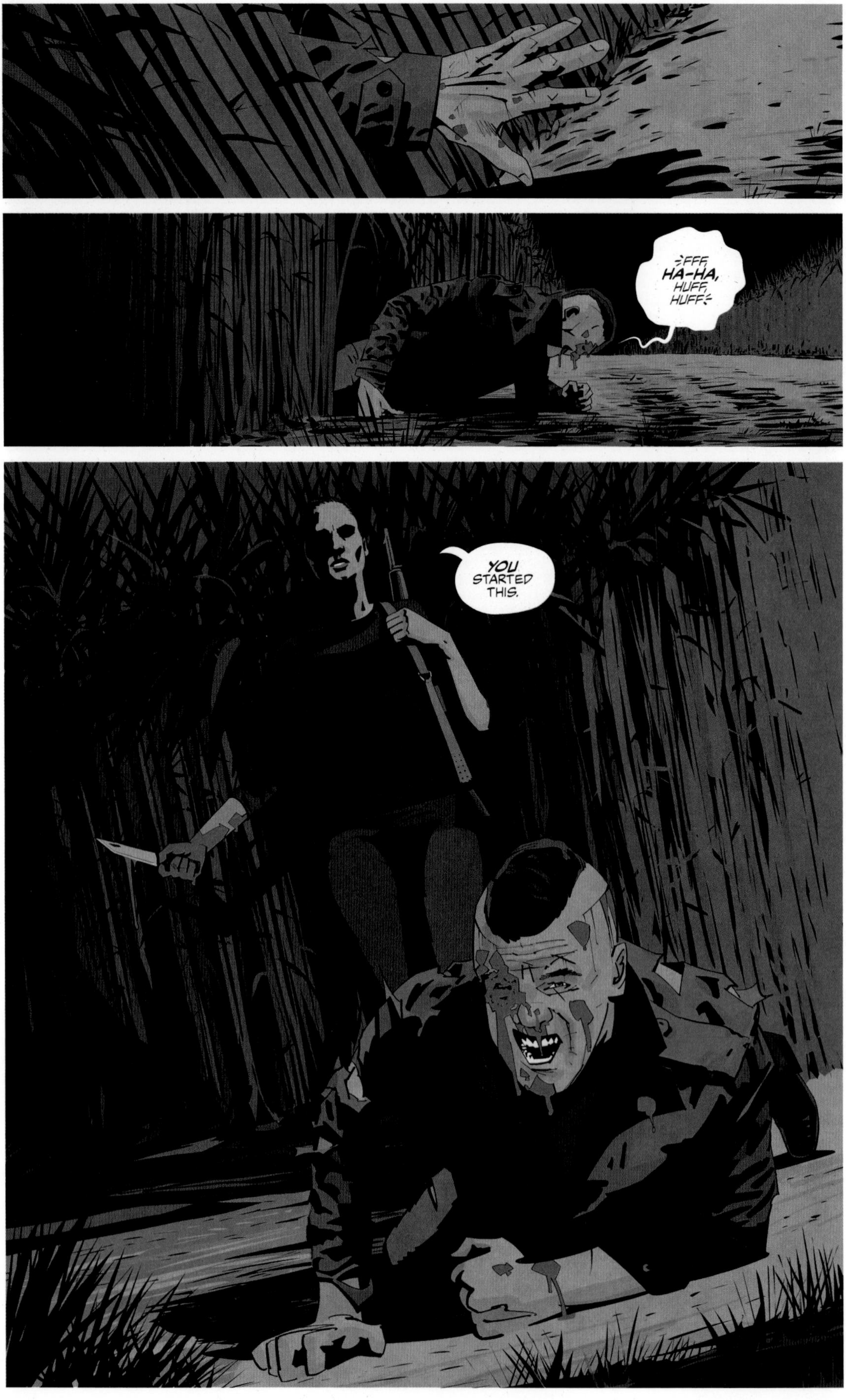
FFF, HA-HA, HUFF, HUFF
YOU STARTED THIS.

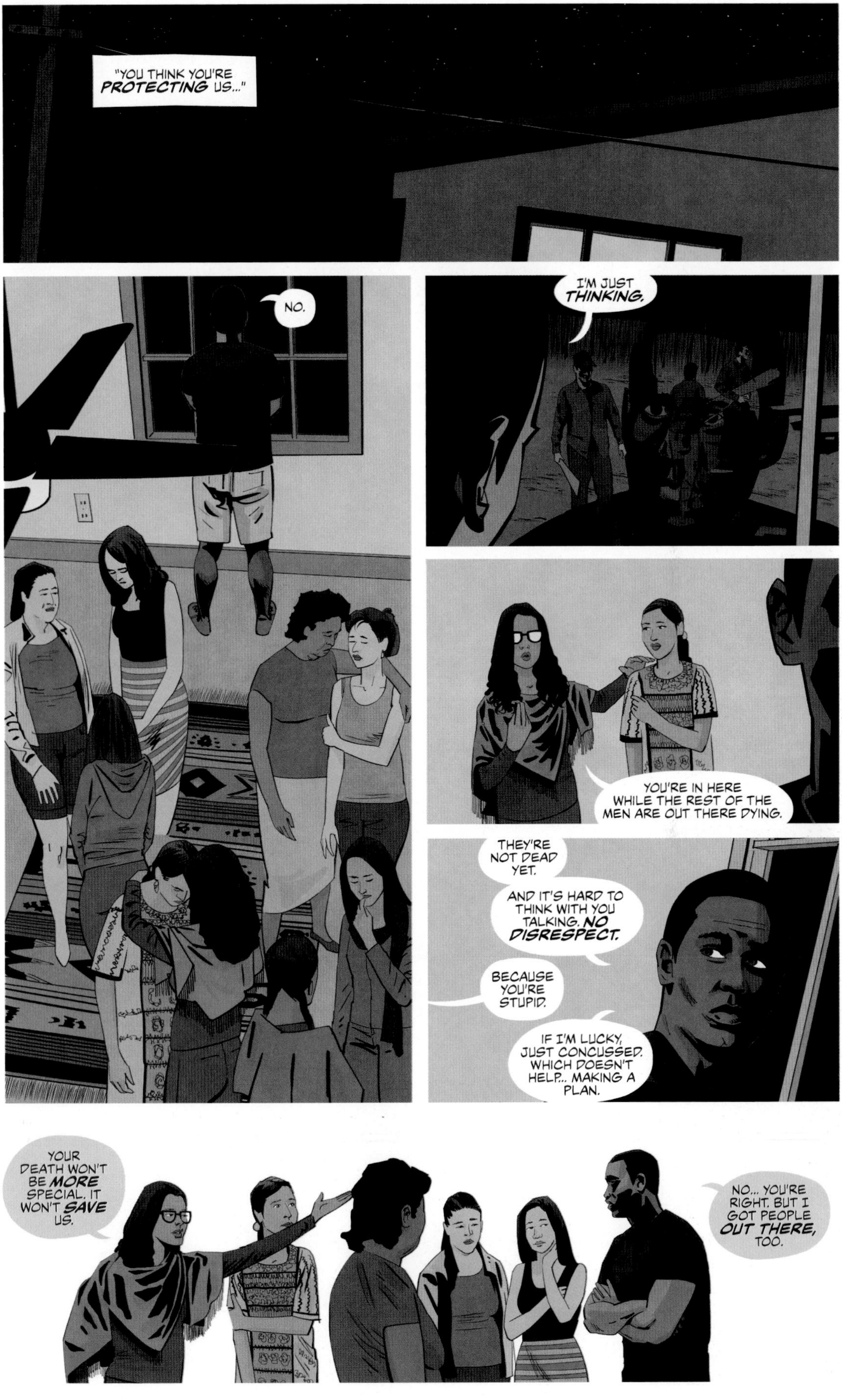
"YOU THINK YOU'RE PROTECTING US..."
NO.
I'M JUST THINKING.
YOU'RE IN HERE WHILE THE REST OF THE MEN ARE OUT THERE DYING.
THEY'RE NOT DEAD YET.
AND IT'S HARD TO THINK WITH YOU TALKING. NO DISRESPECT.
BECAUSE YOU'RE STUPID.
IF I'M LUCKY, JUST CONCUSSED. WHICH DOESN'T HELP... MAKING A PLAN.
YOUR DEATH WON'T BE MORE SPECIAL. IT WON'T SAVE US.
NO... YOU'RE RIGHT. BUT I GOT PEOPLE OUT THERE, TOO.

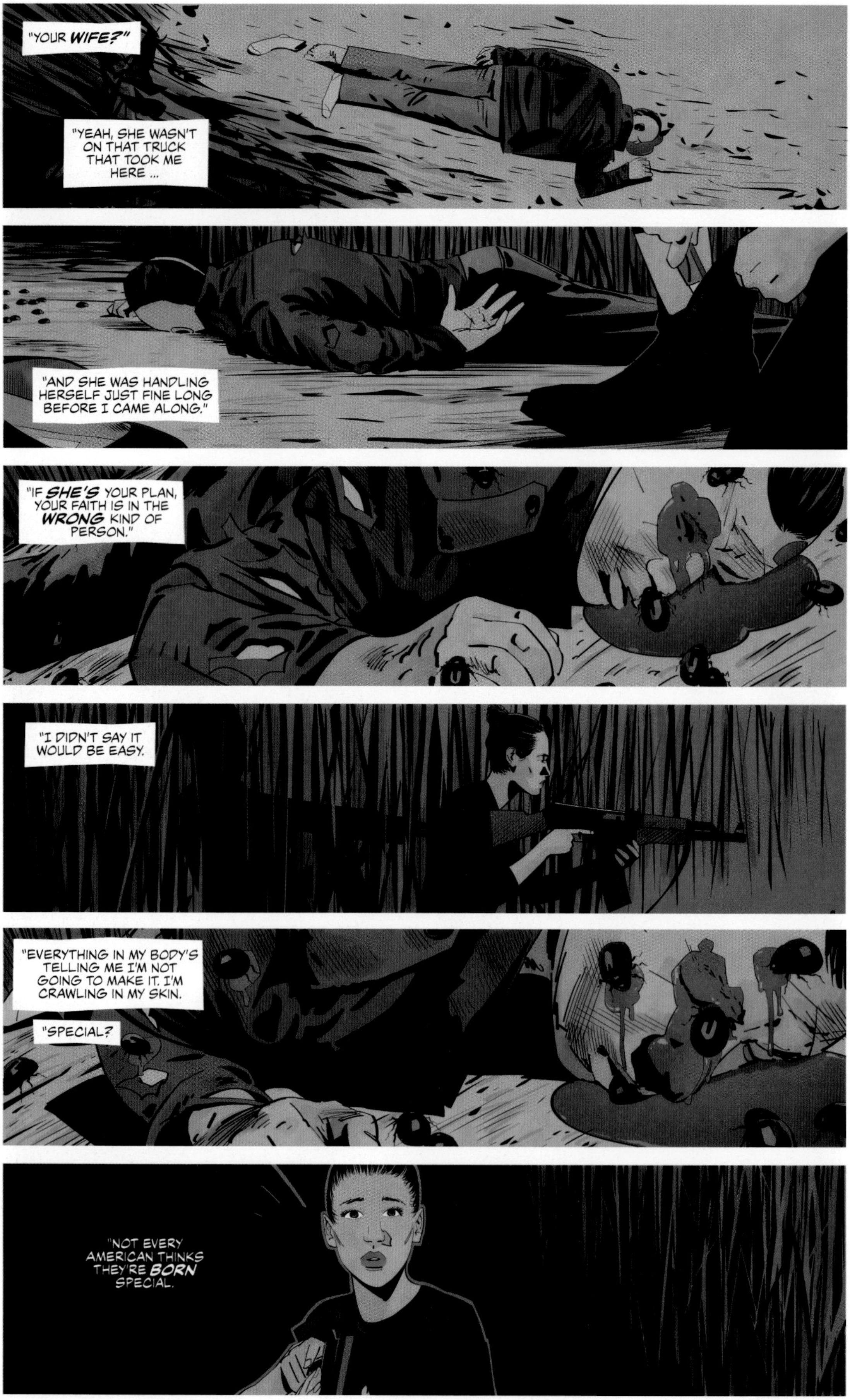
"YOUR WIFE?"
"YEAH, SHE WASN'T ON THAT TRUCK THAT TOOK ME HERE ...
"AND SHE WAS HANDLING HERSELF JUST FINE LONG BEFORE I CAME ALONG."
"IF SHE'S YOUR PLAN, YOUR FAITH IS IN THE WRONG KIND OF PERSON."
"I DIDN'T SAY IT WOULD BE EASY.
"EVERYTHING IN MY BODY'S TELLING ME I'M NOT GOING TO MAKE IT. I'M CRAWLING IN MY SKIN.
"SPECIAL?
"NOT EVERY AMERICAN THINKS THEY'RE BORN SPECIAL.

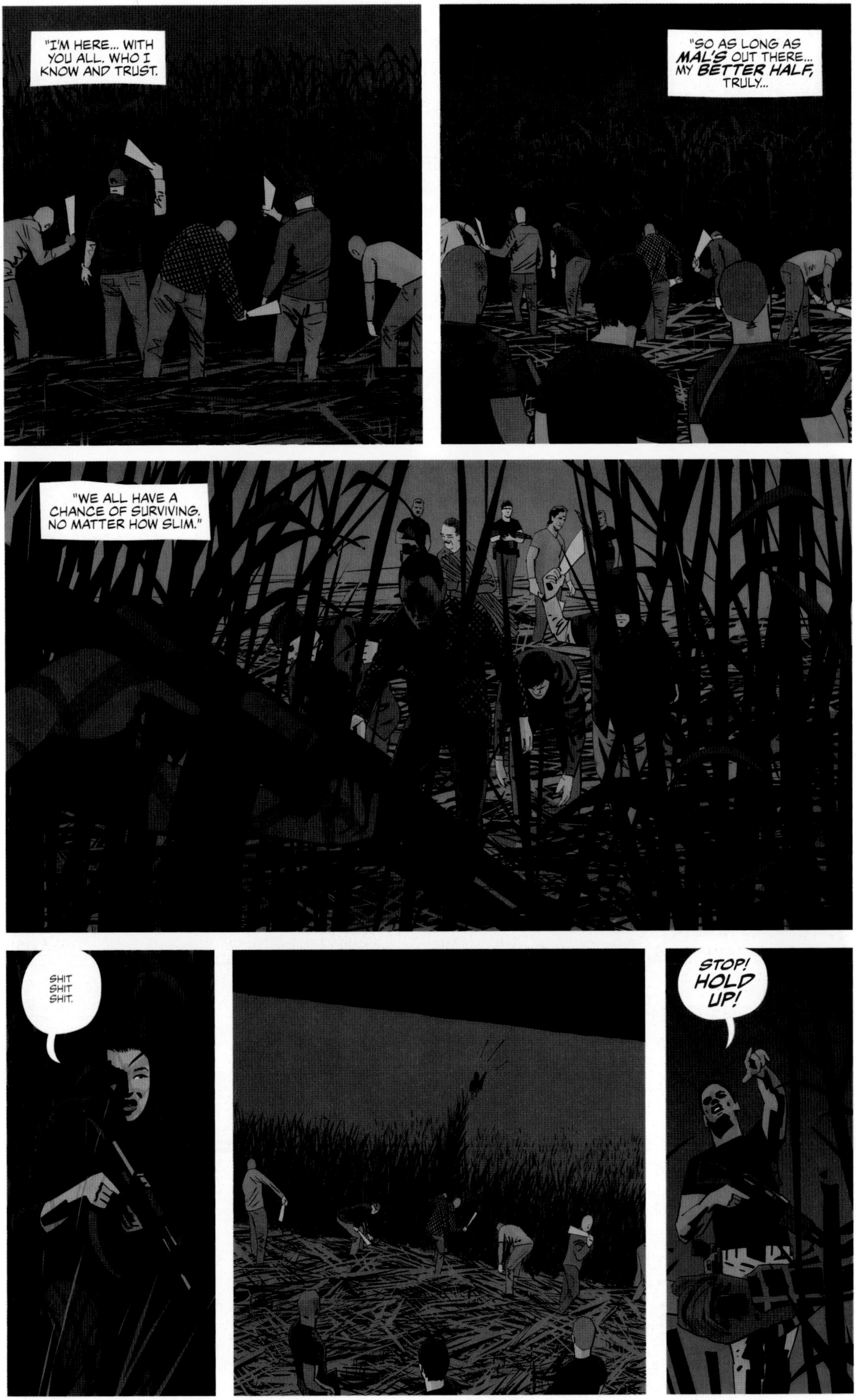
"I'M HERE... WITH YOU ALL. WHO I KNOW AND TRUST.
"SO AS LONG AS MAL'S OUT THERE... MY BETTER HALF, TRULY...
"WE ALL HAVE A CHANCE OF SURVIVING. NO MATTER HOW SLIM."
SHIT SHIT SHIT.
STOP! HOLD UP!

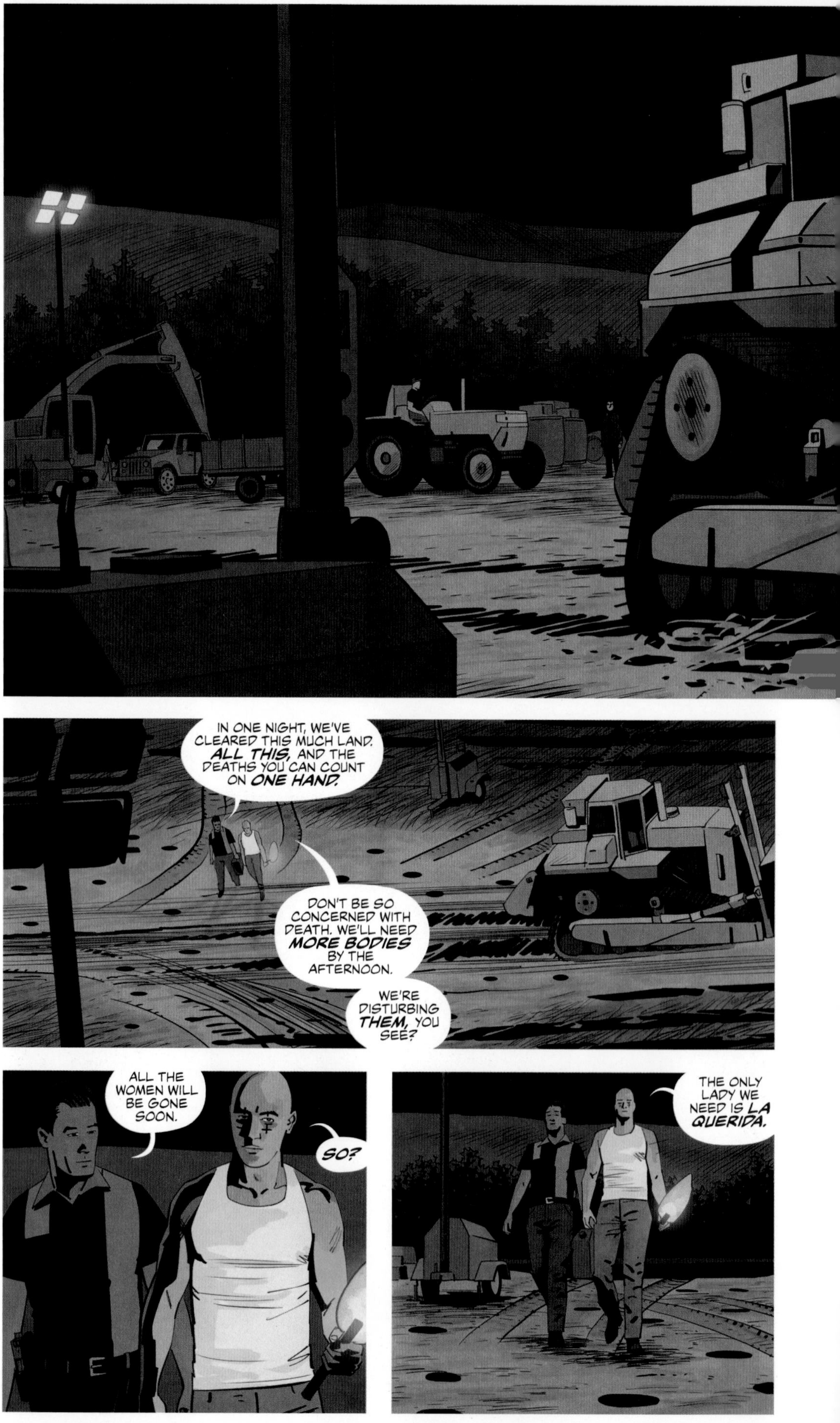

IN ONE NIGHT, WE'VE CLEARED THIS MUCH LAND. ALL THIS, AND THE DEATHS YOU CAN COUNT ON ONE HAND.
DON'T BE SO CONCERNED WITH DEATH. WE'LL NEED MORE BODIES BY THE AFTERNOON.
WE'RE DISTURBING THEM, YOU SEE?
ALL THE WOMEN WILL BE GONE SOON.
SO?
THE ONLY LADY WE NEED IS LA QUERIDA.

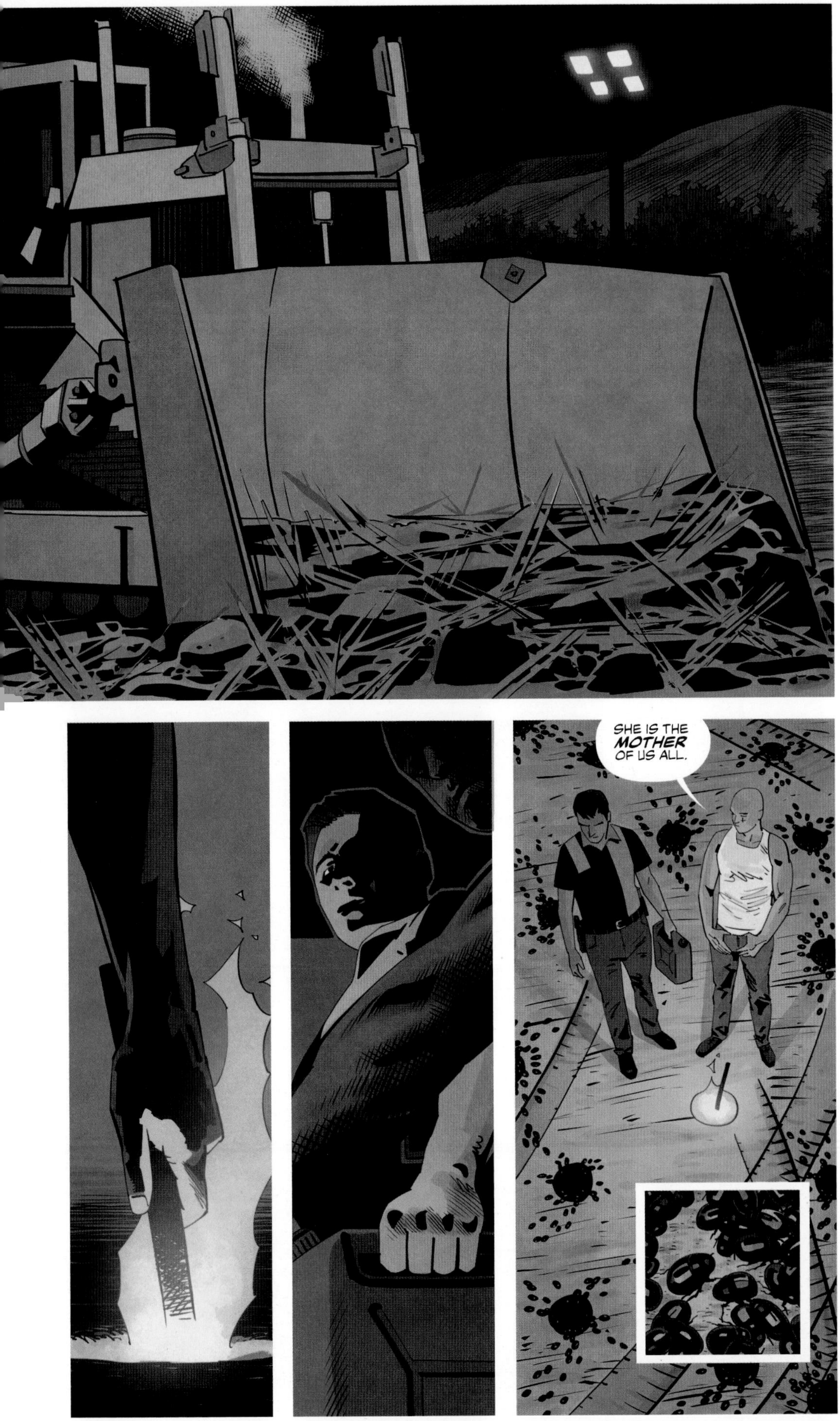
SHE IS THE *MOTHER* OF US ALL.

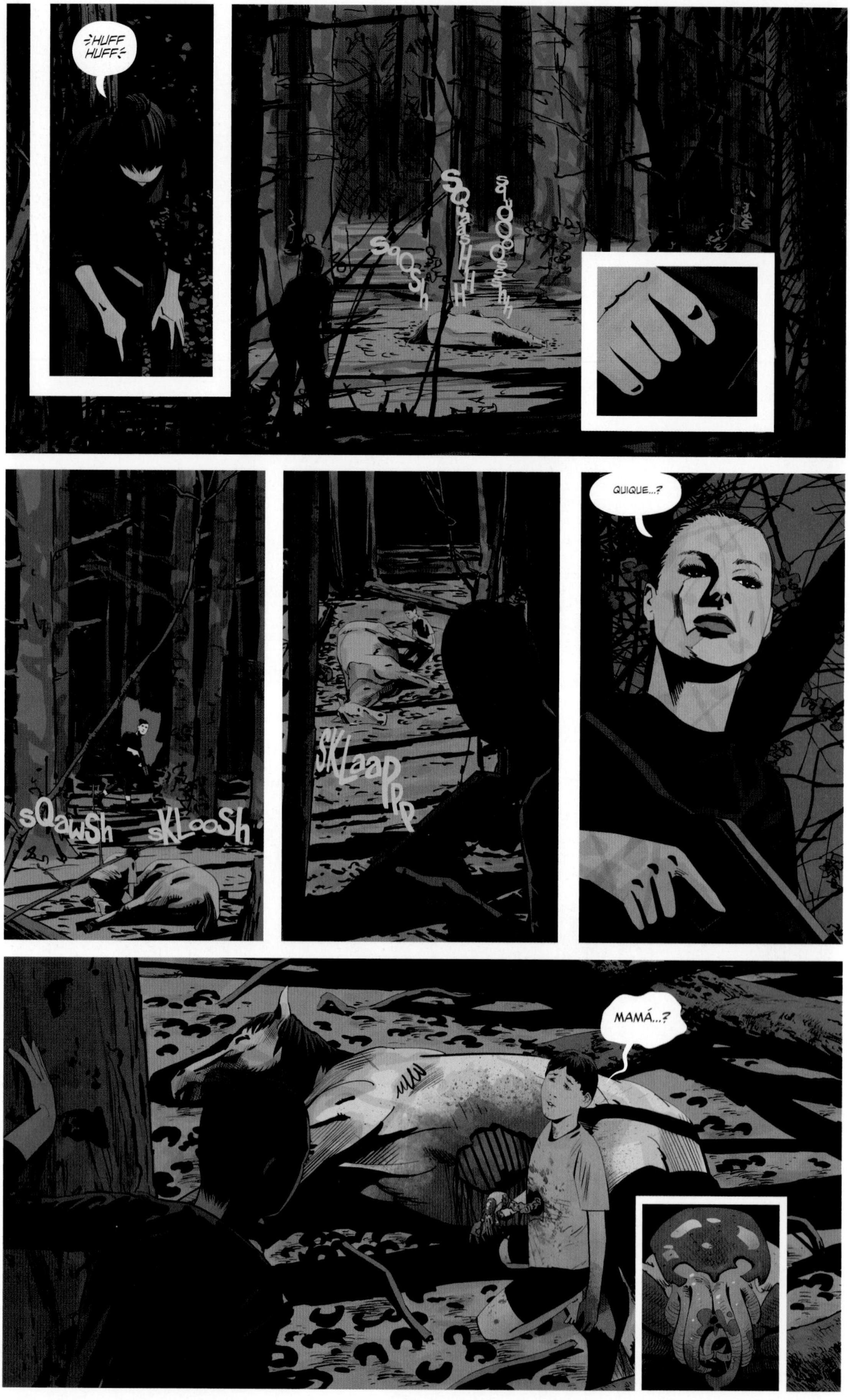
HUFF HUFF
SQOOSH
SQUASHHH
SQUOOOOSSHH
SQAWSH
SKLOOSH
SKLAAPPP
QUIQUE...?
MAMÁ...?

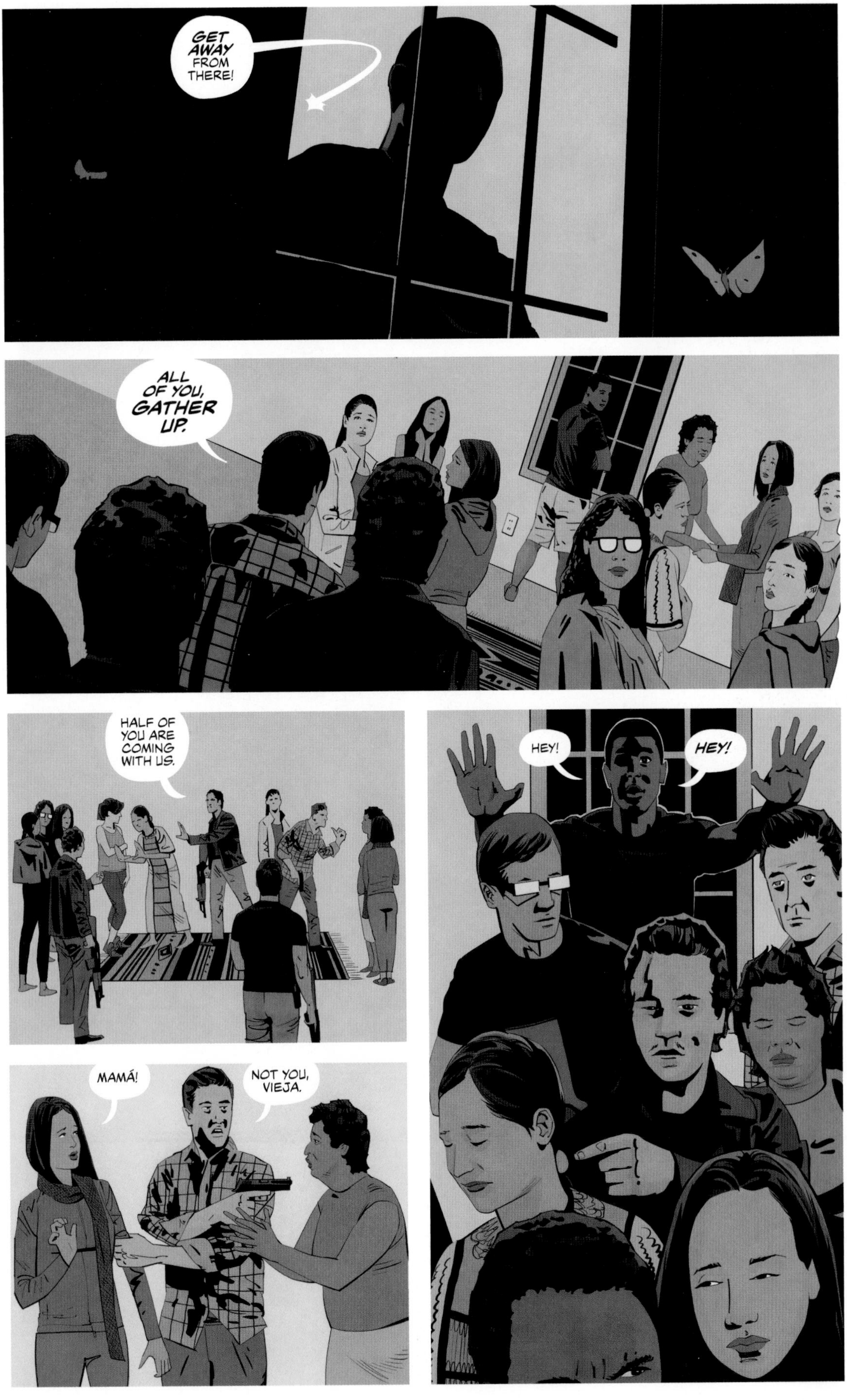
GET AWAY FROM THERE!
ALL OF YOU, GATHER UP.
HALF OF YOU ARE COMING WITH US.
MAMÁ!
NOT YOU, VIEJA.
HEY!
HEY!

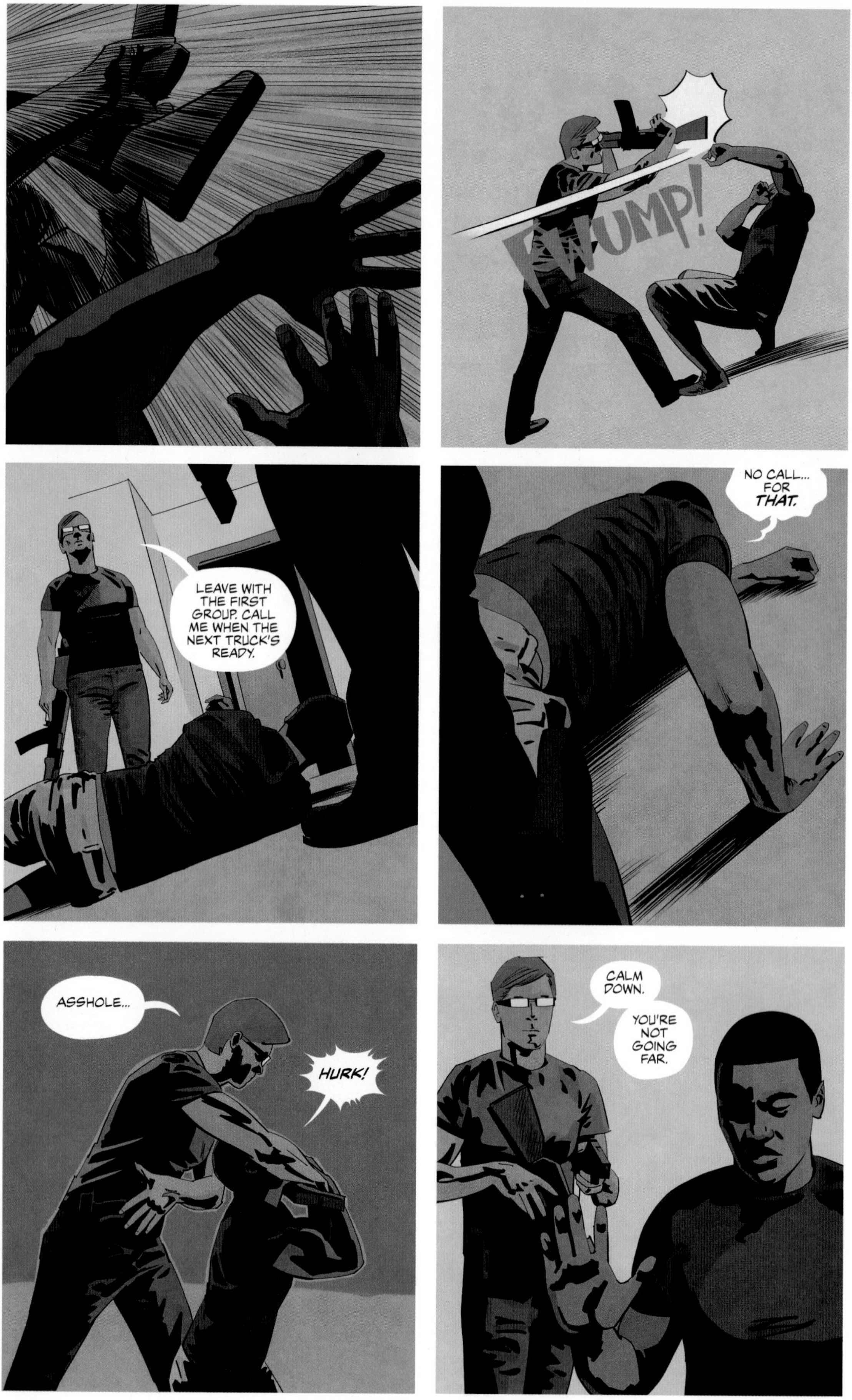
FWUMP!
LEAVE WITH THE FIRST GROUP. CALL ME WHEN THE NEXT TRUCK'S READY.
NO CALL... FOR THAT.
ASSHOLE...
HURK!
CALM DOWN.
YOU'RE NOT GOING FAR.

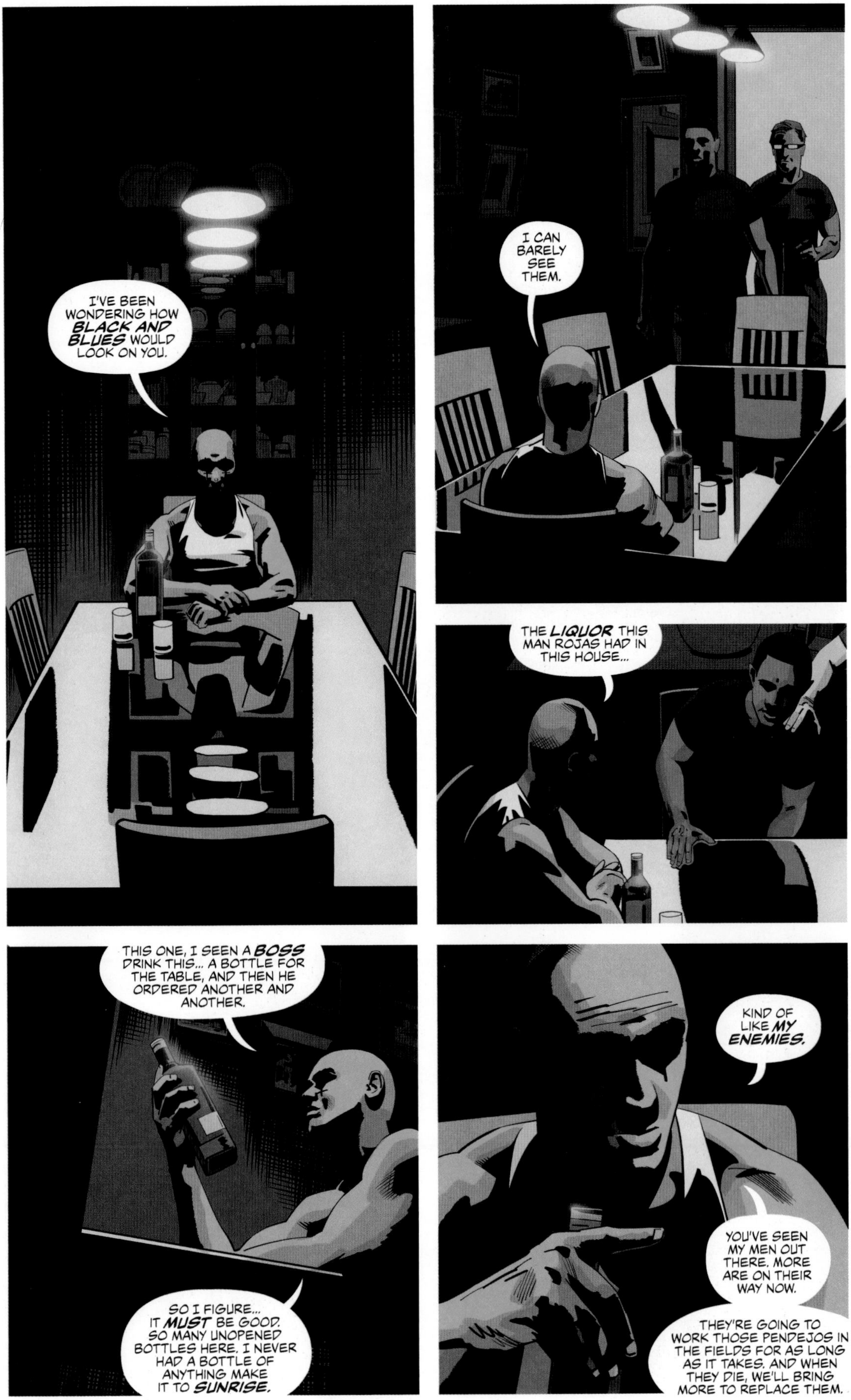
I'VE BEEN WONDERING HOW BLACK AND BLUES WOULD LOOK ON YOU.
I CAN BARELY SEE THEM.
THE LIQUOR THIS MAN ROJAS HAD IN THIS HOUSE...
THIS ONE, I SEEN A BOSS DRINK THIS... A BOTTLE FOR THE TABLE, AND THEN HE ORDERED ANOTHER AND ANOTHER.
SO I FIGURE... IT MUST BE GOOD. SO MANY UNOPENED BOTTLES HERE. I NEVER HAD A BOTTLE OF ANYTHING MAKE IT TO SUNRISE.
KIND OF LIKE MY ENEMIES.
YOU'VE SEEN MY MEN OUT THERE. MORE ARE ON THEIR WAY NOW.
THEY'RE GOING TO WORK THOSE PENDEJOS IN THE FIELDS FOR AS LONG AS IT TAKES. AND WHEN THEY DIE, WE'LL BRING MORE TO REPLACE THEM.

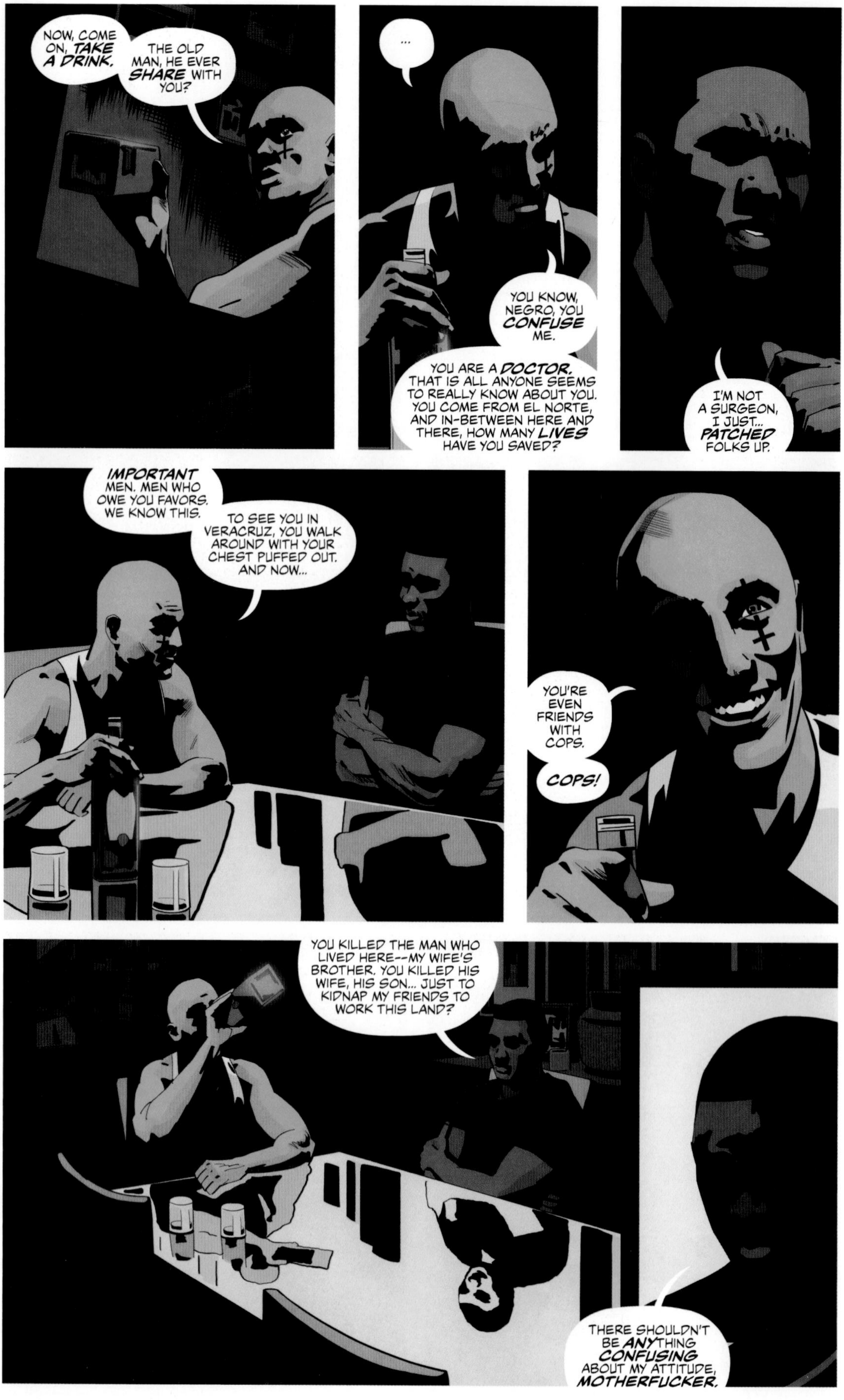
NOW, COME ON, TAKE A DRINK.
THE OLD MAN, HE EVER SHARE WITH YOU?
...
YOU KNOW, NEGRO, YOU CONFUSE ME.
YOU ARE A DOCTOR. THAT IS ALL ANYONE SEEMS TO REALLY KNOW ABOUT YOU. YOU COME FROM EL NORTE, AND IN-BETWEEN HERE AND THERE, HOW MANY LIVES HAVE YOU SAVED?
I'M NOT A SURGEON, I JUST... PATCHED FOLKS UP.
IMPORTANT MEN. MEN WHO OWE YOU FAVORS. WE KNOW THIS.
TO SEE YOU IN VERACRUZ, YOU WALK AROUND WITH YOUR CHEST PUFFED OUT. AND NOW...
YOU'RE EVEN FRIENDS WITH COPS.
COPS!
YOU KILLED THE MAN WHO LIVED HERE--MY WIFE'S BROTHER. YOU KILLED HIS WIFE, HIS SON... JUST TO KIDNAP MY FRIENDS TO WORK THIS LAND?
THERE SHOULDN'T BE ANYTHING CONFUSING ABOUT MY ATTITUDE, MOTHERFUCKER.

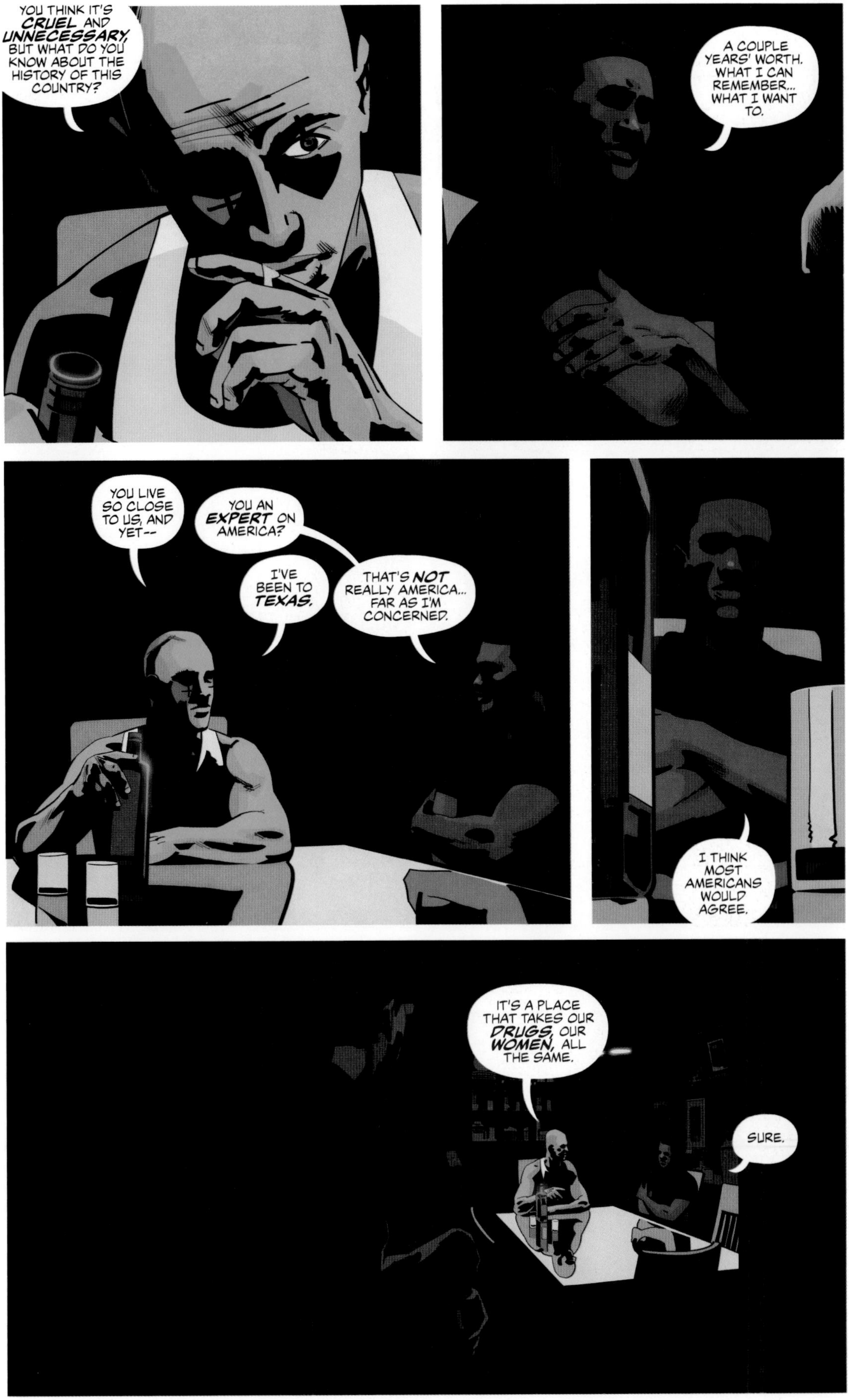
YOU THINK IT'S CRUEL AND UNNECESSARY, BUT WHAT DO YOU KNOW ABOUT THE HISTORY OF THIS COUNTRY?
A COUPLE YEARS' WORTH. WHAT I CAN REMEMBER... WHAT I WANT TO.
YOU LIVE SO CLOSE TO US, AND YET--
YOU AN EXPERT ON AMERICA?
I'VE BEEN TO TEXAS.
THAT'S NOT REALLY AMERICA... FAR AS I'M CONCERNED.
I THINK MOST AMERICANS WOULD AGREE.
IT'S A PLACE THAT TAKES OUR DRUGS, OUR WOMEN, ALL THE SAME.
SURE.

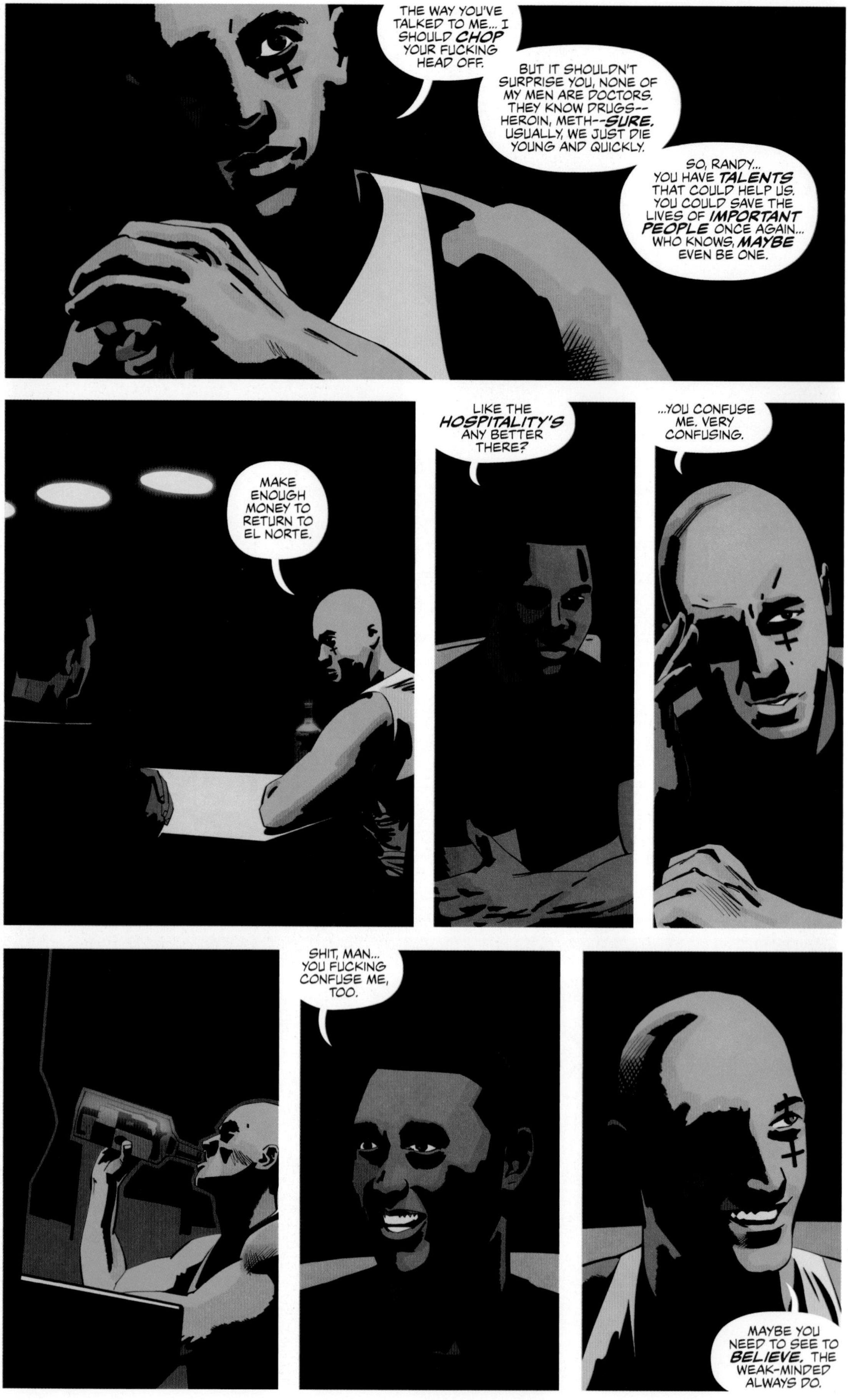
THE WAY YOU'VE TALKED TO ME... I SHOULD CHOP YOUR FUCKING HEAD OFF.
BUT IT SHOULDN'T SURPRISE YOU, NONE OF MY MEN ARE DOCTORS. THEY KNOW DRUGS--HEROIN, METH--SURE. USUALLY, WE JUST DIE YOUNG AND QUICKLY.
SO, RANDY... YOU HAVE TALENTS THAT COULD HELP US. YOU COULD SAVE THE LIVES OF IMPORTANT PEOPLE ONCE AGAIN... WHO KNOWS, MAYBE EVEN BE ONE.
MAKE ENOUGH MONEY TO RETURN TO EL NORTE.
LIKE THE HOSPITALITY'S ANY BETTER THERE?
...YOU CONFUSE ME. VERY CONFUSING.
SHIT, MAN... YOU FUCKING CONFUSE ME, TOO.
MAYBE YOU NEED TO SEE TO BELIEVE. THE WEAK-MINDED ALWAYS DO.

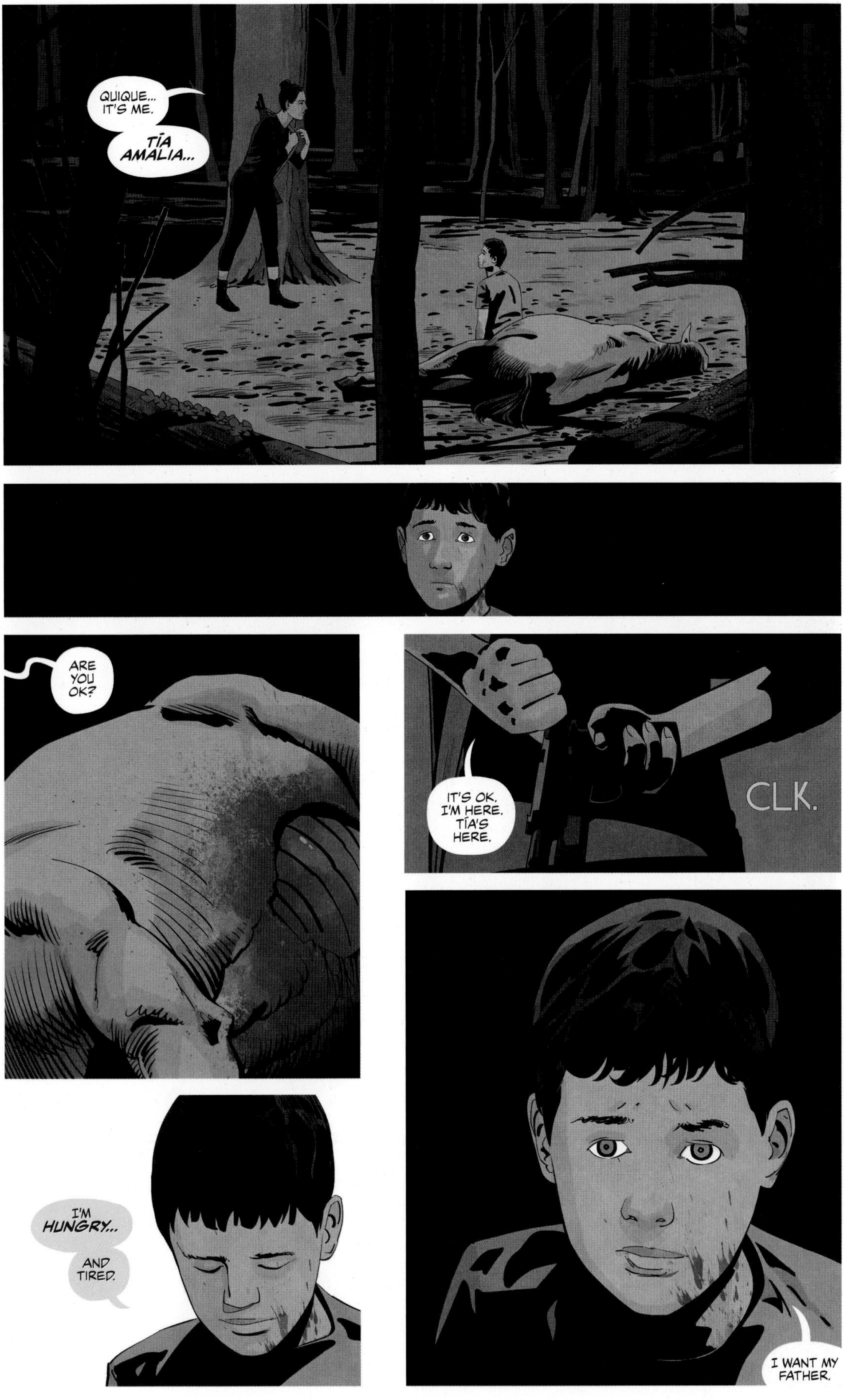
QUIQUE... IT'S ME.
TÍA AMALIA...
ARE YOU OK?
IT'S OK. I'M HERE. TÍA'S HERE.
CLK.
I'M HUNGRY...
AND TIRED.
I WANT MY FATHER.

CHIT CHIT

HOME... YOU WANT TO GO HOME?

A-HUH-HUH...

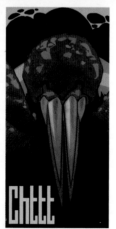

CHTTT

OK, OK...

I HAVE *KIDS*, YOU KNOW. I'M A *MOM*. I'VE BEEN A MOM LONGER THAN YOUR MOM.

I DON'T TALK ABOUT IT, BUT... I WANTED TO *SHARE* THAT WITH YOU.

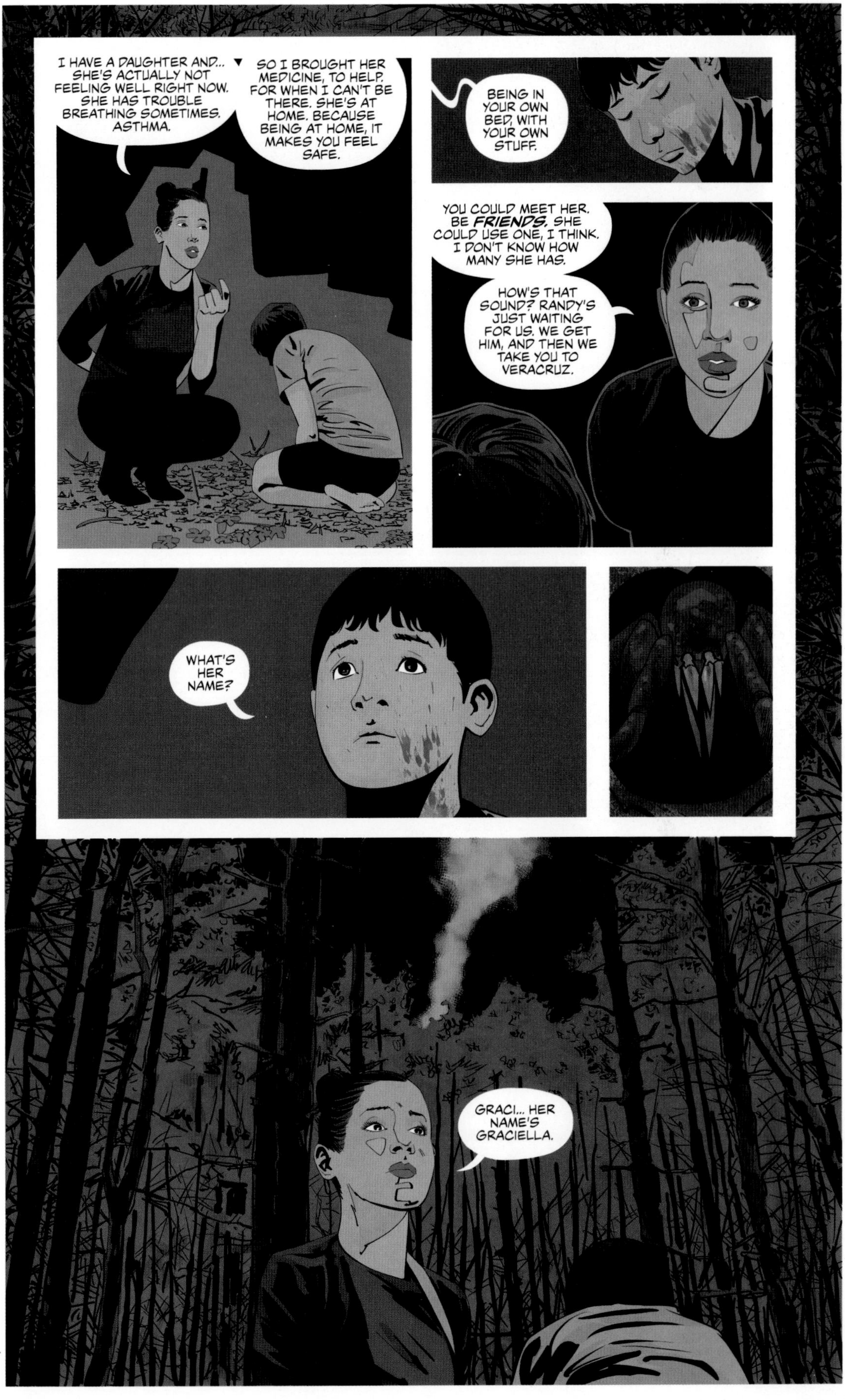
I HAVE A DAUGHTER AND... SHE'S ACTUALLY NOT FEELING WELL RIGHT NOW. SHE HAS TROUBLE BREATHING SOMETIMES. ASTHMA.
SO I BROUGHT HER MEDICINE, TO HELP. FOR WHEN I CAN'T BE THERE. SHE'S AT HOME. BECAUSE BEING AT HOME, IT MAKES YOU FEEL SAFE.
BEING IN YOUR OWN BED, WITH YOUR OWN STUFF.
YOU COULD MEET HER. BE *FRIENDS.* SHE COULD USE ONE, I THINK. I DON'T KNOW HOW MANY SHE HAS.
HOW'S THAT SOUND? RANDY'S JUST WAITING FOR US. WE GET HIM, AND THEN WE TAKE YOU TO VERACRUZ.
WHAT'S HER NAME?
GRACI... HER NAME'S GRACIELLA.

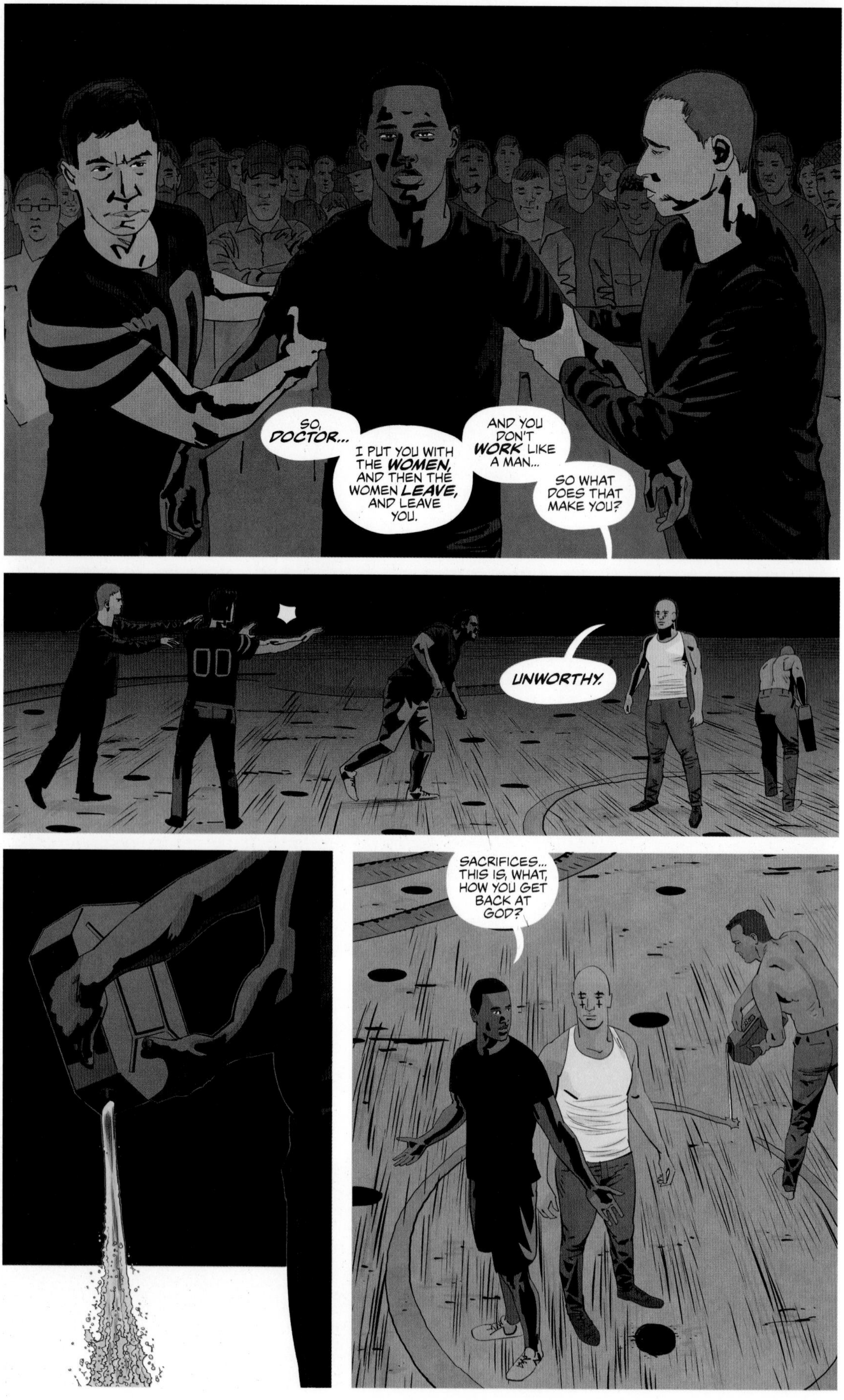
SO, DOCTOR...
I PUT YOU WITH THE WOMEN, AND THEN THE WOMEN LEAVE, AND LEAVE YOU.
AND YOU DON'T WORK LIKE A MAN...
SO WHAT DOES THAT MAKE YOU?
UNWORTHY.
SACRIFICES... THIS IS, WHAT, HOW YOU GET BACK AT GOD?

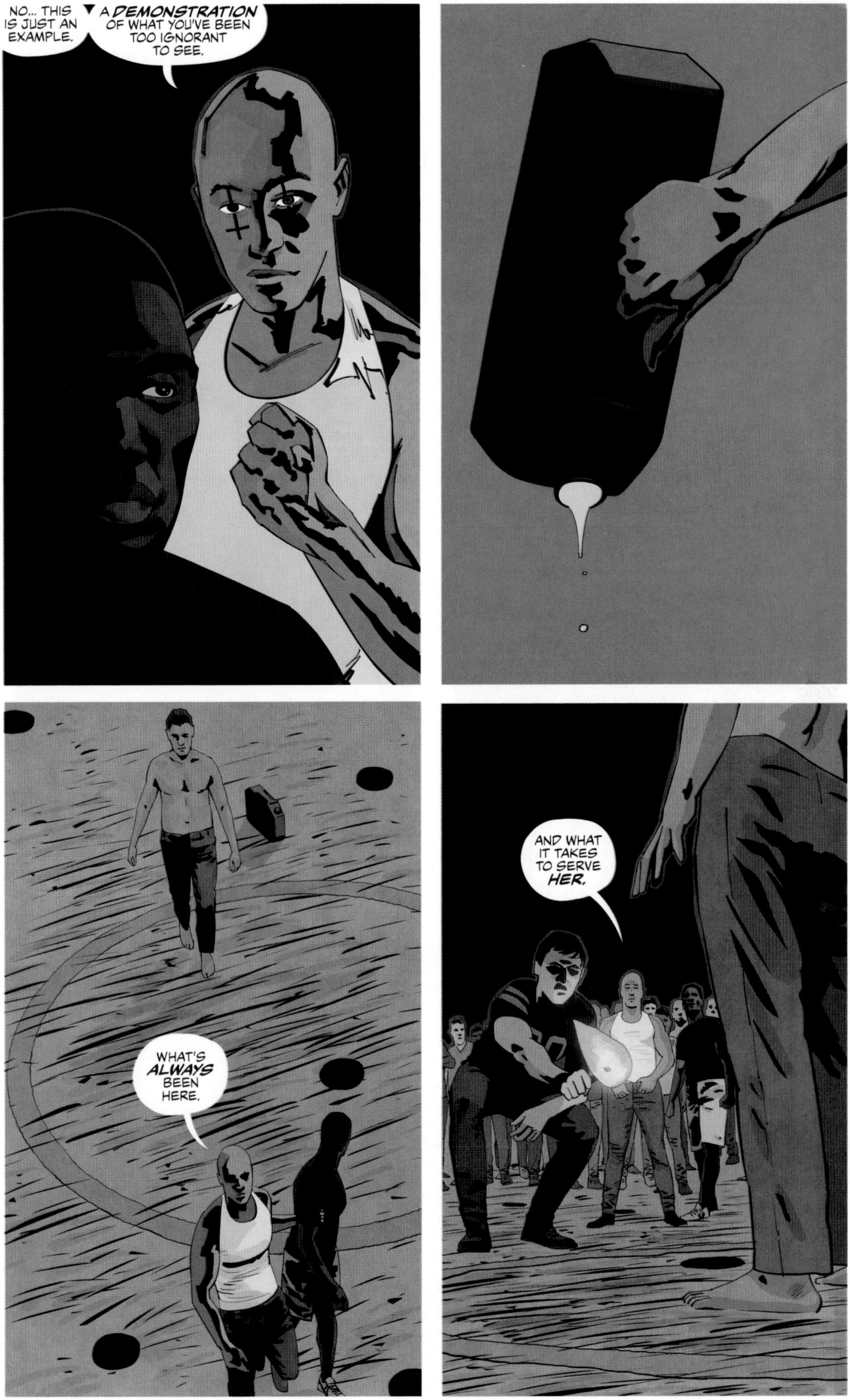
NO... THIS IS JUST AN EXAMPLE.
A DEMONSTRATION OF WHAT YOU'VE BEEN TOO IGNORANT TO SEE.
WHAT'S ALWAYS BEEN HERE.
AND WHAT IT TAKES TO SERVE HER.

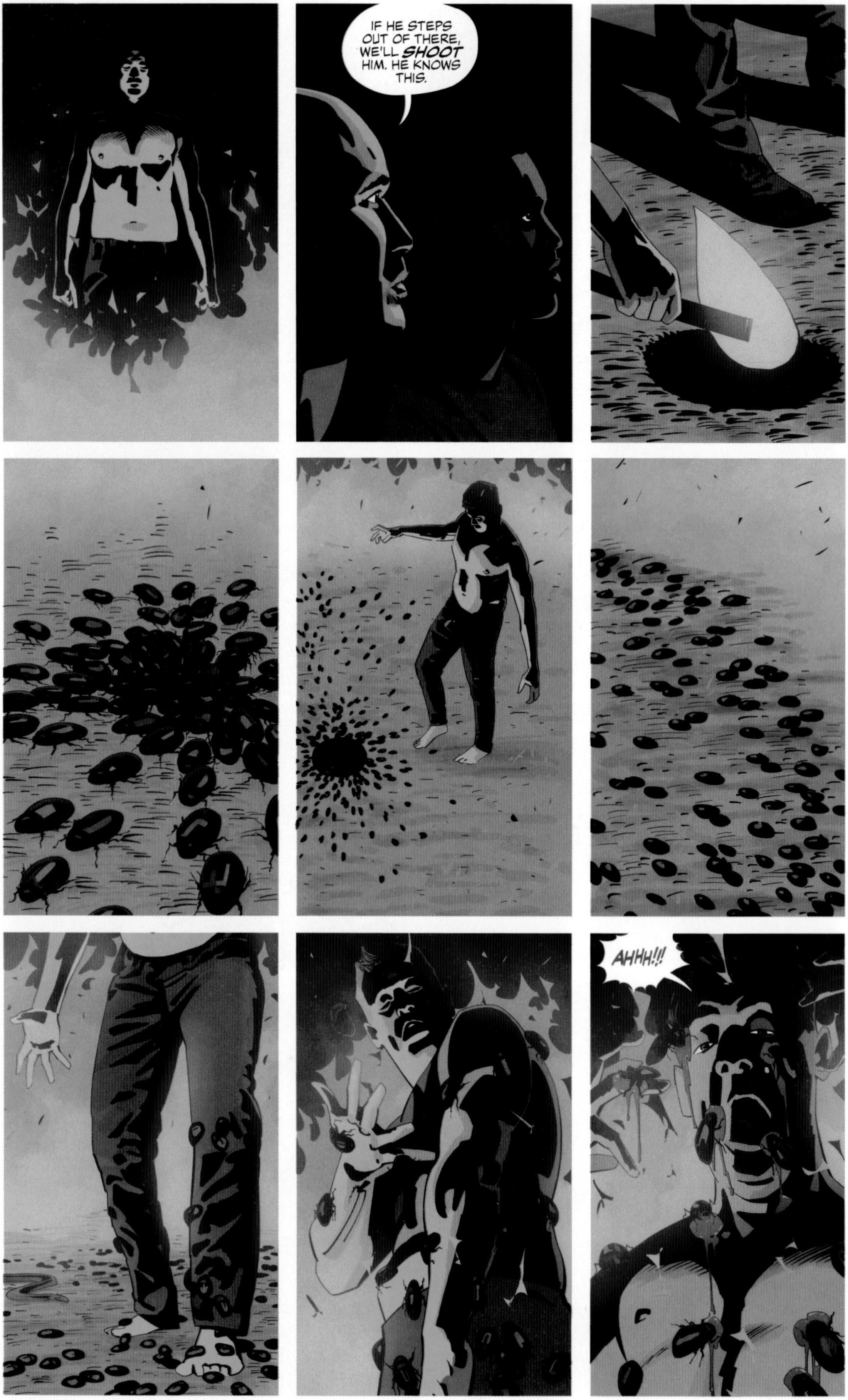
IF HE STEPS OUT OF THERE, WE'LL SHOOT HIM. HE KNOWS THIS.
AHHH!!!

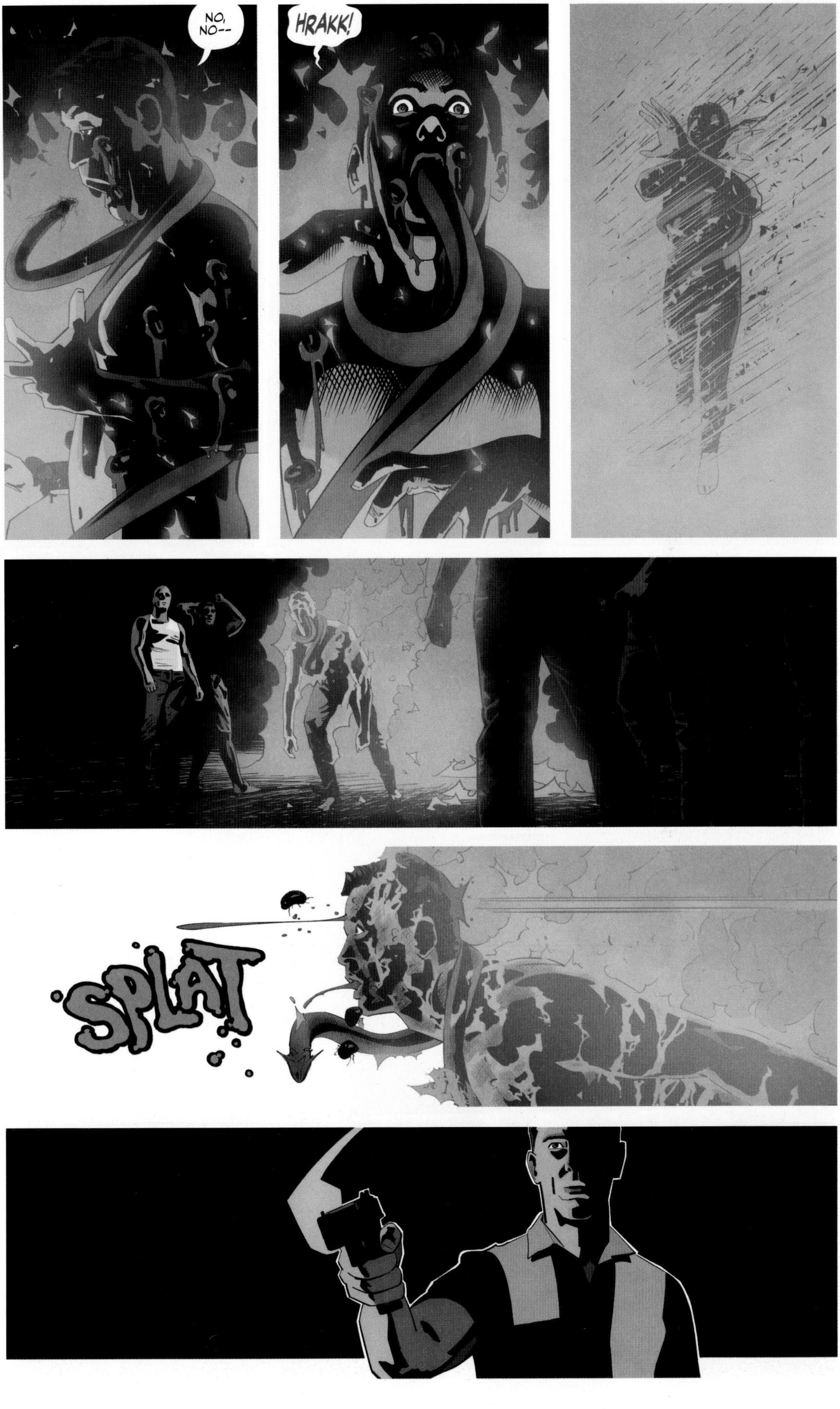
NO, NO--
HRAKK!
SPLAT

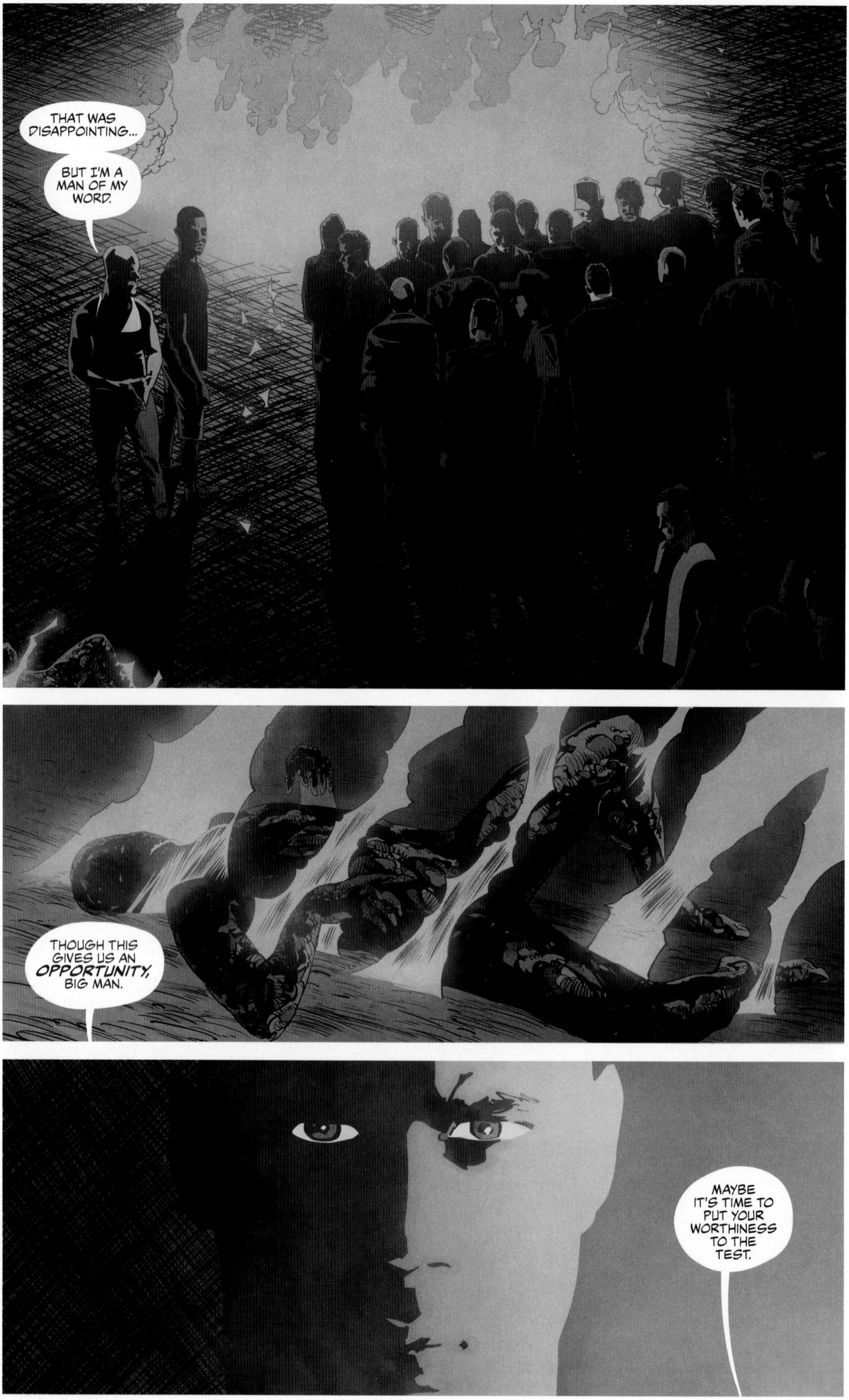
THAT WAS DISAPPOINTING...
BUT I'M A MAN OF MY WORD.
THOUGH THIS GIVES US AN *OPPORTUNITY,* BIG MAN.
MAYBE IT'S TIME TO PUT YOUR WORTHINESS TO THE TEST.

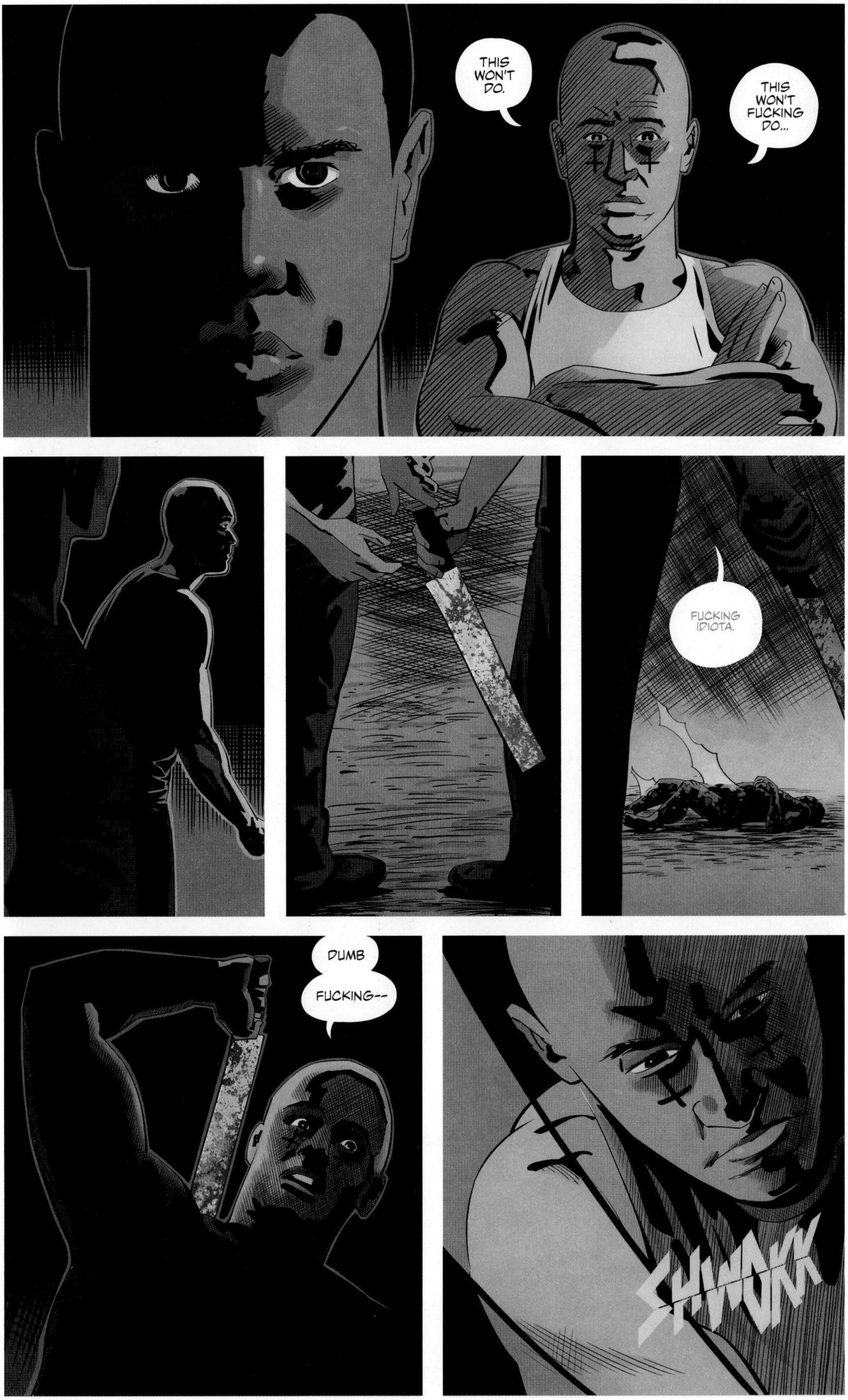
THIS WON'T DO.
THIS WON'T FUCKING DO...
FUCKING IDIOTA.
DUMB
FUCKING--
SHWOKK

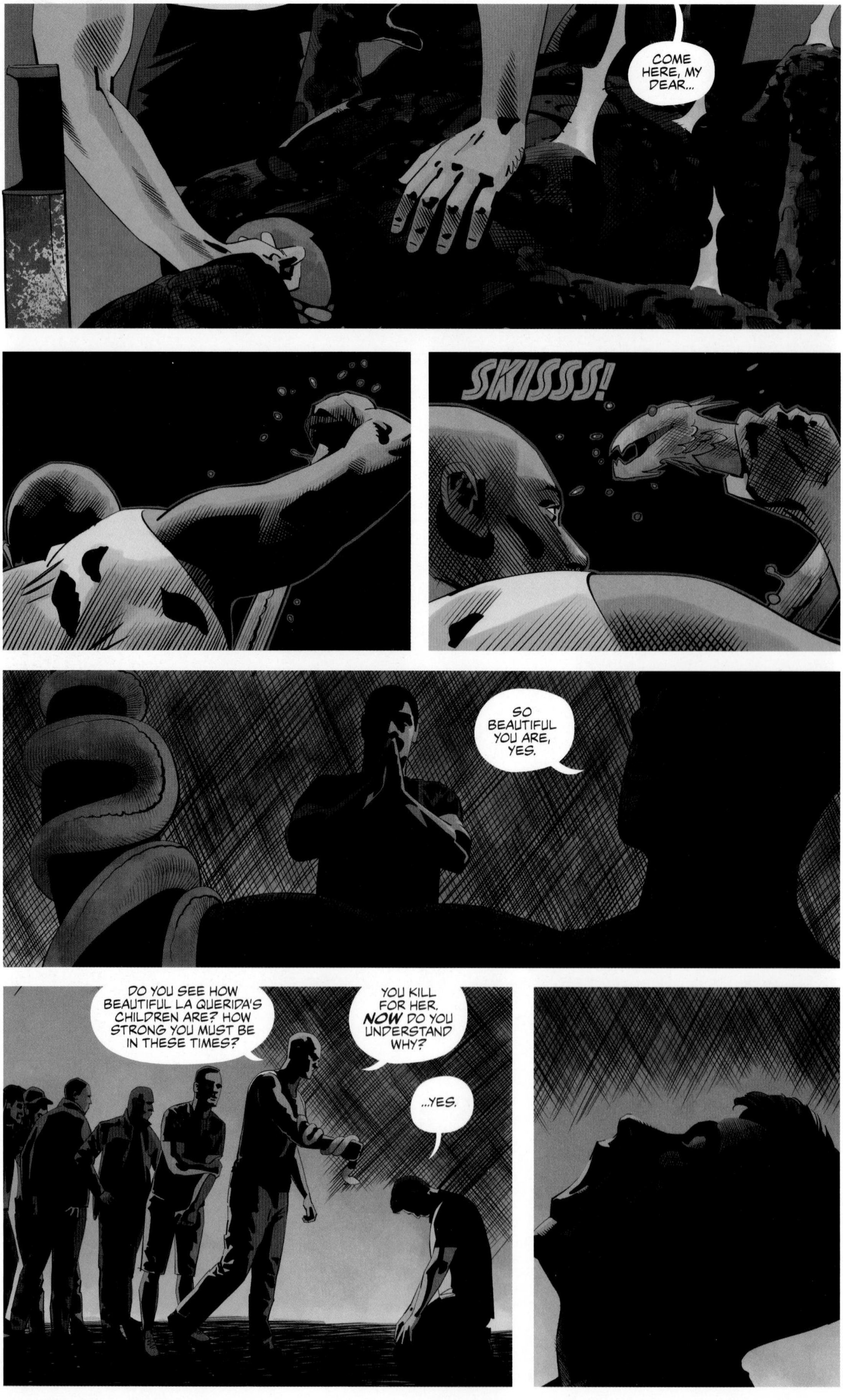
COME HERE, MY DEAR...
SKISSSS!
SO BEAUTIFUL YOU ARE, YES.
DO YOU SEE HOW BEAUTIFUL LA QUERIDA'S CHILDREN ARE? HOW STRONG YOU MUST BE IN THESE TIMES?
YOU KILL FOR HER. NOW DO YOU UNDERSTAND WHY?
...YES.

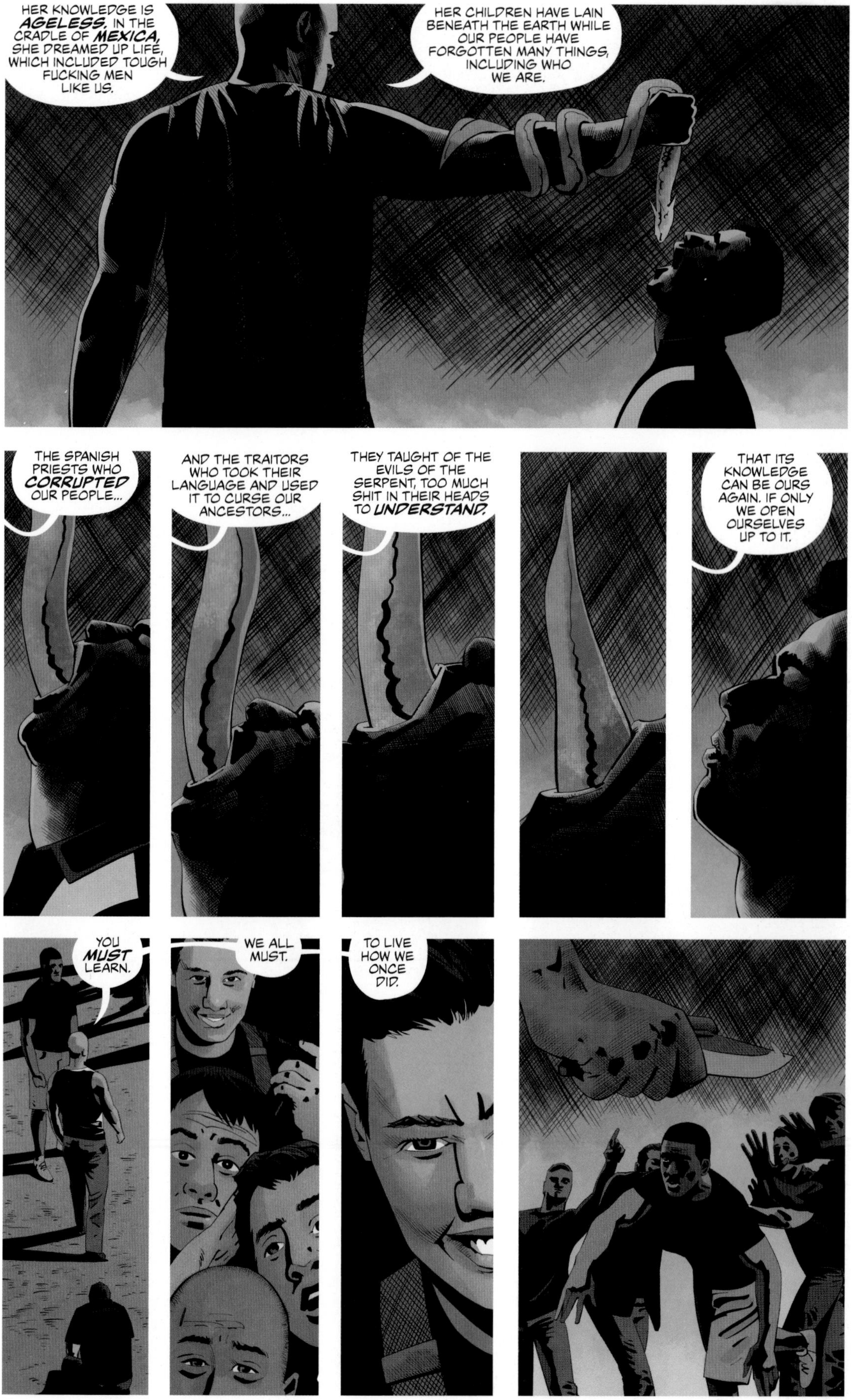
HER KNOWLEDGE IS AGELESS. IN THE CRADLE OF MEXICA, SHE DREAMED UP LIFE, WHICH INCLUDED TOUGH FUCKING MEN LIKE US.
HER CHILDREN HAVE LAIN BENEATH THE EARTH WHILE OUR PEOPLE HAVE FORGOTTEN MANY THINGS, INCLUDING WHO WE ARE.
THE SPANISH PRIESTS WHO CORRUPTED OUR PEOPLE...
AND THE TRAITORS WHO TOOK THEIR LANGUAGE AND USED IT TO CURSE OUR ANCESTORS...
THEY TAUGHT OF THE EVILS OF THE SERPENT, TOO MUCH SHIT IN THEIR HEADS TO UNDERSTAND.
THAT ITS KNOWLEDGE CAN BE OURS AGAIN. IF ONLY WE OPEN OURSELVES UP TO IT.
YOU MUST LEARN.
WE ALL MUST.
TO LIVE HOW WE ONCE DID.

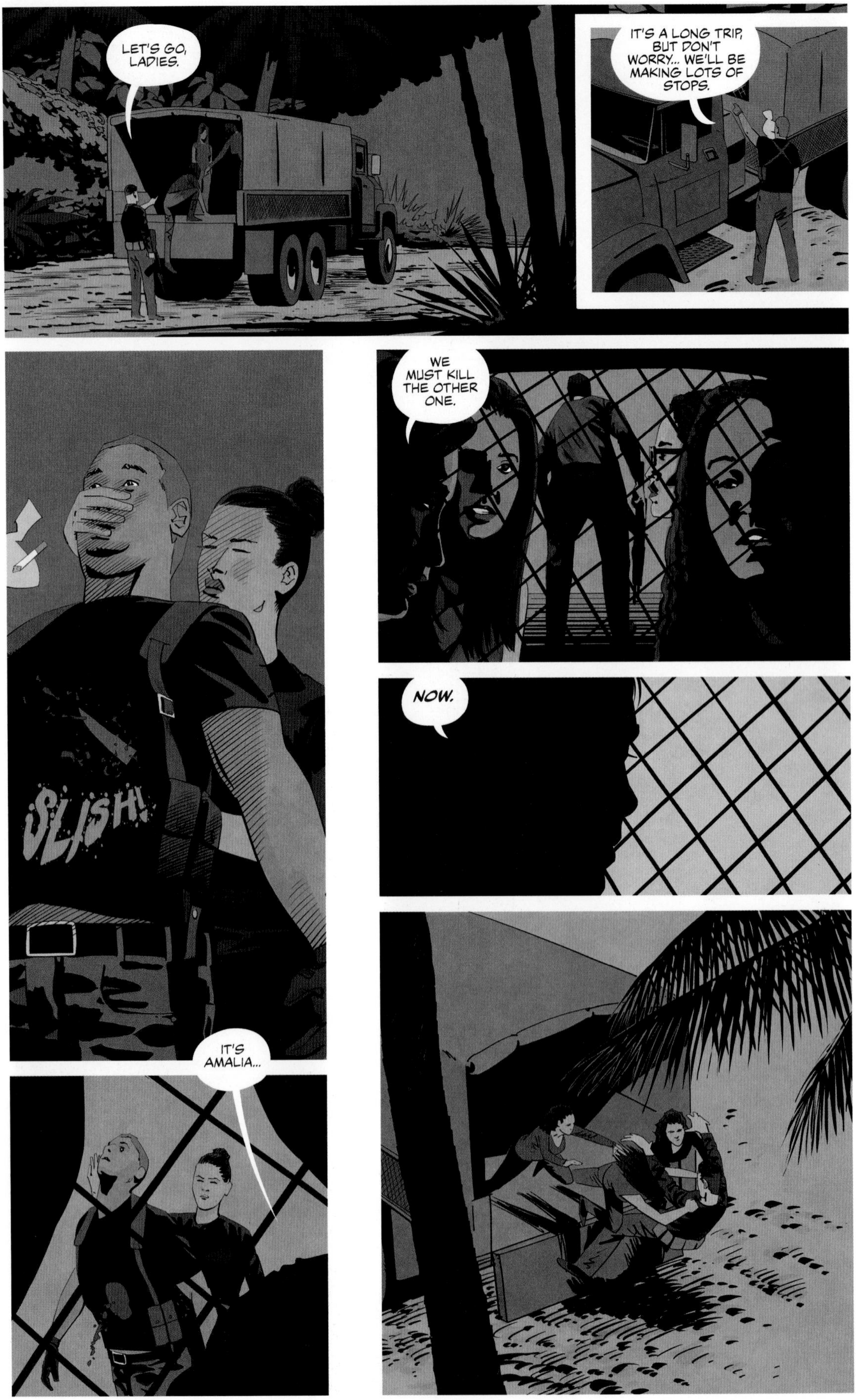
LET'S GO, LADIES.
IT'S A LONG TRIP, BUT DON'T WORRY... WE'LL BE MAKING LOTS OF STOPS.
SLISH!
WE MUST KILL THE OTHER ONE.
NOW.
IT'S AMALIA...

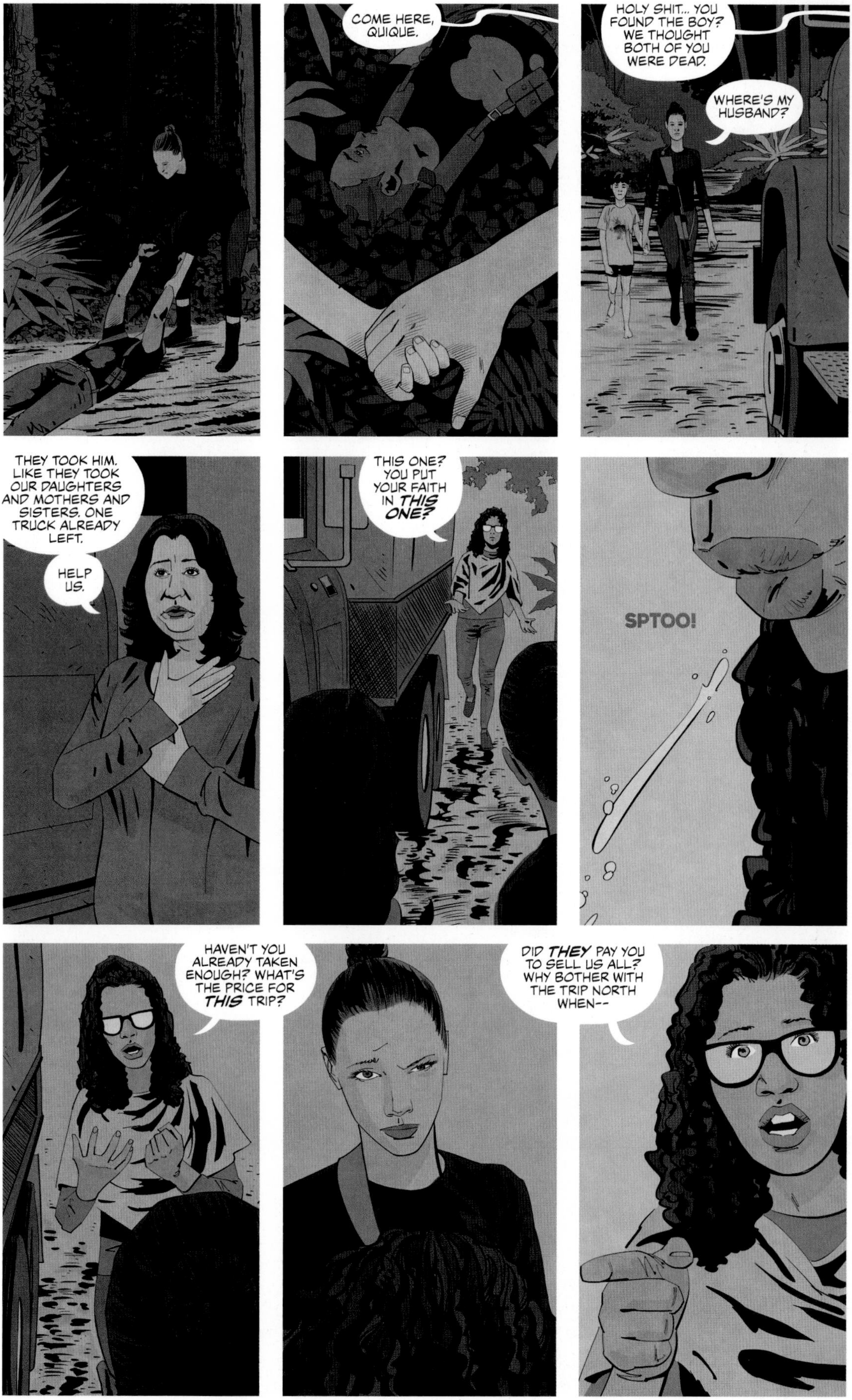
COME HERE, QUIQUE.
HOLY SHIT... YOU FOUND THE BOY? WE THOUGHT BOTH OF YOU WERE DEAD.
WHERE'S MY HUSBAND?
THEY TOOK HIM. LIKE THEY TOOK OUR DAUGHTERS AND MOTHERS AND SISTERS. ONE TRUCK ALREADY LEFT.
HELP US.
THIS ONE? YOU PUT YOUR FAITH IN *THIS ONE?*
SPTOO!
HAVEN'T YOU ALREADY TAKEN ENOUGH? WHAT'S THE PRICE FOR *THIS* TRIP?
DID *THEY* PAY YOU TO SELL US ALL? WHY BOTHER WITH THE TRIP NORTH WHEN--

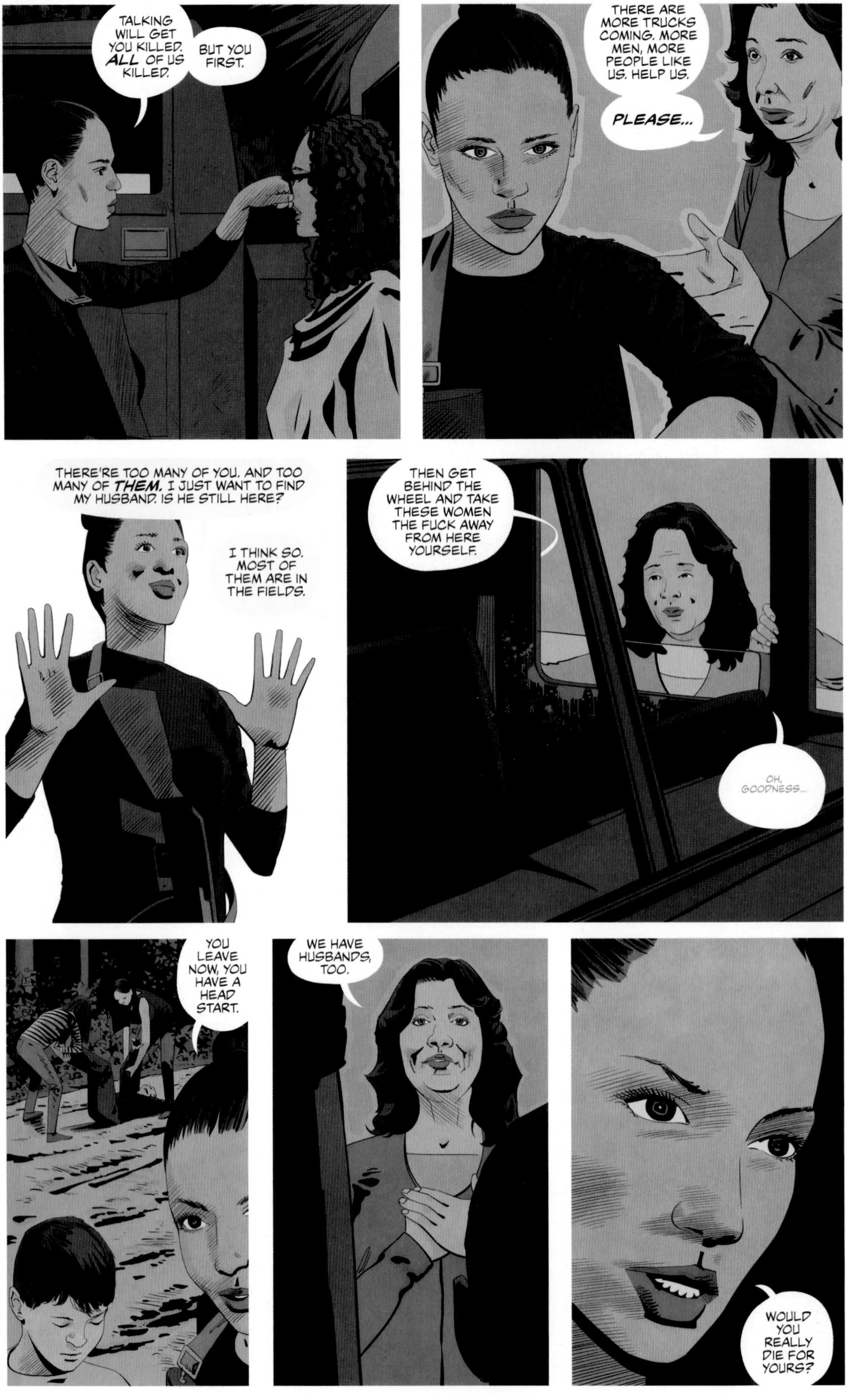
TALKING WILL GET YOU KILLED. ALL OF US KILLED.
BUT YOU FIRST.
THERE ARE MORE TRUCKS COMING. MORE MEN, MORE PEOPLE LIKE US. HELP US.
PLEASE...
THERE'RE TOO MANY OF YOU. AND TOO MANY OF THEM. I JUST WANT TO FIND MY HUSBAND. IS HE STILL HERE?
I THINK SO. MOST OF THEM ARE IN THE FIELDS.
THEN GET BEHIND THE WHEEL AND TAKE THESE WOMEN THE FUCK AWAY FROM HERE YOURSELF.
OH, GOODNESS...
YOU LEAVE NOW, YOU HAVE A HEAD START.
WE HAVE HUSBANDS, TOO.
WOULD YOU REALLY DIE FOR YOURS?

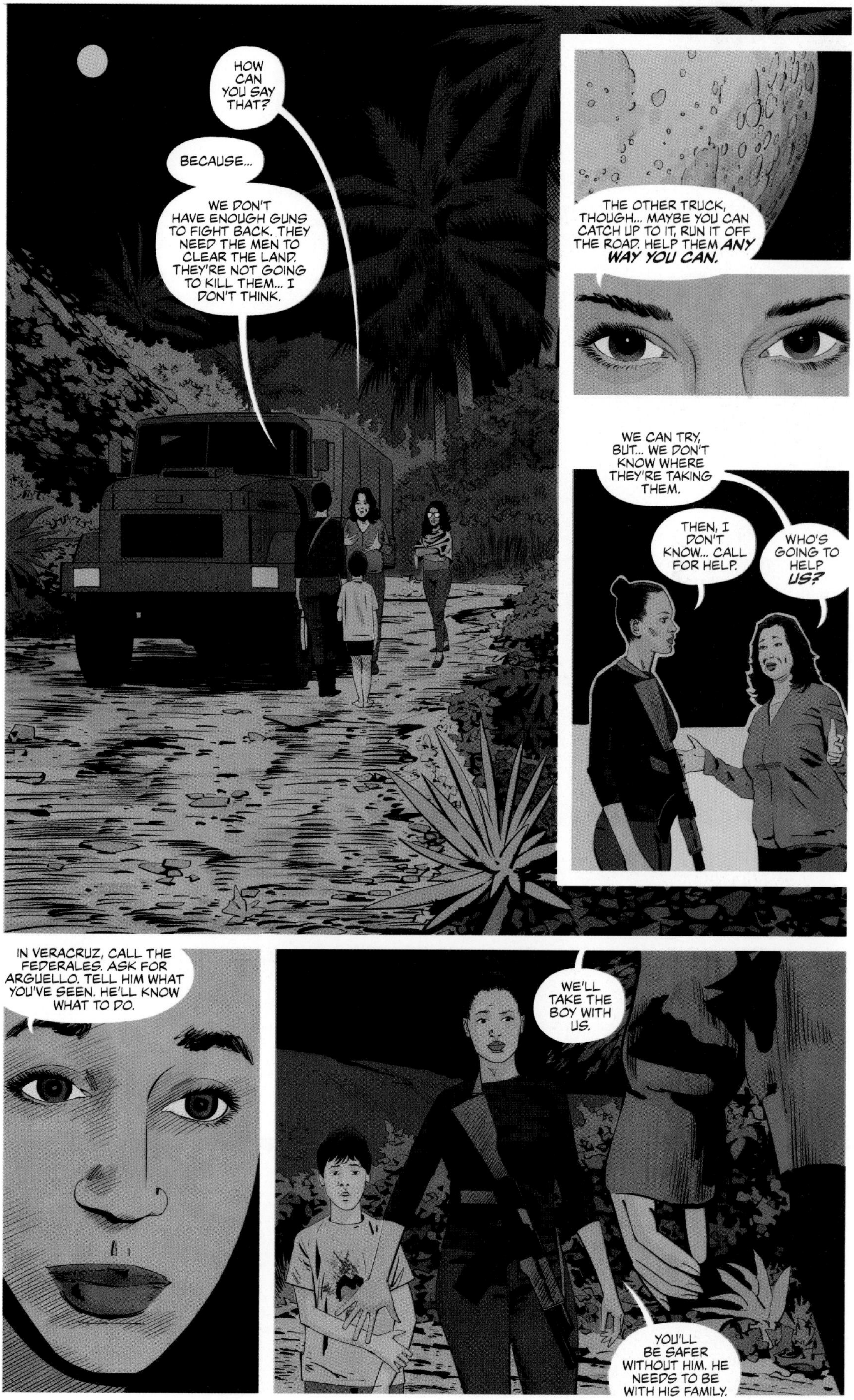
HOW CAN YOU SAY THAT?
BECAUSE...
WE DON'T HAVE ENOUGH GUNS TO FIGHT BACK. THEY NEED THE MEN TO CLEAR THE LAND. THEY'RE NOT GOING TO KILL THEM... I DON'T THINK.
THE OTHER TRUCK, THOUGH... MAYBE YOU CAN CATCH UP TO IT, RUN IT OFF THE ROAD. HELP THEM ANY WAY YOU CAN.
WE CAN TRY, BUT... WE DON'T KNOW WHERE THEY'RE TAKING THEM.
THEN, I DON'T KNOW... CALL FOR HELP.
WHO'S GOING TO HELP US?
IN VERACRUZ, CALL THE FEDERALES. ASK FOR ARGUELLO. TELL HIM WHAT YOU'VE SEEN. HE'LL KNOW WHAT TO DO.
WE'LL TAKE THE BOY WITH US.
YOU'LL BE SAFER WITHOUT HIM. HE NEEDS TO BE WITH HIS FAMILY.

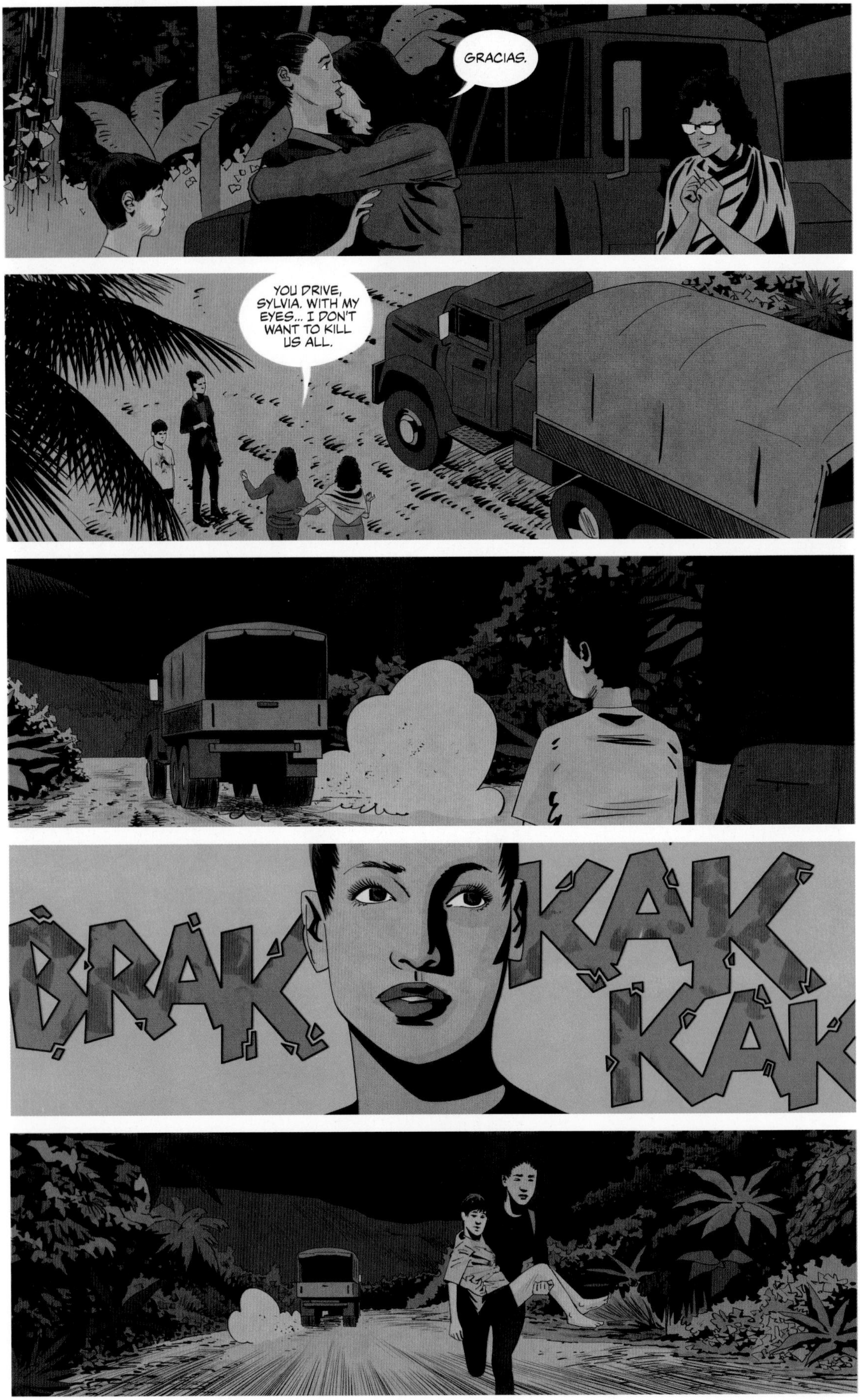
GRACIAS.
YOU DRIVE, SYLVIA. WITH MY EYES... I DON'T WANT TO KILL US ALL.
BRAK
KAK
KAK

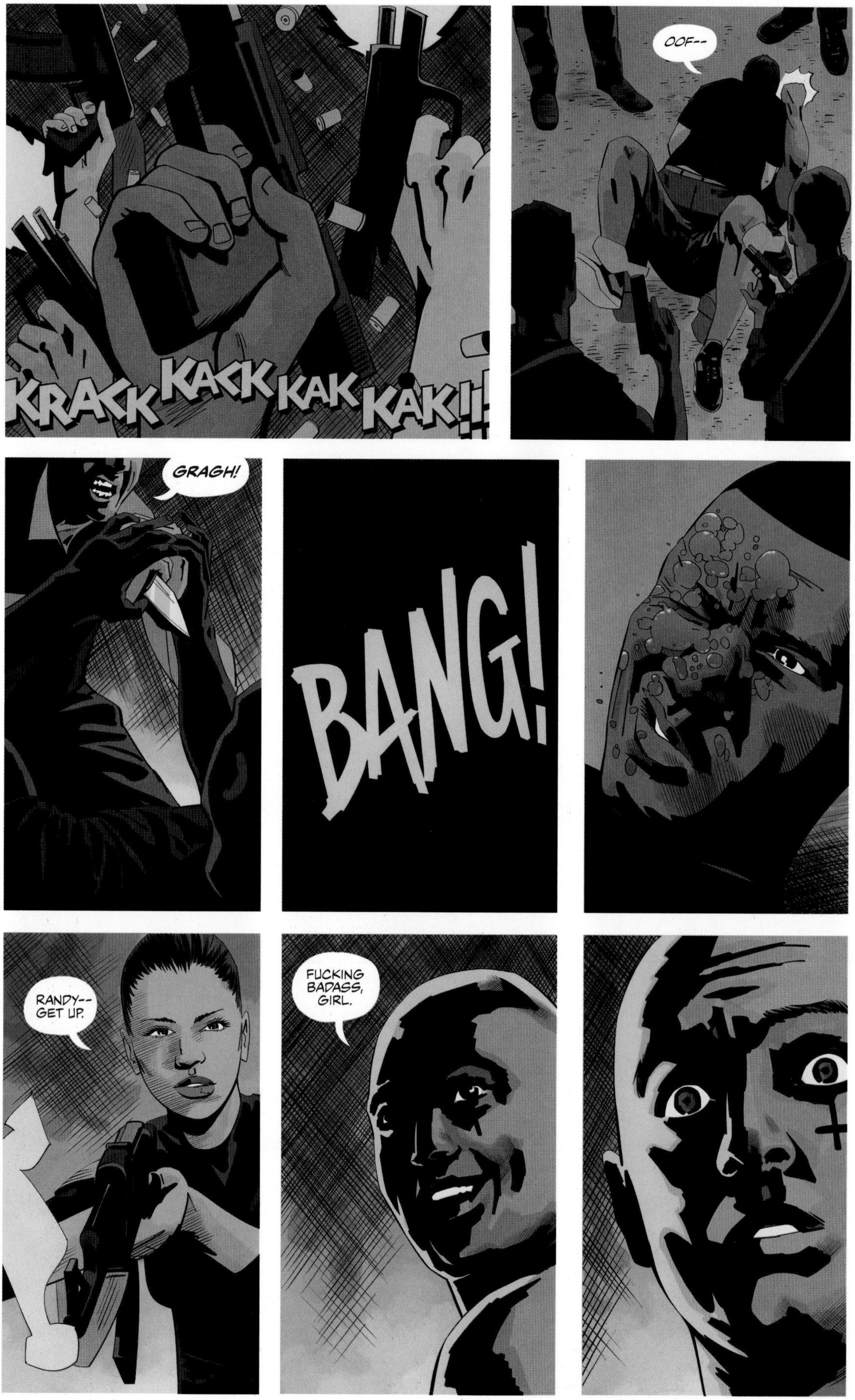
KRACK KACK KAK KAK!!
OOF--
GRAGH!
BANG!
RANDY-- GET UP.
FUCKING BADASS, GIRL.

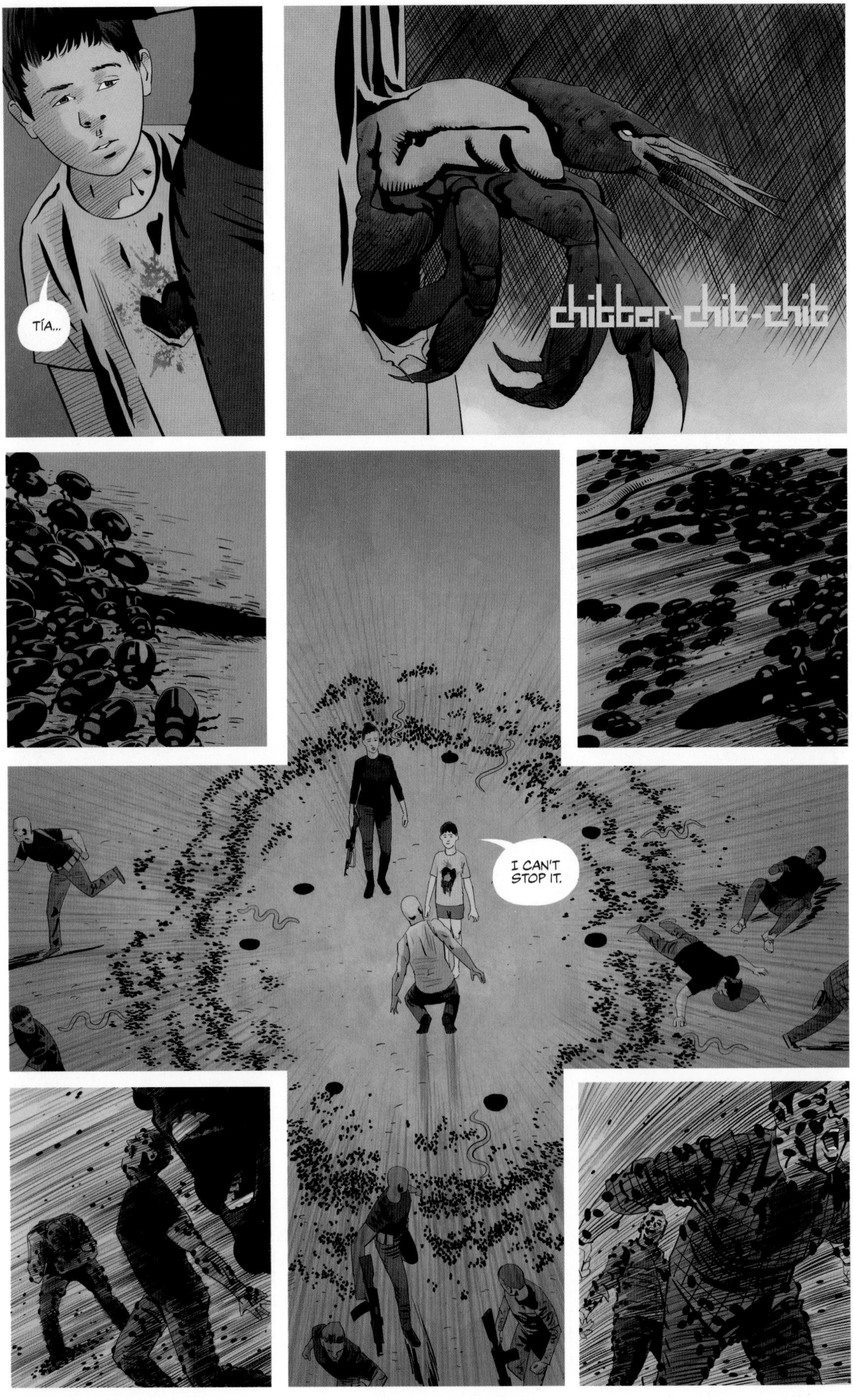
TÍA...
chitter-chit-chit
I CAN'T STOP IT.

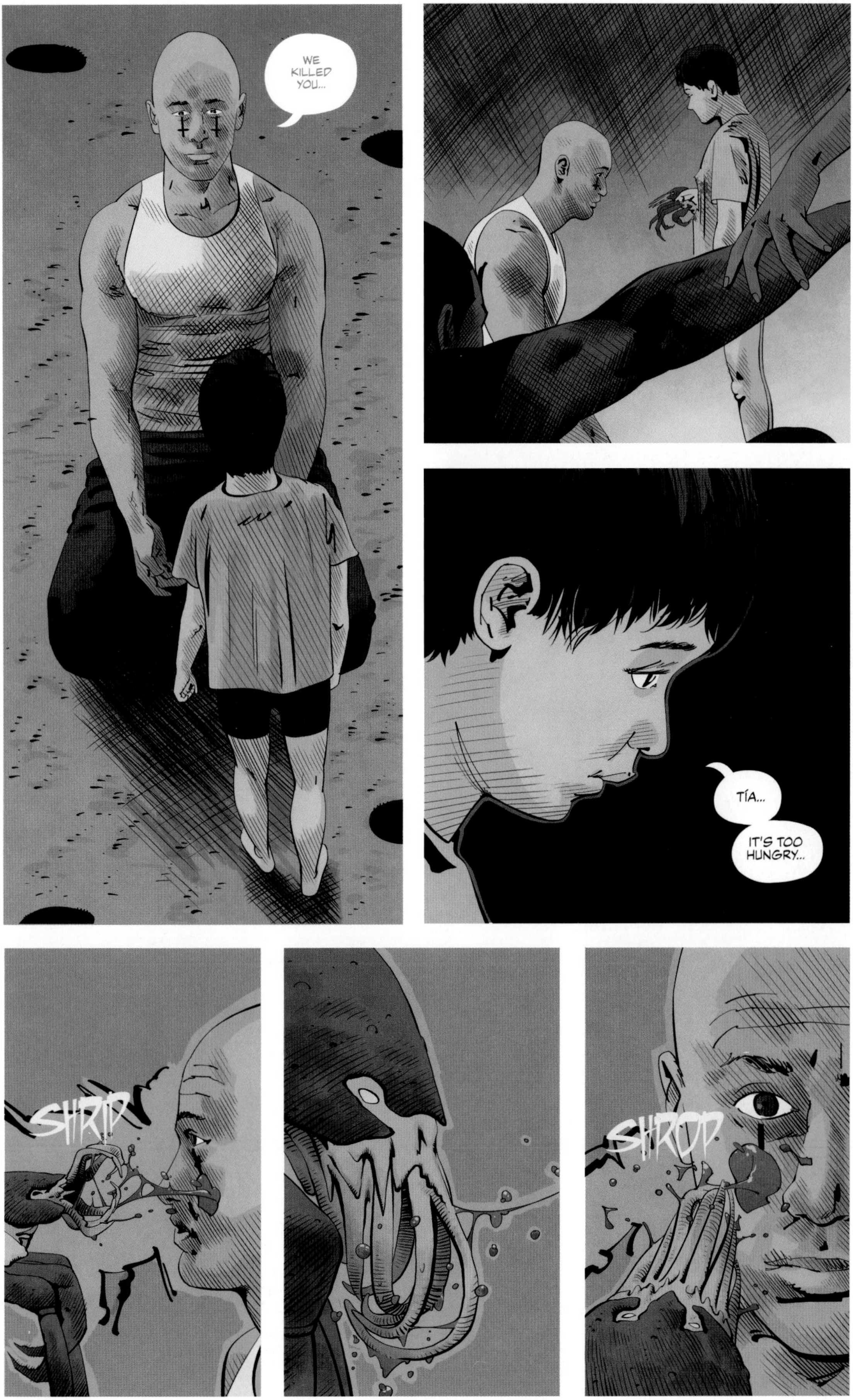
WE KILLED YOU...
TÍA...
IT'S TOO HUNGRY...
SHRIP
SHROP

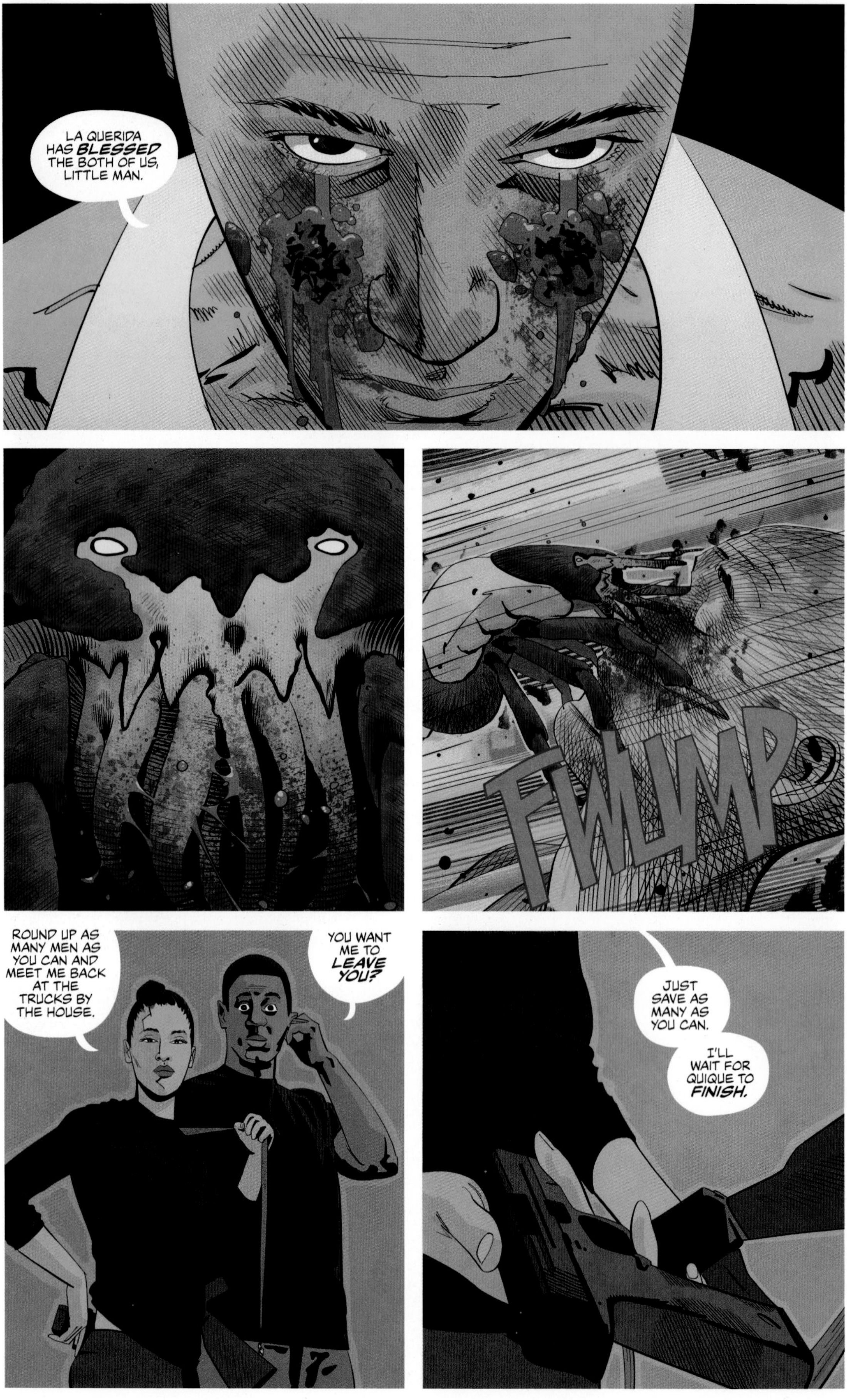
LA QUERIDA HAS BLESSED THE BOTH OF US, LITTLE MAN.
FWUMP
ROUND UP AS MANY MEN AS YOU CAN AND MEET ME BACK AT THE TRUCKS BY THE HOUSE.
YOU WANT ME TO LEAVE YOU?
JUST SAVE AS MANY AS YOU CAN.
I'LL WAIT FOR QUIQUE TO FINISH.

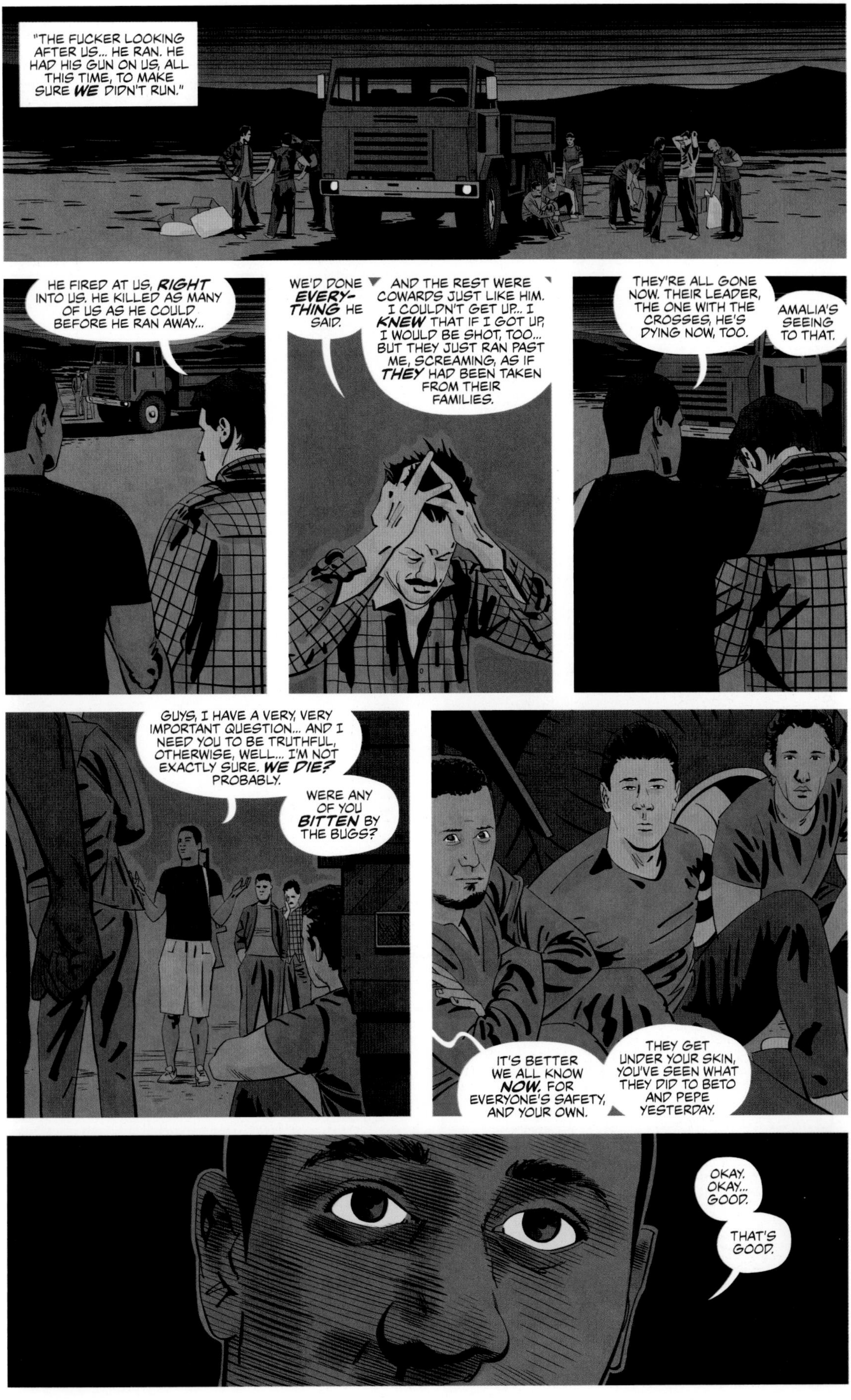
"THE FUCKER LOOKING AFTER US... HE RAN. HE HAD HIS GUN ON US, ALL THIS TIME, TO MAKE SURE WE DIDN'T RUN."
HE FIRED AT US, RIGHT INTO US. HE KILLED AS MANY OF US AS HE COULD BEFORE HE RAN AWAY...
WE'D DONE EVERYTHING HE SAID.
AND THE REST WERE COWARDS JUST LIKE HIM. I COULDN'T GET UP... I KNEW THAT IF I GOT UP, I WOULD BE SHOT, TOO... BUT THEY JUST RAN PAST ME, SCREAMING, AS IF THEY HAD BEEN TAKEN FROM THEIR FAMILIES.
THEY'RE ALL GONE NOW. THEIR LEADER, THE ONE WITH THE CROSSES, HE'S DYING NOW, TOO.
AMALIA'S SEEING TO THAT.
GUYS, I HAVE A VERY, VERY IMPORTANT QUESTION... AND I NEED YOU TO BE TRUTHFUL, OTHERWISE, WELL... I'M NOT EXACTLY SURE. WE DIE? PROBABLY.
WERE ANY OF YOU BITTEN BY THE BUGS?
IT'S BETTER WE ALL KNOW NOW, FOR EVERYONE'S SAFETY, AND YOUR OWN.
THEY GET UNDER YOUR SKIN, YOU'VE SEEN WHAT THEY DID TO BETO AND PEPE YESTERDAY.
OKAY. OKAY... GOOD.
THAT'S GOOD.

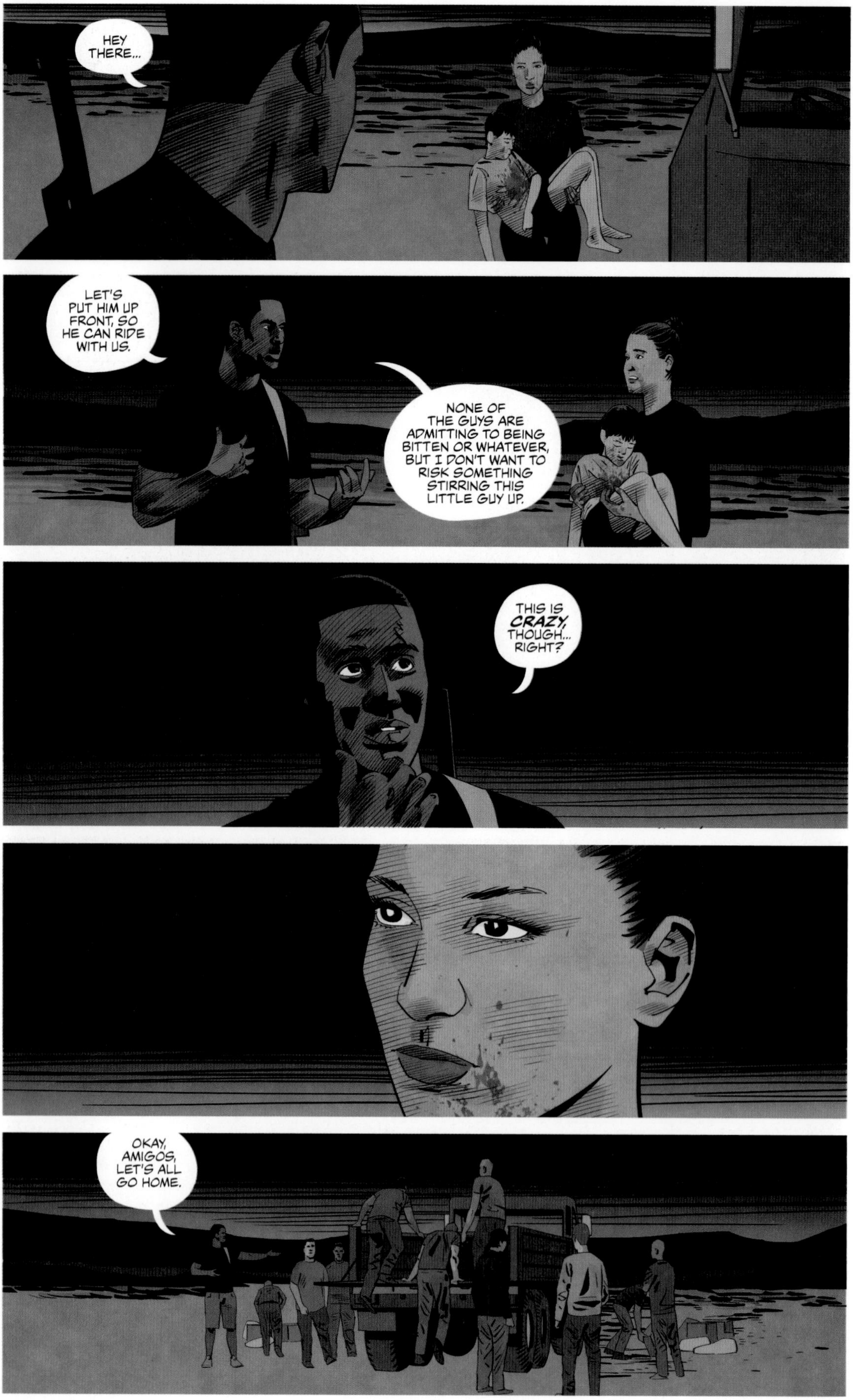
HEY THERE...
LET'S PUT HIM UP FRONT, SO HE CAN RIDE WITH US.
NONE OF THE GUYS ARE ADMITTING TO BEING BITTEN OR WHATEVER, BUT I DON'T WANT TO RISK SOMETHING STIRRING THIS LITTLE GUY UP.
THIS IS CRAZY, THOUGH... RIGHT?
OKAY, AMIGOS, LET'S ALL GO HOME.

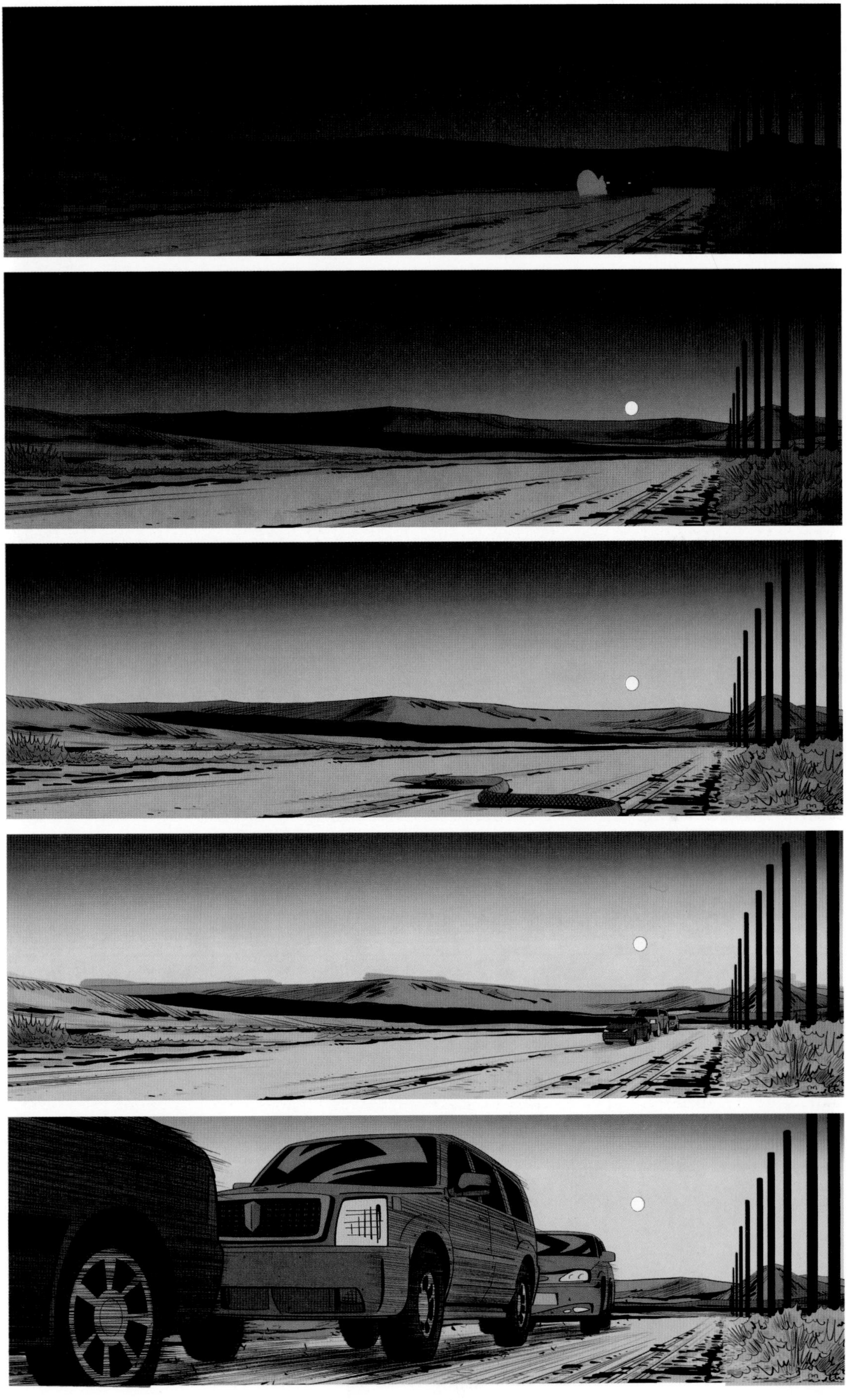

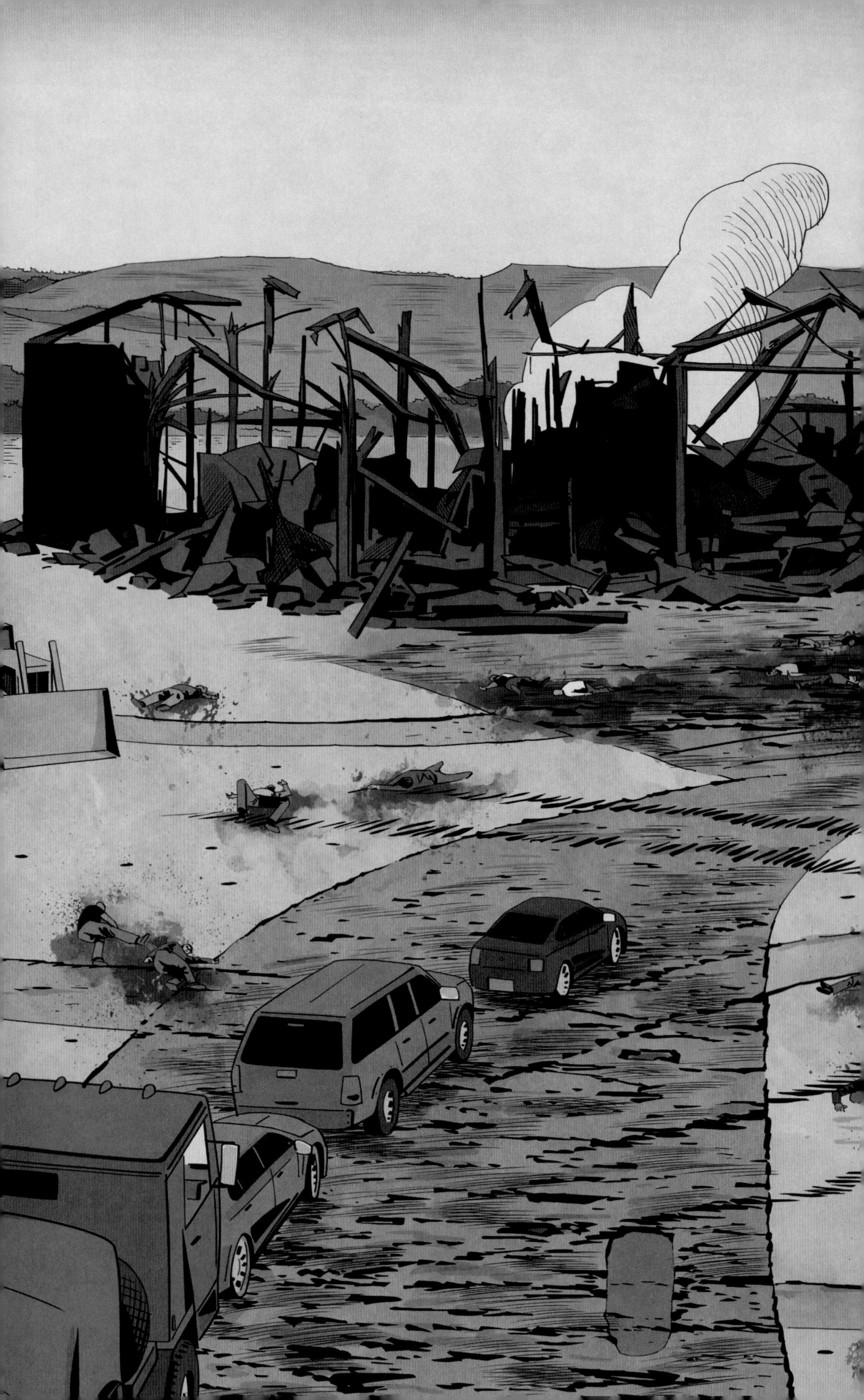

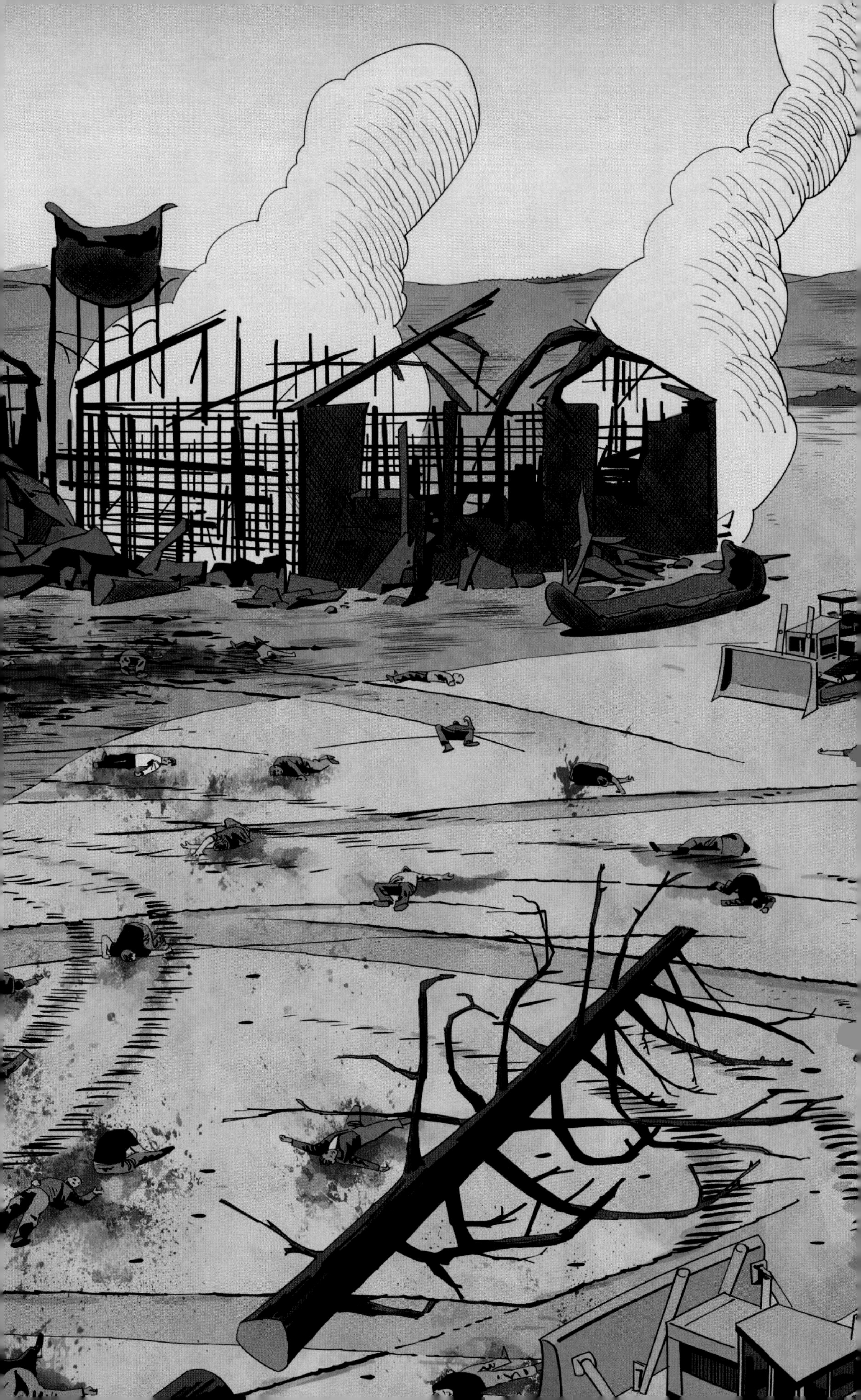

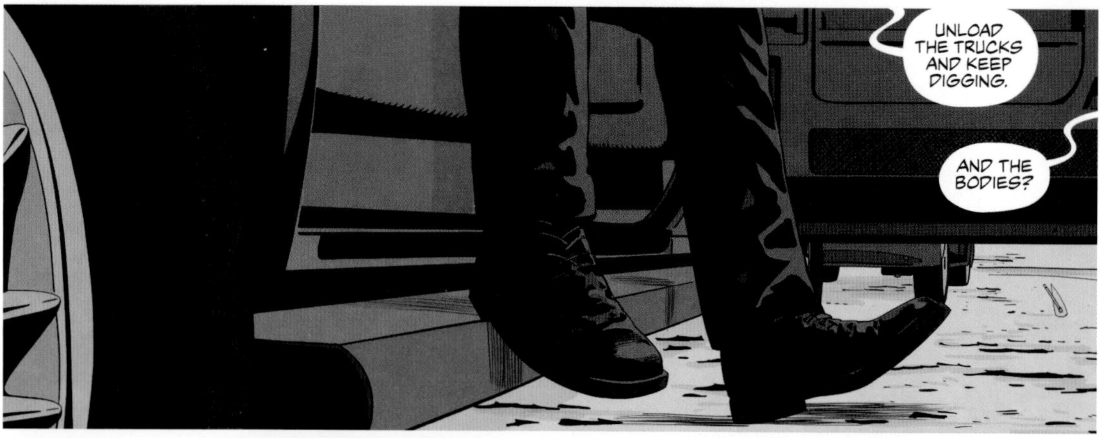
UNLOAD THE TRUCKS AND KEEP DIGGING.
AND THE BODIES?

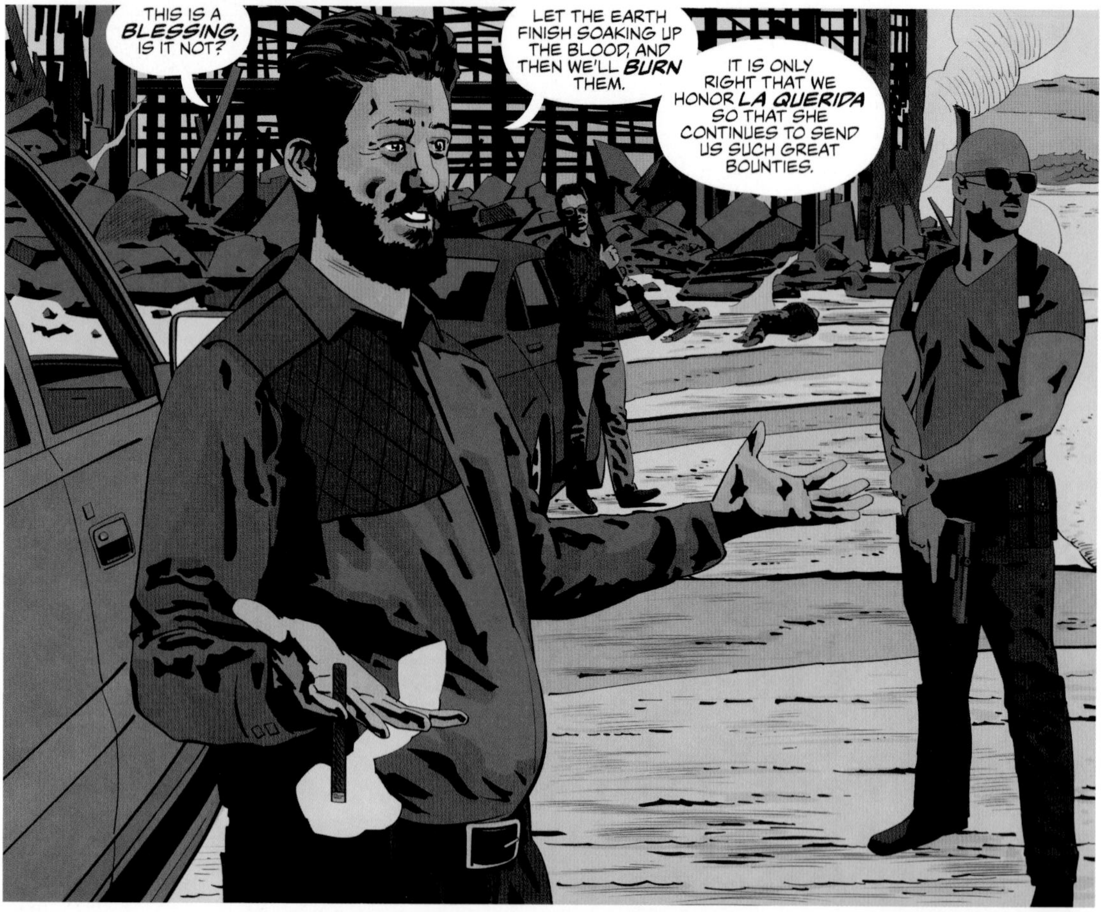
THIS IS A *BLESSING,* IS IT NOT?
LET THE EARTH FINISH SOAKING UP THE BLOOD, AND THEN WE'LL *BURN* THEM.
IT IS ONLY RIGHT THAT WE HONOR *LA QUERIDA* SO THAT SHE CONTINUES TO SEND US SUCH GREAT BOUNTIES.

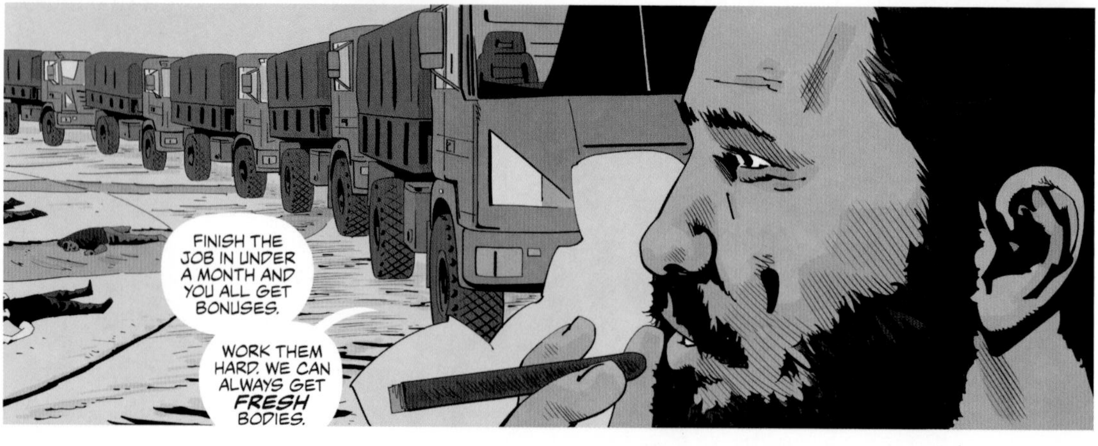
FINISH THE JOB IN UNDER A MONTH AND YOU ALL GET BONUSES.
WORK THEM HARD. WE CAN ALWAYS GET *FRESH* BODIES.

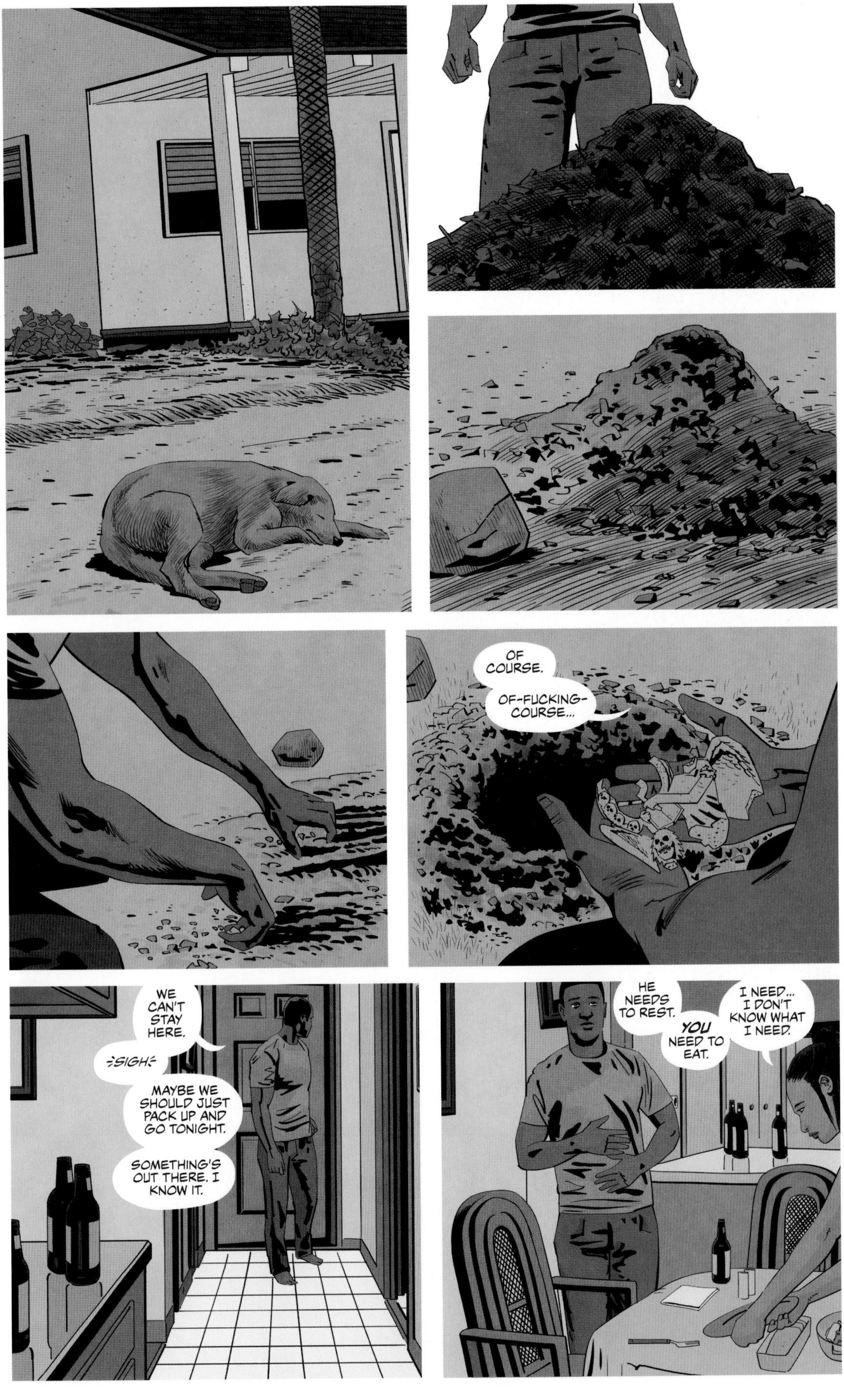
OF COURSE.
OF-FUCKING-COURSE...
WE CAN'T STAY HERE.
SIGH
MAYBE WE SHOULD JUST PACK UP AND GO TONIGHT.
SOMETHING'S OUT THERE. I KNOW IT.
HE NEEDS TO REST.
YOU NEED TO EAT.
I NEED... I DON'T KNOW WHAT I NEED.

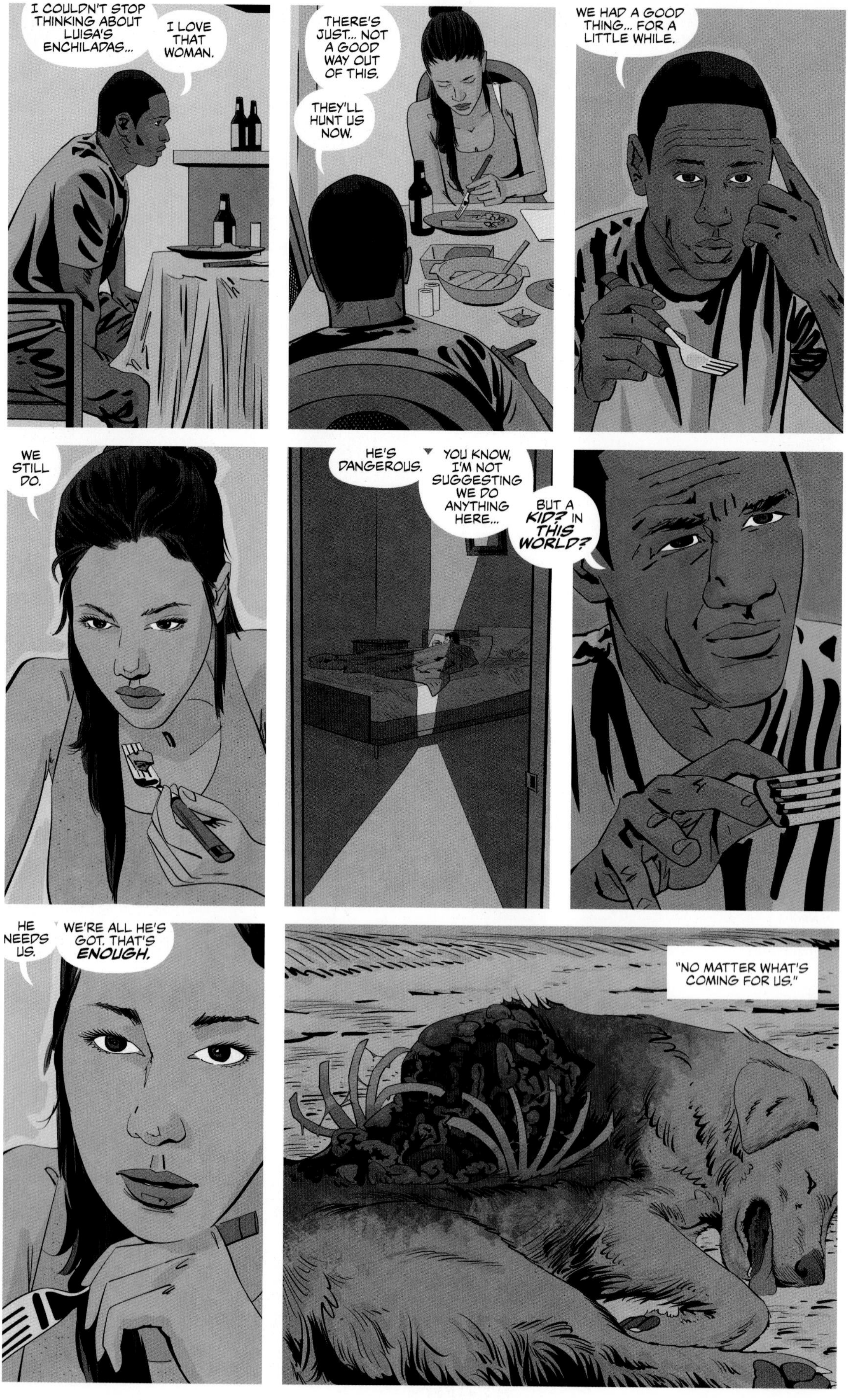
I COULDN'T STOP THINKING ABOUT LUISA'S ENCHILADAS...
I LOVE THAT WOMAN.
THERE'S JUST... NOT A GOOD WAY OUT OF THIS.
THEY'LL HUNT US NOW.
WE HAD A GOOD THING... FOR A LITTLE WHILE.
WE STILL DO.
HE'S DANGEROUS.
YOU KNOW, I'M NOT SUGGESTING WE DO ANYTHING HERE...
BUT A *KID?* IN *THIS WORLD?*
HE NEEDS US.
WE'RE ALL HE'S GOT. THAT'S *ENOUGH.*
"NO MATTER WHAT'S COMING FOR US."

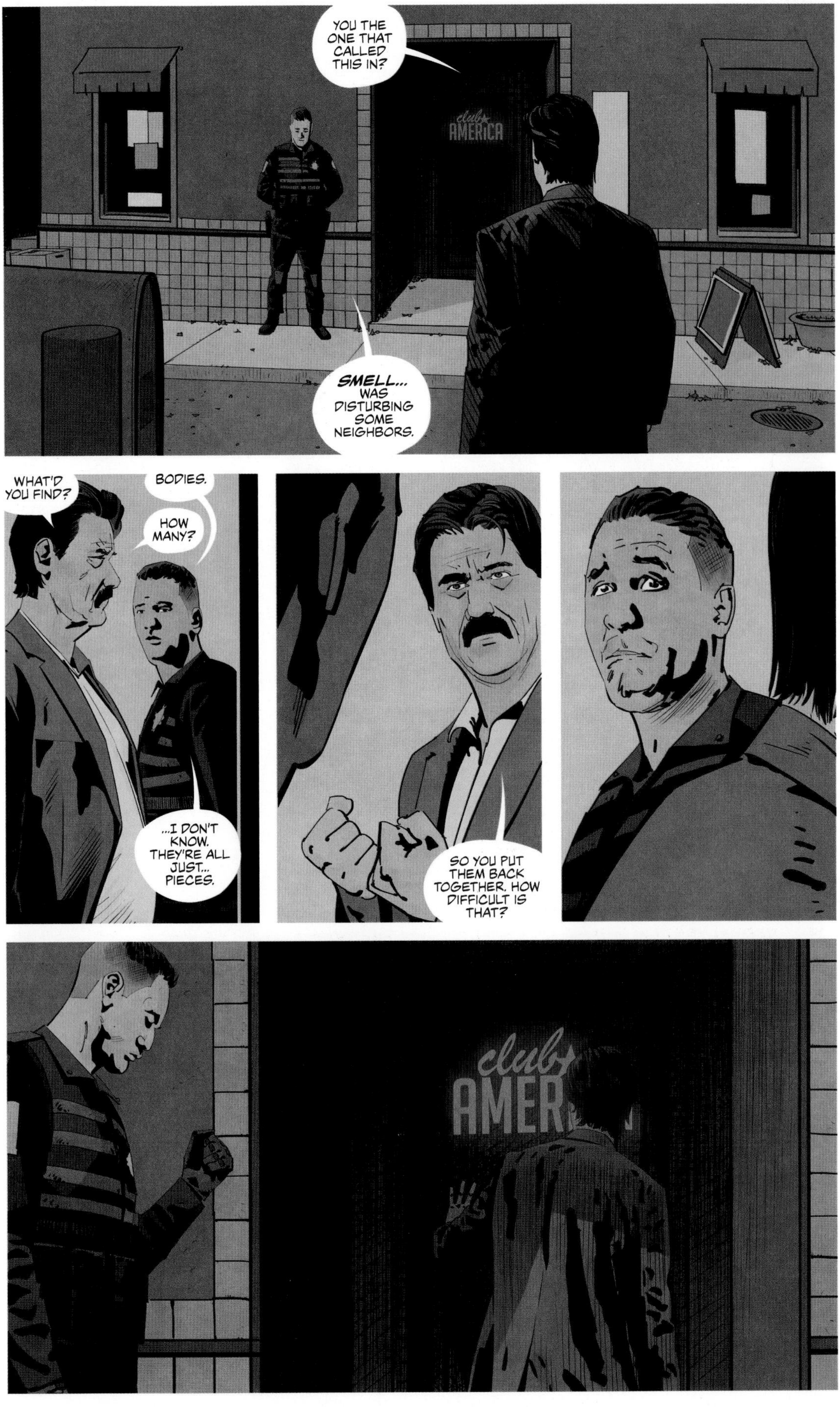
YOU THE ONE THAT CALLED THIS IN?
SMELL... WAS DISTURBING SOME NEIGHBORS.
WHAT'D YOU FIND?
BODIES.
HOW MANY?
...I DON'T KNOW. THEY'RE ALL JUST... PIECES.
SO YOU PUT THEM BACK TOGETHER. HOW DIFFICULT IS THAT?
club AMERICA

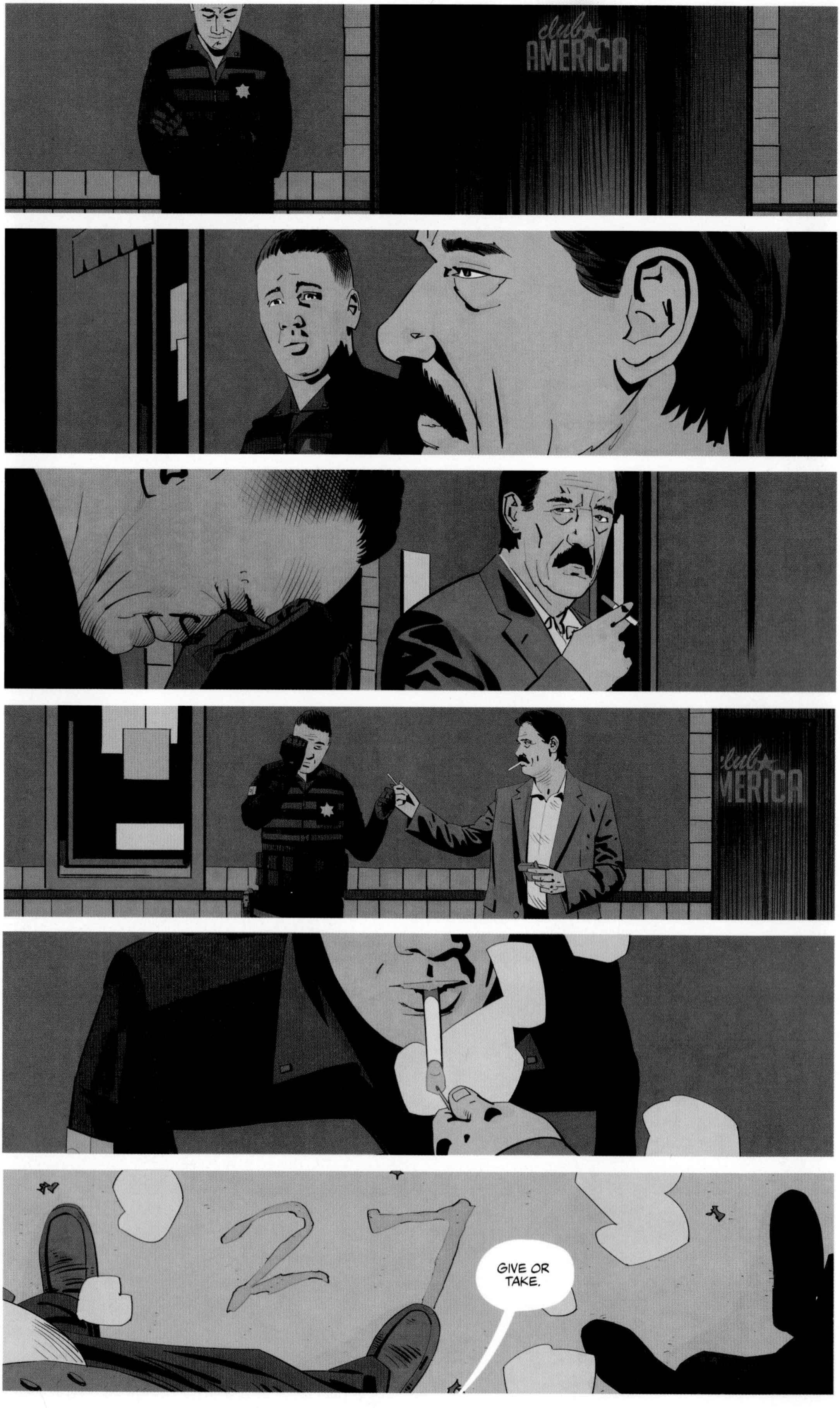
club AMERICA
club AMERICA
GIVE OR TAKE.

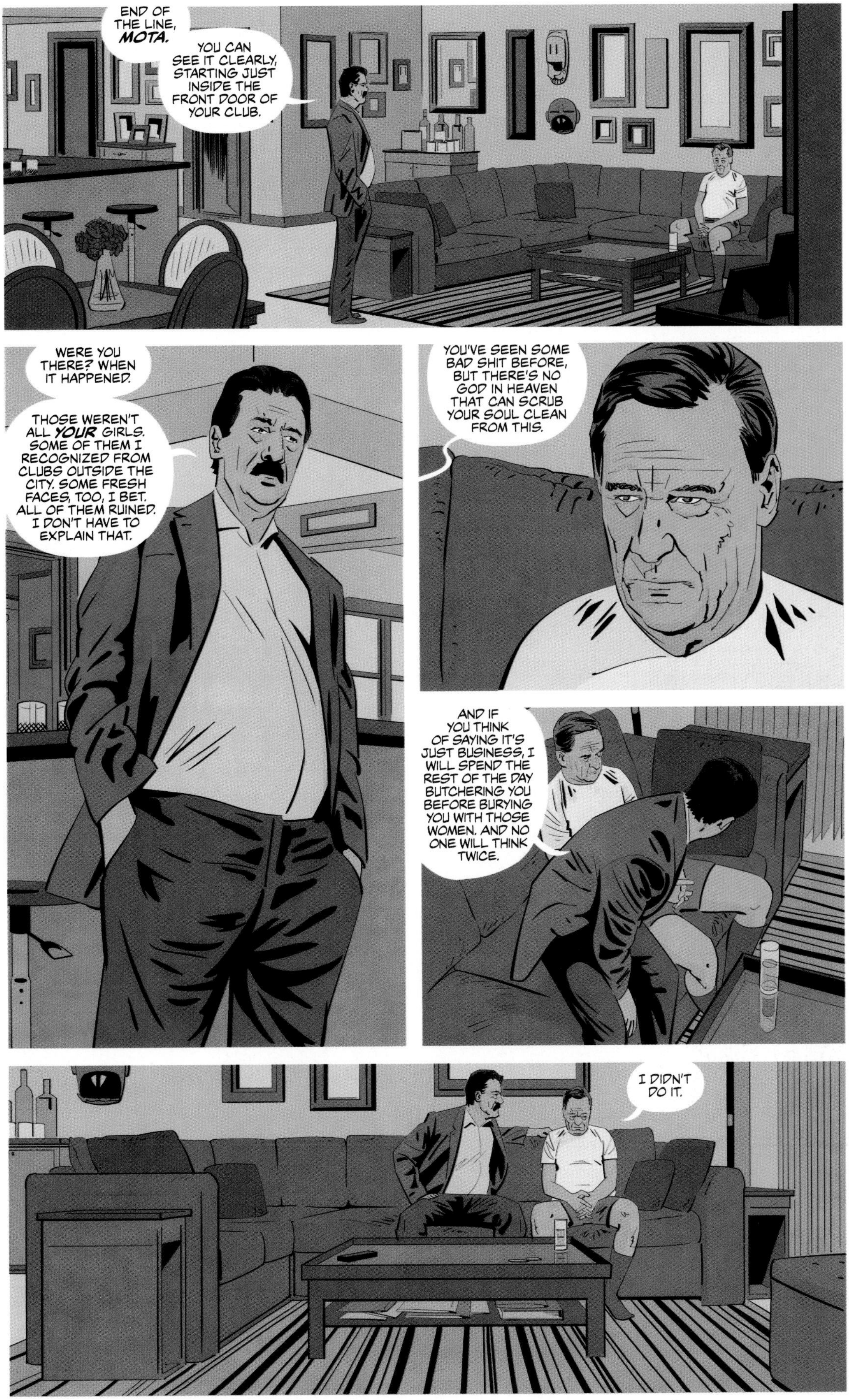
END OF THE LINE, MOTA.
YOU CAN SEE IT CLEARLY, STARTING JUST INSIDE THE FRONT DOOR OF YOUR CLUB.
WERE YOU THERE? WHEN IT HAPPENED.
THOSE WEREN'T ALL YOUR GIRLS. SOME OF THEM I RECOGNIZED FROM CLUBS OUTSIDE THE CITY. SOME FRESH FACES, TOO, I BET. ALL OF THEM RUINED. I DON'T HAVE TO EXPLAIN THAT.
YOU'VE SEEN SOME BAD SHIT BEFORE, BUT THERE'S NO GOD IN HEAVEN THAT CAN SCRUB YOUR SOUL CLEAN FROM THIS.
AND IF YOU THINK OF SAYING IT'S JUST BUSINESS, I WILL SPEND THE REST OF THE DAY BUTCHERING YOU BEFORE BURYING YOU WITH THOSE WOMEN. AND NO ONE WILL THINK TWICE.
I DIDN'T DO IT.

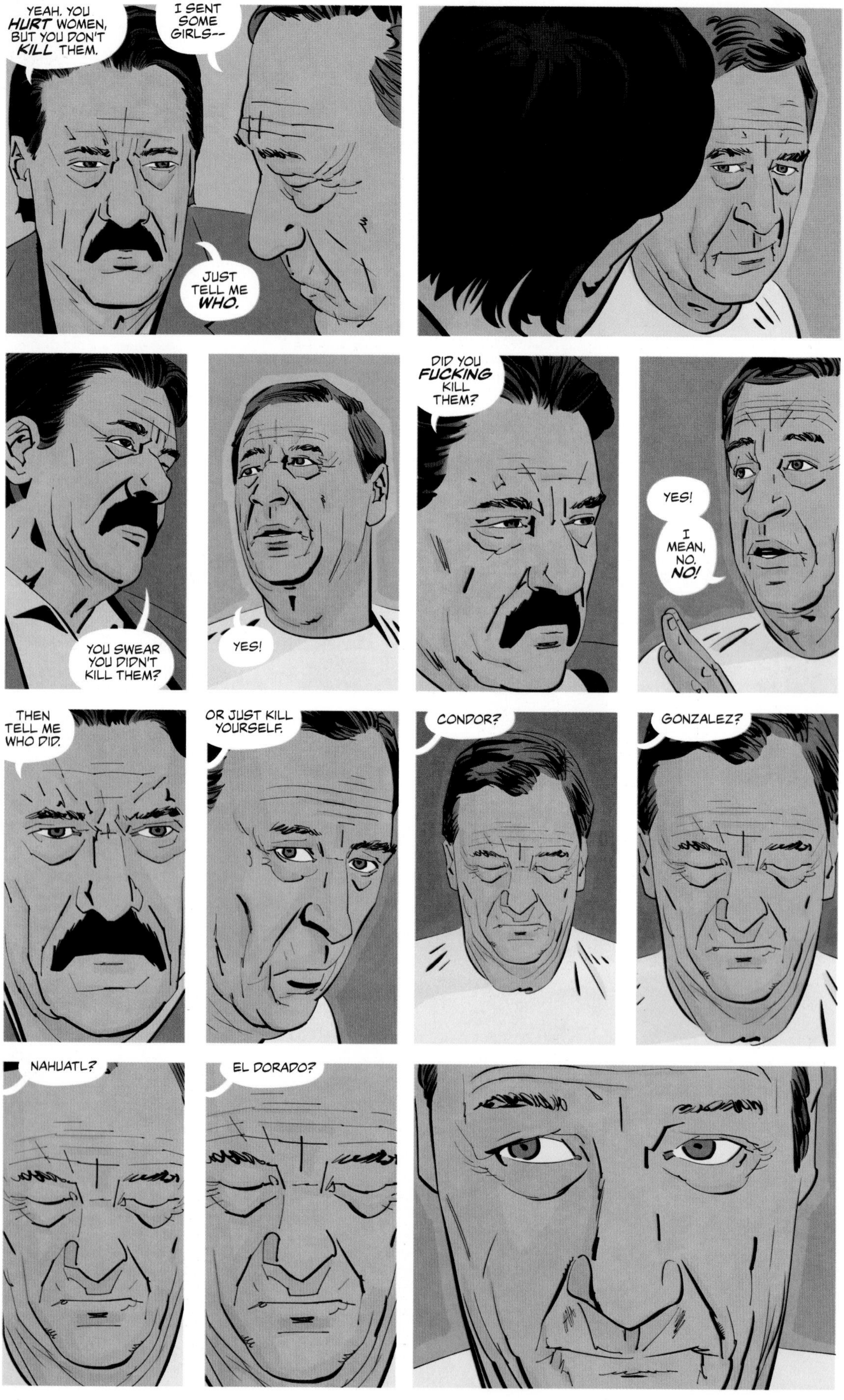
YEAH. YOU HURT WOMEN, BUT YOU DON'T KILL THEM.
I SENT SOME GIRLS--
JUST TELL ME WHO.
YOU SWEAR YOU DIDN'T KILL THEM?
YES!
DID YOU FUCKING KILL THEM?
YES!
I MEAN, NO. NO!
THEN TELL ME WHO DID.
OR JUST KILL YOURSELF.
CONDOR?
GONZALEZ?
NAHUATL?
EL DORADO?

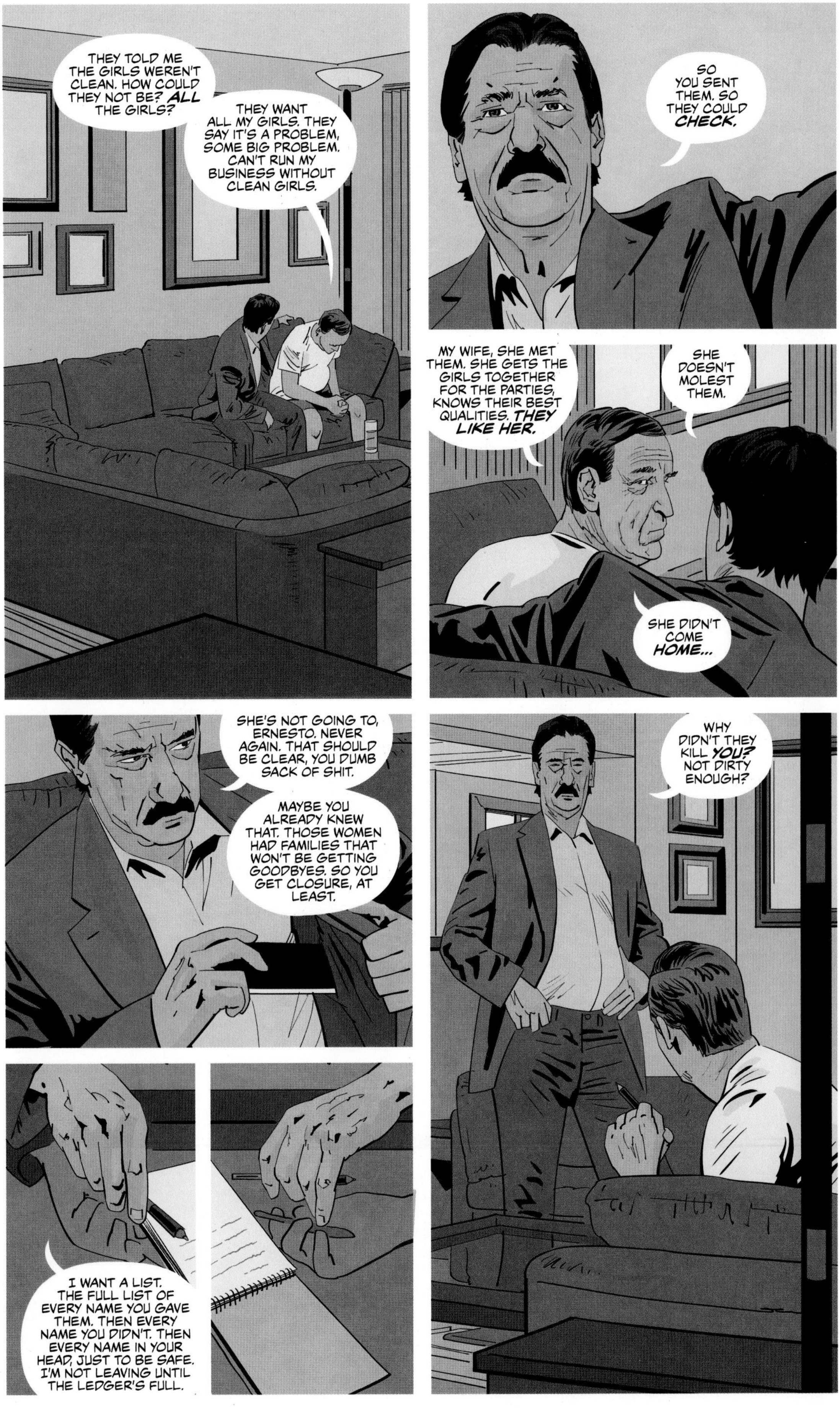
THEY TOLD ME THE GIRLS WEREN'T CLEAN. HOW COULD THEY NOT BE? ALL THE GIRLS?
THEY WANT ALL MY GIRLS. THEY SAY IT'S A PROBLEM, SOME BIG PROBLEM. CAN'T RUN MY BUSINESS WITHOUT CLEAN GIRLS.
SO YOU SENT THEM. SO THEY COULD CHECK.
MY WIFE, SHE MET THEM. SHE GETS THE GIRLS TOGETHER FOR THE PARTIES, KNOWS THEIR BEST QUALITIES. THEY LIKE HER.
SHE DOESN'T MOLEST THEM.
SHE DIDN'T COME HOME...
SHE'S NOT GOING TO, ERNESTO. NEVER AGAIN. THAT SHOULD BE CLEAR, YOU DUMB SACK OF SHIT.
MAYBE YOU ALREADY KNEW THAT. THOSE WOMEN HAD FAMILIES THAT WON'T BE GETTING GOODBYES. SO YOU GET CLOSURE, AT LEAST.
WHY DIDN'T THEY KILL YOU? NOT DIRTY ENOUGH?
I WANT A LIST. THE FULL LIST OF EVERY NAME YOU GAVE THEM. THEN EVERY NAME YOU DIDN'T. THEN EVERY NAME IN YOUR HEAD, JUST TO BE SAFE. I'M NOT LEAVING UNTIL THE LEDGER'S FULL.

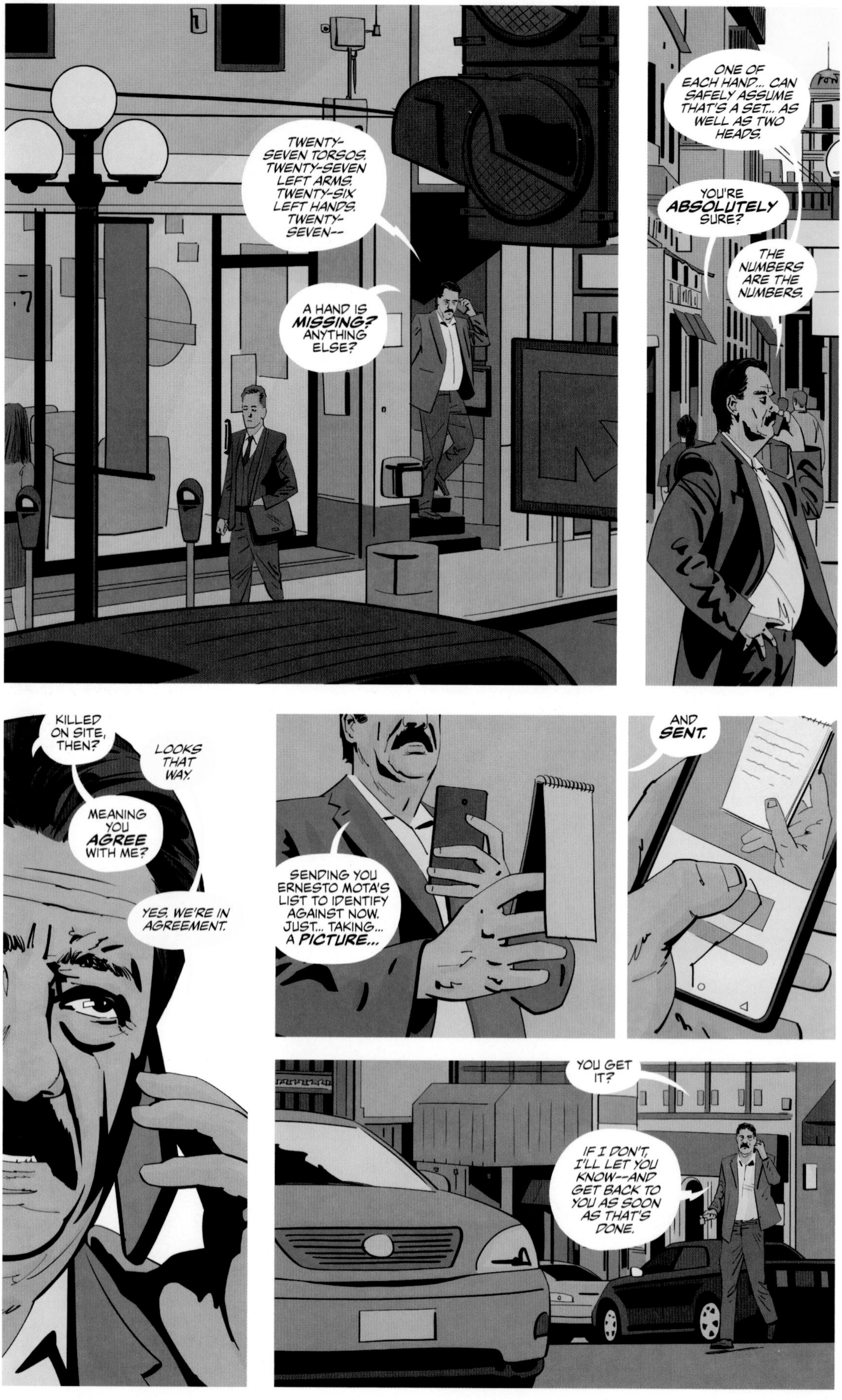
TWENTY-SEVEN TORSOS. TWENTY-SEVEN LEFT ARMS. TWENTY-SIX LEFT HANDS. TWENTY-SEVEN--
A HAND IS MISSING? ANYTHING ELSE?
ONE OF EACH HAND... CAN SAFELY ASSUME THAT'S A SET... AS WELL AS TWO HEADS.
YOU'RE ABSOLUTELY SURE?
THE NUMBERS ARE THE NUMBERS.
KILLED ON SITE, THEN?
LOOKS THAT WAY.
MEANING YOU AGREE WITH ME?
YES. WE'RE IN AGREEMENT.
SENDING YOU ERNESTO MOTA'S LIST TO IDENTIFY AGAINST NOW. JUST... TAKING... A PICTURE...
AND SENT.
YOU GET IT?
IF I DON'T, I'LL LET YOU KNOW--AND GET BACK TO YOU AS SOON AS THAT'S DONE.

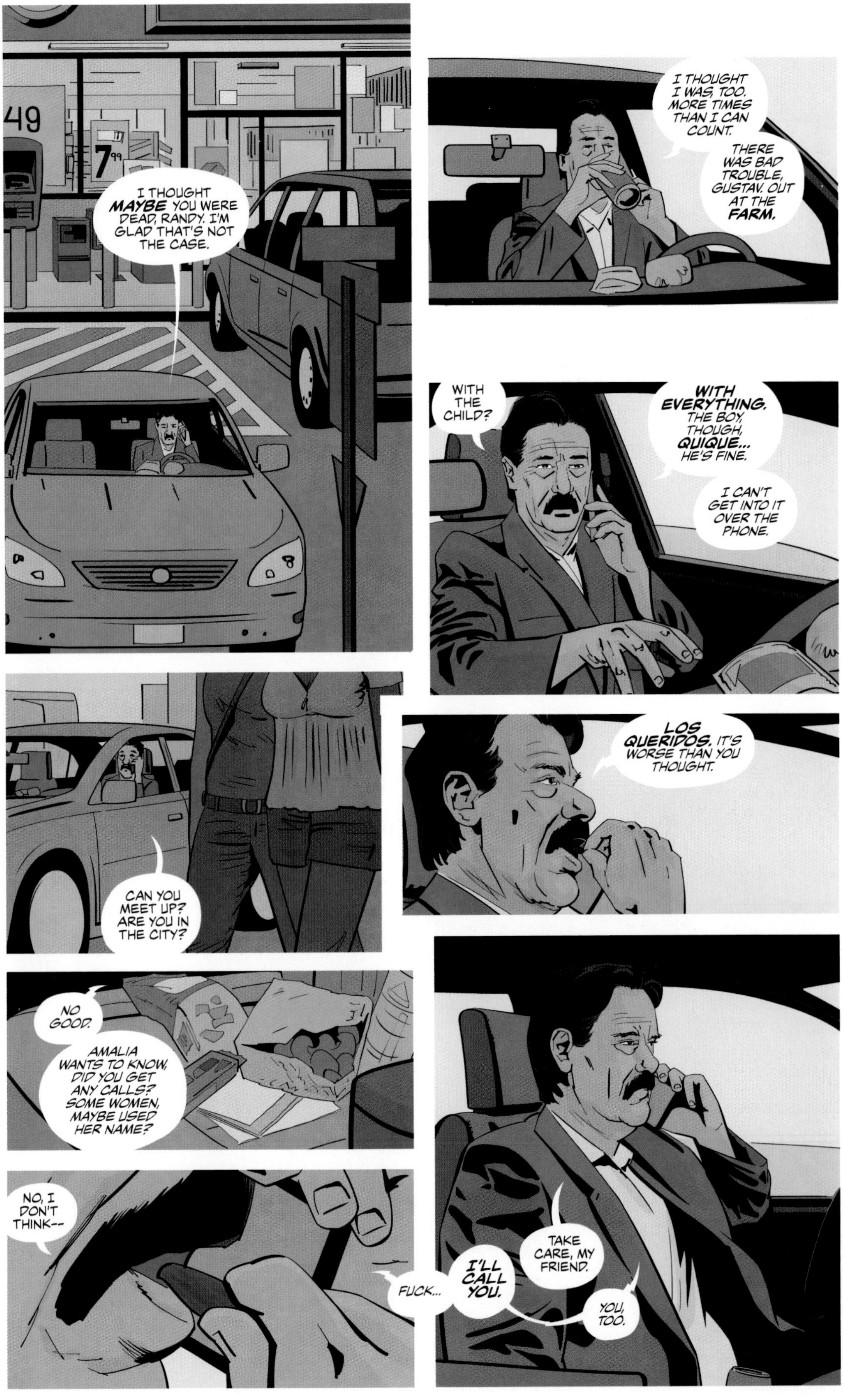

49
7.99
I THOUGHT MAYBE YOU WERE DEAD, RANDY. I'M GLAD THAT'S NOT THE CASE.
I THOUGHT I WAS, TOO. MORE TIMES THAN I CAN COUNT.
THERE WAS BAD TROUBLE, GUSTAV. OUT AT THE FARM.
WITH THE CHILD?
WITH EVERYTHING. THE BOY, THOUGH, QUIQUE... HE'S FINE.
I CAN'T GET INTO IT OVER THE PHONE.
LOS QUERIDOS. IT'S WORSE THAN YOU THOUGHT.
CAN YOU MEET UP? ARE YOU IN THE CITY?
NO GOOD.
AMALIA WANTS TO KNOW, DID YOU GET ANY CALLS? SOME WOMEN, MAYBE USED HER NAME?
NO, I DON'T THINK--
FUCK...
I'LL CALL YOU.
TAKE CARE, MY FRIEND.
YOU, TOO.

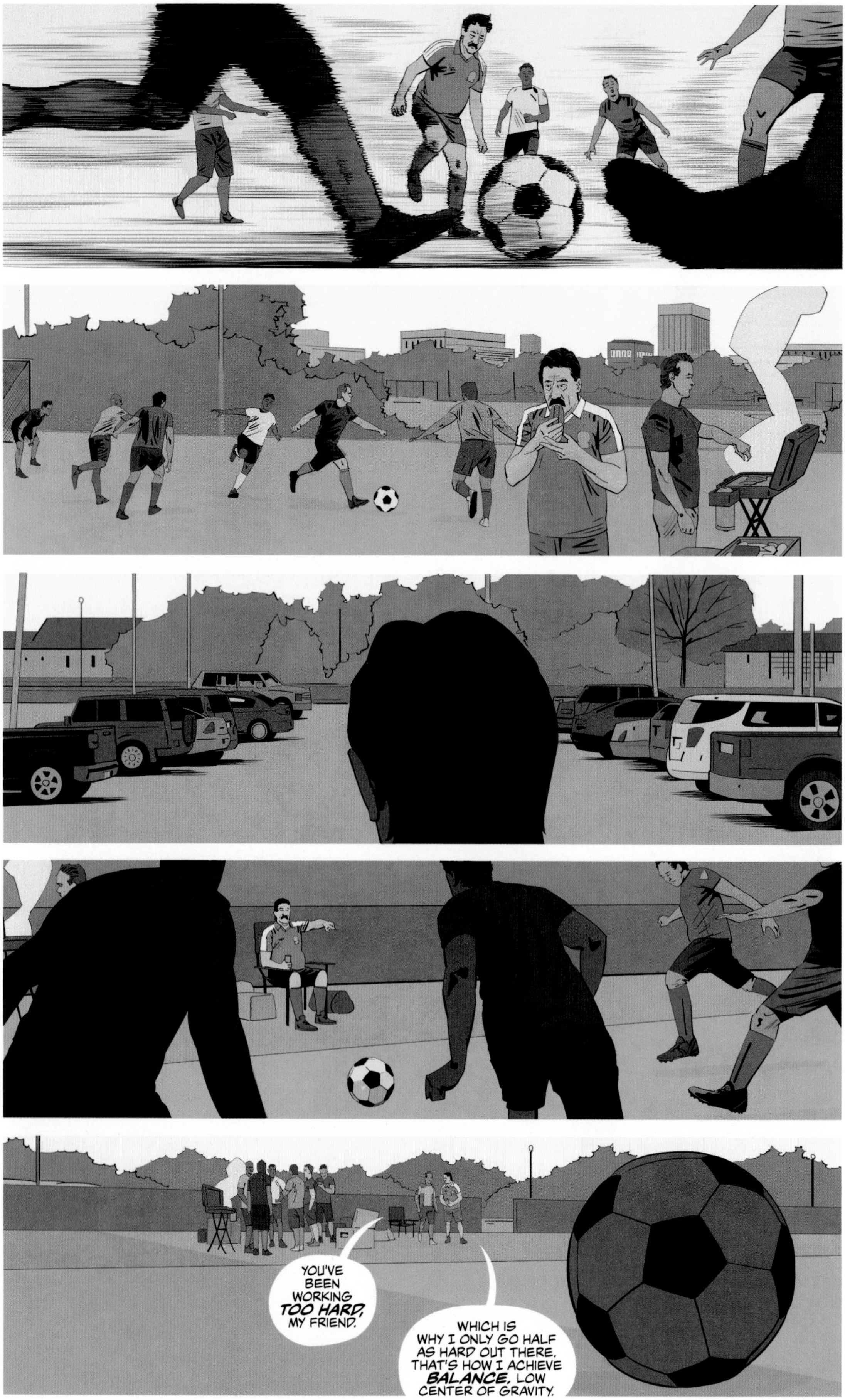
YOU'VE BEEN WORKING TOO HARD, MY FRIEND.
WHICH IS WHY I ONLY GO HALF AS HARD OUT THERE. THAT'S HOW I ACHIEVE BALANCE. LOW CENTER OF GRAVITY.

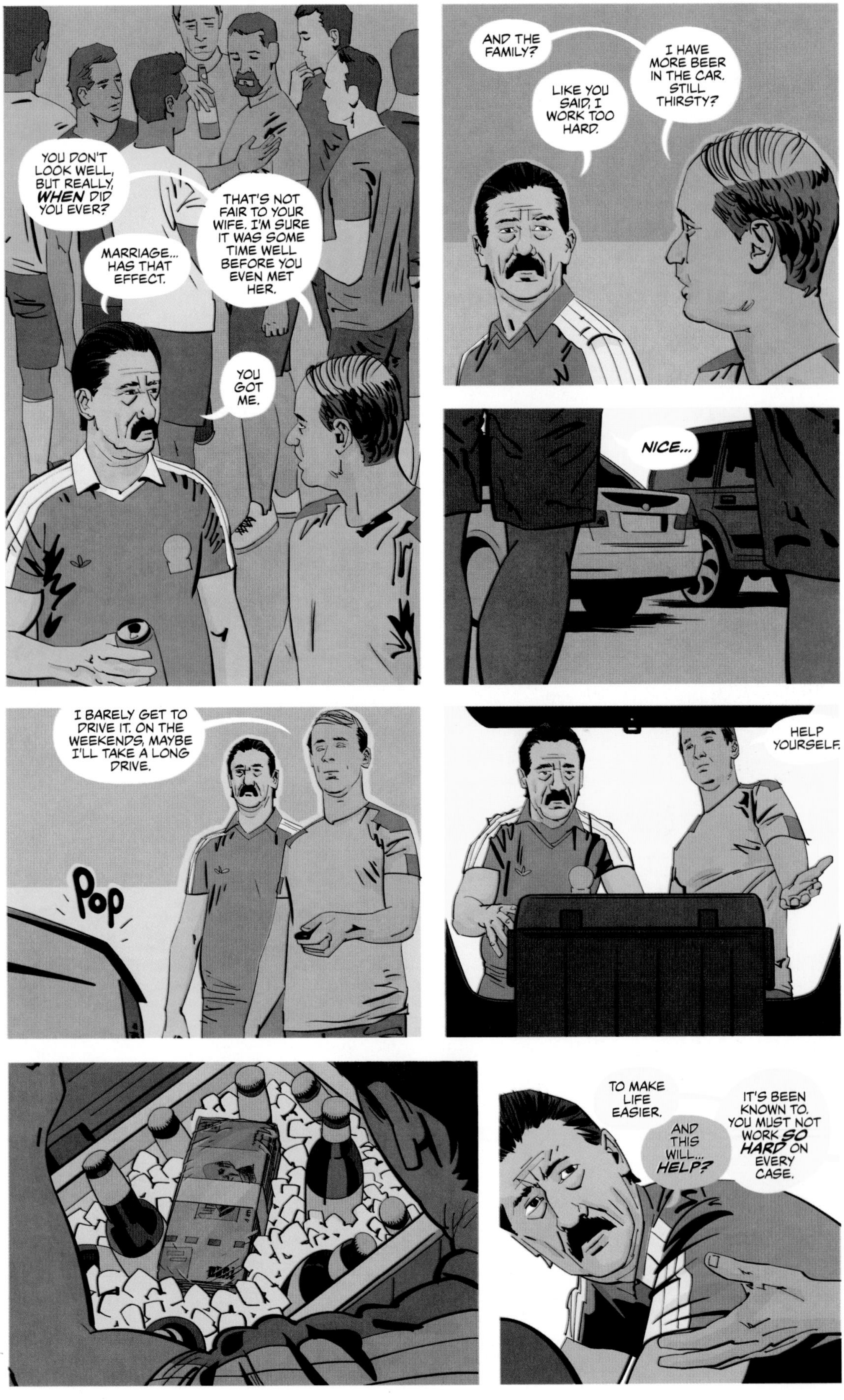
YOU DON'T LOOK WELL, BUT REALLY, WHEN DID YOU EVER?
MARRIAGE... HAS THAT EFFECT.
THAT'S NOT FAIR TO YOUR WIFE. I'M SURE IT WAS SOME TIME WELL BEFORE YOU EVEN MET HER.
YOU GOT ME.
AND THE FAMILY?
LIKE YOU SAID, I WORK TOO HARD.
I HAVE MORE BEER IN THE CAR. STILL THIRSTY?
NICE...
I BARELY GET TO DRIVE IT. ON THE WEEKENDS, MAYBE I'LL TAKE A LONG DRIVE.
POP
HELP YOURSELF.
AND THIS WILL... HELP?
TO MAKE LIFE EASIER.
IT'S BEEN KNOWN TO. YOU MUST NOT WORK SO HARD ON EVERY CASE.

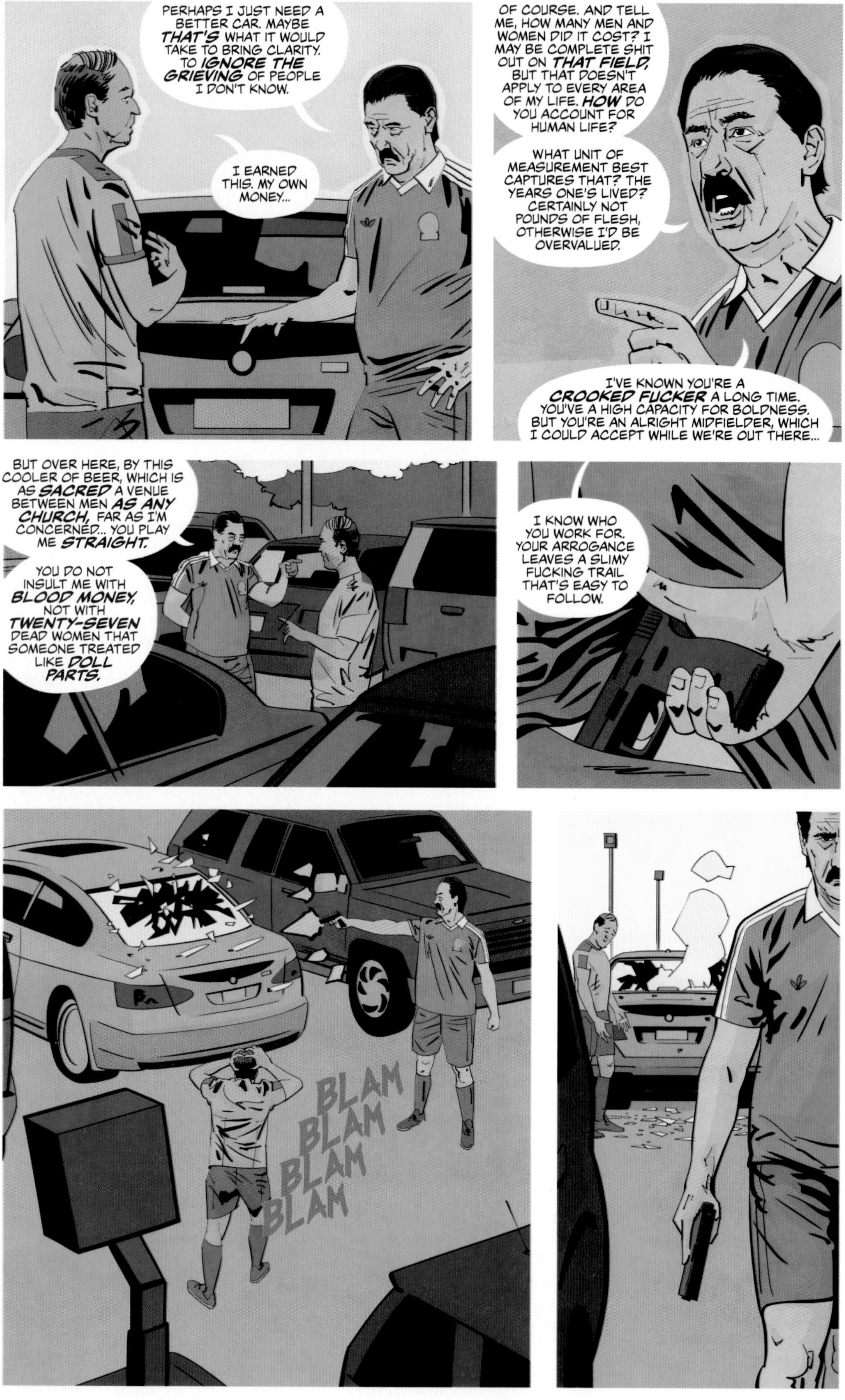
PERHAPS I JUST NEED A BETTER CAR. MAYBE THAT'S WHAT IT WOULD TAKE TO BRING CLARITY. TO IGNORE THE GRIEVING OF PEOPLE I DON'T KNOW.
I EARNED THIS. MY OWN MONEY...
OF COURSE. AND TELL ME, HOW MANY MEN AND WOMEN DID IT COST? I MAY BE COMPLETE SHIT OUT ON THAT FIELD, BUT THAT DOESN'T APPLY TO EVERY AREA OF MY LIFE. HOW DO YOU ACCOUNT FOR HUMAN LIFE?
WHAT UNIT OF MEASUREMENT BEST CAPTURES THAT? THE YEARS ONE'S LIVED? CERTAINLY NOT POUNDS OF FLESH, OTHERWISE I'D BE OVERVALUED.
I'VE KNOWN YOU'RE A CROOKED FUCKER A LONG TIME. YOU'VE A HIGH CAPACITY FOR BOLDNESS. BUT YOU'RE AN ALRIGHT MIDFIELDER, WHICH I COULD ACCEPT WHILE WE'RE OUT THERE...
BUT OVER HERE, BY THIS COOLER OF BEER, WHICH IS AS SACRED A VENUE BETWEEN MEN AS ANY CHURCH, FAR AS I'M CONCERNED... YOU PLAY ME STRAIGHT.
YOU DO NOT INSULT ME WITH BLOOD MONEY, NOT WITH TWENTY-SEVEN DEAD WOMEN THAT SOMEONE TREATED LIKE DOLL PARTS.
I KNOW WHO YOU WORK FOR. YOUR ARROGANCE LEAVES A SLIMY FUCKING TRAIL THAT'S EASY TO FOLLOW.
BLAM BLAM BLAM BLAM

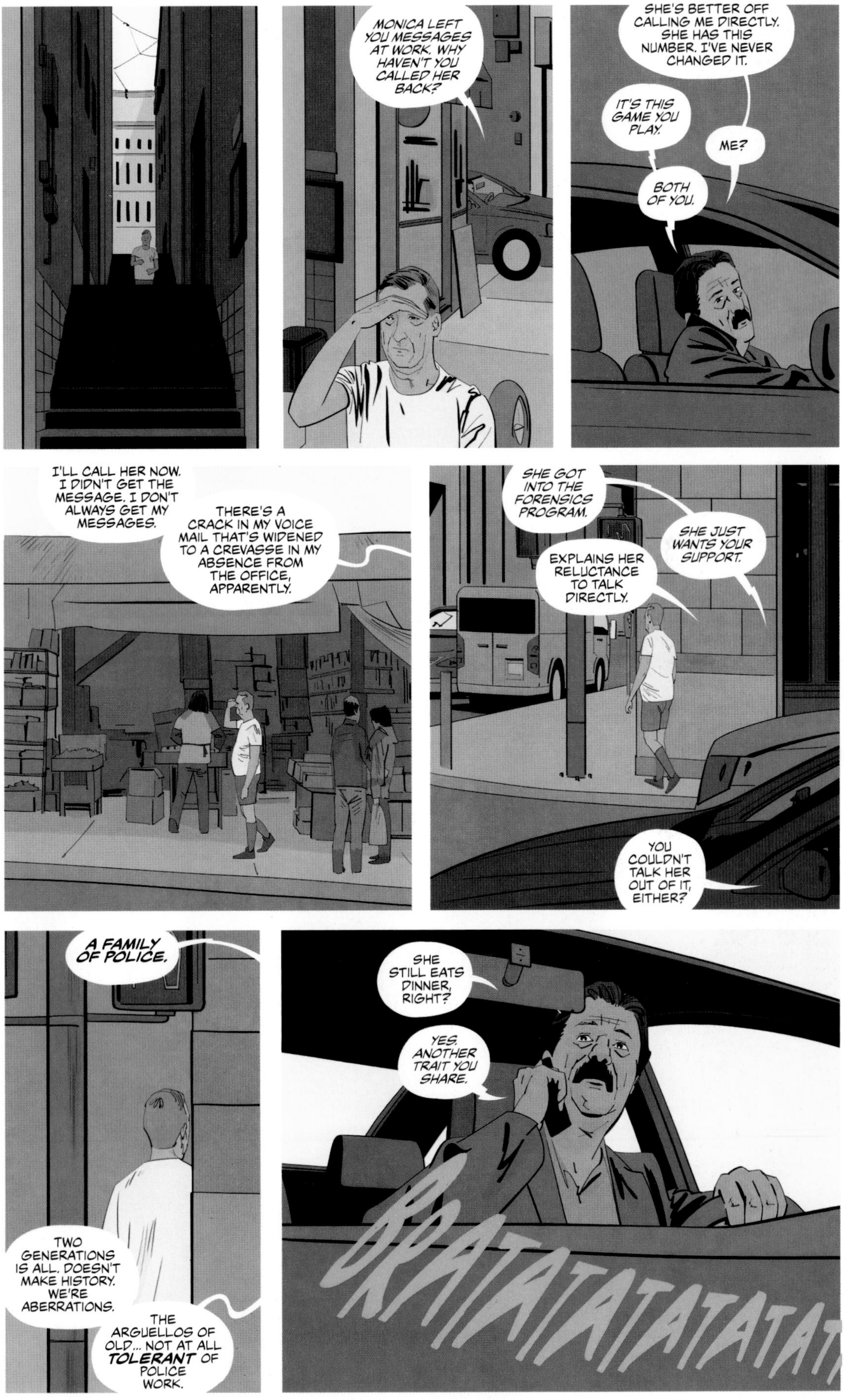
MONICA LEFT YOU MESSAGES AT WORK. WHY HAVEN'T YOU CALLED HER BACK?
SHE'S BETTER OFF CALLING ME DIRECTLY. SHE HAS THIS NUMBER. I'VE NEVER CHANGED IT.
IT'S THIS GAME YOU PLAY.
ME?
BOTH OF YOU.
I'LL CALL HER NOW. I DIDN'T GET THE MESSAGE. I DON'T ALWAYS GET MY MESSAGES.
THERE'S A CRACK IN MY VOICE MAIL THAT'S WIDENED TO A CREVASSE IN MY ABSENCE FROM THE OFFICE, APPARENTLY.
SHE GOT INTO THE FORENSICS PROGRAM.
SHE JUST WANTS YOUR SUPPORT.
EXPLAINS HER RELUCTANCE TO TALK DIRECTLY.
YOU COULDN'T TALK HER OUT OF IT, EITHER?
A FAMILY OF POLICE.
TWO GENERATIONS IS ALL. DOESN'T MAKE HISTORY. WE'RE ABERRATIONS.
THE ARGUELLOS OF OLD... NOT AT ALL TOLERANT OF POLICE WORK.
SHE STILL EATS DINNER, RIGHT?
YES. ANOTHER TRAIT YOU SHARE.

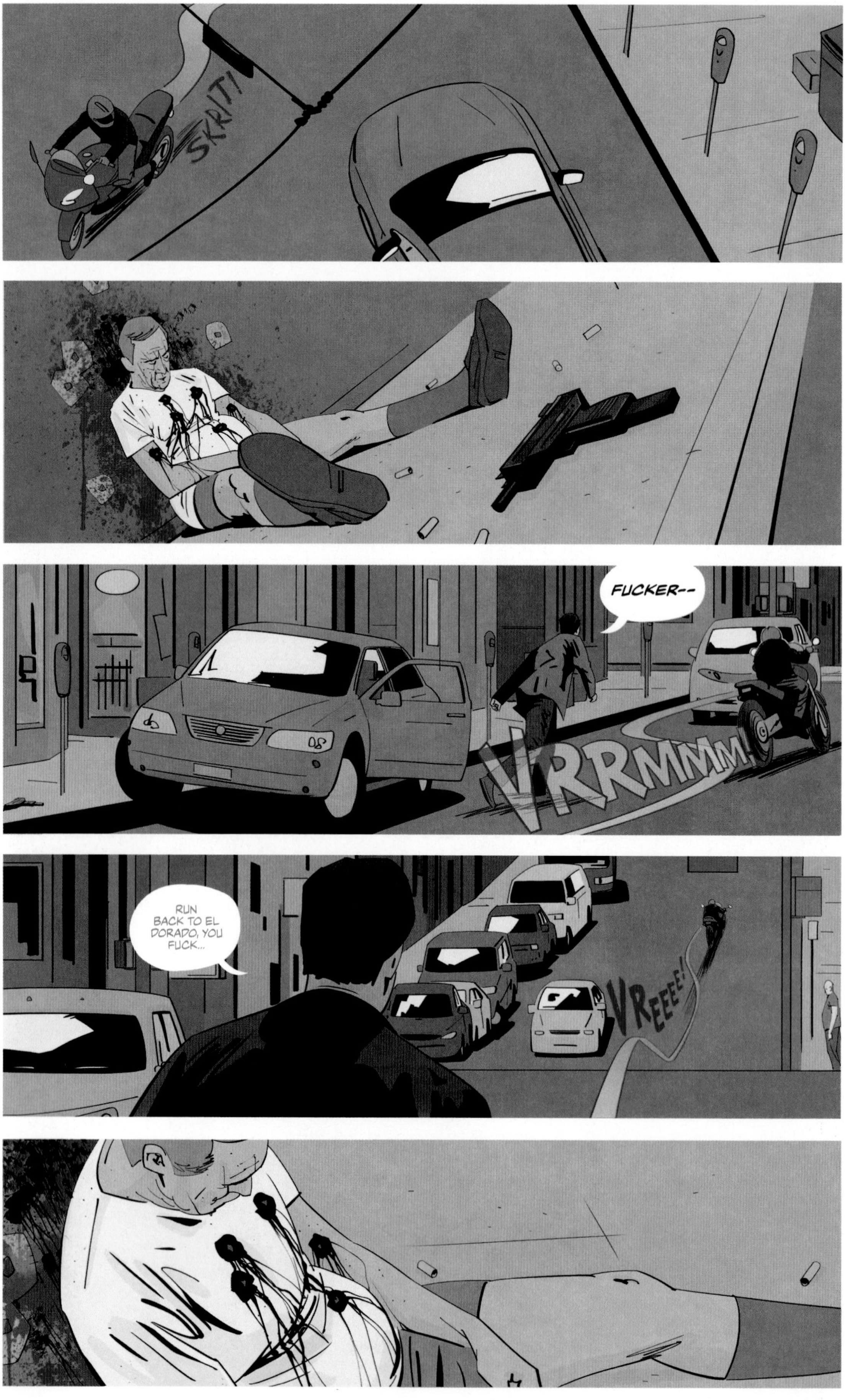
SKRIT!
FUCKER--
VRRMMMM!
RUN BACK TO EL DORADO, YOU FUCK...
VREEEE!

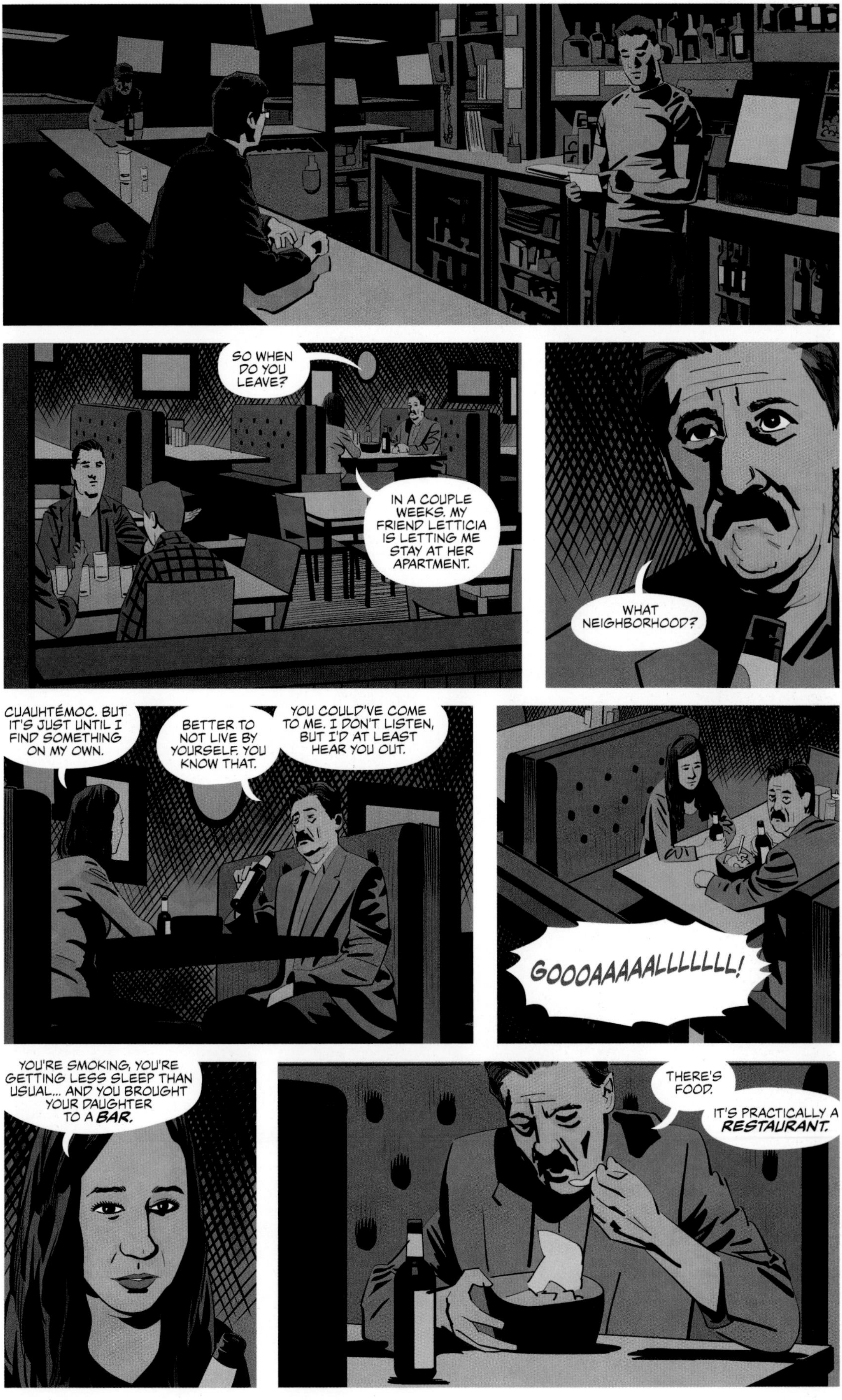
SO WHEN DO YOU LEAVE?
IN A COUPLE WEEKS. MY FRIEND LETTICIA IS LETTING ME STAY AT HER APARTMENT.
WHAT NEIGHBORHOOD?
CUAUHTÉMOC. BUT IT'S JUST UNTIL I FIND SOMETHING ON MY OWN.
BETTER TO NOT LIVE BY YOURSELF. YOU KNOW THAT.
YOU COULD'VE COME TO ME. I DON'T LISTEN, BUT I'D AT LEAST HEAR YOU OUT.
GOOOAAAAALLLLLLL!
YOU'RE SMOKING, YOU'RE GETTING LESS SLEEP THAN USUAL... AND YOU BROUGHT YOUR DAUGHTER TO A **BAR.**
THERE'S FOOD.
IT'S PRACTICALLY A **RESTAURANT.**

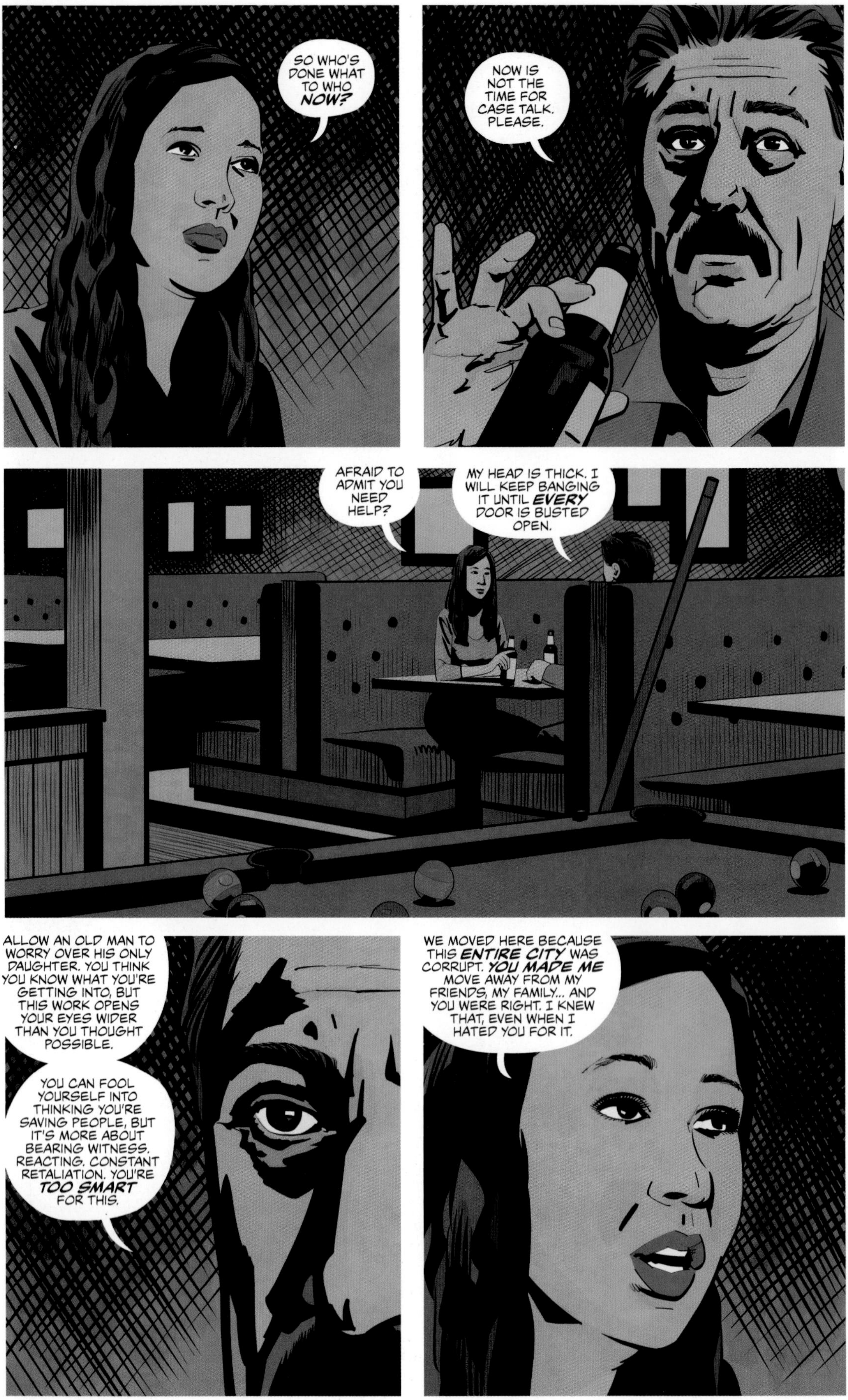
SO WHO'S DONE WHAT TO WHO NOW?
NOW IS NOT THE TIME FOR CASE TALK. PLEASE.
AFRAID TO ADMIT YOU NEED HELP?
MY HEAD IS THICK. I WILL KEEP BANGING IT UNTIL EVERY DOOR IS BUSTED OPEN.
ALLOW AN OLD MAN TO WORRY OVER HIS ONLY DAUGHTER. YOU THINK YOU KNOW WHAT YOU'RE GETTING INTO, BUT THIS WORK OPENS YOUR EYES WIDER THAN YOU THOUGHT POSSIBLE.
YOU CAN FOOL YOURSELF INTO THINKING YOU'RE SAVING PEOPLE, BUT IT'S MORE ABOUT BEARING WITNESS. REACTING. CONSTANT RETALIATION. YOU'RE TOO SMART FOR THIS.
WE MOVED HERE BECAUSE THIS ENTIRE CITY WAS CORRUPT. YOU MADE ME MOVE AWAY FROM MY FRIENDS, MY FAMILY... AND YOU WERE RIGHT. I KNEW THAT, EVEN WHEN I HATED YOU FOR IT.

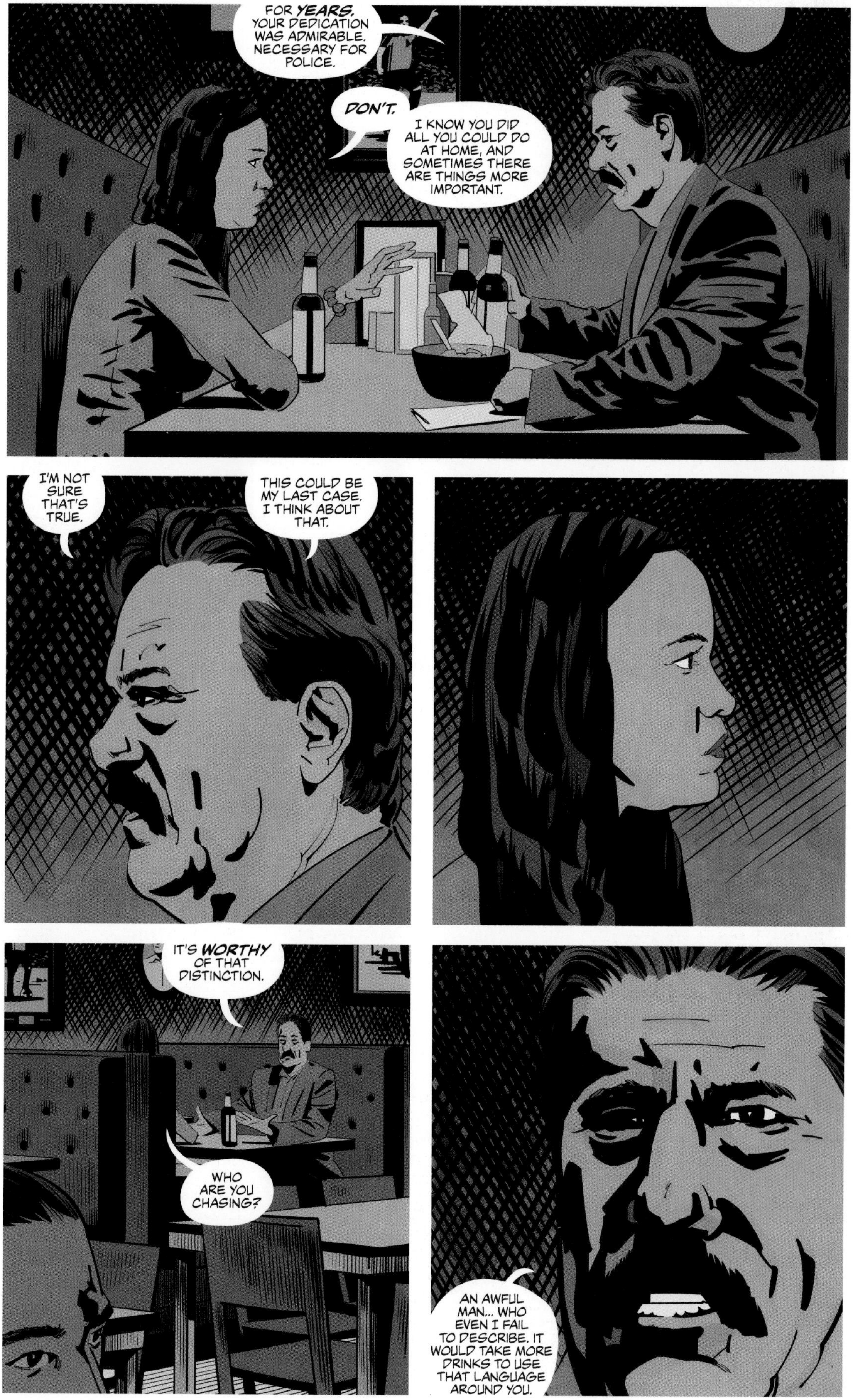
FOR YEARS. YOUR DEDICATION WAS ADMIRABLE. NECESSARY FOR POLICE.
DON'T.
I KNOW YOU DID ALL YOU COULD DO AT HOME, AND SOMETIMES THERE ARE THINGS MORE IMPORTANT.
I'M NOT SURE THAT'S TRUE.
THIS COULD BE MY LAST CASE. I THINK ABOUT THAT.
IT'S WORTHY OF THAT DISTINCTION.
WHO ARE YOU CHASING?
AN AWFUL MAN... WHO EVEN I FAIL TO DESCRIBE. IT WOULD TAKE MORE DRINKS TO USE THAT LANGUAGE AROUND YOU.

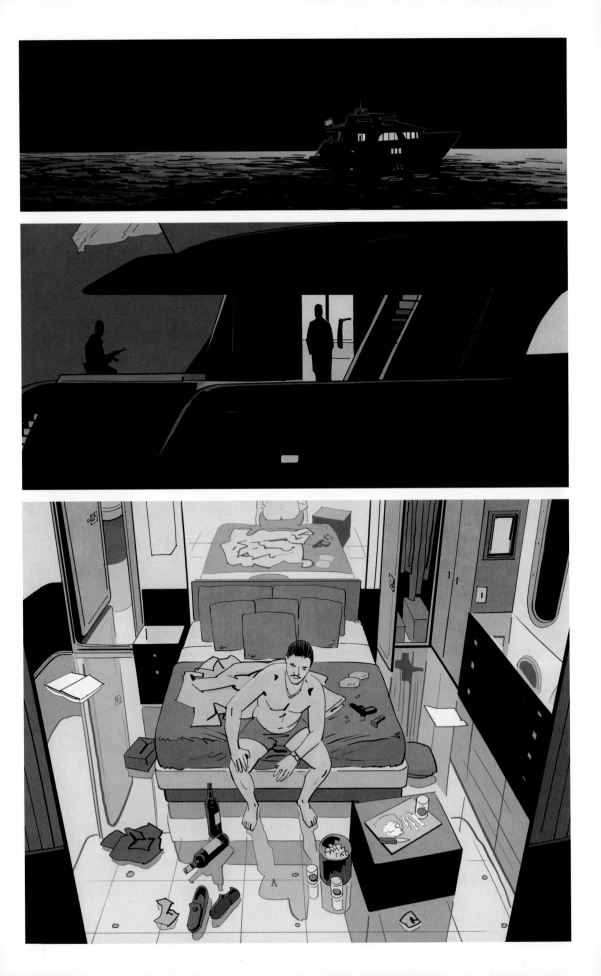

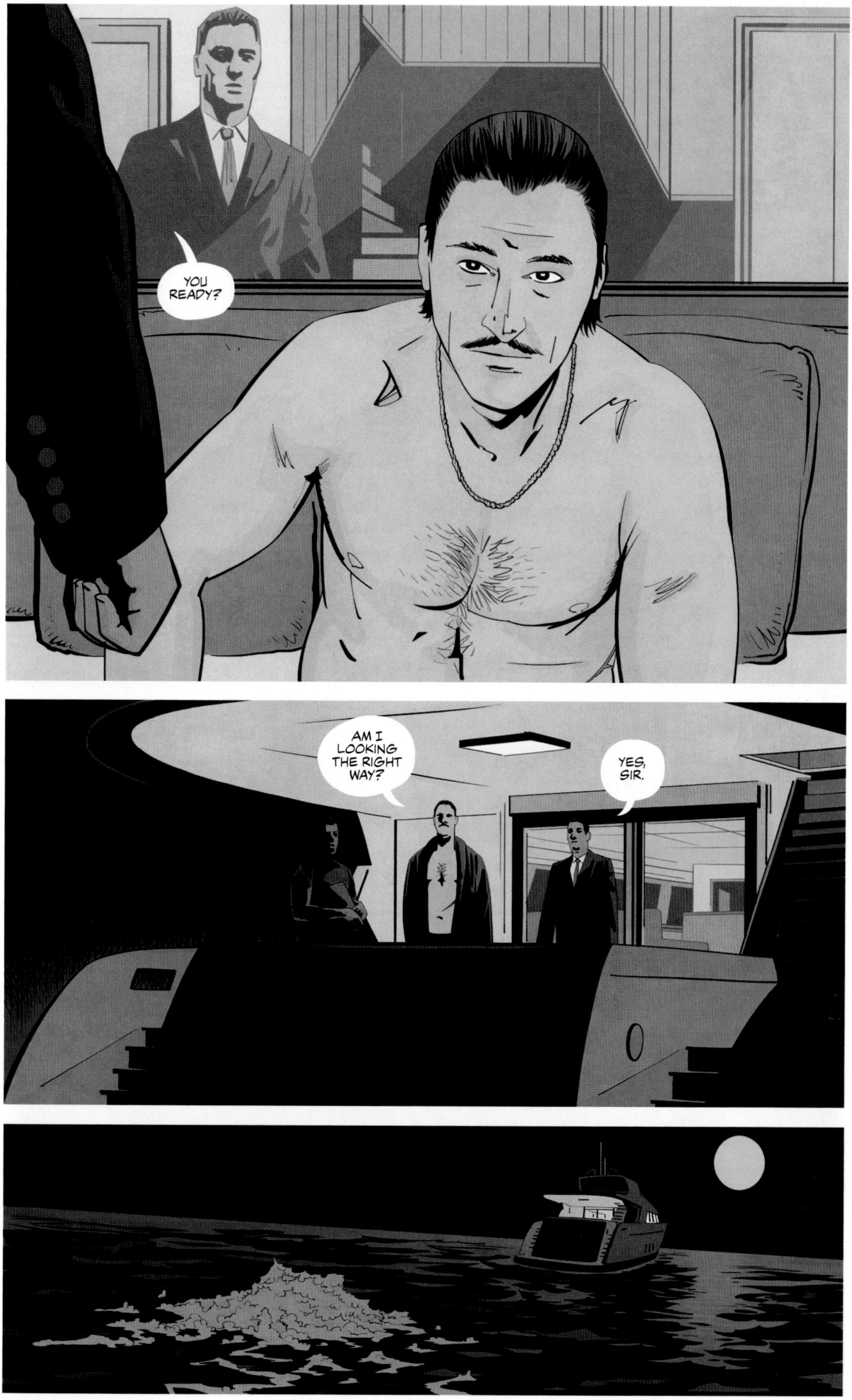
YOU READY?
AM I LOOKING THE RIGHT WAY?
YES, SIR.

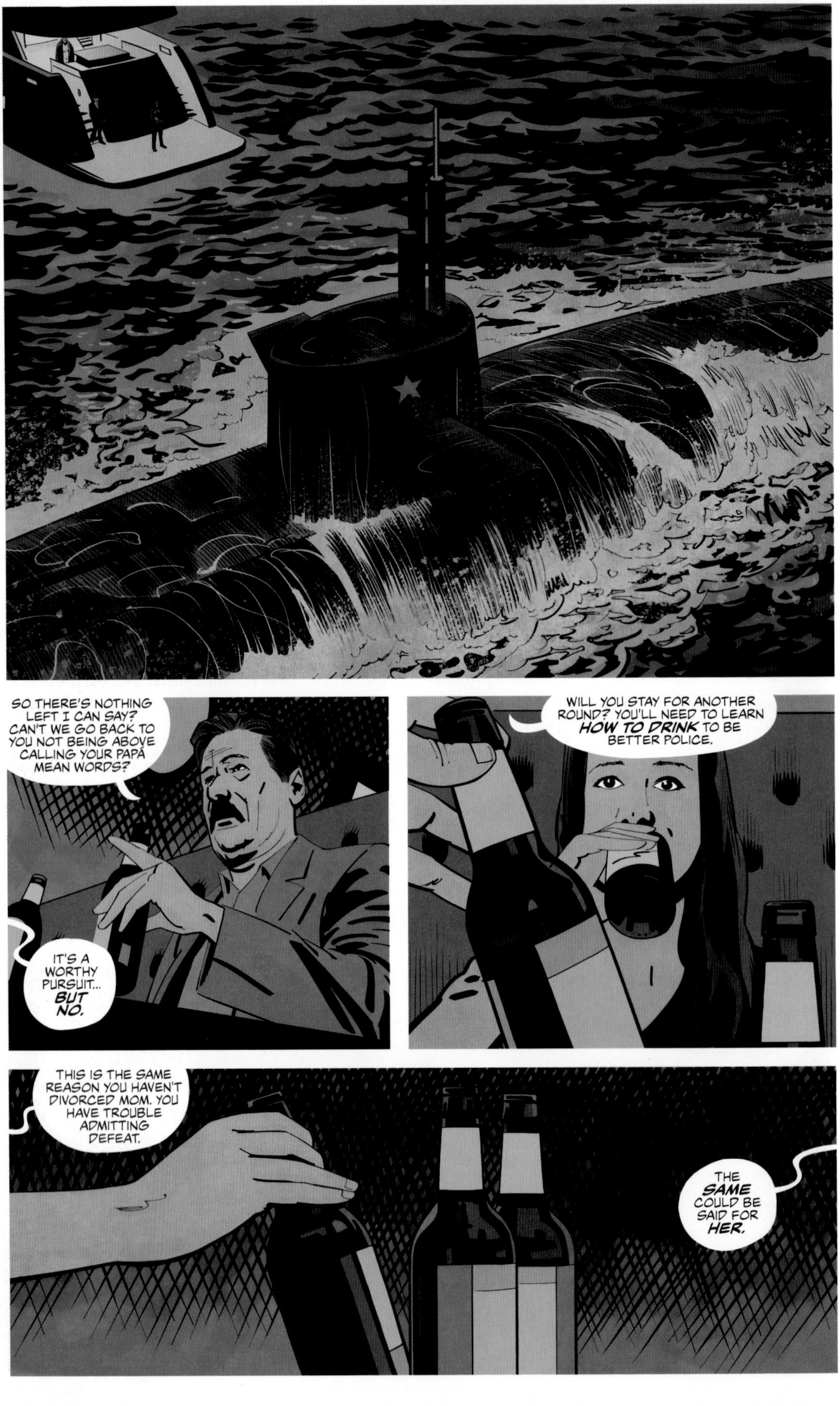
SO THERE'S NOTHING LEFT I CAN SAY? CAN'T WE GO BACK TO YOU NOT BEING ABOVE CALLING YOUR PAPÁ MEAN WORDS?
IT'S A WORTHY PURSUIT... BUT NO.
WILL YOU STAY FOR ANOTHER ROUND? YOU'LL NEED TO LEARN HOW TO DRINK TO BE BETTER POLICE.
THIS IS THE SAME REASON YOU HAVEN'T DIVORCED MOM. YOU HAVE TROUBLE ADMITTING DEFEAT.
THE SAME COULD BE SAID FOR HER.

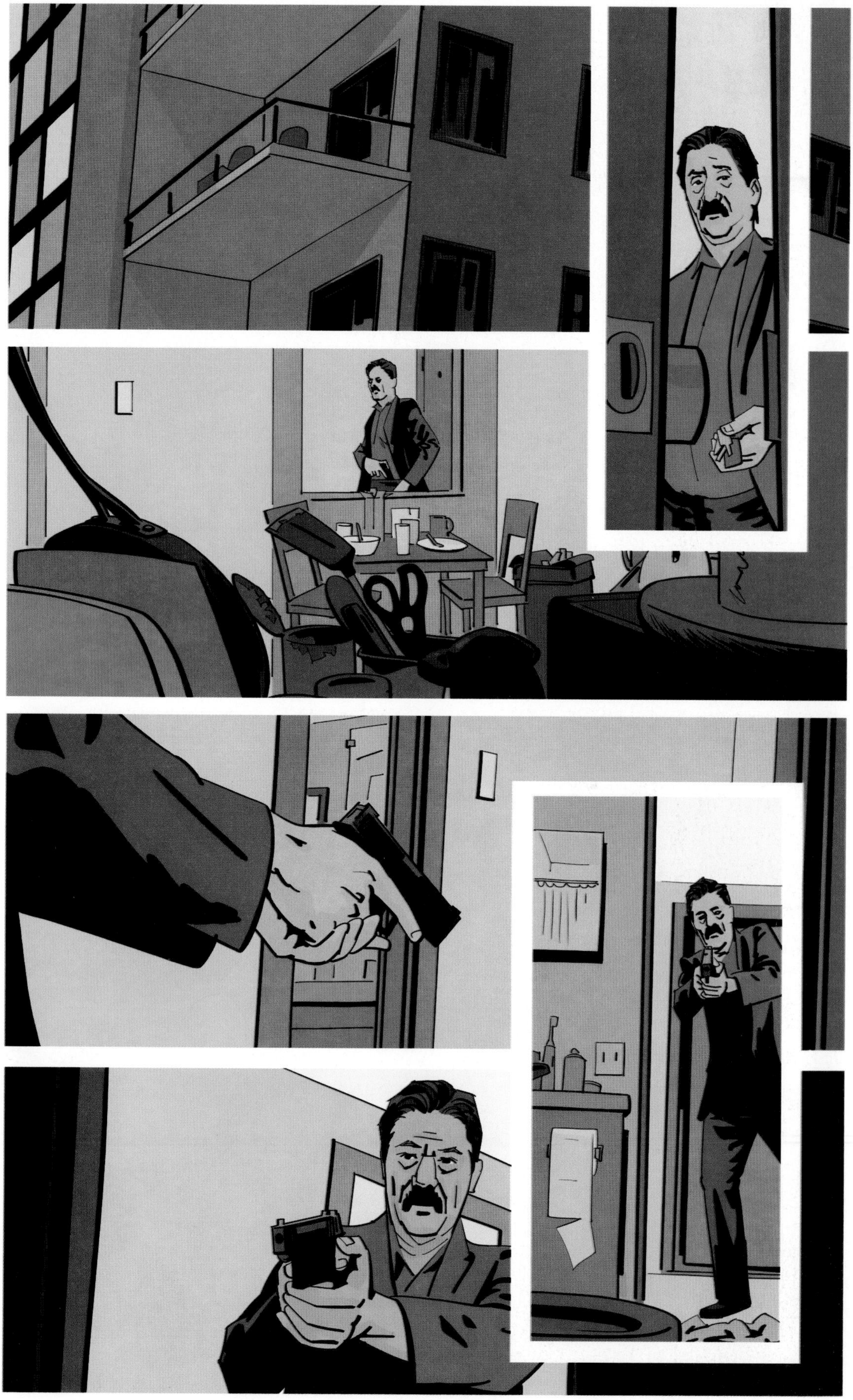

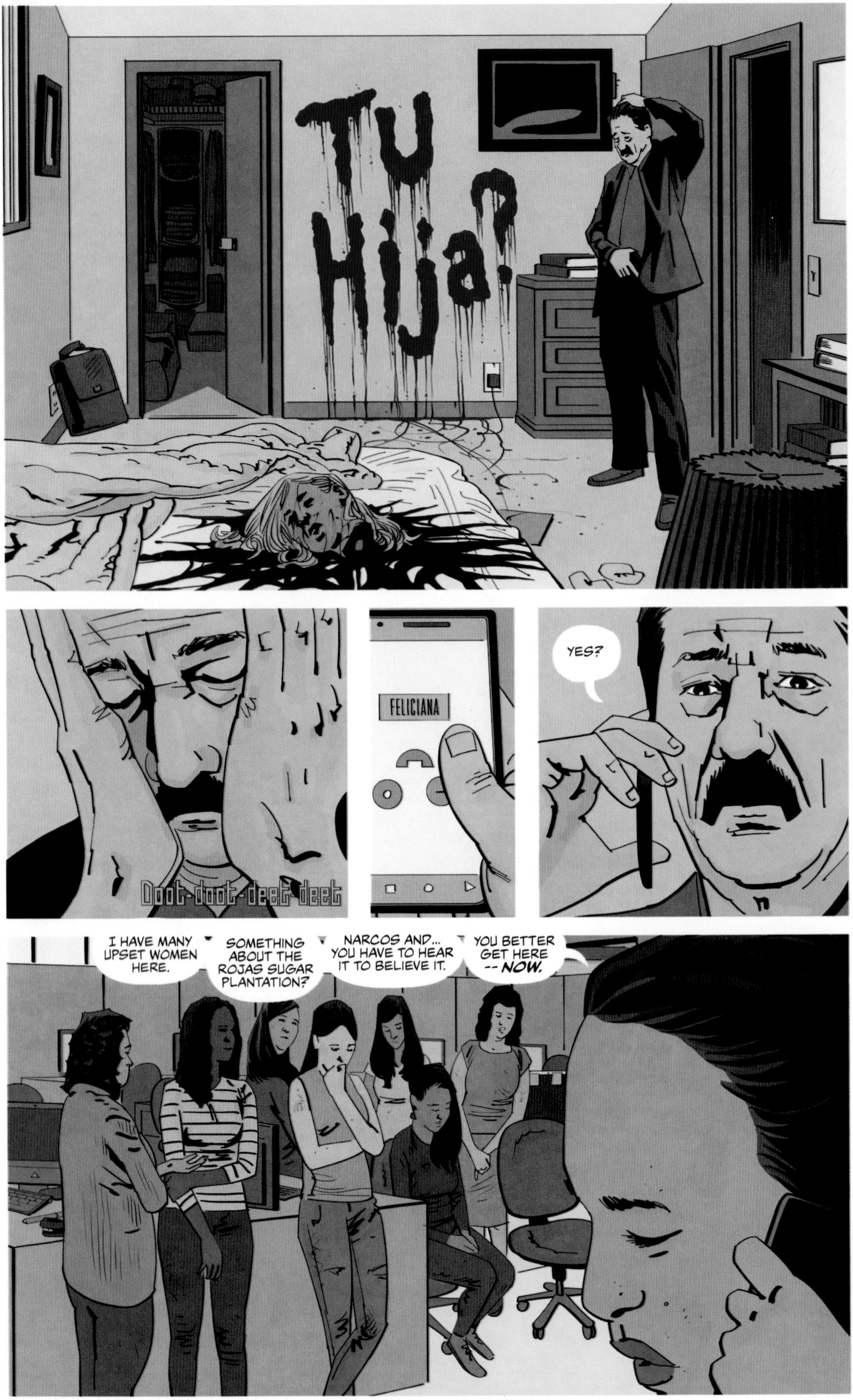
TU
Hija?
Doot-doot-deet-deet
FELICIANA
YES?
I HAVE MANY UPSET WOMEN HERE.
SOMETHING ABOUT THE ROJAS SUGAR PLANTATION?
NARCOS AND... YOU HAVE TO HEAR IT TO BELIEVE IT.
YOU BETTER GET HERE -- NOW.

TO BE
CONTINUED

For more tales from ROBERT KIRKMAN and SKYBOUND

Daniel Warren Johnson Mike Spicer
EXTREMITY
VOLUME ONE ARTIST

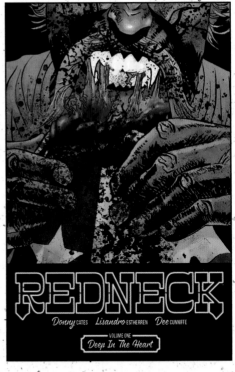

VOL. 1: ARTIST TP
ISBN: 978-1-5343-0242-6
$16.99

REDNECK
Donny CATES Lisandro ESTHERREN Dee CUNNIFFE
VOLUME ONE
Deep In The Heart

VOL. 1: DEEP IN THE HEART TP
ISBN: 978-1-5343-0331-7
$16.99

BRANDON THOMAS JUAN GEDEON MIKE SPICER
HORIZON
VOLUME 03

VOL. 1: REPRISAL TP
ISBN: 978-1-5343-0047-7
$9.99

VOL. 2: REMNANT TP
ISBN: 978-1-5343-0227-3
$12.99

VOL. 3: REVEAL TP
ISBN: 978-1-5343-0487-1
$16.99

CHRIS DINGESS MATTHEW ROBERTS OWEN GIENI
MANIFEST DESTINY
VOLUME 4 SASQUATCH

VOL. 1: FLORA & FAUNA TP
ISBN: 978-1-60706-982-9
$9.99

VOL. 2: AMPHIBIA & INSECTA TP
ISBN: 978-1-63215-052-3
$14.99

VOL. 3: CHIROPTERA & CARNIFORMAVES TP
ISBN: 978-1-63215-397-5
$14.99

VOL. 4: SASQUATCH TP
ISBN: 978-1-63215-890-1
$14.99

VOLUME 5 THE NEW PATH
BY KIRKMAN AZACETA
OUTCAST

VOL. 1: A DARKNESS SURROUNDS HIM TP
ISBN: 978-1-63215-053-0
$9.99

VOL. 2: A VAST AND UNENDING RUIN TP
ISBN: 978-1-63215-448-4
$14.99

VOL. 3: THIS LITTLE LIGHT TP
ISBN: 978-1-63215-693-8
$14.99

VOL. 4: UNDER DEVIL'S WING TP
ISBN: 978-1-5343-0050-7
$14.99

THIEF OF THIEVES
VOLUME 6
"GOLD RUSH."

VOL. 1: "I QUIT."
ISBN: 978-1-60706-592-0
$14.99

VOL. 2: "HELP ME."
ISBN: 978-1-60706-676-7
$14.99

VOL. 3: "VENICE."
ISBN: 978-1-60706-844-0
$14.99

VOL. 4: "THE HIT LIST."
ISBN: 978-1-63215-037-0
$14.99

VOL. 5: "TAKE ME."
ISBN: 978-1-63215-401-9
$14.99

VOL. 6: "GOLD RUSH."
ISBN: 978-1-53430-037-8
$14.99